# EVIL
## IN ALL ITS DISGUISES

**NOVELS BY HILARY DAVIDSON**

*The Damage Done*
*The Next One to Fall*
*Evil in All Its Disguises*

# EVIL
# IN ALL ITS
# DISGUISES

## HILARY DAVIDSON

A TOM DOHERTY ASSOCIATES BOOK
NEW YORK

EVIL IN ALL ITS DISGUISES

Copyright © 2013 by Hilary Davidson

A Forge Book
Published by Tom Doherty Associates, LLC
175 Fifth Avenue
New York, NY 10010

www.tor-forge.com

Forge® is a registered trademark of Tom Doherty Associates, LLC.

Library of Congress Cataloging-in-Publication Data

Davidson, Hilary.
    Evil in all its disguises / Hilary Davidson.—1st ed.
      p. cm.
    "A Forge book"—T.p. verso.
    ISBN 978-0-7653-3352-0 (hardcover)
    ISBN 978-1-4668-0229-2 (e-book)
    1. Travel writers—Fiction.  2. Missing persons—Fiction.  3. Revenge—
Fiction.  4. Murder—Investigation—Fiction.  5. Acapulco (Mexico)—
Fiction.  I. Title.
PS3604.A9466E95 2013
813'.6—dc23

                                                2012038907

First Edition: March 2013

Printed in the United States of America

0  9  8  7  6  5  4  3  2  1

*For my parents, John and Sheila Davidson,*
*with love, affection, and admiration.*
*Every year, I appreciate you more.*

## ACKNOWLEDGMENTS

The third time's the charm, an old saying goes. This is my third novel, but I'm not sure if there's a way to improve on the charmed journey I've been on since *The Damage Done* was published in 2010. I'm incredibly grateful for the warm reception that both Lily Moore and I have had. As always, I owe many people a debt of gratitude.

I'm forever thankful to my wonderful editor, Paul Stevens, for taking a chance on Lily—and on me. His intelligence, instincts, dedication, and humor make him a joy to work with. The entire Tor/Forge team is incredible. In particular, I'd like to thank Aisha Cloud, Patty Garcia, Edward Allen, Seth Lerner, Nathan Weaver, Justin Thrift, and Miriam Weinberg. I'm also fortunate to be represented by the Sobel Weber agency. A huge thank-you to Judith Weber for many hours of reading and discussion, and to Nat Sobel, Adia Wright, and Julie Stevenson for all their help and insight. Many thanks to my Canadian distributor, Raincoast Books— and, in particular, to Dan Wagstaff and Jamie Broadhurst— for their efforts on my behalf. I'm grateful to agent Catherine Lapautre for bringing Lily to France.

Several authors I've long admired have been incredibly supportive of my work. I still pinch myself when I hear that Linda Fairstein has told yet another crowd of readers about my books. A huge thank-you to Linda, and to Laura Lippman,

Megan Abbott, Reed Farrel Coleman, Ken Bruen, and Meg Gardiner. You are my heroes.

The Crimespree Family—the world's best crime family, and the most notorious—has adopted me, and for that I will be forever grateful. In particular, I want to thank Jon and Ruth Jordan, Jen Forbus, and Jeremy Lynch for all they've done. Who knew writing about evil would give me a new extended family?

If you love an author, there's nothing kinder you can do for her than spread the word about her work. On that front, I owe a huge debt to Oline Cogdill, Carole Barrowman, Cullen Gallagher, Jenn Lawrence, Jedidiah Ayres, Katrina Niidas Holm, Chris F. Holm, Janet Rudolph, Chuck Wendig, Elizabeth A. White, Margaret Cannon, Martin Levin, Laurie Grassi, Peter Kavanagh, Clare Toohey, Laura K. Curtis, Bethanne Patrick, Carolyn Cooke, Benoît Lelièvre, Dan O'Shea, Todd Ritter, Becke Martin Davis, Elyse Dinh, Jacques Filippi, and Sarah Weinman. It's impossible to ignore just how much awesomeness there is in the crime fiction community. Yes, I'm looking at you, Todd Robinson, Allison Glasgow Robinson, Robin Spano, Keith Rawson, Brad Parks, David Cranmer, Margery Flax, Bobby McCue, Linda Brown, Steve Weddle, Deryn Collier, Ian Hamilton, Stephen Blackmoore, Aldo Calcagno, and Eric Beetner. (That's just to name a few.)

There are so many booksellers and librarians who've supported my work, and I'm grateful to all of them. Some that deserve special recognition: Scott Montgomery at BookPeople in Austin; Barbara Peters at the Poisoned Pen in Scottsdale; Lesa Holstine at the Velma Teague Library in Glendale, Arizona; McKenna Jordan, John Kwiatkowski, and Sally Woods at Murder by the Book in Houston; Ben Mc-

Nally at Ben McNally Books in Toronto; Otto Penzler and Sally Owen at the Mysterious Bookshop in New York City; Maryelizabeth Hart and David Joslin at Mysterious Galaxy in San Diego; Lisa Casper at the Tattered Cover in Denver; Mary Alice Gorman and Richard Goldman at Mystery Lovers in Pittsburgh; Lisa Forman at the Easton Public Library in Easton, Connecticut; Alan Chisholm at Mysteries to Die For in Thousand Oaks, California; Jessica Perry at Book Passage in San Francisco; Nicole Miller at Book Revue in Huntington, New York; Tracey Higgins at Bryan Prince in Hamilton, Ontario; Georgina Flynn at the McGill Library in Burnaby, British Columbia; Ann Rees at the Richmond Library in Richmond, British Columbia; Dan Ellis at Armchair Books in Whistler, British Columbia; Walter Sinclair and Jill Sanagan at Dead Write Books in Vancouver; Richard Katz and David Biemann at Mystery One in Milwaukee; Guy Dubois at La Maison Anglaise in Quebec City; and Marian Misters and J. D. Singh at Sleuth of Baker Street in Toronto.

Wonderful friends who deserve a special thank-you: Shelley Ambrose, Trish Snyder, Susan Shapiro, Ilana Rubel, Ghen Laraya Long, Stephanie Craig, Darya Arden, Beth Russell Connelly, Helen Lovekin, David Hayes, Kate Walter, Jessica DuLong, Leslie Elman, Tony Powell, and Rich Prior.

Since taking up crime (writing), I've joined Sisters in Crime, Mystery Writers of America, Crime Writers of Canada, and International Thriller Writers, and I'm grateful to all of them. Also, my longtime friends at the American Society of Journalists and Authors and the Society of American Travel Writers have been incredibly supportive of my criminal ways. My thanks to you all.

I've dedicated this book to my parents, John and Sheila

Davidson, because they've encouraged me to follow my dreams since I was born, and they continue to be the best cheering squad ever. (My mom is still my first reader, and how she manages to give encouragement and useful criticism is an amazing feat.) I couldn't do what I do without the support of my husband, Dan, who—I'm thrilled to say—seems reconciled to living with the voices in my head. I also have a wonderful extended family; special thanks to Irene McIntosh, Barry and Evelyn Rein, Sandy and Gerry Katz, and Joanna Hoffman for being so supportive.

Finally, I'm grateful to everyone who reads my work. None of this would be possible without you. When I started writing fiction, I never imagined that much of the joy in the journey would be in making new friends along the way.

# EVIL
## IN ALL ITS DISGUISES

# 1

The snake had coiled itself halfway around my ankle by the time I spotted it. Cool and smooth against my skin, it inched across my sandaled foot, turning its head back and upward to meet my gaze. Its slender body was striped with red and yellow and blackish brown. Even though its eyes were all but invisible in its glossy dark head, I was sure it was regarding me with pure defiance.

"Welcome to Acapulco, Miss Moore." The hotel clerk's voice echoed from far, far away. "Is this your first time here?"

I wanted to answer him—it was my first time in Acapulco, not Mexico—but my tongue had gone sandpaper-dry and my teeth were grinding together. A soft noise escaped from the back of my throat.

The clerk didn't notice. "You will enjoy your stay at the Hotel Cerón very much, I promise you."

The snake gave an excited shiver, and then abandoned its perch atop my foot, slithering toward the shadows under the reception desk.

Stepping back several paces, I took a deep breath that didn't quite fill the pit in my chest. "That snake isn't poisonous, right?"

"What snake?" The clerk's buoyant mood instantly deflated. "Where?"

"Under your desk."

The clerk took a couple of steps back and looked down. The whites of his eyes were startling against his deep tan. The reception desk was a tall wooden counter carved into a series of archways that wouldn't have been out of place in a church; the openings were fitted with wrought-iron grates. The snake was weaving its way through the slits in the metal, as if on an obstacle course. Briefly, it lifted its head and flicked its tongue, seemingly pleased at being the center of attention. When the clerk screamed, a bellman came running in, and I backed away some more. When I looked at the floor again, the snake was gone.

I stared at the tiles, holding my breath and waiting for it to reappear. The clerk and the bellman were on the floor, hunting under the desk and cursing in rapid-fire Spanish. The only word I caught was *venonoso*—poisonous—which wasn't reassuring. I looked around the lobby. The Hotel Cerón had seemed so charming as I'd strolled in five minutes earlier. There were antique wooden tables with clawed feet and chairs with elaborately carved backs fitted between plush white sofas. The room was dolled up like a Technicolor film set from the 1950s, with its pink tile floor, turquoise pillows, and silver vases holding long-stemmed fragrant pink flowers. Scattered around the walls and on the squared-off columns was a series of black-and-white photographs of Hollywood stars who'd famously made this Mexican resort town their playground. There was a print of my idol, Ava Gardner, who'd brought Frank Sinatra to Acapulco on vacation. I also noticed a shot of Elizabeth Taylor and Mike Todd, who'd gotten married at a local villa. The retro atmosphere had immediately made me feel at home, until the snake decided to give me a personal welcome.

"Do not worry, Miss Moore. We will find the snake," the clerk said. The bellman was stretched on the floor, peering under the reception desk.

"I'm sure you will."

"It is very common to see snakes and lizards here, you understand. Even in the water, there are snakes."

"Lovely." I wasn't phobic about snakes, but I preferred them behind glass, as they were at the Bronx Zoo's Reptile House. "I guess it's too late for me to get back on the plane?"

Behind me, someone said, "Lily?"

I turned and saw Skye McDermott standing by a pillar. She was blonder and thinner than she'd been when I'd last met up with her, but her heart-shaped face and wide-set gray-blue eyes were instantly recognizable. Now that her hair was platinum, she looked more like Jean Harlow than ever, though her features—eyebrows full, not tweezed into a thin 1930s line, and lips glossy, not painted into a bow—were modern. If Harlow were making movies today, she'd be a dead ringer for Skye.

"I had no idea you were on this trip!" I was thrilled to see her. We'd traveled together countless times over the years, and even though I rarely saw her outside of press junkets, she was the best travel companion I could ask for.

"It's good to see you, Lily." Her voice was thin, and it quavered on my name. As I went toward her, I noticed her skin was red and blotchy, as if she'd just been running. Up close, her eyes were swollen. Still, she gave me a smile and pulled me into a hug. Skye's shoulder blades cut through the delicate black silk of her dress, making her seem terribly fragile. Barely five foot two, she was wearing four-inch heels that made her almost the same height as me in my low-heeled sandals.

"What's wrong?" I pulled back gingerly, untangling myself from the long, flapperlike strand of reddish orange beads she was wearing. Up close, I could see how heavy her makeup was. She looked gorgeous but exhausted, with purplish half-moons under her eyes that no concealer could cover; I knew, because I'd tried to cover up plenty in my time.

"Nothing. Just, um, allergies. They're awful here." She smiled at me, but I wasn't convinced. Skye had a definite flair for the dramatic, but she wasn't someone who walked around weeping. She was usually gregarious and irreverent, and an incorrigible flirt. "What were you saying about a snake?" she asked, swiftly changing the subject.

"One wanted to get to know me better." I looked at the tiles again, but they were serpent-free. "I don't know where it crawled off to, so keep your eyes peeled. I didn't see its fangs, but the clerk thinks it's dangerous."

"Ugh. There are creepy-crawly things all over the place here," Skye said. "You'd think the humidity would get rid of them, but the only thing that kills is humans."

"Your luggage is already in your suite, Miss Moore." The clerk slid a small envelope across the counter. I retrieved it, stepping lightly near the desk. The number 527 was scrawled on the front; tucked inside were a pair of electronic key cards.

"Thank you."

"If you will go upstairs, a waiter will bring your dinner to you," he added. "The kitchen will have everything ready in less than half an hour."

"But how do they . . . ?"

"Steak, medium rare. Grilled root vegetables. Champagne. Crème brûlée," the clerk recited. If someone had asked me to name a few of my favorite foods, those would all be on the list. "Miss Denny Chiu arranged for everything for you."

That cleared up the mystery. Denny was the public relations person who'd organized the trip, and she knew me well. Before I left my apartment in Barcelona, she'd sent me a travel pillow; when I'd arrived at my friend Jesse's place in New York, I found Denny had couriered over a margarita-mixing kit, complete with a pair of cobalt-rimmed glasses from Mexico. Journalists tended to be spoiled on press trips, but this was above and beyond. Before I could say a word, Skye made a gasping, choking sound and burst into tears.

# 2

I put my hand on her shoulder, and Skye got herself under control quickly. "Sorry. I'm so embarrassed. I don't know what came over me."

"Don't apologize." I rubbed her back, like I used to do for my sister when she was sick, feeling the familiar anxiety welling up inside me.

"I've been . . ." She shook her head, brushing her fingertips across her cheekbones. "Things have been so awful, Lily."

"Do you want to come up to my room to talk?"

She took a shuddering breath. "Would you . . . would you mind coming with me to the bar instead?"

It was close to eight, and the thought of dinner was more appealing than a cocktail. But Skye was distraught and I couldn't say no. "Sure. We can have a drink and talk."

"It's this way." Skye put her arm around my shoulders, leading me under an archway and along an empty hallway decked out with bright blue tiles and gilded moldings.

"Do you want to tell me what made you cry back there?" I asked her once we were out of the clerk's earshot.

"It's just . . . this is going to take a while to explain."

"Should I guess? Either you and Ryan are back together, and you're trying to figure out how to leave him again, or else you're dating someone new and he's making your life hell."

"Wow." She gave me a sidelong glance. "You know me pretty well, don't you, Lily?"

Skye had been engaged to a wealthy hedge-fund manager back when I'd been engaged to a man named Martin Sklar, but neither proposal had resulted in a trip down the aisle. Maybe that was part of the reason Skye and I had bonded so well. We both had strange push-pull dynamics in our personal lives that left us perennially uprooted. No wonder we'd become travel writers.

"So, which is it?"

"Ryan and I will always be close, but I'm never going to marry him," Skye said, leading me up a short set of steps. "It's hard, because he's such a great guy, and he'd be such an incredible dad." Her voice was wistful. "But his dream is to get a house in Connecticut and have four kids and a dog and a white picket fence. The thought makes me feel like I'm being smothered. But the worst part is, every other man I meet is such a rat."

"They aren't all rodents," I said, thinking of a man I knew in New York, a cop named Bruxton. He was part pit bull, but I hadn't detected any rattiness in him.

"Well, the ones I meet definitely are. The latest one takes the cake for being a total bastard. Then I end up crying on Ryan's shoulder, because even though we're not together anymore, he's still my best friend. The times we've gotten back together never work out. I feel so guilty, because he usually dumps whatever poor girl he's seeing, and I keep breaking his heart."

It was my turn to give Skye a sidelong glance. When she described her ex, he sounded like a cross between a hopelessly devoted lapdog and a limp dishrag. I'd met Ryan only once, a couple of years earlier, at a convention of the Society of American Travel Writers in Germany. He'd struck me as shy but intelligent, with old-fashioned manners that made me like him. We'd had dinner together one night with a group of journalists and their partners in Dresden, and I remembered Skye ridiculing Ryan for wearing jeans and looking schlumpy. *You'd never know how much money he makes, would you?* she'd asked everyone at the table, embarrassing us all into silence.

There was an odd kind of intimacy you developed from traveling with other journalists. People revealed a great deal about themselves on the road; taken out of their element, they bonded with strangers quickly, revealing secrets their closest friends back home didn't know. But road-friendships often didn't translate into real-life ones. That dinner in Germany was the only time I'd had a meal with Skye and Ryan together.

"Here we are." Skye pushed open a wrought-iron door filled with panes of opaque red glass.

My stomach rumbled slightly. "Have you had dinner?"

"I can't even look at food these days."

"I noticed you're a bit—"

"Emaciated," she filled in. "I've been kind of sick the past couple of months."

"I'm so sorry. Is it . . ." *Is it serious?* I wanted to ask, but Skye gave a sharp little laugh.

"Don't worry, Lily, it's not contagious."

"I didn't mean—"

"I'm fine. My doctor says a lot of it is stress-induced."

As we entered the bar, the host gave us an extravagant nod—almost a bow—and unfurled his arm to indicate that we could pick any seats we wanted. It was a polite but unnecessary gesture, since the place was empty except for its staff.

The Hotel Cerón's bar was a study in scarlet and black. There were tall wrought-iron gates acting like privacy screens, with crimson and fuchsia flowers climbing through them. The room had an upper level that was dominated by a bar counter covered in mirrored tiles; on the wall behind it, jutting out between bottles of tequila and mezcal, was a giant, genderless face. Its features, shaped in plaster, were human, but the way its eyes popped in opposite directions and its mouth, filled with pointed teeth, opened in a scream startled me.

Skye must have noticed me staring, because she said, "That's copied from the ruins of Xochipala. Have you been there?"

"No. Is it nearby?"

"It's in the same state as Acapulco, but it's a pain in the ass to get to. It was looted decades ago, but there's still some interesting stuff there."

She was quiet while I looked around. The carved wooden tables and ocelot-patterned upholstered chairs around the bar were elegantly tame. The floor at the center of the room was cut open into a smooth oval, guarded by an elaborate, waist-high iron railing. A sweeping staircase led to the level below, which had glittering tiles that I took for a dance floor. There were a few uniformed employees moving about, their footsteps echoing in what felt like a movie set.

"Are we under quarantine?" I asked. "Where is everyone?"

"You don't miss much, do you?" Skye's teasing tone evaporated. "It's quiet as a tomb here. Want to sit on the balcony? I know it's ninety degrees out there and drizzling, but it's the only way to get any privacy." I gave her a curious look, and she gave me a tight smile that didn't quite fit her face. "Plus, that's the only place you can smoke."

"Does that mean you've quit?"

"Mmm-hmm."

"That's great. Is it going to bother you if I smoke?" I asked.

"No, don't be silly. It's fine."

We abandoned the air-conditioned comfort of the bar to sit outdoors, and the hot, clammy air draped itself around me like a shroud. It felt as if I'd walked into a tightly enclosed space, instead of an open, empty one. A waiter trailed after us, lighting a citronella candle as we took our seats. Our table was shielded from the rain by a giant umbrella with a golden, tasseled fringe that must have looked absurdly gaudy in daylight. The waiter offered us menus, lit my cigarette, and took our order, returning a couple of minutes later with a pomegranate margarita for me and an orange juice for Skye.

"So," I said, exhaling smoke, "are you going to tell me what's wrong?"

Skye's eyes were on the table. "It's a long story."

"You mentioned that already." I scanned her face, noticing her mouth quiver, as if tears were building up inside her again. I looked away, wanting to give her space in which to compose herself. "The view from this place must be incredible during the day," I said, staring into the distance. The sun was completely gone, and the sky was an unrelieved expanse of flat blackness, with clouds crowding out the stars that should have been peering down at us. The fronds of towering palm trees rustled as they moved, stirred by salty gusts of ocean breeze that seemed to be the only relief from the merciless humidity. I could hear the water, even if I couldn't see it. The cliffs, caught in shadow, were pitch-black, a jagged silhouette framed by fiery torches. The streaks of vivid orange flames matched the beads around Skye's neck; their colors were as vivid outside, by candlelight, as they were indoors.

"It's a dead hotel in a dying destination." Skye's tone was harsh. "Do you mind if I steal a cigarette?"

"No, but didn't you just tell me you quit?"

"I'm under way too much stress right now," she answered. "Anyway, tomorrow's another day." That made her sound like a peroxided Scarlett O'Hara, but I don't think she realized it; my love of old movies wasn't something Skye shared. She waved the waiter over for a light while I watched her, perplexed by the strangeness of her demeanor. She took a long, deep drag and closed her eyes, sighing as she exhaled.

"Can I ask you something?" she said. "You know how we were just talking about staying in touch with exes? I was wondering if you and Martin Sklar ever—"

"We don't talk." My voice was as flat as the starless sky.

"Because he's in Southeast Asia?"

"What?"

"From what I've heard, he's been there a lot lately. Something about negotiating to open a hotel in Burma or Myanmar or whatever you're supposed to call it these days."

Martin cozying up to a regime to get a hotel concession? That figured. Nothing my ex did really surprised me, though hearing about his unethical exploits made me angry at myself for how much I'd been willing to overlook when we were together.

"I couldn't really care less about what he does," I said.

Skye took another long drag from her cigarette. For the first time, I realized she was nervous. She watched me with an intent expression that made me feel like I was under a magnifying glass. Her mouth shifted into a grin now and then, as if a pair of tiny fishhooks tugged each corner into place, but her eyes betrayed the effort; they were caught somewhere between worry and hope. "You two always seemed like such a great couple." Her voice was tentative, almost wary. I didn't respond, and she went on. "You're both so glamorous. Seeing the two of you together was like watching a movie."

"Sometimes it felt like a movie, but I didn't like the way the script was going."

"So you two really are through?"

"Any particular reason you're asking, Skye?"

The only light was from the candle on the table and the ambient glow of the bar's interior, but I was certain she blushed. "I was thinking you and Martin have broken up before and gotten back together," she mumbled.

"That's not going to happen this time."

"Someone told me you hand-addressed your wedding invitations and were taking them to the post office, when you suddenly threw them in the garbage and flew off to Spain instead."

"That sounds like something Ava Gardner would have done." The truth was, I'd tossed a stack of save-the-date cards, not wedding invitations. Not that Skye needed to know. "You seem awfully interested in Martin."

She took her time answering. Cigarettes were useful props; you could disguise confusion or annoyance or any other reaction with a long, thoughtful drag. I'd done that myself, enough times to recognize when someone else attempted it. "I guess, in a way, I am."

I examined her more closely. There was tension behind her facade. It was knotted around her eyes and mouth, and I saw it in her hands as she reached for another cigarette and lit it with the first. I was about to ask, "Why on earth would you be interested in Martin?" but I immediately thought of a reason: she was involved with him. My mind teetered for a moment, bracing for an agonized revelation, before catching its balance. *I don't really care,* I thought, surprising myself. I wasn't trying to be the bigger person. If they were together, I hoped they were both heart-wrenchingly miserable.

"I feel like my whole life has fallen apart. I haven't . . ." Skye's voice trailed off and she inhaled smoke, staring out at the dark cliffs. The flames of the torches were losing their fight against the rain.

Her words hung in the air between us as I waited for an explanation that didn't come. "You mentioned being sick," I said cautiously. "What else is wrong?"

She gave me a searching look, her face pinched with worry. Applause erupted from the cliffs, and Skye took advantage of the distraction. "You know what's funny? People say there's never been a death here from cliff diving. Just wait until you see them in action. It's impossible to believe."

The spectacle on the cliffs wasn't half as interesting to me as whatever had gotten under Skye's skin. She was normally a cheerful chatterbox; it was unnerving to see her so subdued. "What's going on with you, Skye? Why did you start crying in the lobby?"

"That . . . that was just me being an idiot. I've been seeing this guy for months, and I really thought he was The One, but he's a bastard. He's just . . . evil. There's no other word for it. I'm ashamed I didn't see it before, you know? I should've known something was wrong when he said we had to keep our relationship under wraps. What kind of guy does that?"

"Is he married?"

She shook her head. "No, just seriously screwed up in the head."

Martin and I had agreed to keep things quiet when we'd first started dating, but that had been a mutual decision, inspired—on my side—by fear of being taken for a gold digger and paranoia about reporters dredging up my past. Before I could form a question, Skye started speaking again.

"The thing is, I know how to get even with him." She stopped fidgeting and looked me in the eye. "I'm going to destroy him professionally, and he'll never even see it coming."

"Skye, no matter how much you hate him right now, nothing good is going to come from taking revenge."

"This isn't about revenge. This is about righting wrongs. *Illegal* wrongs, Lily. I can deal with my hurt feelings, but he can't be allowed to keep on doing the things he does."

"Have you gotten the police involved?"

"There's no point. This is too big. I know I'm right about what's going on, but . . ." She exhaled furiously. She sounded as if she were replaying an argument in her head. "When I try to get to the bottom of things, the truth keeps slipping away. I can't get the hard proof I need. Sometimes, I think if I were a real journalist, instead of a fluffy travel writer, I'd have done it already. I'm going to write a feature about—"

She stopped speaking as a man stepped out onto the balcony. In the golden half-light of the bar, I could see he was tall and broad-shouldered, with tanned skin and curly black hair, but the shadows obscured his features. He wore a dark suit with a white shirt that was open at the neck. As he walked by, he nodded at us then stood at the edge of the balcony for a moment. The breeze carried the scent of his cologne, musky and enticing but a touch too heavily applied.

"Good evening, ladies." His English was accented. He passed us again and went back inside. Had he heard us speaking? When I looked at Skye, she was glaring after him with narrowed eyes.

"Who was that?" I asked.

"Listen to me, Lily. You don't want to know that guy."

"Okay, what were you saying about working on a story?"

"I'm not sure I can tell you." Skye crushed her cigarette and pulled an iPhone out of her bag.

"You don't really think I'm going to steal your story, do you?"

Her platinum hair gleamed as she shook her head. "No, no, no. Of course not, Lily. If anything, you're the person who could help me with the story."

"How?" I was mystified and more than slightly exasperated.

"Here, take a look at this." She reached into her bag and handed me a paperback book that I immediately recognized as *Frakker's Mexico.*

"I have this book with me, Skye. I work for them, remember?"

"Just look at it, okay?" She stood. "I just need to call m— uh, someone. I can't explain right now, but I'll be able to soon." She hurried toward the door, leaving her bag behind on a chair.

*Someone?* I thought. She'd been about to say a name but she'd pulled back at the last second.

"I'll be back in a couple of minutes," she called over her shoulder. "Be careful."

Before I could say anything, she was through the door and inside the bar. There was a huge cheer from the cliffs. I got to my feet but couldn't see anything from that vantage point, except the fading glow of the torchlights. That sight didn't pique my curiosity the way Skye had. I looked back at the bar, but she was already gone.

# 3

I polished off my margarita while I waited for Skye to return. Another cliff diver must have jumped, because there was more wild cheering. It was surreal, sitting in a bar so close to the spectacle, yet being removed from the action. Ironically, I could picture the divers thanks to the promotional video clips that Denny Chiu, the public relations executive who'd lured me to Acapulco, had sent my way. I'd been fascinated by the fearless way the men hurled themselves off a narrow ledge. For a split second, they seemed to swoop forward, arms high and torsos arced, defying gravity before plunging into the abyss below. Having seen the sunny highlights on film, I wondered if I'd be disappointed in person, watching under a gray drizzle. That was so often the case in real life.

"Another pomegranate margarita, señora?" asked the waiter.

I looked at my watch. It had been at least twenty minutes since Skye had handed the book to me and gone off to make her phone call. The Frakker's guide had asterisks drawn in the margins next to a few hotels; from what little I'd read by candlelight, there was nothing special about the properties. "No, thank you."

"You did not care for it?" he asked. He was in his midfifties, with neatly combed and pomaded iron gray hair and dark brows.

"It was very good. I'm just a little tired." That was an understatement. Denny had flown me from Barcelona to New York the day before, so I'd spent two days traveling and was seriously road-weary and jet-lagged.

He smiled. "It is only nine o'clock! The night has not even started."

"I've heard Acapulco is one of those towns that never sleeps."

"Oh, we sleep, but only at afternoon siesta. When you are in Acapulco, you should do as the natives do."

"When my friend comes back, will you tell her that I went to my room—number 527—and that I have her purse?" I felt bad about leaving—I imagined Skye coming back to the table just after I left—but I was hungry, exhausted, and more than slightly annoyed that she'd dragged me to the bar only to abandon me there.

Retracing my steps back to the lobby, I found it silent. The clerk looked bored as he pecked at his computer, and I wondered if the snake had been captured and escorted off the premises. I headed toward the elevators, turning from the broad expanse of the lobby down a narrow corridor with a high ceiling. The hallway's walls were populated with black-and-white photographs of Hollywood stars. I recognized a bare-chested Johnny Weismuller and a bare-legged John Wayne. Next to them was a shot of Tyrone Power, who had filmed *Captain from Castile* in Acapulco. I stared at that photo; Martin Sklar looked a lot like him, and the resemblance had been the first thing that had attracted me to him. It was only as I stared at the picture that I started to wonder how the hell Skye knew where Martin was.

My mind churned with bits of our conversation. *He's in Southeast Asia,* she'd said. *Something about negotiating to open a hotel in Burma or Myanmar or whatever you're sup-posed to call it these days.*

I'd dated Martin for two years, and we'd stayed in touch for a year after we broke up. While I hadn't spoken to him in eight months, there were some things about him that I didn't believe had changed. One was that Martin, who wasn't ex-actly trustworthy himself, didn't put his faith in other people. Anyone who'd read about Martin could have figured out that he was at a major art show at certain times of the year—Maastricht in mid-March, Art Basel Miami Beach in early December—because he attended a handful of those annually. But Myanmar? That wasn't just an educated guess. When we'd first started seeing each other, Martin kept quiet about his itinerary; later, I found out that he feared I'd inadver-tently tell someone and spoil whatever he was planning. My ex was nothing if not paranoid. The fact that Skye knew where he was made me wonder how well she knew him.

When I stepped into the elevator, Skye's voice kept rever-berating in my head, distracting me so much that I pressed the wrong button. *The thing is, I know how to get even with him. I'm going to destroy him professionally, and he'll never even see it coming. . . . This isn't about revenge. This is about righting wrongs.* Illegal *wrongs, Lily. I can deal with my hurt feelings, but he can't be allowed to keep on doing the things he does.*

That made something twist inside me. Could Skye have been talking about Martin? If anyone had cause to want re-venge on him, it was me. He'd plotted against my sister, Claudia, and I knew he'd wanted to have her killed back when he believed she was blackmailing him. His plans never came to pass, but that awful impulse was something I'd never be able to forgive him for. For weeks after my sister's funeral,

I'd wanted revenge on Martin, even though he wasn't responsible for what had actually happened to Claudia. I'd lain awake many nights, visualizing what I'd do to get even. But as I crawled out of the pit of despair, I left my fantasies of vengeance behind. It wasn't a conscious decision, but a survival mechanism. Moving forward in my life meant shedding the dark regrets in my past.

When the elevator doors opened, I stepped out before remembering that the fourth floor wasn't the one I wanted. It was dark and silent, and I backed into the elevator, wondering why all the lights were off. Did the hotel have so few guests that an entire floor was empty? As the doors slid shut and the elevator chugged upward again, my thoughts returned to Martin. My ex was amoral and ruthless, but it had taken me a long time to see that. In retrospect, I realized I'd been willfully blind, ignoring what was in front of me. Maybe poor Skye caught on faster than I had. *You don't even know that they were involved,* whispered a voice in the back of my brain. Even so, I wondered what Martin had done to Skye to make her hate him so deeply.

On the fifth floor, I stepped out of the elevator and turned down the hallway, finding my room at the end of a long, curving corridor. *Room* was a misnomer; when I unlocked the door, I found a grand suite that was perhaps a grade below *El Presidente* levels, but only by a hair. The foyer had a circular table in its center, bearing a massive floral display that I had to inch around to avoid it poking me in the eye. A short hallway opened into an expansive living room with a high, molded ceiling. Someone had pulled the heavy drapes almost closed, but I could still make out floor-to-ceiling windows. I stepped forward, setting both my bag and Skye's on a table, and slipped out of my shoes. All of the lights were burning bright, jolting the vivid colors of the room to life. Whoever had decorated this room lived by the motto "more is more." Scarlet and tangerine and yellow and chartreuse rioted together from one end of the room to the other, all screaming for attention.

The phone rang before I got any further. "Miss Moore, we have your dinner ready. May we bring it to you?" A minute later, the doorbell rang, and a trio of waiters bearing covered silver trays and a matching ice bucket came into the room. They marched through the living room and into the dining room.

"This will only take a moment to set up," one said. "Thank you, Miss Moore."

I decided to keep exploring while they laid the meal out. Stepping through another doorway, I found the bedroom. My carry-on bag stood against a wall; I'd almost forgotten that a bellman had disappeared with it when I'd arrived at the Hotel Cerón. The bedroom wasn't as aggressively colorful as the living room, but it did boast a bedspread that was the same shade of red as a chili pepper. Lying against a pillow was a white envelope with the words FOR MISS LILY MOORE written in a calligraphic style on the front.

As I reached for it, a champagne cork popped, making my head turn, and I noticed a framed photograph on the wall. It was a portrait of Ava Gardner. I stopped suddenly and stared, disconcerted. The other art I'd seen in the suite were bright paintings of Mexican landscapes; this black-and-white shot seemed very much out of place. I stared around the room, realizing that there was a shot of Ava with Frank Sinatra, and another that was a publicity still of Ava wearing a leopard-print bathing suit and posing on a leopard-skin rug. The presence of the shots didn't feel accidental; it was hard to imagine that they weren't deliberate choices made by someone who knew of my admiration for Ava Gardner. Had Denny asked the hotel to redecorate my room? She was detail-oriented, but this felt like overkill.

"Everything is ready. Thank you, Miss Moore!" called a waiter. I hurried out of the bedroom, because I'd left my purse in the living room, but the front door was already closing. The fact they hadn't waited for a tip was startling, but the smell emanating from the red-walled dining room distracted me from everything else. On the oval dining table, they'd laid out salad, steak, and vegetables on white china plates with HOTEL CERÓN emblazoned on the edge; the crème brûlée sat in a blue ramekin, and an open bottle of champagne chilled in a silver ice bucket. I took a sip from the glass they'd poured for me and shook my head. Most of the time, travel writing was a job like any other, but there were days I wished I could live at a hotel forever.

I sat down and took a bite of the steak. It was cooked to medium-rare perfection, even if it was slathered in a gravy it could have done without. Someone in the kitchen clearly had a heavy hand with sauces, because the salad was drenched in dressing, and there was even a creamy relish atop the grilled vegetables. I scraped off as much as I could, and I was half-way through the main course when a booming sound from the hallway made me freeze. Someone was banging on a door and yelling. I went to the foyer, silent as a ghost and glad I'd already abandoned my shoes. Through the peephole, I could see a large man. His back was to me; the door across the hall was the one he was attacking. He wore jeans and a black shirt, and his shoulder-length dark hair was shaggy.

"Skye!" he bellowed, hitting the door again, knocking the side of his balled fist against it as if he were hammering a nail. "Skye!"

It was only when he spoke that my heart stopped galloping and resumed its normal pace. I turned the lock on my door and pulled it open.

"Pete, what are you doing?" I asked. "You sound like Marlon Brando shouting for Stella in *A Streetcar Named Desire*."

The man turned, his mouth gaping in surprise. It had been well over a year since I'd seen Pete Dukermann and roughly three years since I'd poured a pitcher of beer over his head in a bar in Prague. He was in his late thirties now, and he hadn't aged well: there were dark pouches under his eyes and his jawline was melting into wobbly jowls. He'd put on weight, too, though the way his arms bulged against the thin fabric of the shirt showed that there was muscle under the fat.

"Lily Moore? I'll be damned." Even though he was standing several feet away, he reeked of his usual overripe scent of sweat, marijuana, and musk. Among travel journalists, he was known as Pepé le Pew, but the smell was only part of it; he'd earned the nickname for his unrelenting pursuit of anything in a skirt. He was a photographer notorious for asking women to pose naked for him, always with the caveat *Don't worry, my wife won't mind, we have an open marriage.* Pete was the punch line to many a joke in the travel industry.

"That's Skye McDermott's room?" I asked.

"Yeah. You seen her around?"

"I had a drink with her downstairs, but she left to make a phone call. She never came back."

"She seem kinda weird to you?" Pete asked.

"Weird?" That wasn't the word I'd have chosen, but it fit. The crying, the bone-thinness, the revenge talk, none of that was like the Skye I knew. Still, Pete was low on the list of people I'd confide in, and I wasn't going to tell him what Skye had told me.

"I don't know how to explain it. She's such a nice girl, real friendly. Not like some stuck-up travel writers I could name." Pete's unsubtle barb made me smile; at least I didn't have to worry about him coming onto me again. "But she's all freaked out. It's obvious something big is going on with her, you know?"

I nodded. I did know. A wave of exhaustion and nausea washed over me, and I leaned against the doorframe for support.

He rapped on Skye's door again. "There's a doorbell," I pointed out. Pete grunted, then pushed it a couple of times. I noticed his hand was marked with red scratches, as if he'd had a run-in with an alley cat. The bells echoed faintly back at us.

"So, I guess you and your hotel zillionaire boyfriend got back together, huh?" Pete asked.

"What? No! Why would you think that?" The question caught me completely off guard, and Pete chuckled. He'd managed to rattle me, and that made me angry. "How the hell did you manage to get on this press trip, anyway? I thought you were on everyone's blacklist by now."

"I wasn't invited on the press trip," Pete admitted. "I was already down here. I ran into Skye at the zocalo yesterday, and she mentioned it. I called Denny, and the snobby bitch told me no, the trip was already planned, the hotel was full, blah, blah, blah. So I called corporate HQ and got myself into the hotel without her. People in the industry know I do great work."

"I'm sure Denny is thrilled. As are we all."

That made him scowl. "Don't know why I'm wasting time talking to you, anyway. You should get a life." He turned back to Skye's door, ringing the bell one more time. We both waited for her to answer.

"I don't think she's home."

"No shit, Sherlock," he shot back. He shrugged and started down the hallway, his movements loose and shambling, as if alcohol and pot had set him up on casters and were gently wheeling him away.

I was glad to see him go. Ducking back into my suite and locking the door, I realized he'd only made me worry about Skye. I bumped into a doorknob and noticed that my hallway had a connecting door with the room next to it. *Too bad that's not a door to Skye's room. It would be so much easier to get inside.* I'd assumed her call went on for longer than expected, or that she'd run into another journalist and lost track of time. But seeing that even a drunken, drugged Pete was concerned about her set off alarm bells in me. Skye had admitted she'd been ill, though she hadn't given me any details. My mind immediately jumped to the worst possible place, picturing her unconscious and incapacitated.

*There's probably a key card in her bag,* whispered a voice that sounded suspiciously like my sister's. It often suggested things that weren't exactly appropriate. Feeling bold, I unsnapped the top of Skye's bag and peeked inside. Just as quickly, I closed it. I'd grown up with a mother and a sister who had no regard for my privacy, and I'd resented them for it. My concern about Skye didn't give me the right to dig through her purse, or to go into her room.

*But what if she needs help?* That voice was so persuasive, because it played on my unspoken fears. It reminded me of the time I'd found Claudia on the floor of my apartment after an overdose. Skye wasn't a junkie—she wasn't even drinking alcohol—but it was possible that she was in trouble.

That settled it. I opened her bag, feeling both shame and exhilaration. Under a layer of damp, wadded-up tissues was a fold-out map of Acapulco, a beaded change purse stuffed with coins and a few hundred-peso bills, a comb, a lipstick case, a bottle of chewable multivitamins, a hand sanitizer spray, a half-empty bag of ginger candies, and a book of matches. At the bottom, I found some seashells, a few crumpled twenty-peso bills, and another Frakker's travel guidebook. This one was for Eastern Europe, which suggested Skye had just been there, or was about to head in that direction. Finally, my fingers brushed against the zipper of an inner pocket, and I found a plain beige room key.

I stepped into my shoes and ventured out to the hallway, ringing Skye's bell. For a moment, I thought I heard footsteps inside, and I waited for her to open the door. She didn't, and I rang again. Resting my palm against her door, I leaned forward and turned my head, which let me listen for noises inside the room and keep an eye on the corridor in case someone stumbled across my eavesdropper pose. There wasn't any sound I could discern: no television, no radio, no conversation, no heels tapping on the floor. Still, that didn't mean anything; Skye could have been lying down, or reading, or . . . I pressed the doorbell, counted to ten, and buzzed again. Only emptiness echoed back at me. When I finally tried the key card, I was stunned to find it didn't work; instead of flashing green, I got an angry red evil eye blinking at me.

So much for that. I went back to my room, picked up the phone, and dialed Skye's room number. After a minute of ringing, my call went to an impersonal hotel voice mailbox.

"Skye, it's Lily. Please call me as soon as you get this message. It doesn't matter what time it is. Just give me a call. I'm in room 527, right across from you."

Setting the receiver down, I had a change of heart, and I picked it up again and pressed zero. A clerk picked up, greeting me in English. "Can you connect me with Denny Chiu, please?"

"Of course," he answered, but her line also rang and rang before dropping me back in the voice mail ether.

Thwarted on all fronts, I still wasn't ready to give up. Skye might be back in the bar, wondering where I'd gone and when I was coming back. I had to check, at least. But on my way downstairs, I had what seemed like a better idea. Instead of taking the winding passageways that led to the bar, I went to the reception desk.

"Hello, Miss Moore. You will be glad to hear we found your snake friend," the clerk said.

"I hope you got him some better accommodations."

"All I can say is that he is in a better place."

I felt a moment of sadness for the snake. It wasn't the creature's fault that it had slithered indoors. "I'd like to speak to the hotel's manager. I know it's after ten on a Friday night, but is there some way I can reach him?"

"He is here, Miss Moore. He is always here. Let me call him for you." The clerk picked up the receiver and pressed a button. "Mr. Stroud? I apologize for disturbing you, but

Miss Lily Moore would like to speak with you. Yes. Yes? Thank you, sir." He hung up.

The name had caught my attention. It wasn't just that it was an obviously Anglo one, rather than a Mexican one; I knew enough about Mexico to realize it was a multicultural society. But the name *Stroud* had made me flinch in recognition when I heard it. It was like a puzzle piece that suddenly clicked into place. Before I could catch my breath, the door behind the reception desk opened and Martin Sklar's right-hand man stepped out.

# 5

Gavin Stroud seemed faintly amused by my startled expression, and the sharp angles of his face eased into a smile. He was always so measured and tentative around Martin, but he looked oddly delighted to see me. "Lily!"

"Gavin." I wanted to smile back, if only to pretend I was unfazed, but his name came off my tongue with the arid chill of a night in the desert.

"It's been such a long time, Lily. Much too long for my taste." He came around the counter, moving with the stealth of a jaguar. He was just shy of six feet, with broad shoulders that spoke of his dedication to the gym. I put out my hand for him to shake, but he clasped it in both of his. The gesture was warm even if his hands were cool. "Of all the hotels, in all the world, you walk into mine!"

It sounded as if he hoped to channel Humphrey Bogart in *Casablanca*. *Of all the gin joints, in all the towns, in all the world, she walks into mine.* The way the phrase sprang from his lips made it appear as if he'd been practicing it in front of a mirror. His crisp English accent didn't help it seem natural, either.

"It's good to see you again, Gavin." I hoped my voice sounded more sincere to his ears than it did to my own.

He stared at me, suddenly leaning forward to kiss my left cheek, then the right. How Continental of him. How forced and awkward it felt to me. To be fair, any meeting with a close associate of Martin's would be difficult, but this was especially hard. I'd never felt a hint of warmth from Gavin, and his pretending we were old friends made it seem as if he were following a script instead of his true feelings.

"I'm honored that you remember me, Lily." His smooth baritone was suddenly intimate. "I never thought I made much of an impression on you, not with Martin around."

Gavin's words hung in the space between us, and I carefully extracted my hand from his grip. I didn't want to talk about Martin, especially not with a man who worked for him. Even if that man was the one he called Robo-Rex. Martin was shameless in mocking both Gavin's obsessive workaholism and his more obsequious qualities, even though Martin relied on him professionally. In that uncomfortable pause, something shifted in Gavin's expression, and I knew he wasn't pleased with my icy reaction. He went on, speaking swiftly as if aware that he might have made a misstep, doubling down on flattery. "You're even lovelier than I remembered. I hope you don't mind my saying so, Lily. I was surprised—very pleasantly surprised—to learn that you would be staying here."

"*You* were surprised?" I didn't even try to keep my disbelief out of my voice. "You're hosting the press trip, aren't you?"

"No, it's the Mexican Tourism Board's trip. Everything happened at the last minute. You were supposed to be at another hotel, one in the Diamante Zone, I believe, but they discovered bedbugs there."

"Bedbugs?"

"Horrible, isn't it? They only decided this morning to put you up here. I hope no one will mind that we're basically closed for renovations. I must say, I was absolutely delighted when I saw your name on the list. It was a surprise to me, a wonderful surprise."

It sounded plausible enough, but what he said didn't add up. Pete Dukermann had told me he'd run into Skye the day before and she was already at the Hotel Cerón. When Pete mentioned calling "corporate HQ," he'd clearly meant Pantheon Worldwide's headquarters. No wonder Pete had asked if Martin and I had gotten back together—I was staying at a Pantheon hotel. The way Gavin kept repeating that he was surprised made it sound like a fact he wanted to convince me of. That made me suspicious, and for the first time, I wondered if Martin had deliberately lured me down to Mexico. *Don't be paranoid*, I chided myself; *Martin hasn't bothered you in eight months, so why would he start now?*

"I had no idea Pantheon owned the Hotel Cerón," I said.

"It's a recent acquisition. We're going to upgrade the property before we start publicizing it."

"I see." That was the Pantheon way. The riot of color in my suite wouldn't survive after the company made its mark on the hotel. Everything would be muted to shades of sand and beige. The only vivid colors would be those you saw through a window: a sunset stretching across the sky, or torchlight on the cliffs. "I'm sorry, Gavin, but I never would have agreed to be on this trip if I'd known I'd be staying at a Pantheon property. I'll go upstairs to gather my things. If you could recommend another hotel where I can stay tonight, I'd appreciate it. Otherwise, I'll find one online."

"Lily, please. You simply can't do that."

"Just watch me."

"What I mean is that it isn't safe, Lily. You have no idea how dangerous it is here." Gavin's slate-blue eyes were serious.

"I can't, in good conscience, let you leave tonight. It's after ten, and the locals won't even drive on the roads at this time of night for fear of carjackings and kidnappings. Thugs have literally killed people and piled up their decapitated bodies at Plaza Sendero at night."

I knew that Acapulco had a seedy side, but my mind had been brimming with visions of Hollywood stars vacationing there, the glamour and luxury of it all. Apparently, those carefree images were hopelessly out of date. "Gavin, I can't stay here. Isn't there a hotel down the road?"

"There's nothing nearby. Part of our charm is our very remoteness in such a densely populated destination. We have our own guards patrolling the grounds, so I can assure you you're safe here, but it would be hazardous to leave. In the morning, you'll be able to go wherever you like, and I'll make sure the tourism people find you an excellent spot. I'm sorry about this situation, Lily. I'm very happy to see you, but I understand that this is less than thrilling for you."

"I know it's not your fault, Gavin." I felt petty and small for taking out my frustration on him. "Just tell me one thing: is Martin here at the hotel?"

"No. Why would he be?" Gavin's brow furrowed and smoothed itself out. "Ah, you think this is some trick of Martin's to get you near him? I promise you, Lily, nothing could be further from the truth. He's off on a jaunt to another continent, actually."

"I heard he was in Burma."

For the first time, I'd surprised Gavin. Like me, he knew that Martin's schedule was a closely held secret. "How did you know . . . ?"

"Skye McDermott mentioned it."

He blinked twice. "Did she really?" There was a sharp edge beneath his deep, polished voice. "What else did Skye tell you?"

"She's the reason I wanted to talk to you. I had a drink with her at the bar tonight, a little after eight. She left to make a phone call and never came back. She's not in her room—or, at, least, she's not answering the door."

"I don't see why that's any cause for worry." Gavin's tone reverted to its familiar soothing blandness. The blade underneath that had flashed briefly was already sheathed.

"She mentioned that she's been sick, and at one point, she burst out crying. I've known Skye for a long time, and that's not like her." I bit my lip. "I'm worried. Given what you said about how dangerous things are in Acapulco, maybe we should call the police?"

"Let's sit down for a moment, Lily." Gavin put his hand behind my elbow and guided me to one of the lobby's pristine white sofas. His gray suit was neatly pressed, his pale blue shirt was uncreased, and his tie was knotted with Duke of Windsor–like precision. He'd undoubtedly been at work since early in the morning, but he looked as if he'd just gotten dressed. *Just wind Gavin up and point him in any direction, and he'll get the job done. I wish I could keep him in a box.* I could hear Martin's voice in my head, as clear as if he were in the lobby with us.

"I've been in Acapulco long enough to know that the local police are not people you want to deal with. They tend to be corrupt, and they look at travelers as cash machines. They're badly underpaid, and it's not unusual for them to extort money from travelers who cross their path. The honest ones have their hands full dealing with the drug cartels."

Gavin's accent gave his words sharp points that felt like thorns. "Acapulco might look like fun in the sun, but this city is a minefield."

He reminded me of something my friend Jesse had told me while we were traveling in Peru in the spring. Jesse had been partially right: there were some elements of that country's police force that were corrupt. Still, it was far from being the rule. "Skye could be in trouble."

Gavin patted my hand. "You can't file a Missing Persons report on a woman who went missing a few minutes ago. Especially someone as temperamental and flighty as Skye McDermott."

"She can be dramatic, but I've known her for years, and I've traveled with her many times. She's reliable, not flighty."

His expression was cautious. "Well, you clearly have a better sense of her than I do. I only know Skye through her relationship with Martin, so perhaps I don't have the most accurate impression."

My ears took his words in, but my brain stopped processing them after Gavin said, *I only know Skye through her relationship with Martin.* Relationship?

Gavin read my expression perfectly. "You did know that they had dated, didn't you?"

I cleared my throat. "No. That never came up."

"I don't know that it was ever serious, but they were going out, hmm, perhaps a year ago? I don't know what's happened since I relocated to Mexico to run Pantheon's operations here. I used to be so closely tied to Martin's orbit, but that's not true anymore."

"How exciting that you're running things here." My voice was calm, even though my pulse was racing. I got to my feet.

"Thank you for having me stay here tonight. I'll be leaving as early as I can in the morning."

"There's no rush, Lily. Keep in mind that time in Acapulco moves more slowly than it does in New York or even Spain." He stood. "Let me walk you up to your room."

"No need. Goodnight, Gavin." My sandals clacked on the tile as I headed through the lobby. I was hoping to see another venomous snake, because I had a sudden impulse to pick it up and deposit it in Skye's room.

The kicker was, I knew I was an idiot. That thought kept me company as I rode the elevator up to the fifth floor and stormed down the corridor. I was a fool and I hated myself for it. In the back of my mind, I could picture my sister, Claudia, ruefully shaking her head at me. *Deep down, you're pretty superficial.* She'd told me that so many times, the phrase was tattooed on my brain. She'd been right.

I stopped at the end of the hall, in front of my door, then turned so that I was facing Skye's. Suddenly, I had the oddest feeling that eyes were watching me. Trying to get my heartbeat under control, I stared straight ahead, as if I could make her open up. Maybe that was why the key card hadn't worked—she'd bolted it from the inside. I pounded on her door with the heel of my hand, then rang the doorbell for good measure. Nothing but the echo of my own racket came back to my ears.

"Coward," I called, turning to unlock my own door.

What did it matter to me, who Martin dated? The memory of our relationship was agonizing, not so much because of any particular incident—though the events around my sister's death still pained me—but because I'd been so eager to believe that he was the man of my dreams. That was proof positive I'd watched too many movies from Hollywood's Golden Era. I hadn't had one moment's doubt since our last parting, and my emotions toward him were equal measures of loathing and disgust. No, that wasn't quite true: if they could be weighed on a scale, the tilt in favor of loathing would have been impossible to disguise.

As I stepped into the living room, I grabbed Skye's black leather bag, tossed it on the floor, and kicked it across the room. The bag hit the fragile leg of a decorative end table, slamming the marble top against the wall, in turn dislodging a painting that had its crash landing broken by the bag. I froze, staring at the cartoonish wreckage. Whatever glint of satisfaction I had was instantly crushed. Somewhere, somehow, Claudia was laughing at me and the faint hiss of that sound made me both nostalgic for her and ashamed of myself. I used to be much better behaved.

I crossed the floor, set my own bag on the sofa, and lifted the gilded frame. I'd taken the scene inside it for a painting when I'd first seen the room, but now it was obvious that it was just a print with brushstrokes applied over it. The paper was so flimsy that it had ripped, even though the sturdy frame still held it. I hung it back up on the wall, noticing the plaster was covered in spidery hairline fissures. I hoped I wasn't going to have to take the blame for that, too; it was bad enough I'd busted up a picture. I picked up the tabletop and set it back in place. The surprise came when I lifted Skye's bag. It wasn't any heavier than I remembered, but a large black rectangle poked out of it. I eased it out, turning it over in my hands. The piece was flat and thin, yet completely solid. How had I missed it?

Setting it down, I knelt and lifted the yawning mouth of the bag. I pulled out the guidebooks and bits and pieces I'd noted earlier before finding something unfamiliar. It was a U.S. passport, one that was thicker than usual because it had been loaded with the extra pages that a travel writer needed, plus an assortment of visas and stamps. I opened it and saw a photograph of Skye, her face a little fuller and entirely free of the anxiety I'd glimpsed in the bar. Flipping through the pages made me remember how hard it had been to replace my passport when it went missing in Peru. So frustrating. So time-consuming. I got up and went to the desk, tucking Skye's passport inside a drawer. It was a petty, mean trick to pull, yet oddly satisfying. My best friend, Jesse, wouldn't approve, but I knew Claudia would.

I rooted through Skye's bag with a deepening curiosity. What else was in there? I found a nylon wallet that contained three credit cards—two in Skye's name, and one belonging to her former fiancé, Ryan Brooks. There was also a New York driver's license and some cash, both American dollars and Mexican pesos. It took me a minute to understand how I'd missed all this the first time around: that strange black rectangle was the false bottom of Skye's bag. Under it had been a wide but shallow compartment. It was clever on Skye's part, and I felt a grudging admiration for her. Travel writers got scammed just as often as normal tourists did, mostly through opportunistic pickpocketing. Skye managing to keep her documents and money with her, yet out of reach from a thief's eager hand, was smart.

When I reached into the bag again, I retrieved two small, tinted vials of pills, both locked under childproof caps. There was nothing inherently sinister about them, but my hands quivered so that, for a split second, it sounded as if I were shaking a pair of maracas. Skye was sick, or at least she had been recently. The fact she'd left her medications behind made me worry for her. Was she so reluctant to see me that she'd decided she could do without them?

The labels matched: both bottles were from Pasteur Pharmacy on East Thirty-fourth Street in New York, and the prescriptions had been filled ten days earlier. One bottle was for something called promethazine, the other for trimetho-benzamide. The instructions were disturbingly dull, giving no hint at what they were for. When I typed the names into a search engine, I found them quickly in the database of the U.S. National Library of Medicine: *Promethazine is used to relieve the symptoms of allergic reactions such as allergic rhinitis (runny nose and watery eyes caused by allergy to pollen, mold, or dust), allergic conjunctivitis (red, watery eyes caused by allergies), allergic skin reactions, and allergic reactions to blood or plasma products.* Skye had mentioned allergies when I'd first seen her, so that fit. The other was more disturbing: *Trimethobenzamide is used to treat nausea and vomiting that may occur after surgery.* Surgery? Was that what Skye had meant when she said she'd been sick?

My heart had been thudding when I'd entered my suite, but now its beat felt slow and faint. I was lightheaded and more than slightly nauseated myself. Minutes before, I'd been furious at Skye. Now, for the first time, I was truly afraid for her.

# 7

It look took me a while to find Denny Chiu. Gavin had already made it clear that he wasn't concerned about Skye, so I went to the one person I was sure would share my apprehension. The front desk confirmed that Denny was in the suite next to mine, but she wasn't answering her phone. I went to her door and rang the bell, planting myself there to wait. Finally, I spotted her in the hallway, coming toward me.

"Lily? What are you doing out here? You should be sleeping!" Denny's face was flushed and her expression was slightly dazed, but she smiled and air-kissed me on both cheeks. It was a lot more natural than Gavin's gesture. "It's so good to see you! You must be completely exhausted, but you look fantastic."

Denny herself looked fresh and chic, as if she'd just dressed, the opposite of me, who smelled like someone who'd been traveling all day. She was casual in jeans and a black silk T-shirt, sporting a red scarf at her throat and the de rigueur stiletto heels of a New York City–based public relations executive. Behind squared-off Prada frames, she had wide-set eyes with catlike lashes swooping upward. Her long, ebony hair cascaded around her shoulders, accentuating her delicate features. Whenever I saw her, she brought to mind the actress Nancy Kwan. The only unlovely thing about her appearance was a taupe bandage wrapped around her right wrist and forearm.

"I'm a little tired," I admitted. "What happened to your arm?"

"Ugh. I sprained my wrist from grabbing my suitcase." She glanced down at the bandage and shook her head. "First carpal tunnel syndrome, now this. I think my body started falling apart when I turned forty." Her rueful expression switched to a smile. "How has everything been so far?"

"The suite is lovely, and it was very thoughtful of you to arrange for dinner, Denny. But I never would have agreed to this trip knowing that Pantheon was a sponsor."

"You have no idea how sorry I am." Denny knew me well enough to realize why I wouldn't want anything to do with Martin's company. "It was totally out of my control. There was a problem at the sponsor hotel, and—"

"Gavin already told me. Bedbugs."

Her eyes widened. "He said that? I'm going to kill him. Rule One is don't scare the journalists." She sighed. "Everything about this trip has been total hell. Two journalists dropped out at the last minute, and . . . oh, I don't want to bore you with the details. Let's just say this has been the press-junket equivalent of a swamp. Nothing is working out the way it's supposed to. But don't worry. I'm staying up all night fixing everything."

"You don't have to—"

"We won't do breakfast together in the morning—I thought you could do with some room service, and you've got a spa appointment at eleven. I hope that's okay. I figured you could use a massage."

"That's kind of you, but I'm heading off to another hotel in the morning."

"Oh! Of course! I'm such an idiot. Listen, the Fairmont

Princess is gorgeous. They have a stunning hotel-within-a-hotel called Pearl, and I'm going to arrange to get you in there." She lowered her voice. "I'm not a fan of Pantheon, either."

"Why not?"

"I used to work in their London office," Denny said. "Let's just say it wasn't a great experience. They actually inspired me to start my own PR company."

"I had no idea you'd worked for Pantheon." The idea startled me.

"Well, you were probably in college at the time. And I wasn't there for long. I've never worked on staff for another large hotel chain. They burned me out on that front." She shook her head. "Enough about that. Ruby and Roberta get in tomorrow. I think I'll move the three of you to another hotel."

"What about Skye?"

"Make that the four of you. But I am *not* moving that creep Pete Dukermann. There are limits."

"I'm glad to hear that." I'd been angry at Denny, but knowing that her feelings about Pantheon mirrored mine mollified me, at least a little.

"Are you okay?" she asked.

"I'm fine. Just tired." And nauseated, but I kept that to myself.

"You should go to bed. We've got tours planned for tomorrow afternoon, and on Sunday we'll be doing the all-day trip to Taxco, the silver capital of Mexico. You need to get some rest."

"I will, but first I need to talk to you about Skye."

"Sure. What's up?"

"We went for a drink at the hotel bar tonight, and she got

up and vanished in the middle of it. She was acting strange before that. . . ."

"Strange how?"

"She was nervous, and she kept talking about her evil boyfriend, but she wouldn't tell me his name. She was secretive about everything, and she burst into tears at one point." I didn't want to mention what Skye had said about getting revenge; that felt like a breach of confidence.

Denny sighed. "I used to know Skye really well, but not anymore. She's changed completely. She . . ." Her voice trailed off. "Look, I shouldn't be telling tales out of school. Let's just say there's nothing she can do that would surprise me now."

"Well, she left her medication and her money behind with me." I held Skye's black bag up. It had its original contents, mostly. I'd held back the guidebooks, since I still didn't understand why Skye had insisted I take one. After much internal wrangling, I'd left her passport in the desk drawer. It was low on my part, but it also made my ethical line clear: I didn't mind creating a time-consuming problem for her—as far as I was concerned, she deserved it—but I wasn't going to do anything that might jeopardize her health. I could always quietly return the passport later. "I want to put Skye's bag in her room."

"Oh, good idea," Denny said. "I'll take care of that."

"I'd feel better putting it in her room myself."

Denny cocked her head to the side, examining my face. "You want to see if she's in there, don't you?"

I nodded, realizing I'd just been busted.

"Okay, I'll call housekeeping. Wait here." Denny went into her room and closed the door. A minute later she came out, and we waited for the maid to materialize. It didn't take long; an elderly woman with her gray hair pulled back in a net opened the door when Denny pointed to it.

I hesitated, but Denny charged right in. "Skye?" she called, her bright, cheery voice echoing through the rooms. Skye's suite was a mirror image of mine. A long hallway opened to a living room—another free-for-all of color—and instead of turning right to find the bedroom, this layout took a twist to the left. There was nothing to suggest anyone was staying there at all. Maybe I was projecting too much, but since she'd gotten to Acapulco before me, I expected she'd have settled in a little more. In the bedroom, all was serene, except for a pair of open-toed black pumps half-hidden by the bed-spread. Obviously tiny—Skye and I had gone shoe shopping together in the past, so I knew she wore a size five—yet seri-ously vampy, with a towering heel, they could only have be-longed to Skye.

"Skye?" Denny called again, her own heels clacking into the bathroom.

I looked around the bedroom for any sign of Skye. There were only the shoes. Following Denny into the bathroom, I saw an empty counter and used towels.

"Did she say anything about leaving the hotel?" Denny asked.

"No." I was mystified. Looking into the shower, I spotted hotel toiletries but nothing personal. When I turned around, I saw a toiletry kit hanging on the back of the bathroom door; that hadn't been visible from the doorway. "Look," I pointed.

Denny's face registered shock before she plucked it off the hook. She set it on the counter and opened the compart-ments while I watched. There was nothing sinister, just a tube of sunscreen surrounded by compacts filled with face powder, eye shadow, and blusher.

"Where are the rest of her things?" I wondered aloud. Walking back into the bedroom, I opened the closet, but it was empty. There was something forlorn about the pair of heels by the bed; they were almost ghostly, as if Skye had stepped out of them and vanished. The room smelled slightly of Skye's perfume, but otherwise it felt as if there wasn't a trace of her left behind.

**8**

After leaving Skye's suite, I went back to my own while Denny headed downstairs to talk with people and make some calls. I wanted to go with her, but she turned me down flat, insisting that I was unnaturally pale and must go to bed. Her concern over Skye's disappearance eased the throbbing behind my temples a little. When I'd talked to Gavin, I'd felt as if I were swimming upstream, clashing with the current of his disbelief. I would have expected him to be more concerned about his boss's girlfriend but, for all I knew, Skye was just another addition to Martin's Ziegfeld Follies–like parade of dates. At least Denny knew Skye well, and she was as rattled by the idea of Skye suddenly checking out of the hotel as I was.

While getting ready for bed, I finally opened the white envelope that had been lounging against my pillow all evening. The popping of the champagne cork had distracted me from opening it, and afterward I'd forgotten about it. I tore it open and found a heavy white card, edged in gold, with the words FROM THE DESK OF MR. GAVIN P. STROUD engraved at the top. Mentally, I kicked myself for not opening it sooner; it would've saved me from being startled by Gavin in the lobby. Written on the card, in the same elaborate hand as the envelope, was this note:

*My Dearest Lily, it's an honour to have you with us in*
*Acapulco. I am so very happy to see you again.*

*Fondest regards, Gavin*

*Maybe that explained all of the Ava Gardner photos in*
*the room,* I thought. That idea made me shudder and I tore
the note into a hundred pieces before crawling under the
covers. I was bone-weary and sore, but I couldn't sleep.

I lay quietly for a long time, first with my eyes shut and
then, when that obviously wasn't working, I turned on the
bedside lamp and stared at an image of Ava Gardner on the
wall. It was a studio portrait, one of those perfectly posed
and lighted visions that looked beautiful, yet held her personality and vibrancy so tightly in check that it almost
seemed shot from inside a cage. In a way, it was: Ava hated
the endless photo sessions that were demanded by her studio
bosses at MGM. The candid shots of the real-life Ava Gardner from the same era were striking by comparison. So often
her hair was mussed or her dress was creased, and often she
wasn't wearing shoes. But her vitality, her voracious appetite
for life, and her carefree spirit were in plain view and they
were overwhelming. In this photograph, Ava's face was
turned to the side so that it captured her flawless profile.
While she was clearly recognizable and obviously beautiful,
the image was stiff and formal and not like her at all.

Pushing back the sheet, I got to my feet and went to it. Up
close, I recognized the photo as a promotional still for *One
Touch of Venus.* Ava had, of course, played the goddess of
love. In the movie, she was a statue brought to life with a
kiss. It was a silly, frothy romantic comedy, one that show-
cased Ava's beauty but made little room for her considerable

talent as an actress. It was also, oddly enough, the one Ava Gardner film I remembered watching with Martin; he was always in motion, and couldn't sit still for the two hours it took to watch a movie. Skye's words about us floated through my mind: *You're both so glamorous. Seeing the two of you together was a bit like watching a movie.*

There was something wistful in her voice, but I hadn't sensed an undercurrent of jealousy. It was a strange observation, but she wasn't wrong. My relationship with Martin was like something out of an old movie, complete with lovely props, wardrobes, and settings. If it had been on celluloid, no doubt it would have been perfect. In the real world, it was as tenuous as an old film reel, with a climax that was ragged and torn.

Barefoot, I padded to the living room, planted myself on the sofa, and opened my laptop. My fingers hovered over the keyboard while my brain creaked along. What I wanted was a website that would explain what was going on in Skye's head. What was she up to? I'd been so preoccupied with her romance with my ex that I hadn't stopped to consider the other discordant notes in our conversation. *I've been seeing this guy for months, and I really thought he was The One, but he's a bastard. Just . . . evil. There's no other word for it. I'm ashamed I didn't see it before, you know? I should've known something was wrong when he said we had to keep our relationship under wraps. What kind of guy does that?* I'd assumed she'd been talking about Martin, but it bothered me that Gavin was well aware they were dating. Martin wasn't one for confidences with his lieutenants, so if his dalliance with Skye was well known, what did that mean? I couldn't get over the fact that Skye was holding onto a credit card that belonged to her ex. Why would Ryan let her do that? And why would Skye even want it? Maybe it had been taken, not given. It could be useful for shopping online, but I imagined she'd be caught quickly if she did.

I'd never thought of Skye as a person who held grudges, but either I was wrong or something had changed dramatically in her. *I know how to get even with him. I'm going to destroy him professionally, and he'll never even see it coming.* It was hard to discern whether her rage was like a lightning strike—powerful, overwhelming, yet finished in a flash—or if it was something she nurtured that had taken root in her heart and poisoned her mind.

*This isn't about revenge. This is about righting wrongs.* Illegal *wrongs, Lily. I can deal with my hurt feelings, but he can't be allowed to keep on doing the things he does.*

What worried me was the story she was working on. That suggested she'd started on this vengeful trail some time earlier, and that it wasn't a white-hot impulse that would burn itself out.

*When I try to get to the bottom of things, the truth keeps slipping away. I can't get the hard proof I need. Sometimes, I think if I were a real journalist, instead of a fluffy travel writer, I'd have done it already.*

Those words made me feel as if at least some of her anger was directed at herself. When she'd said "real journalist," I'd thought of an amazing man I'd met in Peru in the spring, one I'd initially despised. Felipe Vargas was so dismissive of my writing guidebooks and fluffy articles. He'd told me that I should be an investigative journalist, which had a certain appeal—that was my childhood dream—but it was work I wasn't sure I had either the smarts or stamina for. Worse, who even paid for investigative pieces anymore? Not that travel writing was getting any easier. Pico Iyer had famously described it as "covering eighty towns in ninety days while sleeping in gutters and eating a hot dog once a week," which summed up the business pretty well. I'd turned thirty in February and I was ready for a change, but I had no idea what I'd do for my next act. Skye and I were the same age; was part of her drama over the fact that she was at a crossroads and had no idea which way to turn?

Thinking about her exhausted me in the same way that my sister's crises did. I spent way too much time trying to figure out people's motives. With that in mind, I typed a quick email:

> Skye, I don't know why you ran off last night, but that was a ridiculous thing to do. It's fine if you don't want to talk with me, but you might want to let the hotel know you're still around before they call in the police.

All I really needed to know was that Skye wasn't in trouble. Then I could go back to being furious at her, which was what I really wanted.

When I finally managed to fall sleep, my dreams broke apart into strange fragments. In one, Skye was jumping off a cliff, just like Acapulco's famous divers. Another had me wearing a pair of shoes that kept falling off, which made no sense but was profoundly annoying. The worst dream had me walking through a door outside the Hotel Cerón's bar, then finding it led to an intimate, candlelit cocktail lounge; Skye was standing at the bar with Martin, staring into his eyes with adoration. I jolted awake, sitting upright and discovering I'd hurled two pillows onto the floor.

There was no way I could get back to sleep after that. It was five forty-five in the morning, and my headache had mostly receded, though it still lightly tapped out a code from behind my temples. I wanted to call Denny and ask if Skye had actually checked out of the hotel, but I knew I wouldn't be able to do that for another hour, maybe two. I had to wait, which was something I'd never been good at—if anything, my patience had slipped precipitously over the past few months. It was as if some filter that modulated my responses had fallen away; I was still puzzling over whether that was a good or bad thing.

I'd stopped in New York for one night before continuing on to Acapulco, and while I'd stayed at my best friend's apartment, he'd loaded my music library with songs he insisted I would love. While Jesse hadn't actually told me I was in a rut, musically speaking, he not-so-subtly pointed out that I needed to broaden my "listenin' spectrum," as he put it. After my shower, I started up one of his playlists on my laptop. The singer was identified as Madeleine Peyroux, but the sound coming from her mouth was pure Billie Holiday. I would've thought Jesse was playing a joke on me, but the song was one I'd never heard before. I towel-dried and combed my hair, feeling shivers of pleasure at the sound of her voice.

It was too early for me to switch hotels, but I'd go stir-crazy sitting inside a Pantheon property. The sky was stormy and forbidding, though there were hints of sunlight on the horizon. It was a perfect time of day to stroll on the beach without being overwhelmed by crowds. I needed to go some-where to clear my head. Maybe salt air would stop the ham-mering inside it.

I put far too much energy into getting ready to go out, for reasons that were purely vain: I didn't want to look sad or sick in case I bumped into Gavin or someone who reported to him. My visit would eventually get back to Martin's ears, and I could picture my ex's smug expression if he thought I was pining for him. That got me to pull on a sleeveless green wrap dress with a belted waist. I snapped the latch on my silver bangle bracelet and slipped into a pair of jeweled flip-flops. That was enough glamorous armor, at least for this early in the day.

Downstairs, everything was silent. Outside, the humid-ity dial was turned up full blast, and my silk dress wilted against my skin, clinging to me for dear life. The only person around was a man standing a dozen yards away, under the shade of a palm tree. He was wearing a shirt with the Hotel Cerón's name on it, but he didn't seem to be doing much except smoking a cigarette and watching me with suspicion.

The hotel's exterior was painted an unrelenting white that might have gleamed in sunshine, but under a gray sky, it had a sickly pallor. There were rows of navy and turquoise ceramic tiles at the base of the first story, and it was hard to tell whether the design was an artistic decision or simply a lack of commitment to finish the job. The main building looked like a plain rectangular box that had grown to a full four stories before anyone realized it resembled a minimum-security prison in Florida. To save face, the architect had added a more dramatic fifth story with arched windows. Then he'd tacked on a round tower, presumably allowing its owners to call it a castle. There were statues on the roof, posted like sentries.

Around the first corner, the view became less charming, with a sprawling parking lot and a plain service entrance. The scene improved after the next corner: at the back of the building was an Olympic-sized swimming pool tiled with aquamarine glass, surrounded by row upon row of white flagstones and fringed by palm trees that protected the eyes—if not the ears—from the road beyond. I looked for snakes but found only lizards, and they seemed content enough to ignore me. Continuing on, I passed the terrace where I'd sat with Skye the night before. In the dark, it had felt as if we were up on a balcony, but in reality it was a mere four feet above the level of the pool; if anyone had been swimming the night before, the illusion would have been dispelled.

Her words came into my head suddenly. *It's a dead hotel in a dying destination.* Every time I turned around, I was reminded of something she'd said.

As I stood there, staring at the balcony, it was easier to acknowledge why Skye kept haunting me. I was obsessing about her because, not long ago, I'd felt exactly the way she did. I'd been consumed by an aching desire for revenge that was unlike anything I experienced before; the only parallel in my mind was my sister's craving for heroin. It clawed at me through every waking moment, and during many unconscious ones. The urge had hit me with the force of a tornado after I left Peru; I'd been full of fury at the way a select few never faced justice, no matter what crimes they committed. I wanted Claudia's ghost to be laid to rest, and the only way to do that was to hurt those who had harmed her. Then, one day, I'd gotten a package in the mail, postmarked from London. It contained two sketchpads filled with my sister's artwork. There were also notes and cards and torn-out pages tucked inside. The note with them said simply:

> *My Dear Lily, I stole these from our girl some time ago, before she could destroy them. Now, I must return them to their rightful owner, who I know will cherish them.*
>
> *Sincerely yours, Tariq*

I spent days going over them, feeling as if I'd been given a road map to Claudia's mind. Her artwork was invariably disturbing. She had once drawn a picture of a woman killing two small children, and she'd burned it after seeing my horrified reaction. One of the notebooks had a rough study of that scene, along with a postcard of the painting that inspired it. On the back of the card was printed MEDEA, 1838, EUGÈNE DELACROIX, MUSÉE DES BEAUX-ARTS DE LILLE. I knew the Greek myth, and I finally understood the lone word my sister had written on her sketch: *Revenge.*

After that, the urge for vengeance stopped coursing through my veins. Perhaps not completely, but it went from being a mighty river to a trickle of a stream. What I'd said to Skye on the balcony was, *No matter how much you hate him right now, nothing good is going to come from taking revenge on him.* I meant every word.

I turned away from the hotel, telling myself I needed to stop rehashing every detail of the night before. From the silence of the cliffs, it was clear there were no divers performing at this early hour. The soft rumbling of the water had a magnetic quality that drew me toward it.

The walk wasn't as scenic as the call of the surf promised. I found myself in a barren dirt landscape dotted with a few palm trees. There was a ruin of a grand villa, but that building was charred to a skeletal frame and obviously uninhabited. A dirt path led me to the cliffs, and it was only when I got to the ledge that I realized I'd fallen prey to an optical illusion the night before. The Hotel Cerón wasn't that far from where the divers jumped—which was why I'd been able to see torchlight—but there was water between the two cliffs. My eyes followed the jagged edges of the land and I realized it would be quite a challenge to walk around, with no obvious path to follow. In the distance, I saw a metal fence that blocked off this patch of dirt from its neighbor. Much farther off, I could see the crests of white towers; those were the newer, taller hotels that had sprouted along Acapulco Bay. They seemed a world away.

There was a wooden staircase leading to a narrow strip of sand; the jagged black rocks edging the water didn't make it look like a great place to swim. I took a few steps down and realized I wasn't alone. There was a tall, broad-shouldered man standing on the beach; it took me a moment to recognize Pete Dukermann. I watched him pull one arm back and throw something forward with the coiled tension of a baseball pitcher. I couldn't see what it was, only a quick glint of gold before it sank into the water and vanished.

# 10

Pete stared over the water, as if whatever he'd cast into the clapping waves and churning foam might be tossed right back at him. He was wearing a black T-shirt and black jeans, and looked even more ragged than he had the night before. He crouched, reaching for a giant black duffel bag resting on the concrete beside him. I held my breath, wondering what he was up to. On press trips, photographers were often out of bed hours before everyone else so they could reach some stunning, remote location before the sun rose over it. But if Pete was carrying any camera gear, it was hidden. He put his hand into the bag's side pocket and started to pull a cord out when he froze. It was as if something beneath his skin had started itching under my gaze, because Pete whipped his head around and stared up at me. He was wearing sunglasses, but his expression was stormy. He stuffed the cord back into the pocket, grabbed the bag, and charged up the staircase toward me.

"Are you spying on me?" he shouted. His long legs had already carried him a good part of the way up.

"Why would I bother?" I turned and walked back up to the cliff; I wanted to be on solid ground to deal with Pete.

He didn't say another word until he reached the top of the staircase. "Then what are you doing here?" He was breathing hard as he strode toward me, moving so quickly I thought he wanted to knock me over. Pete was known for his indiscriminate passes, but he wasn't someone who got angry easily. Even that time in Prague, when I'd poured a pitcher of beer over him, he'd laughed and told everyone I was mad because he'd dumped me. His nickname, Pepé le Pew, was cartoonishly demeaning, suggesting a bumbling character. Now, he was seething, and the role of the unkempt, would-be Lothario he usually played was replaced by something raw and ominous. His enormous dark silhouette blotted out most of the sky as he loomed over me. I could smell booze on his breath.

"Did you end up finding Skye last night?" I asked.

That unsettled him. "Skye?" The way her name crept out of his mouth was like a rasp of sandpaper.

"Did you see her?"

"No."

"So you don't know if she checked out of the hotel?"

Even though I couldn't see his eyes behind the mirrored lenses, I felt them boring into mine. "She what?"

I took a step back. The lingering smell of gin mixed with sweat made my empty stomach churn. "Last night, I found Skye's money and passport and medication. Denny and I went to her room, and it looked like she'd cleared out. There was a pair of shoes and some toiletries in there, but that was all she left."

"Maybe she went to her other room." His anger had softened around the edges and as it ebbed away he seemed to deflate.

"Where is that?"

"In the hotel." His voice was dull. "The suite at the end of the hall."

"I just told you her stuff was gone last night."

"No, not the room across from yours. The other one."

I put my hands up. "Pete, she's in the room across from mine. What other room does she have?"

"After I checked in, I saw Skye come out of a room a couple doors down from mine. She freaked when she noticed me. Later, she told me there was a dead bird on the balcony. It made her flip out, and she changed rooms."

"But if she did, she would've taken her things to the new room with her," I pointed out. There was something else that was shaky about his story, a detail that didn't jibe with what I knew, but I couldn't quite put my finger on what it was.

"Yeah, I guess." He shrugged. "Whatever."

He was drifting back to being his usual lunkheaded, adolescent self, and that made me want to shake him. "No, not whatever. You thought something was wrong last night. You were looking for her. Why?"

"I don't know." He turned away from me to stare at the horizon. He wasn't exactly drunk, but he was in that paranoid state some alcoholics fell into as the effects of inebriation wore off and reality started to intrude. It was almost as if you were waking them from a bad dream, one that they blamed you for. My mother had been like that, which meant that I understood the situation, even if I had no patience for it.

He reached up to rub his chin, and I noticed two long, rusty scratches on the side of his forearm. When I'd seen him the night before, hollering outside of Skye's door, he'd been wearing a long-sleeved shirt. I wondered how long those red stripes had been there, and what he'd done to earn them.

"I took some photos of her," he said finally.

Photographers often took photos of journalists on a press trip; they always carried release forms in their pockets, so they could sell the images afterward. "And?"

"We talked."

This was excruciating. "Okay, what did you talk about?"

"The business. You know, how it just gets worse and worse every year, how shitty the pay is now. Skye said she was sick of it and she was gonna become a real journalist. And I said that was stupid because they don't get paid any better, and at least you get free trips when they cover travel. But she said it's not worth it to stay at a hotel like the Cerón. I told her about places I've stayed that were even worse." He shrugged. "She mentioned her big-shot boyfriend. She said they were going to have a big talk, and everything hinged on that."

"Everything? What does that mean?" Now, the catch was in *my* throat.

"Your guess is as good as mine." He stared at the water. "She said they had to keep their relationship quiet, for professional reasons. I could tell that pissed her off."

Pete looked down at his hands, and I did, too. His ring finger was bare, and there was a broad swath of tan line where a ring must have been until recently. That started me wondering, until I noticed a big, jagged cut that looked red and raw. His hands had been scratched up when I'd seen him in front of Skye's door, but this mark was a new addition to his collection.

"What happened to your hand?" I asked him.

Pete stared at me silently. It was disconcerting, seeing my own reflection in his mirrored lenses. I looked anxious and apprehensive.

"Lily," he said. "Is that guy following me, or you?"

"What are you talking about?"

Pete gestured with his chin and I turned to look. A man in a ball cap was standing maybe fifty feet away, by a palm tree, speaking quietly into a cell phone. He could have been the same man I'd spotted when I'd left the Cerón, but his appearance was so unremarkable I couldn't be sure.

Pete spoke again. "If anyone asks, you haven't seen me, okay?" Without waiting for me to respond, he started on the dirt path back to the hotel. As he got close to the interloper, the man in the cap moved around the tree, still talking on his cell. Pete halted, reconsidered, and kept moving along the path. I watched his hunched shoulders and retreating back with a growing sense of unease. As I followed Pete, I noticed that the man in the cap fell in line behind me, keeping a wary distance between us.

# 11

I retraced my steps back to the grounds of the Hotel Cerón, but Pete had already disappeared from sight. Looking at the path behind me, I saw that the man I'd thought was following me—or Pete—had vanished, too. I stood in place, waiting and watching for the man to reappear, but he didn't. I couldn't be imagining all of this, I told myself. If I were, that would mean I'd lost my marbles. The other option was that everyone else had lost theirs; that didn't make me feel any better.

My watch told me it was a quarter past seven, and I made a mental note, in case that was important later. It was an awful way to think, but my brain had opened up a dossier called Things to Tell *la Policía*, and it was filling up quickly. It was hard to imagine what Pete could have to do with Skye's disappearance, but his strange behavior grated on me. More than that, why did Pete look as if he'd been on the losing side of a bar fight?

Sheltered in a grove of trees, I stared at the facade of the Hotel Cerón. The sky had turned several shades darker, and instead of sunlight warming the structure's stark edges and angles, the gray veil of menacing weather made it more grim. It looked as if the life had been sucked out of the place and all that remained was a neat stack of hollow bones.

It didn't help that there wasn't a soul moving around the hotel. I stared at window after window, my eyes tracing up its full five stories, expecting someone to appear at any moment. The drapes were drawn in all but a handful of rooms, but the ones that were exposed had no lights on inside. The glass looked dark; perhaps it was tinted to compensate for what was surely blazing sun for most of the year. The only indication that I wasn't completely alone was the occasional sound of a car on the road, which was hidden by a tall hedge with a wall backing it up.

There was an opening on the other side of the property and another pathway, and I wanted to see where it led. The stone pathway was slick from the rain, and I moved as quickly as I dared. The hotel's windows were like a hundred black eyes on me; once my back was to them, I was filled with the heavy, unshakable sense of being watched. *Stop being ridiculous,* I told myself, looking around yet again. *There's no one there.*

The pathway on the other side of the hotel was a short one, but it changed styles in the middle, so that the Cerón's slippery stones were replaced by wide flagstones that made it easier to move forward. The path opened suddenly to a small clearing that was filled with the skeletal remains of three dozen small bungalows. No, not remains, I realized, taking in the scene; there were construction supplies and equipment littering the ground. The bungalows were still in the process of being built.

They didn't have proper pathways between them, just rows of packed-in mud. My pretty flip-flops were going to be goners after this, I realized, as I stepped through the muck. Maybe the earth was used to the constant precipitation it got at this time of year, which was why I didn't sink into it, though mud clung to my shoes and slowed me down. I peered into one bungalow, which seemed almost ready for human habitation; all someone had to do was tear off the clear plastic that shielded the window openings and fill them with glass instead. The next house I looked at was further from completion; the inside needed drywall, but it already had a snake lying on the floor. I was about to look into the next one when a hand grabbed my shoulder and pulled me back, off-balance.

Turning my head, I saw a man who was about my height. His pie-round face and sparse scraps of beard made him look like a kid starting high school. But he was holding a gun and pointing it at my chest, and once I noticed that, his age didn't matter.

He watched me and I watched the gun. That standoff went on for an eternity. I felt as if I were sinking, but I couldn't take my eyes off the gun. When I tipped to one side, I looked down and saw that one of my feet was completely submerged in the mud.

His eyes followed mine, and he started to chuckle. The gun bobbed from side to side.

"It's not funny," I muttered.

He gave me a broad grin, flashing yellow teeth, and lowered the gun so that the muzzle could brush against his jeans.

"Soy un huésped en el hotel Cerón," I said. *I'm a guest at the Hotel Cerón.*

"Lo sé," he answered. *I know.* His tone was careless, as if the difference between shooting me and not wasn't such a big deal.

I looked down again and tried to pull my foot out of the mud. That was easy enough, except that the flip-flop stayed planted. I tried to lift it out with my toes and failed. Finally, I bent down to retrieve it. He went from chuckling to laughing in earnest, making his belly wobble. When I finally extracted the shoe, I moved to one side, and he got serious again, gesturing with the gun to move to the other side. He kept that up while we retraced my original steps along the path, stopping briefly to stuff my muddy foot into the unrecognizable flip-flop.

He shadowed me all the way back to the front door of the Hotel Cerón, frequently mumbling to himself and giggling along the way. The man-boy seemed like a perfect fool, but he was a fool with a gun, and there was a peculiar terror in that. It wasn't unreasonable that a guard would be watching over the construction site. Mexico was a poor country, and even in a wealthy one, it wouldn't be unusual to have someone watching over building materials that weren't locked up. But the giddiness made him seem out of control, and even if he didn't plan to shoot me, there was a fifty-fifty chance of it happening anyway.

When we reached the hotel's front door, a bellman stood there, and the two nodded at each other. The bellman held the door open, staring at my feet and the mud I tracked in. The guard said, "La premia"—sarcastically calling me a prize, or perhaps something worse in Mexican slang—and he laughed, but the bellman didn't join in. Inside the double doors, soaking in the cool air, I turned back and saw the bellman yelling at the guard. I couldn't hear a word, but I watched as the bellman shoved him, knocking him to the ground.

"What happened to you?" the clerk at the reception desk said. It was the same man who'd been there the night before.

"Long story," I murmured. When I turned back to look at the scene outside, both the bellman and the guard were gone.

# 12

By the time I got the mud scrubbed off me in my second shower of the morning, Denny had called and left a message. After I called her back, she came to my room. I was in a fluffy white robe with my hair piled into a towel-turban. Denny was wearing an elegantly simple white linen sheath with taupe suede heels that made her tanned legs enviably long. Her long, dark hair was pinned up with a tortoiseshell clip, matching the frames of her glasses. I'd never managed to look effortlessly chic like that in my life. I wanted to take notes as she sauntered in.

"Morning, Lily." She touched my arm. "How did you sleep last night?"

"Fine," I lied. "What about you?"

"I was up late trying to figure out if Skye left the hotel. She didn't say anything to anyone, and she didn't check out. None of the staff saw her leave, but that doesn't mean much because there's just a skeleton crew on duty here. But she's definitely gone. She cleared her stuff out of her room."

"We saw that last night."

"No, I mean I asked a housekeeper to let me in to her room half an hour ago. The bag you put in there is gone. So's her toiletry kit. For some reason, her shoes are still there."

"You're saying Skye came back to the room and picked up her things?"

"I don't know if Skye did it herself, or if someone else went into her room. But her things are definitely gone." Denny sighed. "Was there anything, anything at all, she said to you about leaving the hotel?"

"No, nothing."

"Is there a chance she could have been meeting someone?"

"She mentioned the man she'd been seeing, but only to say how much she hated him." For some reason I couldn't quite explain, I didn't want to mention Martin's name. "She gave me the impression that he wasn't at this hotel, or even on this continent right now."

"Hmm. I know I'm grasping at straws, Lily, but did Skye say anything about knowing people here? Or maybe she said something about a hotel?"

"No, there was nothing like that." Bits of conversation spun through my head like snippets of film reels. "Wait, there was a man who came out to the balcony while we were there. All he said was 'good evening,' but it was obvious Skye knew him."

"Why do you say that?"

"She warned me off him. When I asked who he was, she said I didn't want to know him." I tried to picture his face; he'd been handsome, but there was a lounge lizard quality to him that wasn't attractive at all. "She got up to make her phone call right after he left the balcony."

Denny's brows shot toward the ceiling, but her voice was calm. "Could she have been following him?"

"I . . . I never thought about that. I really thought she was making a call." Looking back, it suddenly seemed clear that the man was the real reason Skye had run off suddenly. The call was just a ruse. Then another thought jolted me. "Pete

Dukermann said something about seeing Skye come out of a room at the other end of the floor. She must have been coming out of someone else's room. That's why she made up a story about switching rooms."

Denny's lips were pressed into a firm line, and her arms were crossed in front of her chest. "Okay, this is all starting to make sense. It's a lousy thing for her to do, but at least we know what's up."

"What do you mean?"

"One of the hotel's drivers took a couple to the airport in the middle of the night. The woman was wearing dark sunglasses, a black scarf over her hair, and a black raincoat, and she never spoke. I don't know for sure that it was Skye, but that's my guess. This is just like her. Nothing with Skye is ever simple or straightforward. She thrives on drama and she invents some when there isn't any to be had."

"You don't mean that her boyfriend was here, do you?" The hairs on the back of my neck were bristling. Had Martin been in the hotel last night? That thought unsettled me, but more than that it made me angry. It made me feel as if Martin and Skye were toying with me.

"That guy she left with is not her boyfriend." Denny's voice sounded weary.

"How do you know?"

"Because I know the whole awful story about the boyfriend," Denny said. "Skye and I used to be a lot closer than we are now. I care about her, but she . . ." Denny's voice trailed off. I could hear her taking breaths, trying to compose herself. "Skye is one of those people who seems wonderful until you really get to know her. Then you realize she's abusive toward the people who care most about her."

"Abusive?" In my mind, the textbook definition of the word was my mother; the drunker she got, the more she lashed out at my sister and me. "Not physically?"

"I don't mean she hits anyone, Lily. She's manipulative. I think the person who gets it worst is Ryan. He's such a sucker for her. She breaks up with him, sleeps with strings of guys, tells him all about it, then asks him for money. And he gives it to her." Her tone went beyond disapproval, edging into disgust.

"She had one of Ryan's credit cards in her wallet." As the words came out of my mouth, I felt ashamed for going through Skye's things. It had seemed like the right thing to do at the time, but in the light of day it was just nosy. "I found it accidentally when I knocked her bag over and the false bottom fell out and—"

"You don't have to explain, Lily. Look, if someone takes off without a word, any normal person is going to look at the stuff she left behind to try to get a clue." Denny reached her left hand to her left shoulder and stretched her neck to the right. "Sorry, just thinking about their psychotic relationship ties my muscles up in knots. I'm supposed to be her friend, but I feel terrible for Ryan. He's a really good guy. He deserves better."

"When she talks about him, it's as if she thinks he's her puppet."

"Or her slave."

We were both quiet for a moment. "Do you have any idea who the guy she left with is?"

"No. Just another guy she's sleeping with. This is the point where I say it's none of my business."

"Denny . . ." I wanted to ask her about Skye's boyfriend. Clearly she knew; she had to. Her gaze met mine briefly and swept away. "About Skye's boyfriend . . ."

"Please don't ask me about that, Lily. She swore me to secrecy and I . . . I just can't say anything about it, okay?"

"Sure," I said, backing off instantly. Did I really want to hear about whatever drama Skye was involved in with Martin? My brain buzzed with curiosity, but my gut said *hell, no.*

Denny smiled. "Now, we have to figure out what hotel to move to. I've already sent a couple of messages out, but it's so early, and this isn't an early-morning place. My guess is that we'll be moving hotels around lunchtime. Is that okay?"

"That's fine." Sooner would be better, but I didn't want to act like a petulant brat.

"It's possible that I may have to move Pete Dukermann with us. I don't want to, but now that we're down one journalist, the tourism people are probably going to insist. Would you mind if he does?"

"I honestly don't care. You might have issues with him because he's being weirder than usual."

"I know he's slimy," Denny said.

"It's more than that. Last night, he was banging on Skye's door, looking for her. This morning, I ran into him outside, by the cliffs. He was throwing something into the water, and he looked like he'd been in a fight. There were scratches on his arms and a cut on his hand."

Denny breathed in sharply. "You think maybe he came on too strong to a woman and she . . ." She closed her eyes and shook her head. "No, I don't want to go there. Now I need brain bleach. I'm going to figure out a way to leave him here." She smiled at me. "Don't worry about anything. This isn't your problem, Lily. I'm going to get things sorted out while you have breakfast and that massage."

"Thanks, but I've got work to do, so I'm going to pass on the spa appointment." The truth was that I didn't want to enjoy anything at a property owned by Martin.

"There's no getting out of the massage, Lily. You need one after the stress caused by Skye's little stunt. And it's Saturday, so you should be off work and on the beach, not stuck in front of your computer in a hotel room."

"When you're self-employed, you're never off work." I glanced at my computer screen, noticing that I had new email. When I clicked into the inbox, I saw that there was a message from Skye. "Denny, you won't believe this."

She moved closer and glanced at my screen. "Speak of the devil."

I opened the message.

Hi Lily!

I feel SO guilty about leaving Acapulco without saying goodbye. I'm in a complicated situation right now, and I had to come home. I feel TERRIBLE about this and I hope everyone won't hate me for screwing up the press trip. I'll talk with you soon and explain everything!

Skye

"Well, at least she finally said something." Denny's tone suggested she wasn't impressed. "I wonder if she's bothered to email me."

"Denny," I said. "Something is seriously wrong here."

"What do you mean? I'm pissed off at her, but I feel better knowing nothing terrible has happened."

"There's something very wrong." I went to the desk, pulling out Skye's passport and handing it to Denny. Her face froze.

She looked at Skye's photo, leafed through the pages, then went back to staring at Skye's photo. "I . . . I don't understand." Her expression was blank, as if she couldn't process what was happening. "How did you get her passport?"

"Denny, the only thing that matters right now is that Skye doesn't have it. Her email says that she went home, but there's no way she could have done that. Not without her passport."

# 13

Denny was shell-shocked when she left my room. She murmured something about finding Gavin, and talking to the tourism people, and getting to the bottom of this. But the story her face told was very different. Denny was a take-charge type who was convinced that every problem had a solution. That confidence normally made her unflappable, but this situation wasn't something she knew how to fix. She was suddenly cast adrift, and it was clear that she didn't have any sense of which direction to go in.

With Denny gone, my suite suddenly felt much colder. I read and reread the email, wanting to believe it; things would be so much easier if I didn't know the message couldn't possibly be true. There had to be an explanation for this bizarre situation, one that wasn't sinister. But each time I looked at the laptop's screen, my heart plunged a little deeper down into my chest. The only thing I felt sure of was that Skye was in trouble.

The message, brief as it was, sounded like something Skye would write. The email had come from her account, too, which made it seem legit. But why would she lie about going home? Why did she want everyone to think that she'd left Mexico? Her deception made my nerves crackle. Reflexively, I opened and closed the latch of my silver bracelet, the two clicks reminding me of my sister's shaky relationship with the truth, but also all that she had done to try to make up for that. Claudia's falsehoods were self-serving, hastily constructed to meet immediate needs. *No, I'm not using drugs. I just need money for food. No, I'm not in trouble again.* As much as I hated hearing them, I'd at least understood the purpose they served. What I couldn't grasp now was what purpose Skye could possibly have for telling lies that were so easily disproven.

I leafed through her passport. No airline in the world would let you board a flight to the US without proper documentation, because that airline was responsible for the cost of deporting you when American immigration barred you from entering the country. Skye had to be in Mexico.

On impulse, I pressed "reply" and typed a hasty message:

Skye, Where the hell are you and what are you doing? I'm worried about you. I know you didn't fly back to the US, because I have your passport. Where are you?

There were a hundred other things I could have added. *What's the story you're working on? Why did you say I could help you? Is this just some crazy game you're playing?* But I kept those thoughts to myself and pressed "send."

I went back to my inbox. There were plenty of other missives to distract me from the worry spiraling through my mind. There were already a half-dozen emails from my friend Jesse, who liked to send along anything I might find amusing, as well as advice about health, gossip about people we knew, and assorted style questions and advice. The most recent one read:

What do you think of this shirt? It's great, right? But if I get it, everyone will know I shop from the L.L.Bean catalog. What to do?

There was a lone email from Bruxton, an NYPD detective I'd met in January when I was searching for my sister. I'd seen him while I was in New York, right before flying to Acapulco. The only trouble was, we hadn't been alone; Jesse had been there the entire time, like a chaperone. His message had no subject line and contained only two words: *Miss you.* That was enough to make me smile and reach for my phone.

"Hey," Bruxton said when he answered.

"Hey yourself." Even long-distance, I was shyly self-conscious with him. "Do you have a minute?"

"Yeah. Everything okay?" His voice was harsh and ragged around the edges, but his concern still registered.

"I'm fine. It's just . . . something's going on and I don't know what I should be doing about it."

"You only call when you have ulterior motives, Lily."

"That's not true!" I chewed on my lip. Hmm, maybe he was right.

"Whatever. I'm used to it. What do you want?" In the background, I heard a lighter snap and hiss, and that made me crave a cigarette. It was ridiculous, being that suggestible. I'd made some rules for myself, and one of them was no smoking before noon. Instead, I picked up a pen and twirled it around.

"There's another writer on this trip, someone I know fairly well. Her name is Skye McDermott. I ran into her in the lobby last night, and we had drinks in the hotel bar. Then she said she'd be back in a minute, and she never came back." When I paused, he didn't say anything. It was a cop trick, sitting back and letting the other person fill up the empty air; even though he wasn't interrogating me, it was second nature to him. "She left her bag with me. I thought it just had beach shoes and junk in it, but later I found it had a false bottom, and her wallet and passport and other things were hidden inside."

"I love how you said that," Bruxton said.

"Said what?"

"You 'found' her bag had this stuff in it. Like you didn't snoop through it looking for evidence."

"I was worried about her!" My face felt warm; Bruxton had made me blush. I almost spilled the fact that I'd only discovered the false bottom of Skye's bag because I'd kicked it in a fit of rage, but I managed to keep that to myself. There were certain things Bruxton didn't need to know.

"I know you were, Lily." Under the harsh rasp of his voice, there was a hint of amusement that was almost sweet.

"Anyway, the point is that she vanished. Denny—that's the public relations person who set up the trip—and I went to Skye's room last night, and her suitcase and most of her things were gone. This morning, all of her stuff is gone. I just got an email from her that says she went home, but she couldn't have gone home because I have her passport."

My words picked up speed as they tumbled out. I'd expected Bruxton to get as worked up as I was, but his voice was skeptical. "Who's the guy mixed up in this?"

"The . . . guy?" I asked. My mind went to Martin and I snapped it back, like an unruly dog on a leash.

"What you're telling me sounds off. Half the time, people who are reported missing are actually shacking up with someone. Call it the horizontal mambo theory. She could be with some guy right now."

"Why wouldn't she just say that?"

"Maybe she's too embarrassed to say it. Look, people do all kinds of shit without a second thought. You know what makes them feel bad? Having to admit what they did.

People spin all kinds of explanations for what they do in their heads. It can seem legit until you actually have to say the words to another human being. Then it's clear they're full of crap."

"I guess that makes sense. It's just that this isn't like her." But that wasn't true. I kept thinking that Skye hadn't been herself the night before, but all that meant was that she wasn't the way she was when I normally saw her.

Bruxton's next words made me feel as if he were reading my mind. "Lily, by now you've learned people never really know someone as well as they think they do, right?" His voice was almost too gentle, as if he knew his words carried thorns deep inside. The more I saw of people, the less I knew about them, it seemed. Wishful thinking had a tendency to override my instincts. I braced myself for a pointed example, but when Bruxton failed to deliver one, I nudged those thoughts aside. This wasn't about mistakes I'd made; this was about Skye.

"There's one more thing I have to tell you," I said. "Skye told me she's working on a story. Not a travel story, a real one. She said I could help her with it, but she didn't say how. She said she was going to tell me what she was working on, but she had to check with someone first."

There was a pause, during which Bruxton's calm tone fled. "You got any idea what she's writing about?"

"No. Why?"

"I'm trying to figure how much danger she's in."

I dropped the pen. "What do you mean?"

"You got any idea how risky it is to be a journalist in Mexico? Something like fifty journalists have been murdered or disappeared in the past five years. Any chance your friend was working on a story about drugs or the cartels?"

*If anything, you're the person who could help me with the story.* That's what Skye had said to me on the balcony. Drugs and the cartels that sold them weren't my area of expertise. "I think the odds of that are pretty much zero. She did say she had been seeing someone—someone evil—and she was going to bring him down."

"This girl sounds like she was looking for trouble. What's the guy's name?"

"She wouldn't tell me." It would be wrong to tell him that I thought the man in question was Martin; that would make Bruxton blow his very short fuse and it wouldn't get us any closer to the truth. Bruxton had a rough manner and was easily annoyed, but he rarely got angry at me. Still, the mere mention of Martin Sklar made his eyes bulge and his skin flush red; that much, I'd seen for myself. If anything, it would keep Bruxton from looking at other possibilities, and that would be a terrible mistake. That was what I told myself, to justify holding Martin's name back. "I got the impression that he works in the travel business, but I could be wrong. Skye was determined to give me as little information as she could."

"You want to hear the truth? Your pal was involved with something sketchy and she knew it. She wanted to drag you into it because she was scared."

"She was crying last night, Brux. She told me she'd been sick, and she definitely looked unwell."

"Drugs?"

"I don't think so. She was painfully thin, but she wasn't spaced out and there were no marks on her."

"Lily, I get why you're worried. It sounds like something the local PD needs to hear about. Wait, let me translate that for you: get the hotel to talk to the police. You don't need to get dragged into this."

I didn't want to tell him that I was already involved, emotionally speaking. That was the part of the story that I was leaving out.

"Does the hotel have security cameras?" he asked.

"Yes." There had to be; that was a given in a Pantheon property.

"Okay, the police should look over the tapes, make sure your friend wasn't taken from the hotel against her will. They can also do forensics on the message, to figure out where it was sent from."

"Forensics on email?"

"I've seen them narrow it down to an apartment in a giant building. They're magicians." He coughed. "Look, you can send the email to me. One of the techs owes me. I'll make him take a look at it."

"Thanks, Brux."

"I'll add it to your tab. You want to do me a favor?"

"Name it."

"Stay the hell away from trouble. Don't go anywhere looking for this girl. There are professionals to do that, okay?"

"Okay."

"Plus, she's probably screwing some guy and having a great time."

I laughed. I couldn't help it.

"I need to get back to work. I'll call you or email, okay?"

"Thanks, Brux. Oh, by the way . . ." I stopped speaking and let the silence stretch on until he couldn't stand it anymore.

"What?" he demanded.

"I miss you, too."

I hung up the phone as soon as I said it, which simultaneously made me feel daring and about thirteen years old again. Bruxton was so abrupt, especially on phone calls, that he usually hung up without saying goodbye. I found that jarring, but was mildly amused with myself for hanging up first this time. He was probably staring at the phone, wondering what had happened.

Putting my cell down, I turned to my laptop and refreshed the inbox. My breath caught in my throat at the sight of a new email from Skye. I wasn't expecting that. My fingers trembled as I opened it.

Hey Lily,

I'm fine! Stop worrying and ENJOY ACAPULCO!!!

xox Skye

It looked and sounded like something Skye would write, making me wonder if she wasn't holed up in one of those white towers that ringed much of Acapulco Bay. That was a comforting thought, in a way. Otherwise, I had to wonder who else had access to her email account. I forwarded that email to Bruxton, along with the first.

A few minutes later, Denny called my room. "Can you meet us in Gavin's office at nine?" she asked. "I'm trying to get him to call the police, but he wants to talk to you first."

"Of course."

"Okay, good. Lily, please bring Skye's passport with you, and anything else of hers you still have."

That remark made me flush. I'd known I was doing wrong by holding back Skye's passport, and now Gavin would hear about that, too. I couldn't regret my bad decision completely; if I hadn't kept the passport, I would have taken Skye's email at face value. The only other things I had of hers were the books. Skye had given me the Mexico guide, telling me to look at it, so I didn't feel obliged to return it. There were several hotels marked with asterisks in that book, but they were all over Mexico, so they offered little information as to her whereabouts.

The other guidebook was something I'd held back out of curiosity and a vague sense of it being out of place. It still struck me as odd that I'd found *Frakker's Eastern Europe* in her bag. Why bring that to Mexico? I leafed through the book, noticing that Skye had scrawled asterisks next to a few hotels. Looking closer, I realized that the hotels she'd singled out all had something in common. Wherever they were located—Hungary, Poland, Ukraine—every single one was owned by Pantheon.

# 14

Gavin's office was spacious and luxurious yet almost devoid of natural light. The lone rectangular window had a white Venetian blind pulled over it. The walls were a stark, bright white that wanted to compete with the hotel's facade; it was so freshly painted that a harsh, acrid smell still lingered. Recessed lights dotted the ceiling, casting a cool, clear glow over the space. Mahogany bookcases lined two walls, and they were already filling up with an extravagant collection of art books. That didn't surprise me at all; I remembered Gavin accompanying Martin to a couple of art fairs, eager to get close to the masterworks. His taste was nothing like his boss's though, and while Martin gravitated to works by grand masters—for his personal collection—and by contemporary artists better known for creating controversy than art—for his hotels—Gavin sought out romantic nineteenth-century painters with names like Dicksee, Rossetti, Waterhouse, and Burne-Jones. I'd never heard of the Pre-Raphaelites before that, and I owed Gavin a debt for introducing me to their work. His taste, at least when it came to art, was superior to Martin's.

There were two small, framed sketches on the wall behind his desk, flanking it. As I got closer, I realized that they were studies of women's faces, made in the same evocative, dreamlike style of the Pre-Raphaelite painters. The room also held a conversation area with four chairs and a beautiful rug that looked as if it had been imported from nineteenth-century Persia. The grandiosity felt like every other Pantheon-owned hotel I'd been inside, but the details were very different from the aesthetic I was used to and associated with Martin.

Denny was staring out the window through a slit in the blinds, her arms crossed in front of her chest. When she turned, I saw she was frowning; whatever was going on in her head was grim. Gavin, by contrast, was unruffled. His angular, grave face seemed too sharp to hold a smile for more than a nanosecond, but he didn't seem perturbed by the things that had upset Denny. He was wearing a charcoal suit with a faint pinstripe, and his cufflinks bore a coat of arms.

"Good morning, Lily. Don't you look lovely this morning? Thank you for making time for this." He pulled back one of the chairs in the conversation area, holding it for me to sit in. It was a formal gesture, which was in character for Gavin.

"Of course," I said. "I'm worried about Skye."

Gavin cleared his throat, as if readying himself for some grand pronouncement. "I suspect she rather enjoys having people fussing over her, actually. I know she's a friend of yours, Lily, but in my experience, she's rather high-strung."

"Even if she is, Gavin, I think it's important that we make sure nothing is wrong," Denny said. "That's more important than the press trip."

Gavin's gaze shifted to Denny, and it was cold enough to frost the air between them. "I've always thought you professional, Denny. I would hate to be disappointed."

I hoped Denny would say something to puncture his arrogance and ego, but instead she answered, "I *am* professional, Gavin."

"I'm glad to hear it. Now, why don't you go back to doing your job while I speak with Lily." Gavin turned to me. "Our head of security will be here in a moment. He would like to ask you a few questions, if that's all right."

"I'd like to stay for that," Denny interjected. "I've known Skye for a long time. It might be useful if—"

"No." Gavin's voice was sharp. "Please do us the favor of shutting the door on your way out."

His rudeness toward her startled me. I'd never really seen Gavin outside of Martin's shadow; in its shade, he was ingratiating and unctuous. But I was starting to see that without his boss hovering nearby, Gavin was a different man. Martin, for all his many faults, never spoke brusquely to the people who worked for him. The lower you were down the totem pole, the kinder Martin was; he was famous for chatting with waiters and bellmen, and remembering them by name. It was a trait he shared with Frank Sinatra, and it had impressed me when we'd met. Clearly, Gavin had a different role model. Bruxton's words came to mind. *You've learned people never really know someone as well as they think they do, right?*

His last remark to Denny made her straighten her spine. "I'll be happy to, Gavin. Please excuse me, Lily. I'll be making arrangements for us to move hotels later today."

Gavin bristled at that, but he didn't say a word. Clearly, the two of them had been arguing before I'd come in, and the tension between them was palpable. Was it only because of Skye, or was there something more? Denny had told me she'd worked in Pantheon's London office years earlier; Gavin had worked there, too. I wondered if their antipathy was new, or if it stretched back more than a decade.

Denny shut the door with a soft click, and Gavin gave me his brief, rueful smile. "I apologize for that, Lily. Denny and I have some differences of opinion about Skye."

"Which are?"

"Denny is her friend. By contrast, I tend to look at everything through a rather critical, skeptical prism. It's a family trait, I'm afraid. My father was very much like that."

Before I could say anything, there was a knock on his door. "Come in," Gavin called.

The man who opened the door was wearing a well-cut black suit with a lavender shirt, open at the neck. His skin was deeply tanned and his hair was a wavy dark brown. He wasn't as tall as Johnny Weissmuller, whose image hung near the elevator, but he had the athlete-turned-actor's broad shoulders and narrow waist, the build of a swimmer.

As the man came toward us, I got a whiff of his cologne, and I realized where I'd seen him last. This was the man who'd stepped out onto the balcony the night before, moments before Skye vanished. *Listen to me, Lily. You don't want to know that guy.* Before I could say anything, Gavin spoke.

"Apolinar, this is the lovely and immensely talented Lily Moore," he said. "Lily, I'm pleased to introduce you to Apolinar Muñoz, our head of security."

# 15

"I've heard so much about you, Lily Moore, all of it charming." Apolinar's English was slightly accented, but flawless. He stepped closer and took my hand. As he stared into my eyes with the intensity of a Marlon Brando, I noticed that his own eyes were so dark that the iris almost matched the pupil; the effect was unnerving, as if that inky blackness was swallowing him from inside. "It's truly a pleasure to meet you."

If my heart could've galloped out of my chest, it would have made a break for freedom right then. *This* was the Hotel Cerón's head of security? Suddenly every paranoid fear I'd had about Skye's safety seemed justified.

"You were on the balcony," I blurted out. "You were there when Skye and I were having drinks."

"You were there last night, Apolinar?" Gavin's eyes narrowed. "Why didn't you tell me that?"

Apolinar was unfazed. If I'd hoped for an anxious denial or some show of guilt, I was disappointed. "Yes, I was there," he said. "For all of, perhaps, ten seconds. I saw the two ladies having drinks while I was making my rounds through the property." The man's voice was warm and his delivery was smooth, but Skye's words reverberated in my head. *Listen to me, Lily. You don't want to know that guy.* What did she learn about Apolinar Muñoz that would make her issue a warning like that?

"You're the head of security at the Hotel Cerón?" I asked, trying to wrap my mind around that fact.

"For all of Pantheon's operations in Mexico, actually." Apolinar's smile gave a sense of just how pleased he was with this news. He gazed at me, clearly pleased that I couldn't take my eyes off him. He had an aura of preening smugness, as if he expected the attention.

"Have you called the police?" I asked.

"I am the police," Apolinar stated. He put his hands on his hips, and I saw that he had a gun in a holster at his waist.

"You're a security guard. That's not the same thing."

Gavin cleared his throat. "Ah, as it happens, Apolinar is our liaison with the police. He served on the force for several years." His face was serious. "There's a rather porous line here between private security and police. I'm afraid that's simply how things are arranged in this country."

"If there truly is a problem, I will make sure this gets the attention it needs," Apolinar said. "Now, I have been told that you have Skye McDermott's passport. Is that it in your hand?"

"Yes." I glanced at Gavin, because I didn't want to hand the passport over to Apolinar. Gavin took it from me, opened it and stared wordlessly for a moment, then passed it into Apolinar's hands.

"How did this come into your possession, Lily?"

"Skye left it with me when she left the bar to make a phone call."

Apolinar cocked his head. "I am to understand that your friend handed you her passport?"

"No, she left her bag with me."

"And where is the bag?" Apolinar pressed. "I do not see it here."

"I left Skye's bag in her room last night. Denny had someone open the door for me. That was when we saw most of Skye's things were gone."

"Wait, one moment, Lily." Apolinar's use of my name was grating on my nerves. It was falsely intimate, as if we were confidantes. "How did the passport make its way out of the bag? Why was it not left in Skye's room?"

That was an embarrassing question with no good answer. "I went through her bag when I thought she was missing." I hoped I wasn't blushing. "When I found the passport, I put it away so it wouldn't get lost or stolen. It was much later when I saw Denny and got the idea to put the bag in Skye's room. I forgot about the passport."

"You . . . forgot?" Apolinar grinned, revealing movie-star-quality teeth. It was hard to picture how he'd paid for that on a cop's salary. Their gleam was particularly striking against his sun-browned skin.

I didn't respond, mostly because I didn't have an answer that wasn't ridiculous to my own ears. I was also trying to channel the cop trick of the silent stare.

Gavin broke the silence. "I think Lily has already explained how she obtained the passport. Are there any real questions you need her to answer?"

Apolinar sighed. "What was your conversation with Skye about?"

"We were just catching up. I hadn't seen her in a while."

"When I was coming through the door, she was telling you about a story she was writing, wasn't she?"

The man must have ears like a fox. Skye had said, *I'm going to write a feature about . . .* just as Apolinar had appeared.

"Yes, she mentioned she was writing an article."

"A feature, she said," Apolinar corrected me. "What *exactly* did she say to you about this story?"

"Nothing. She didn't tell me the subject." But she'd said, *If anything, you're the person who could help me with the story.* At the time, it hadn't made sense. Now that I'd seen the guidebooks she was carrying, my mind reeled. Skye had marked several Pantheon hotels in Eastern Europe, and she'd circled some properties in Mexico as well. None of the Mexican ones were Pantheon's, at least not at the time the book was last updated, more than a year ago. But Skye had noted seven, including the Hotel Cerón, which left me wondering. Had Martin's company suddenly started locking down hotel real estate in Mexico, and why would that interest Skye? How did the European hotels fit into the picture? Skye had thought I was still in touch with Martin; I'd assumed her interest was personal, but maybe it had to do with her story. In any case, I was in a room with a pair of Pantheon employees, and I was keeping this bit of intelligence under wraps.

My stubbornness forced them to move on. "Did she mention anyone?" Apolinar prompted.

The reason for Skye's interest in Martin wasn't clear to me anymore. Were they involved, or was she writing about his company? For all I knew, there was some overlap between business and pleasure. I kept my unruly ideas to myself. "She mentioned Pete Dukermann," I improvised. "Skye spent some time with him yesterday."

Apolinar looked at Gavin. "I will need to speak with him as well."

"Fine."

"You are remembering more, aren't you?" Apolinar said to me. "What else did Skye say to you?"

I was feeling badgered by him at this point. "I can't think of anything else."

"There is *always* something else." Apolinar's tone brooked no argument.

"Lily is telling us everything she knows, I'm *sure*." Gavin's statement was conciliatory, but his tone was glacial. His emphasis on the last word announced his annoyance with the clarity of a megaphone.

"People always leave something out. They always do." Apolinar stared at me. He wasn't giving up. "What else do you remember?"

I had the strangest sensation creeping up my spine, as if I were a suspect in Skye's disappearance. It was patently ridiculous, but it was there, pulling at my skin with all the tenderness of a fishhook. *Stop it,* I warned myself, but my blood tapped against my skin as if it were rising to a boil.

"Well, Martin Sklar's name came up," I said. "He used to be my fiancé."

That piqued Apolinar's interest. "What about him?"

"Well, we didn't discuss sexual positions or anything like that." I gave him a coy smile. For the first time, Apolinar's expression was uneasy. Gavin seemed mildly bemused. I decided I'd had enough of their interrogation. "Actually," I added, "I have a question for you, Apolinar. Why did you come out to the balcony last night?"

"It is my habit to walk through the hotels I protect. It is a point of pride."

"Right, you're the head of security. So, have you checked out the security tapes from last night?"

"Tapes?" Apolinar's blank look made it clear he hadn't.

"The ones from the cameras trained on every door into the hotel. The ones from the cameras in the lobby and in the bar. I didn't see one on the balcony, but there are quite a few others." I kept my eyes on Apolinar; I still didn't understand why Skye had warned me away from the man, but her dislike of him spoke volumes and made me suspicious. "It's Pantheon's policy to keep those tapes for a month. No one has actually established whether Skye left the hotel last night. Is she still in the hotel, or did she go somewhere else?"

Apolinar's expression shifted as I spoke. Under his controlled demeanor was a ripple of unease coupled with anger. He glanced at Gavin and back at me. "Thank you for your advice on doing my job. Any other suggestions?"

"I'll let you know if I think of anything."

"I'm sure you will." Apolinar headed for the door, stopping and half-turning back to me as he touched the handle. "Please don't go too far, Lily. I want you to be available to answer questions. You never know what may come out of this."

# 16

"I must apologize, Lily," Gavin said, after Apolinar marched out. "I had no idea Apolinar would be so rude. He clearly needs to learn his place."

"I just hope he finds Skye."

"If she wants to be found."

I gave Gavin a searching look. "What does that mean?"

"She's a friend of yours, isn't she? You must have noticed the way she likes to play games with people."

"No." Then I thought of Skye's strange twisted relationships with the men she dated. "I think whatever games she's involved in are played out in her romantic life."

"Ah." He nodded. "I don't want to speak out of turn, but I understand. I suspect Skye was upset with someone, and she decided to cause trouble because of it. She's probably cooling her heels for a day or two, not realizing the chaos she's caused." He left that cryptic comment hanging in the air as he walked to his desk. When he looked at me again, there was a smile at the edge of his mouth. "I hope you won't mind, but I made plans for us to have breakfast together, Lily. I'm going to let the kitchen know we're ready."

I didn't want to have a meal with him, but no excuse to avoid it came to mind. Gavin didn't wait for my response, in any case. He picked up the phone. "Hello? This is Mr. Stroud. I want a plate of breakfast pastries for two delivered to my office. Pan dulce filled with coconut cream, and a couple of savory breads—the one with ham and, what's the other called, the one with cheese? Yes. Hold on." He covered the receiver with one hand. "Lily, is there anything in particular you'd like? An omelette, perhaps?"

"What you've ordered sounds fine."

He gave me that funny little fleeting smile, the one I wasn't quite sure was there until it was gone. "Bring sliced fruit as well, and fresh-squeezed juice and tea. Oh, also coffee." His hand went to the receiver again. "You take your coffee black, don't you, Lily?"

I was surprised he remembered. "That's right."

"Yes, coffee and tea. That's everything. No, wait. Bring the tray to the Urdaneta Room. Not my office, the Urdaneta Room. Got that?"

The brittle, commanding tone in his voice vanished as he put the phone down. "I have something to show you, if you don't mind. Denny mentioned that you have a date with the spa at eleven, but I'd love for you to see the Urdaneta Room first. I know you'll appreciate it, Lily. Shall we go there now?"

Standing, I tried to smile at him, but it was impossible not to feel self-conscious around Gavin. That was what I remembered: he always tried too hard. *He can win a battle, but he'll never understand what the war's about.* That was what Martin had said of him, and I understood what he'd meant.

As we walked out of his office and he locked the door, I asked him if there was any significance to the name Urdaneta. That earned a dry laugh. "There is, indeed. Does the name Andrés de Urdaneta mean anything to you?"

"I'm embarrassed to say no."

We strolled down a long corridor. All of the doors were shut, and there were no windows. "It was Urdaneta who solved the problem of how to sail east on the Pacific," Gavin said.

"I'm even more embarrassed, because I didn't know that was a problem."

"I had no idea either, until I went to school in Mexico." Gavin took in my curious look and smiled to himself. "I spent two years of secondary school—what an American would call high school—in Mexico City."

"I'm jealous," I admitted. "I would've loved to go to school in another country."

"I only did because my mother married a Mexican," Gavin said. "In any case, it gave me an entirely different perspective on history. Magellan was able to sail west on the Pacific, because he had the trade winds at his back, but he failed to sail east. Another explorer, Álvaro de Saavedra Cerón, also failed, as did Bernardo de la Torre. It was Andrés de Urdaneta who finally succeeded in finding the way in 1565. He sailed from Cebu City, in the Philippines, to Mexico. His voyage opened up the trade route that came to be known as the Manila-Acapulco galleons. Of course, most of his crew died on that initial voyage, because they didn't have the provisions for it."

Gavin opened a door and held it for me to walk through. "So why is this hotel called the Cerón instead of the Urdaneta?"

"Cerón was better connected. He was related to Hernán Cortés, you know." Gavin sighed. "It's a good question. Why does history honor some and forget others? It's not about accomplishment. It often seems like the vulture who swoops in and claims credit makes off with the glory, too." He stopped suddenly. "We're here. Close your eyes for a moment, Lily. I want you to experience this properly."

He unlocked the door—like his office, it locked with a metal key, instead of an electronic key, like the guest rooms—

and I closed my eyes. He put his hands on my shoulders, edging me inside. The door clicked shut behind us.

"All right. Open your eyes, Lily."

When I did, I gasped. The Urdaneta Room was stunning, with floor-to-ceiling windows covered with wrought-iron trellises and blooming pink flowers. They gave off an intoxicating scent that made my head swim, but in a delightful way, as if I were just slightly tipsy. It took me some time to notice that, on one wall, was a magnificent painting in a tremendous gilded frame. In it, a beautiful, dark-haired woman wearing a blue dress and a forlorn expression held a red fruit—a pomegranate—in one hand.

"Is that . . . ?"

"Dante Gabriel Rossetti's *Proserpine*? Yes, it is." Gavin's smile was as broad as I'd ever seen it. "She's better known to most people as the goddess Persephone."

"But that painting is in the Tate Museum!"

"One version is. He painted this copy himself. Isn't it brilliant?" He sighed. "You know the poem, don't you?"

"No."

"Rossetti wrote it himself. Part of it goes, 'Dire fruit, which, tasted once, must thrall me here. Afar those skies from this Tartarean grey that chills me: and afar, how far away, the nights that shall be from the days that were.' "

"I think I remember reading the Greek myth," I said. "Hades kidnapped her and forced her to become queen of the underworld."

"It's sadder than that. She was going to be rescued, but Hades had tricked her into eating four pomegranate seeds. So the gods decreed she could never really leave him. She had to return to hell and be his wife for four months of every year." Gavin's voice got softer. "The model for the painting was Jane Morris, wife of the artist William Morris. She felt trapped in her marriage, apparently, not unlike Persephone herself." He gave me that all-too-brief smile of his. "So, what do you think of my private oasis?"

I walked around it in a slow circle. "It's incredible. This room is absolutely magical." When I looked at Gavin, his eyes were closed and he was breathing deeply.

"I love it here. I really do," he said, finally opening his eyes. "I think I'm in love with the idea of having a room that makes you feel as if you're out of doors." He looked at me, his face darkening. "What do you think of the hotel, Lily?"

"It's lovely."

"I'd love to hear your professional opinion, not a polite one."

I smiled. "I like the vintage Mexican design on the main floor. The tile and the wrought-iron doors are beautiful. This room is incredible. But the guest rooms are dated, and I say that as someone who prefers vintage styles."

"They're bloody ugly, aren't they?"

It was a relief, hearing stolid Gavin say that. I never thought of him as possessing a sense of humor. "They look like Carmen Miranda put them together, or else a giant fruit bowl exploded in there."

He made a barking noise that startled me, until I realized it was a laugh.

"Carmen Miranda? That's a good one," Gavin said. "Martin always says that you have a brilliant sense of humor."

"Does he?" I aimed for nonchalance, but my heart thudded, beating so hard against my ribs that it felt like it was making a bid for freedom. First Skye had mentioned Martin to me, and now Gavin had. What did I expect? Gavin only knew me through my ex. We were standing in a hotel Martin owned. Sooner or later, his name was bound to come up.

"You have very impressive taste. You always dress so elegantly." It was almost flirtatious, the way he said it, and that surprised me. Gavin had always remarked on my clothes whenever we met, but he took such a keen interest that I wondered if he might be gay. *Oh, Robo-Rex's not gay, just English,* Martin had told me once, when I'd mentioned it.

"Thank you."

There was a lull in the conversation, in which we both looked around the room as if the combination of Martin's name and Gavin's awkward compliment had rendered us mute. The spell was broken by a waiter who knocked on the door. When Gavin opened it, the man wheeled in a trolley. He set the contents on a carved wood table, removed a couple of silvery shells, and poured my coffee and Gavin's tea into red-and-white china cups. The waiter made a brief bow and walked out of the room, shutting the door behind him, and leaving us alone.

# 17

Gavin pulled out a chair for me before taking a seat for himself, and I had a fleeting vision of us being on the world's most uncomfortable first date. He made an effort, one that was far greater than Martin's offhand charm, but it felt contrived. He was so eager to please. I wondered if he was doing this for Martin's benefit somehow, even though his boss was on the other side of the world. Maybe he thought I was in touch with Martin and might report back to him one day. He had no reason to know the truth.

"What do you think of the china? Exquisite, isn't it?"

"Stunning," I agreed. "Where did you find it?"

"My friend Josef sent it from Prague. He has the most impeccable taste of any man I know."

I continued to stare at the china, desperately trying to think of something to say. As if reading my mind, Gavin said, "Lily, I hope you don't mind my speaking about Martin. I know you two didn't part on good terms, but I feel as if he's the elephant in the room with us."

"It's fine. It just feels strange to meet up with someone I only knew through him," I admitted. "I don't think I've ever even seen you except with Martin around." I took a bite of the savory cheese bread. It was every bit as good as it smelled.

"He left me watching over you at Pantheon's Christmas party one year. He had a business call."

I'd forgotten about that completely. Gavin had hovered over me like a mother hen. "Yes, about that hotel in Shanghai. I'd forgotten that." Of course, I couldn't tell him about the conversation Martin and I had had afterward. *Did Robo-Rex take care of my girl, like I told him to?*

*You shouldn't call him that,* I'd said, but I'd also laughed.

*Just wait till you see him roll over and do tricks.*

*Well, he did fetch me champagne.*

*Bet he had his tongue hanging out the whole time. You should've had him roll over and play dead.*

*Martin, you really shouldn't call him that.*

*All right. What about Gavin the Gray? Is that a better title?*

*I don't understand why you're mean when you talk about him. He must be doing good work, or you'd fire him, right?*

*He doesn't do good work. He does great work.* Martin drained a glass of scotch. *Wish I could fire him, but I need him around. Sometimes, I think he'd be better at running the company than I am. All he does is work. He doesn't care about anything else.*

Gavin's voice broke into my thoughts. "I prefer it this way."

"Sorry. What?"

A shadow passed over his face. He cleared his throat. "I only meant that it's nice to get to speak with you, without having Martin burble on all the time with his humble brags."

I realized belatedly that Gavin had been trying to give me another compliment in his stiff-necked way. I blushed slightly, but all I said was, "His what?"

"You know. 'Oh, poor me, I have to go to this awful dinner so some silly people can give me another award.'"

"You forgot to add the part about the award being for all of his selfless humanitarian work."

A dark look full of understanding passed between us. We both knew the score, and we were in full agreement. I took a long, satisfying hit of black coffee. That was just what I needed.

"I take it that you two aren't speaking at this point," Gavin ventured.

"No. It's been a long time since we've been in touch." I doubted that Martin had told Gavin anything about what had happened back in January; he had plenty of reason to bury that. For all intents and purposes, he'd planned to kill my sister; the fact that he was mistaken in the identity of the woman he wanted dead was just a technicality to me.

"I suppose I should mention that Martin hasn't stopped talking about you. He still thinks you'll end up together one day."

"That will never happen." I set my cup down with more emphasis than I'd planned, and a little coffee sloshed out. "Damn," I muttered. Most of it had ended up in the saucer—the cups were made for tea, not coffee—but a dark brown spot wound up on the table. I dabbed at it with my napkin. Gavin didn't seem to notice.

"Not that it's any of my business, but I'm extremely glad to hear that, Lily."

I glanced at him, wondering if the lapdog had been re-placed by something more assertive, or if these sentiments had been roiling underneath an unflappable surface for a long time. Martin took a sly amusement in Gavin's awkward manner that was hard to hide. Maybe Gavin had finally caught on.

"It sounds like you two aren't getting along as well as you used to."

"I don't know that we've ever been that close," Gavin said. "Martin has been rather dependent on me. Of course, he also loves to make fun of me, but I don't take that personally. That's just Martin's style. He . . ." There was bitterness in Gavin's tone, but he reined it in. "He'd love for everyone to think he does a great job running Pantheon, but the truth is he's just extraordinarily talented at claiming the credit for other people's work." His head was down, but he was watching closely for my reaction.

"That doesn't surprise me," I said.

"I didn't think it would. I knew you would understand." He didn't smile at me, but the muscles in his face relaxed considerably. Instead of the guarded, unemotional man I was used to, this one seemed like someone I could relate to. "You should have seen him at the board meeting in Paris. He was crowing about how he'd increased revenues in a terrible global climate. The truth is, *I'm* the one who has increased the revenues. The numbers overall are terrible. The only reason we're showing a profit is because of the Mexican hotels I've acquired. Martin is so weak-willed, he wouldn't even go into the Mexican market, you know."

"I remember," I said. "He came down here, years ago, and someone tried to kidnap him. He told me he'd never set foot in the country again, because it was run by drug cartels."

"Exactly. It was only when I went in, with a plan and with all of the necessary connections, that Pantheon opened a Mexican division. We're behind every international chain here. I can't tell you how much catching up we've had to do. Yet we're already in the black. At the company meeting, I had to bite my tongue bloody not to shout that in front of everyone. Pharaoh was too busy patting himself on the back, in public."

"Pharaoh?" I almost choked on a piece of cantaloupe.

Gavin's face paled. "I'm sorry, Lily, I shouldn't have assumed—"

"No, that's hilarious." I chewed thoughtfully. "Jesse, my best friend, used to come up with nicknames for Martin, but none of them ever fit so perfectly. I love it."

We gazed at each other as I weighed his words. Part of me wondered if Gavin might be plotting against Martin for control of the company. A vengeful section of my brain lit up at the thought of that, even as the rational side said it was none of my business. *Go for it,* I thought. Dimly, I could hear the sound of Claudia's wicked laughter. She would have been impressed.

"So what did Martin have to say about *this* place?" I asked. "I can imagine him becoming apoplectic when he saw the guest rooms or the bungalows."

Gavin's head turned to me sharply. "You saw the bungalows?"

"I went for a walk this morning."

"Did you know that every one of them is fully rented for the next two years?" The pride in Gavin's voice was unmistakable.

"That's . . . incredible." It didn't seem polite to point out that none of the bungalows was ready for guests, unless the occupants liked the idea of plastic-sheeted windows or a lack of interior walls.

Gavin picked at some sliced fruit, sawing it with a knife. "Martin just enjoys the profits we're raking in here. He hasn't seen this hotel, or any of the others in Mexico."

"But he always checks out properties himself before making an offer."

Gavin gave an elaborate shrug. "He used to do that. Lately, Pharaoh has been sloughing off the real work. I know he's been globe-trotting, looking for new business opportunities, but nothing has materialized in months."

A year and a half had gone by since I'd broken my engagement to Martin; it had been nine months since I'd seen or spoken to him. That was more than long enough for circumstances at Pantheon to change. "It must be hard for him to see this division outshining the others, when he's had nothing to do with it."

"Especially because he's petrified of Mexico," Gavin added. "He truly believes if he sets foot in this country, he'll be kidnapped."

"That sounds paranoid, even for Martin."

"I suppose. To be fair, there was a kidnapping threat against him last year. That happened when I was opening our first Mexican hotel in Cabo."

"That's terrible. Martin's already paranoid about safety. He doesn't need anything to push that further."

Gavin's lips tightened into a grimace. "Of course, Martin was perfectly fine with sending me here in his stead."

**18** It was only later that morning, when I was lying naked, facedown on a massage table—my senses blurred by the sound of soft guitar music and the mingled scent of papaya and cocoa and a flower I couldn't identify—that Gavin's words sank in. I hadn't had time to think about them before that; after breakfast, I had a headache, and went up to my room. I woke up more than an hour later when the phone rang; it was the spa calling to tell me I needed to come down early to fill in a medical history and sign a waiver. I was discombobulated and achy, and I started to wonder if I'd picked up some kind of bug on the plane. It was hard to tell how much of the problem was my stressing out over Skye. Thinking about her seemed to hurt my head, because I couldn't decide whether I was afraid for her or furious at her.

In the spa, I started to puzzle out which was the lesser of two evils: stay a little longer at the Hotel Cerón until I understood what was going on with Skye, or move to another hotel and check out Acapulco like a responsible travel journalist. What I really wanted to do was abandon the city entirely and grab the first flight back to New York. The latter option was truly tempting: New York was my hometown and my first love, my best friend was there . . . and so was Bruxton. Something caught my breath, just a little, every time I thought of him, a part of me that was hopeful in spite of everything in my life that pointed the other way.

*You can run,* whispered a voice from the far reaches of my brain, *but you can't hide.*

*I'm not trying to hide,* I shot back.

There were plenty of reasons for me to go back to my hometown. It meant visiting my sister's grave, as well as my father's. While I wasn't in touch with Martin, I was on speaking terms with his teenage son, and I owed him a visit. Ridley's mother had disappeared from his life when he was small, and he'd come to learn enough about his father's Machiavellian ways that he despised him. For a time, Ridley had turned to my sister, who—in spite of being an addict—had nurtured him in her own way. Claudia had thought of Ridley as a little brother and, partly because I wanted to honor her memory, I tried to as well. I'd seen him once in the spring, while I'd been playing Florence Nightingale to Jesse. Ridley had come to Jesse's apartment, bearing a bag of old-fashioned candies and a compact disc he'd burned for me with songs by different artists, basically a modern analog of the mix tape boys had sometimes made for me when I was in high school. I hadn't recognized any of them except for Johnny Cash, but Ridley's choice—"Sunday Morning Coming Down"—only made me sad. Talking to Ridley was depressing, too. It wasn't so much what he said, because he spoke very little. It was his difficulty making eye contact and his stubborn silence. It was the way he'd suddenly thrown his head on my shoulder while we were sitting on the sofa, as if he were a young boy and I was his mother. There was something in his frantic need for contact that drained me.

Ridley's face hovered in my mind, and when I remembered his father was in Burma, my shoulders hunched up.

"Is okay?" the masseuse asked, kneading my upper back and summoning the only two words of English I'd heard her speak. She repositioned a couple of the heated stones that she'd lined up with my spine.

"Don't worry, I'm fine." My face was mashed into what spas called a cradle, a horseshoe-shaped cushion that kept my spine straight. When I opened my eyes, I could see the masseuse's foot with its bunions. I closed my eyes again.

"Is okay?" she repeated.

"Is okay," I said. That was true of the massage, but not of the thoughts racing through my brain. Ridley was undoubtedly in New York while his father traveled for work. Ridley, with his issues with drugs and violence and all his emotional baggage. Of course, Martin left him with a guard to watch him, because of kidnapping threats, but Ridley had ways of giving his minder the slip. When Ridley had visited me in the spring, he—

My upper body jolted up and the flat, hot stones clattered to the floor. It was as if someone had shot an electric current into my body. The masseuse leapt away, a torrent of rapid-fire Spanish pouring out of her, but I wasn't listening. I sat up straight, hearing Gavin's voice in my head. *There was a kidnapping threat against Martin last year. That happened when I was opening our first Mexican hotel in Cabo.*

For a moment I couldn't breathe. *Kidnapping threat.* It all fell into place so suddenly that I felt cold shock, as if I'd just jumped into ice water.

"Que pasa?" the masseuse asked me. *What's wrong?* Her voice was sharp. I'd scared her.

"Pido disculpas. Tengo que vestirme." *I'm sorry. I have to get dressed.*

"Estás enferma?" *Are you sick?* She was looking at me as if I were demented.

"No, estoy bien. Tengo que ir." *I'm fine. I have to go.*

She pulled up the sheet, holding it in front of me until I grasped it, realizing she wanted me to cover up my breasts. I was so shell-shocked I hadn't given a thought to the fact I was naked. Then she opened the door, shaking her head and muttering something that sounded a lot like *loca,* before disappearing with a sharp click.

Sitting there, on a table, Skye's disappearance started to make sense to me for the first time. If she was involved with Martin, and Martin was in danger of being kidnapped, there was a very real reason to fear that that was what had happened to Skye. It would explain why she'd disappeared so suddenly: someone had snatched her. She'd never planned to ditch me; she was coming back to the table, but she didn't get the chance.

I swung my legs down, putting the puzzle together in my mind. Where had Skye been going? Was it possible that she had gone up to her room with someone? Maybe that was why her suitcase was missing, as well as her laptop and camera and valuables.

What if Skye were being held for ransom because of her connection to Martin?

I slid off the table and into the terrycloth robe the spa provided me. My feet went into the plastic slippers, and I opened the door and rushed down the hall. I could hear the massage therapist talking about me, and the part I could translate wasn't flattering. *She was crazy! She threw the stones everywhere!*

I needed to talk to Gavin and Denny immediately, but I knew if I made a break for it in my robe and slippers, I'd be restrained by the staff. I rushed down the hall to the changing room, found the key for my locker, and got dressed in under a minute. Bra. Panties. Simple royal blue dress without mud stains on it. I panicked for a moment when I realized my bracelet wasn't there, before remembering it was upstairs in my room, sharing space in the safe with my necklace and laptop.

The emails. What about the emails? My gut instinct was that Skye hadn't written them. They looked like something she'd send, and they'd come from her account, but there was something off about them. Was it crazy to think that Skye might have been forced to send the emails? Maybe the emails were to throw people off her trail, and the ransom demand would come in later.

I hurried to the hallway, but I tripped and fell against a wall; everything was spinning around me, and I felt faintly nauseous. But the sensation passed, and I headed out of the spa and down a deserted hallway. I passed a series of tiny boutiques, all barricaded with signs saying they were closed. The eerie isolation of the Hotel Cerón was getting to me. I raced to the hotel's reception area, desperate to find someone, anyone, who could help Skye.

# 19

My mind was reeling as I raced along the hallway. I'd been wondering if Skye was playing some kind of game with me; for all I knew, she wanted me to think she'd left Mexico while she was holed up in another room at the same hotel. Stranger things had happened. But with each step I took, that possibility seemed more remote.

I was desperate to talk to Gavin. However unpleasant Apolinar was, I needed to see him, as well. Suddenly, the security tapes were of the utmost importance. They would reveal who Skye was with when she left the hotel, if she'd been drugged, and whether force had been applied. But when I got to reception, the first person I saw was Denny. She was hugging a tall woman with burgundy hair, olive skin, and figure-hugging jeans. When Denny pulled back I saw it was Roberta Needleston, and I felt the urge to run back to the spa. But Roberta spotted me before I could.

"Is that Lily? Lily Moore! Lily! Lily!" she called, her shrill voice reverberating from the tiles. "Hello, beautiful, how are you?" She stumbled forward, grinning and throwing her arms wide for a hug.

"Roberta. What a surprise." I inhaled her wine fumes, but they were immediately squeezed out of my lungs by her bear hug.

"It's good to see you, Lily! It's been a long time." Roberta, to be fair, was a sweet-tempered person who never said a cross word to anyone, at least not while she was drunk, which was virtually all the time. She was the publisher, editor, and main writer behind a wedding magazine that came out every six months. As far as I could tell, it pretty much repeated its content with every issue, obviously relying on a new crop of engaged ladies to buy the recycled material.

"It's good to see you, too, Roberta. Denny, I'm sorry to interrupt, but I need to speak with you."

"Aren't you supposed to be having a massage right now?" Denny's voice was almost chiding me.

"Maybe that's why Lily's got spa shoes on!" Roberta added.

I looked at my feet. Holy hell, as Jesse would say. Roberta might have been pickled in booze, but she wasn't blind. I was still wearing the plastic flip-flops from the spa. "Damn," I muttered. "I was just at the spa, but I realized something about Skye."

"I don't think there's going to be much we can do for her," Denny said, looking away.

"What do you mean?" I asked, but at that moment, another woman walked into the lobby. She was petite, with iron gray hair roped into some kind of crazy corkscrew perm. She was in her late sixties, and she walked with a slow, deliberate pace that was intended to be graceful but actually resembled a crab walk. Her name was Ruby Lazarus, and whenever I encountered her, she was invariably cranky. I'd first crossed paths with her years earlier in Barbados, when I started writing about travel; she'd called me "newbie" and had told me horror stories about the industry. She was on the warpath now.

"That was the crappiest flight I ever had!" she shouted, making heads swivel in her direction. "If I'm crippled from it, I'm gonna sue your keisters off."

"I'm so sorry," Denny tried to soothe her.

"I thought it was a good flight," Roberta said.

"Yeah, because you spent the whole time getting liquored up."

"You guys are picking up the bar tab, right?" There was a slight hint of panic in Roberta's face as she looked at Denny.

"Sure. Of course we will."

"You know what? You could take the money from her bar bill and get us some airplane seats that aren't totally craptastic," Ruby said. "Whaddya think of that plan?"

I made for the reception desk, hoping to get what I needed before Ruby and Roberta started to check in. "Excuse me. I need to speak with Gavin Stroud."

"Mr. Stroud is at a meeting. I could take a message, if you like?"

"No, I need to speak with him right now. It's urgent."

"I'm sorry. Mr. Stroud left the hotel."

"When will he be back?" I asked.

"I don't know."

I sighed and turned back to the knot of people in the middle of the lobby.

"Acapulco's kind of a dump these days," Ruby was saying. "It's not like the glory days when movie stars came down here. John Wayne had a place down here. I'd sure like to see that."

"Of course," Denny said. "We'll make the itinerary fit whatever you want to see."

"While you're at it, look up the hotel Johnny Weissmuller owned. Co-owned, I should say. Bunch of movie stars went in together and bought it. Duke did, too, I think."

"Duke?" Denny asked.

"That's what John Wayne's friends called him," I explained.

"That's right." Ruby gave me an approving nod. "Finest man who ever walked this earth." Ruby's voice got dreamy whenever she mentioned John Wayne. When the moment passed, it went back to shattering glass. "It's not like there's anything else to see here."

"Don't be silly, there's plenty to see," Denny said.

"Like what?" Ruby shot back.

"Well, the bay has been cleaned up in the past few years. It's much better now," Denny offered.

"Better than what? It's still a dump," Ruby said.

People who didn't know better often assumed that all travel journalists loved travel. In my experience, the opposite was often true. Travel writers carried their prejudices wherever they went, and many of them managed to be dissatisfied even when they were being spoiled. It was a bit like traveling with a pack of fussy babies.

"Denny, I need to talk with you right now," I said.

She gave me an exasperated look, but she said, "Excuse me for a minute, ladies." She stepped over to me and whispered, "What's wrong, Lily?"

"Have you heard anything about Skye?"

"Nothing. Gavin made it completely clear that he doesn't want to go there."

"Then we're going to have to find her without his help."

She let out a long breath that was tinged with frustration. "He reminded me of Skye's history. I don't think we'll hear from her for a few days. But she's an adult, so she can make her own decisions."

"Skye's *history*? What does that mean?"

Denny shook her head. "Look, I'm still her friend. I can't tell you things Skye told me in confidence."

"Denny, I'm starting to think that you care as little about finding Skye as Gavin does."

"That's not fair."

"The fact that Skye has lousy relationships with men is not a reason to think her disappearing like this is just some trick she's pulling. She wouldn't do that!"

"How the hell do you know?" Denny hissed. "She got into a car accident out on Long Island back in the spring, and she was arrested for driving under the influence. She didn't go to jail, because it was her first offence, but she had to go to rehab." She glanced around the lobby. "I don't want anyone else to know about this, Lily. Promise me you won't tell."

"I won't. I had no idea, Denny."

"She's been having a rough time in her personal life for a while now. Ryan keeps bailing her out of things—he was the one who paid for her rehab at Betty Ford—but I think that's just making everything worse. She knows he'll always catch her, no matter how far she falls."

"Denny, I think there's a possibility that Skye has been kidnapped."

"Kidnapped?" Denny's face froze. Her eyes were wary, as if she were pondering my mental state. In a way, I couldn't blame her, because the same ideas that fit together so well in my head sounded like pieces of a half-baked melodrama when they tumbled out of my mouth. But I had to forge ahead; I owed Skye that much.

"Gavin told me that a kidnapping threat was made against Martin last year, and it kept him from coming to Mexico. I think that, because Skye is close to Martin, she may have been kidnapped. They could be using her to get to him."

She stared at me, long and hard, before finally blinking.

Her eyes moved over my face, as if she were assessing how seriously to take me. "How did you find out?"

"It wasn't hard to do," I bluffed.

Denny shook her head. "Skye would murder me if she thought I was the one who told you she went out with Martin. But since you know, that's strictly past tense. She really made a play for him, but I don't think he was interested, even though Skye would never admit that."

That was the confirmation I'd craved, but it left me cold. I didn't understand why Skye would want to date my ex; I'd never taken up with any friend's former lover. To my mind, that would be disloyal. But I wasn't going to say any of that to Denny. Instead, I shrugged. "Skye wasn't herself last night. I thought she might be tangled up with Martin, but now I can't tell whether she was more interested in him or Pantheon."

Denny's expression registered alarm. "What did she say about Pantheon?"

"Not much. It's just . . . she told me she's working on a story, and I think it might be about Martin and the company." *The thing is, I know how to get even with him. I'm going to destroy him professionally, and he'll never even see it coming.*

"Lily, if that's what Skye was up to, Martin Sklar would make her disappear."

Denny's voice got far away, and the ground seemed to shift under my feet. She was right, I realized. That's exactly what Martin would do.

# 20

Dazed, I returned to the spa to retrieve my shoes, then wandered back to the lobby. I watched Denny chat with Roberta while Ruby occasionally tossed in some complaint. The clerk tried to put Ruby in room 513, but she balked at the "unlucky" number and, after much debate, was booked into 517 instead. I was standing with them, but I had nothing to say. Mentally, we were worlds apart. They chattered about the spa, lunch, and upcoming zocalo tour. Travel journalism was the last thing on my mind.

As foolish as it seemed, the idea that Martin might have a hand in Skye's disappearance had never occurred to me. In spite of everything that happened with my sister, I hadn't thought Martin capable of that kind of brutal callousness. He'd wanted to get rid of Claudia, but that was because he believed she was a danger to his son. Terrible as that was to contemplate, part of me understood it. I'd done some awful things when I was looking for my sister, and the memory of them shamed me. But motive meant everything to me. Claudia's longtime love, Tariq, had once told me anyone could kill, under certain circumstances. I'd argued with him at the time, but as weeks and months had passed, I'd realized that, deep down, I'd come to believe he was right.

Gavin's words about Skye from that morning came back to me: *She's a friend of yours, isn't she? You must have noticed the way she likes to play games with people.* How well did he know her? What had happened during her relationship with Martin that had made such a strong impression on Gavin?

I turned to the clerk. "Can you tell me where Apolinar Muñoz is, please?"

"I believe he is in his office," she answered. "Let me check."

"No, I'd rather surprise him. Where is his office?"

Her big brown eyes went wide. "Señor Muñoz does not like surprises. I will call him." She tapped three digits into the phone. She cupped her hand over the phone. "Your name, señora?"

"Lily Moore. He knows me. We met earlier this morning."

The clerk whispered into the phone, so quietly that I couldn't catch anything except her soft "Sí, señor. Gracias, señor" at the end of the call. She put the phone down and gave me a shadow of a smile. "He would like you to wait for him. He will be here very soon."

"Can't I go to his office?"

She shook her head. "He prefers here. Please, take a seat."

I didn't want to do that. Instead I strolled around the lobby, scanning it every couple of moments, until my eyes landed on a large, framed black-and-white photograph of John and Jackie Kennedy. It took up a fair part of one wall, and it looked as if it were taken years before they got to the White House. They were tanned and relaxed and JFK was boyishly slim. Jackie was the only one facing the camera, and there was a gigantic fish hoisted between them, suspended by a rope, with its tail in the air.

"Ah, you have found my favorite photograph," Apolinar said, appearing suddenly beside me. "The honeymooners."

"The what?" I tried to hide my annoyance that he'd succeeded in sneaking up on me.

"Jack Kennedy and his wife honeymooned here, in Acapulco. It was 1953, I believe." He stared at the picture. "They seem as if they are truly happy, don't they?"

"They do." The grudging tone in my voice had nothing to do with the vibrant, charming image in front of me.

"For many years, Acapulco was a retreat for wealthy Americans. But few Americans come here anymore," Apolinar added, turning away from the photograph. He led me to a couch, sitting down beside me and pulling his trousers slightly to prevent them from creasing. He wasn't wearing his suit jacket anymore, which made his lavender shirt, still open at the throat, seem like a playboy's affectation. For the first time, I noticed he was wearing a silver chain around his neck. Mostly hidden under his shirt, it fit with his image and obvious taste for fine things.

"Acapulco is a wonderful place to visit, and a wonderful place to live." His voice was warm. I wondered why he suddenly sounded like a public relations rep from a tourism bureau. "Many people are buying condos here. Or they rent a villa. People want to stay longer than a weekend."

"Even with the crime rate?" My tone couldn't have been more pointed. A derisive grunt escaped from his throat and his eyes slithered over me. It felt almost predatory, but not in a sexual way; it was more like an assessment, as if he were weighing every detail on an imaginary scale.

"The U.S. State Department is telling people not to come here. Why? There is crime, but people who are not involved with the cartels have nothing to fear." He shrugged. "I'm sure you will not see anything but the best side of Acapulco."

"You sound very attached to the place."

"I grew up here," he said.

I'd wondered why he was trying to spin me, and now I

understood. Acapulco was his city, and he had a native's pride in it. For the first time, I wondered if I were judging him too harshly.

"Really? In the city?" I asked.

"In Barra Vieja. Do you know where that is?" I shook my head and he continued. "Close to the airport, on the east side of the bay. Not many tourists go there." He glanced over my face, watching my reaction. "I wanted to be one of the divers at La Quebrada when I grew up."

There was something intriguing in his manner; he wasn't flirting with me, but he was watching me with a hawklike intensity, as if recording every word and gesture. "I heard the diving last night, but only from the bar. I can't wait to see it, but I can't imagine how they do it."

"*I* did it." The pride in his voice was unmistakable. "I started training when I was thirteen. I knew Teddy Stauffer." He was watching me so closely he caught the complete lack of comprehension in my face. "Teddy Stauffer!" he repeated. "Mr. Acapulco. You don't know him? He was Swiss, a bandleader, a hotelier, a nightclub owner. He made Acapulco popular with the stars. All these famous people you see on the walls here"—he made an expansive gesture with one hand—"all of them came to Acapulco because of Teddy."

I stared at his hand, noticing the crosshatching of scars on the knuckles. There could have been any number of explanations, really, but it made me think of a man I'd met in Peru, one with a propensity for violence. Beating people could build up scar tissue. I buried the thought under what I hoped was a reasonable facsimile of a smile. "You were one of the divers? I can't imagine having the nerve to do that."

"It does take *huevos*. But you learn, like everything else, with practice. Perhaps we could go see them together. It's a highlight of any visit to Acapulco. They will be performing at one o'clock this afternoon. Will you come with me?"

His voice was casual, and there was nothing dangerous in his tone, but his suggestion unnerved me. I felt as if he were trying to get me alone, outside of the hotel, and that set alarm bells off in my head.

"I wish I could, but there's a press trip lunch at twelve-thirty."

"Of course. The press trip." His words were edged with contempt.

For a moment, we sat in silence, and I glanced at his hands again. There was a jagged scar up the side of one palm. My eyes were only on it for a second, but when I looked at his face again, I could tell he'd noticed. There was something serpentine about his unblinking gaze, and it made me uneasy. Everything about him did. *Listen to me, Lily. You don't want to know that guy.*

I cleared my throat. "I want to talk to you about Skye McDermott. I think there's a possibility she may have been kidnapped."

"Kidnapped?" He stared at me with the icy impassivity of a stone statue. In a way, his control was admirable; I wished sometimes that I could display so little emotion. But it reinforced my dislike of him.

"Gavin mentioned that there were kidnapping threats made last year at another Pantheon hotel."

"Yes, that was in Cancún."

"No, Gavin said it was in Cabo. That's where Pantheon opened its first hotel in Mexico, from what he said."

"Cabo. Of course. You were saying?"

"That made me think Skye might have been abducted." I was only giving him the smallest sliver of what I really thought. It had been on the tip of my tongue to mention the likely connection between Martin and Skye, but my instincts told me to hold back.

"That is not at all likely."

"How can you say that?"

"The threat was only to Pantheon's board of directors, and in particular to Mr. Sklar. There was never any threat to guests at the hotel."

"What about other executives?" Gavin's angry jibe rattled in my head. *Of course, Martin was perfectly fine with sending me here in his stead.* Gavin may have been a reliable foot soldier for Martin to use, but he wasn't a happy one.

"I am here to keep everyone safe," Apolinar said.

"What about Skye? Is she safe?"

"I'm sure she is." Everything about Apolinar—his expression, his demeanor, his tone—told me that he didn't give a damn. It was worse than that; the darkness behind his eyes belied his calculated words and surface polish. I was sure he knew more about Skye's disappearance than he would say.

"Have you reviewed the security tapes from last night?" I asked, well aware I was poking at a hornet's nest.

His smile was frigid. "Miss Moore, I understand that you wish to help—"

"Please call me Lily."

"Lily." He gave me a full-wattage movie-star smile. His mouth was full of capped teeth, white as the Hotel Cerón's own facade. It didn't look attractive so much as expensive. "I can assure you that all necessary steps are being taken."

"Have you even looked at the tapes yet?"

There was a pause, as if he were weighing his options. "There are no tapes."

"That's impossible. There are security cameras everywhere!" I pointed at one of the black spheres embedded in the ceiling. "What do you think that is?"

"That is where there will one day be a security camera," Apolinar said. "That day is not yet here."

I bit my lip. "Is this a joke?"

"No. But keep in mind, there is still a great deal of material to review."

"Such as?" I asked. He didn't answer. "I'd be happy to help."

That earned a frown. "That will not be necessary." He stood, adjusting the front of his trousers, smoothing creases out of them aggressively. One cuff caught on something and Apolinar freed it, but not before I caught a glimpse of a gun in an ankle holster. Was his job so dangerous he needed to carry a gun at his hip and another hidden under his clothing?

"I hope you will enjoy your stay here, Lily," he announced as he walked away. From Apolinar's mouth, it sounded almost like a threat.

**21** More than anything, I wanted to be alone to think. When I went upstairs, I found my room had been tidied by a maid—bed newly made with fresh linens, cushions fluffed, toiletries rearranged. I should have been glad to see that, but I wasn't. The lock on the door of my room gave me the illusion of privacy, but an illusion was all it was. A dozen people might have a key card, and any of them could come inside whenever they felt like it. A maid. Gavin. Apolinar.

I kicked off my shoes and collapsed on the sofa. What I wanted was a cigarette, but I lay there, staring at the ceiling and trying to work through the web of secrets and lies and evasions that I'd let myself become ensnared in. What bothered me most at that moment was the fact that I hadn't even asked Skye about Apolinar. *Listen to me, Lily. You don't want to know that guy.* I should have asked why, but she was rushing off to make her phone call and I hadn't stopped her. What did she know about him? Or was I looking at it the wrong way? What did Apolinar know about her? Was that why Skye warned me away from him?

What if Skye was working on a story about the corruption at Pantheon? Anyone tied to Pantheon—Martin, Gavin, Apolinar, maybe even Denny—would have a motive to shut her up. Of course, there was also the possibility that Skye had slept with Apolinar. His snakelike qualities aside, he was handsome enough—and undoubtedly vain enough—to seek out new, temporary conquests.

*Oh, Honey Bear. Deep down, you're pretty superficial,* Claudia taunted me. *Get your mind out of the gutter.* That edgy little voice in my head was right. Why had I leapt to the conclusion that Skye had gone to bed with Apolinar? I needed a better working theory, one that didn't make her out to be a cheap seductress. Skye may have looked like Jean Harlow, but that didn't mean she was mimicking the actress's vile, deceptive character in *Hell's Angels.*

I couldn't dismiss the idea that she had been kidnapped. Gavin was strangely unworried about her disappearance. *I don't want to speak out of turn. It's just that I suspect Skye was upset with someone, and she flounced out of the hotel because of it. She's probably cooling her heels for a day or two, not realizing the chaos she's caused.* He seemed so confident about that idea. Did that mean he knew something, or was it wishful thinking on his part?

I rubbed my temples and sat up. Counting on other people was getting me nowhere. I had to do something to help Skye. If that meant calling the local police myself, so be it. I got my laptop out of the safe and looked for a number to call.

It wasn't as straightforward as I'd assumed it would be. The first thing that came up was a Facebook page dedicated to reporting the extortion of tourists by police in Acapulco. Next, a news story of how eleven people were killed in Acapulco the previous weekend; the police had no leads in any of the cases. Five bodies had recently been found on a beach, all of them headless. Sites in English and Spanish warned me away from having any contact with local police, claiming that people who looked to them for help often ended up extorted for cash or in jail themselves. The exception were the federal police, who were a relatively recent addition to the three other layers of police in the city, but the *Federales* only dealt with street crime.

The only useful bit of advice I found recommended contacting the consulate for help. Acapulco didn't have a U.S. consulate, but it had a consular agent who was tied to the embassy in Mexico City. I dialed the number, listened to a long series of messages as I went through the electronic switchboard, and landed in voice mail. I left an urgent message, and hung up with a heavy heart. The office was only staffed for four hours a day on weekdays, and it was a Saturday. What were the odds anyone would call back before Monday?

Every move I made felt futile, because without the hotel or the police helping in the search, Skye's trail was pretty damn cold.

There was one other call I realized I had to make. Thanks to Skye's passport, I knew her home address. I'd handed the passport over to Gavin and Apolinar, but I remembered what it said: 75 Livingston Street, Brooklyn. It was a prominent landmark, also known as the Court Chambers Building, a 1927 neo-Gothic office tower with a pyramid at its peak. I'd included it in a Brooklyn walking tour I'd once written for a British newspaper. Not that you could go inside, since it had been converted to residential apartments decades ago. It was a beautiful—and very expensive—place to live.

It took me a minute to find the telephone listing—for R. Brooks and S. McDermott. Skye had filled the contact information in her passport in ink. Technically, you were supposed to change those details when you moved, but most people didn't bother. It turned out that Skye hadn't either. The voice-mail message said, "You've reached Ryan Brooks.

Unfortunately, I'm not available at the moment. Please leave me a message so that I can return your call."

The formality of his message caught me by surprise. "Hello," I said. "You won't remember me, but I'm a friend of Skye's. My name is Lily Moore, and I'm another journalist who's on the press trip with Skye right now. I'm calling because Skye has disappeared. We don't know what's happened to her, and we're worried. I wanted to ask if there's any chance she's called you. Please call me as soon as you get this message." I left my cell phone number and hung up.

I had a few minutes until lunch with the group and nothing to do. That wasn't quite right: I had the uncomfortable feeling that there were things I should have been doing to help Skye, but I had no idea what they were. Thinking about what might have happened to her made me panicky and more than a little paranoid. Broken bits of worst-case scenarios flicked through my head like film clips run through an old projector. They stopped and started, rolling back and forth, jagged at the edges and shimmering in and out of focus. Skye being abducted. Held hostage. Injured. In pain. By the time the headless bodies on the beach started to swirl into view, I had to bolt. As much as I'd craved solitude to think things over, my own ideas were driving me mad.

Heading out again, I made my token knock at Skye's door. I knew she wouldn't answer, even as I waited. After giving it a minute, I made for the elevator. It arrived at the fifth floor, but before I could step in, Pete Dukermann stepped out. His eyes were still bloodshot, but he looked steadier on his feet than he had early that morning by the water.

"You again." He sounded more like his usual self, too.

"Always such a charmer."

He brushed by me, then turned around. "Have you found Skye yet?"

"No. They're supposed to be looking for her," I answered, hoping that really was the case but having less than complete confidence in Apolinar.

"Where would she go?"

"Pantheon had a kidnapping threat at another of its Mexican hotels," I explained, leaving Martin's name out of the equation.

Pete wiped his mouth with the back of his hand. "What's going on with her, huh? I mean, something coulda happened to her. . . ." His voice rose, sounding odd and strained.

"I don't know. You haven't gotten any strange emails that claim to be from her, have you?"

"Email? I dunno. I've been unplugged all morning." He frowned. "You said *claimed* to be from her. You think someone hacked Skye's account?"

"I got a couple of emails that were supposed to be from Skye but they were . . . strange."

"Well, then she's okay, right?" His bloodshot eyes darted over my face.

"One of the emails said she'd flown home, but we know she didn't do that because she left her passport with me last night."

"Shit. This is serious." He stared at me. "You think this has anything to do with her story?"

"I don't know anything about her story. Do you?"

"No. No, nothing." He said it quickly, as if determined to get that out of the way, before I could delve in further. "I can check my email now, see if there's anything from her."

I startled both of us by saying, "Can I come with you?"

"Um. Uh." He rubbed his chin, eyes darting to the side, then back at me. Just as he was studying me, I was judging him. The red scratches on his arms were in plain sight, and I wanted to know how he'd gotten them.

"It will just take a minute, right?" My curiosity outweighed my revulsion at the thought of going back to Pete's room with him.

"Okay," he muttered. "Come on."

I trailed after him, down the corridor in the opposite direction from my suite. No noise emanated from the rooms we passed. The only sound was of Pete's footfalls on the red carpet, which barely registered, yet seemed to boom in the silence.

"Do you think there's anyone else around?" I whispered.

Pete slowed down, glancing over his shoulder at me. "Skye asked me that yesterday." He was whispering, too. "I said it was like a ghost town. And she said . . ."

"What?"

"Never mind. It didn't make sense."

We were at the end of the hallway now, and Pete fished a key card out of his jeans. His door had a DO NOT DISTURB sign hanging on the handle. Pete opened the door an inch, but held it so I couldn't see inside. "Could you wait here for a minute? I need to, uh, put some stuff away."

"Okay," I said, envisioning a porn stash and blow-up doll. Whatever Pete had lying around in there, I didn't want to know. He went inside, closing the door behind him so quietly that I was surprised. What had happened to brash, drunken Pete? Was it just the heavy atmosphere of the empty hotel weighing down on him, as it did me, or was there something else?

Finally he opened the door. "Okay. Come in," he muttered, grudging and stern, pulling the door back just enough for me to enter.

I edged by him carefully, not wanting to have any physical contact with him, and headed through the hallway. As I walked into the living room, I stopped dead, astonished, at the same time Pete locked the door behind me.

# 22

"What the hell happened in here?" I said, staring around the room in shock. Pete's suite looked as if a cyclone had hit it. There was trash on the carpet, including a smashed ashtray with butts scattered far and wide. There were empty bottles of tequila and crushed cans of a Mexican beer called Tecate. One tall lamp lay on the floor, bent in two; its shade was a few feet away, making it look like a party guest who'd finally passed out. There was a fist-sized hole in the plaster of a tangerine wall.

"Nothing."

"Pete, this place looks like . . ." Something crunched under my shoe. "Is that glass?"

"Maybe, yeah, I broke a glass last night."

I turned to stare at him. "Did you get into a fight with someone?"

"How'd you know that?"

"Because your room has been trashed, you've got a cut on the side of your hand, and you look like you've been through the wringer." There was nothing diplomatic in my answer. The truth was brutal, but Pete needed to hear it. There was something about his manner that brought out the sharpest, roughest edge of my personality.

"Yeah, well, you don't know shit." His face was getting red. "I wasn't in that kind of fight."

"What kind of fight were you in?"

"I don't want to talk about it. You better not mention this to anyone, or I'll . . ."

"You'll what, Pete?"

His threat hadn't been articulated, but it hung in the air between us. My instinct was to run from the room, but he was between me and the door, and making a sudden move like that seemed riskier than staring him down. But, before my eyes, Pete drew back, deflating. His face, so furious and red a moment before, seemed to bleed out color, leaving him ashen, and he shrunk back into himself, muttering.

"My computer's in the safe." His head was down; he stared at the floor. "I'll get it."

I couldn't help but wonder what Pete's bedroom looked like. He pulled the door behind him but he didn't shut it completely. From the living room, all I could really see was that the bed was unmade, which was hardly a surprise. I heard him open the closet door. These suites were laid out in identical ways; the safe in my room was in the bedroom closet, too. Walking to the window, I stared outside, but I was really watching for him in the reflection I saw in the glass. What the hell had Pete gotten himself into? Why was he so erratic, and what was eating away at him, under his skin?

He came out of the bedroom carrying his laptop and shut the door. That only increased my suspicion. What was he hiding from me? Was there something worse than a trashed room?

"Okay, I'm opening my email," he announced. I turned to face him, but I couldn't catch a glimpse of his screen.

"Anything?" I prompted while he silently scanned his email. He clicked on something and read it, his lips moving as he did. "Is there anything from Skye?"

"Uh, no, I don't think so. Lot of junk in here. Let me check my spam." A couple of clicks, and he shook his head again. "Nope. Nothing from her." He stared up at me, looking so fearful and wary that it caught me by surprise. "Do you think she's in trouble?"

"Yes. Don't you?"

He wiped his forehead. "Yeah. She was weird yesterday."

"Weird? How?"

"She swore me to secrecy."

"About what?" I demanded. "Pete, she's missing. She might have been kidnapped. If you know anything about what was going on with her, you need to speak up."

"I don't know anything." His tone was petulant. "It was just a couple things that popped outta her mouth, you know? Like, she was bugging me yesterday about the hotel."

"What about it?"

"She asked me if I noticed anything odd about the hotel. I was all, like, what? It looks kinda cheesy, I mean, the whole fortress thing they got going on, but that's not odd, right?"

"No. So what was it?"

"She didn't tell me. She just kept asking me questions."

"Like what?"

"Okay, she was like, what do you think of the other hotel guests? And I was, like, *what* other hotel guests? This place is like a ghost town. And she said . . ."

"Pete." I started to reach out my hand to touch him, but recoiled. "What did Skye say?"

"She said, 'They're all ghost towns.'" He stared at me, turning his hands palm up. "That make any sense to you? 'Cause it didn't to me. I asked her what the hell that meant, but she wouldn't say anything about it. I mean, *what* ghost towns?"

*They're all ghost towns.* An idea tickled the back of my brain, but it seemed so preposterous that I didn't want to acknowledge it. "Did she ask you anything else about the hotel? Anything at all?"

"She kept going on and on about the hotel's prices. I thought that was funny, 'cause, hey, we're on a press trip. We don't pay for squat."

"You might pay for breaking your room, Pete."

He shrugged. "Probably not. You know how it is."

I nodded. Yes, I did know, and he was probably right. So long as he produced material that showed the hotel in a good light, everything would be forgiven. "So, Skye was talking about hotel pricing. Room rates?"

"Yeah, and she asked what I thought the flowers cost. You know, the flowers in the lobby. She asked if they were worth ten thousand a month. I'm, like, this is Mexico. Are you crazy? I don't know." He shrugged. "Who thinks about what the flowers cost? Who cares?"

That was odd. A travel journalist needed to know what it cost to book a room, but why would anyone care about the flowers? "Pete, you were with Skye yesterday. She talks. She talks a *lot*. She must have told you something about the story she was working on."

"She swore me to—"

I hit my hand against the desk and he flinched, pulling his head back like a turtle. "Pete! She's missing. Whatever she told you might be the reason why. What did she say?"

"She said she was going to get even with somebody—she didn't say who. She said this article would settle a lot of scores."

"How?"

"I don't fucking know, okay? She told me she knew she was right and she just had to prove it."

"You don't have any idea what she meant?" My voice was pleading now. "There must have been some clue."

"She freaked out, made me swear I wouldn't say anything to anyone." He ran both hands through his shaggy hair. "What do we do?"

"I don't know." I stared out the window. There was a small crack in the gray sky, just enough to remind me there was light behind it. "Pete, were you serious this morning when you asked if that guy was following one of us?"

"I was just feeling paranoid. You'd already surprised me. I didn't expect to see anyone around at all."

"What about yesterday?" I prompted. "When you were with Skye. Was anyone following you then? Maybe someone trying to eavesdrop?"

He shook his head. "No. It was just a hinkey feeling I had this morning. Like when the hairs stand up on your neck. I can't really explain it."

Great. One paranoid person egging on another. At that moment, I would have given anything to have Jesse beside me. Through so much of my life, he'd been the wisecracking voice of sanity. Without him, I was becoming unnerved and, I feared, unhinged.

"Where did you and Skye go yesterday?"

"Nowhere. She just wanted to hang around the hotel. We walked around, sat in the bar. I took some photos of her."

That piqued my interest. "You did? Can I see them?" Photographers often used attractive journalists or PR people as impromptu models on press trips, so there wasn't anything untoward about it. But I had an overwhelming desire

to see Skye again, to look her over in case there was something I'd missed that would explain everything.

"Sure." Pete started clicking away at his laptop, and I came
closer, sidestepping the glass on the carpet, so I could stand
beside him. He opened a photo library and I saw dusky shots
of a midnight-blue sky with streaks of torchlight against it.
There was a shirtless man staring down with great intensity;
Pete had somehow framed the shot so that you saw the
flames reflected in the man's eyes.

"That's an amazing photo."

"One of the divers. I took that last night." He was scrolling away, going back through his shots from the day. "There
she is."

I leaned forward, taking in an image of Skye staring into a
mirror as she tried on a large silver necklace with onyx beads.
It was shot at an angle from behind her shoulder, so it captured the edge of her face as well as her expression, making it
feel intimate. Whatever else I thought of Pete Dukermann, I
had to admit he had an astonishing talent for composing a
shot, and for capturing odd angles and reflections. I understood why Jesse, also a photographer, admired Pete professionally even though he didn't like him at all.

Pete clicked through a series of photos, all featuring Skye.
Nothing jumped out at me. It was only when I glanced up
and spotted the black duffel that I froze. It was the same bag
Pete had carried that morning. He'd been pulling something
out of it when I'd surprised him at the cliff. Now, I finally
saw what it was: a necklace of fiery red and orange beads,
exactly like the one that had been around Skye's throat when
she vanished.

I must have made some kind of sound, because Pete looked up at me. "You look like you just saw a ghost, Lily."

My chest felt tight, and I couldn't get any air into my lungs. A tiny wheeze escaped from my throat, a dull, half-strangled sound.

"Are you okay? Maybe you should sit down." He stood, leaving the desk chair for me to sink into. Instead, I made my way across the room, reaching for the beads and easing them out of the bag. Even as I did, I tried to tell myself I was mistaken, but I wasn't. It was a long, flapperlike strand of beads, just like Skye's.

I held it up. "Where did you get this, Pete?"

His face was petulant again. "That was Skye's idea."

"*What* was her idea?"

He muttered something I couldn't catch.

"Where did you get this necklace?"

"From Skye."

*Liar,* I thought, but I was shaking with rage and too stunned to say a word. Instead, I moved on pure instinct, rushing to the bedroom door. The area behind it was more chaotic than the living room.

"What are you doing?" Pete yelled.

I ignored him and pulled the closet doors open. In my mind's eye, I saw Skye lying there, unconscious, but there was nothing inside except a rucksack on the carpet, the safe, and extra pillows and blankets on a shelf at the top. The door to the bathroom was closed, and I ran to it, pushing it open just as Pete grabbed my arm.

There was no one in the bathroom.

Pete's fingers dug in to my shoulder, and he pulled me off balance so that I tumbled into the doorway. As I caught myself, I shifted sideways and jabbed my elbow as hard as I could into his stomach. Even with his extra padding, he doubled over.

"Where's Skye?" I demanded.

"Don't . . . know . . ." He panted the syllables out, his breath escaping in small puffs as he rested his palms on his knees. He didn't lift his head.

"You have her necklace."

"She . . . gave it . . . to me."

"She was wearing it last night when I saw her!"

He stood up, shaking his head. I had to fight an overwhelming urge to elbow him again. "She gave it to me," he insisted.

"You can stick to that story if you like, but I know you're lying. And you're not going to get away with it. I'm going to bring people up here, and you're going to be locked away for a very long time in a Mexican jail."

As the words poured out of my mouth, I realized I was being stupid. All I had to do was quietly inch out of the room and bring reinforcements; instead I was daring Pete to stop me, and given that he was six foot four and on the heavy side, that wouldn't go well for me. Instead of trying to intimidate me, he sank to the floor, crouching with his head in his hands. "She gave it to me, Lily. She did."

"Why would she do that? Did she think you were going to wear it somewhere? You're so pathetic you can't even come up with a lie that makes any sense!"

"It's for my wife," Pete whispered.

"Your wife? Why would Skye send her anything?"

"I . . . she . . . we separated. We've had a lot of tough times, but this is the worst." He took a couple of deep breaths. "Skye and me talked about it. She's been having all these problems with her boyfriend. He won't acknowledge their relationship. It's all top secret with him. She hates that. He won't even let her call him her boyfriend in private. He says they're grown-ups, not boys and girls."

I'd expected more stupid lies from Pete, not a story that resonated with what I knew to be true. Skye had told me the same thing, but in different words. "What does her boyfriend have to do with this?"

"He buys her jewelry. Like, they argue, and next thing he'll give her a necklace or a bracelet."

It felt as if someone had just lowered the temperature in the room by twenty degrees. That was Martin's modus operandi. "Go on," I said.

"She's seriously pissed off at him. She wouldn't tell me why." He looked up at me. "I swear, Lily, I'm telling you the truth. We had dinner, and when I was telling her my problems with my wife, she pulled off the necklace she was wearing and gave it to me. She said the stones were fire opals, and they were supposed to reignite passion." He shook his head, looking down. "Like that'll work for me and Donna."

"Your wife left you?" I asked.

"Worse than that," he answered. "Why'd you think I threw my wedding ring into the water this morning?"

I remembered the glint of gold I'd seen. "Are you crazy? Why would you do that?"

"Look, I don't want to talk about it, okay?"

"How did your arms and hand get scratched up?"

That question filled him with fury I could read in his face and in his movements as he got to his feet. His skin was almost pulsing with anger.

"I told you, I don't want to talk about it!" He was almost yelling now. "Just get out of my room."

I took a last look around the room and realized why Pete had been so secretive. There was the residue of white powder on the wooden surface of a night table next to the bed, along with a razor blade.

"Oh, please," I said. "You don't think I care about your drug habit, do you? Get over yourself."

I could see a series of small glassine envelopes on the night table. That brought Claudia back with a rush in my brain; I associated those little packets with her, and with heroin. "You running some kind of business on the side, Pete?"

"It's for personal consumption. That means it's all legal."

"You've got to be kidding."

"Check for yourself. Mexico decriminalized coke and a bunch of other shit in 2009, so long as it's only for personal possession."

"Even if that's true, I bet there's a limit on what counts as personal possession."

Pete grunted. "I told you to get out."

That was exactly what I planned to do. I walked to the doorway between the bedroom and living room, then turned back. "Do you have any idea what Skye is sick with?"

"No, except that she said she couldn't eat. It made her want to vomit."

"What about drinking? Did she say anything about having a problem with that?"

"She wasn't drinking at all!" Pete sounded affronted. "Who told you she has a problem with booze?"

I didn't want to answer that.

"I bet it was Denny," he said. "She's full of shit. You know what she told me when I asked to join the press trip? She said the hotel was all booked up."

"Focus, Pete. Skye. Think about Skye."

"I am. She told me she feels terrible about what happened with Denny."

"What was that?" I asked.

"I dunno. Skye was cryptic as hell. She kept dropping all these hints yesterday, but she wouldn't answer a direct question."

"Okay, what room did you see her come out of?"

"End of the hall. Don't know for sure." He rubbed his stomach, right where I'd elbowed him.

I turned and headed out of the room, back into the chaos of the living room. I turned down the long hallway that led to the suite's front door.

"You're a real bitch, Lily Moore!" Pete shouted after me.

I didn't turn around. "I know."

# 24

No one answered when I knocked on the door at the end of the hallway. I rang the bell, waited, then tried the suite across the hall. The bells echoed through rooms that were obviously empty. I wondered if the key card in Skye's bag would've opened one of these doors, and I wished I'd held it back.

Pete was a liar. I just wasn't entirely sure which parts of his stories were fabricated. There were bits of truth mixed in there, glimmering like silver threads, and they complicated everything. Did I believe that Skye had given Pete her necklace, and that she just happened to have one exactly like it, which she was wearing when I saw her? No. But I knew Pete wasn't lying about Skye's frustration with her secretive boyfriend, or the story she was writing. She'd said similar things to me. She could be lying to both of us, but that was a different issue.

Giving up on my fool's errand, I turned back toward the elevators, shooting Pete's door the evil eye as I went past. Part of me regretted venturing into Pete's room. I should've known that would be a huge mistake, but I was desperate for any word about Skye, even a dubious email. I was also deeply suspicious of Pete. I'd never known him to be violent, but the combination of cocaine and the disaster zone he'd created in his room was frightening. He'd admitted his marriage had broken up. *Worse than that,* as he'd described it, whatever that meant. He was spiraling out of control, and I wondered what he was capable of. His concern for Skye struck me as genuine, but even that troubled me.

When I got to the elevator bank, my knees buckled and I fell against the wall. I took a few shuddering breaths to steady myself. It wasn't the confrontation with Pete so much as a feeling of helplessness. I had no idea where Skye was, or what had happened to her, but I knew that she hadn't just run off, and she wasn't safe. Pete could have had a hand in her disappearance—clearly, he'd been involved in something violent—but who did I turn to in order to report him? The police were not an option. The consular office was closed. Denny would be concerned, but she had no more pull with the local authorities than I did. I could go to Apolinar, who also happened to be someone I thought might have had a hand in Skye's vanishing trick. Gavin seemed determined to play the ostrich, clinging to the idea that Skye had taken off in a huff.

Who else could I turn to?

The only person I could think of was Martin.

It was a devastating comment on my predicament that my ex was the closest facsimile to a person I could trust. That thought stabbed my temple, mocking me.

*You think he'll come in and fix everything,* Claudia whispered from the back of my brain. *That's what you want him to do.*

*No,* I argued back, *I don't want Martin here. Yes, I want him to find Skye, but I don't want anything else to do with him. I want him to force people who work for him into helping Skye.*

*What makes you think he'll want to help anyone except himself?*

I had no answer for that. If history was anything to judge by, Martin would protect his son, and he would take care of himself. He didn't care about anyone else, not really.

Standing straight, I pressed the call button for the elevator. It creaked and groaned on its trip down to the first floor. For a split second, as the doors reluctantly pulled apart, I thought I might catch sight of Skye. It was superstitious of me, but I imagined if I kicked up enough of a fuss looking for her, she'd be bound to reappear and I'd look like an idiot for being worried. But she wasn't there.

I slipped through the lobby and went through the glass doors, feeling instant regret as I abandoned the air-conditioned climate for an al fresco steam bath. The sun was doing its damnedest to burn through the cloud cover, but the result was a hazy sky that was hard on the eyes. A pair of bellmen watched me as I lit a cigarette. They talked in low voices to each other, occasionally chuckling conspiratorially. What purpose did they serve, standing in front of a near-empty hotel, waiting to greet guests who never arrived? Gavin had mentioned renovations, but I saw no signs of work in progress. Maybe construction was set to start after the press trip ended, and Pantheon kept on the full staff to impress the journalists. It was all just window dressing, for our benefit, and it looked as artificial as it felt.

Staring through the glass into the lobby, I tried to picture Skye as I'd seen her the night before. She'd been beautifully dressed and her hair was perfect. But her face was red and there'd been dark circles under her eyes and she'd looked exhausted. I'd never asked her where she was going. There were strange shadows hiding in the planes and hollows of her face. Yes, she may have been sick, but that wasn't why she burst into tears in the lobby.

The contradictions in her bothered me. I hadn't seen them clearly before; I'd been too distracted by the possibility she was sleeping with Martin. But Martin was half a world away, and Skye was all dressed up in her seductive finest. It wasn't as if she were going outside of the hotel. I'd asked her to come up to my room, but she'd wanted to go to the bar. The only man who'd shown up at the bar was . . . Apolinar. Right after he left, so did Skye. Was that a coincidence?

If the past few months had taught me anything, it was that there was no such thing as a coincidence.

Dimly aware I was making a decision I'd regret, I dropped my cigarette on the asphalt and rooted through my bag for my phone. Once it was in hand, I chewed on my lower lip, steeling myself for what I needed to, then wincing in pain as I bit down too hard. Even thousands of miles away, it seemed Martin Sklar still had the power to hurt me.

Goosebumps ran up the back of my bare legs. How did you get past the fact that someone you thought you loved had wanted to kill your sister? And yet, I had to. My fingers tapped out Martin's cell phone automatically, as if we'd been in touch yesterday.

As it rang, I wondered what time it was in Burma. Just as it seemed the call was sinking into the voice-mail ether, Martin answered, his voice so muffled I almost missed his quiet hello.

The air I'd been holding in my chest rushed out of my lungs. I turned my back to the bellmen; I wanted privacy. "Martin, it's Lily."

Time slowed down to a crawl as I waited for him to answer, then sped up again as I heard his voice for the first time in months.

"Lily, sweetheart . . ." There was a pause, and I could hear him breathing heavily, as if he'd just been running. "It's so good . . . to hear your voice."

His words were exactly what I would have predicted, yet Martin sounded strangely subdued. No matter what happened, he maintained a front of resolute cheerfulness. At least, he had when I'd known him. Maybe that facade had folded up and skipped town. *Or maybe you just woke him up, Honey Bear,* that voice in my head pointed out. *Why do you have to read deep meanings into things with simple explanations?*

I didn't have time to argue with both of them. "This isn't a social call. I'm at your hotel in Acapulco, on a press trip. Skye McDermott has been missing since last night." My voice was hard but brittle, as if it were about to break.

"Skye?"

"Don't you *dare* play dumb with me, Martin. You know exactly who I'm talking about." All the anger inside me turned darkly cold. The anxiety I'd felt the night before, thinking about Skye being with Martin, evaporated. Martin had never been honest with me, and that realization drew whatever sadness I was carrying around inside me out like the poison of a snakebite. I'd wasted years playing along with his games. The person I'd been back then was buried just as surely as my sister was.

"I haven't seen Skye in quite some time," Martin said.

"Were you involved with her?"

The silence stretched like a chasm between us. "I took her out to dinner. Once or twice."

I didn't want to ask if he'd slept with her. At last, I was holding onto a bit of truth, a puzzle piece that actually fit.

"Martin, just listen to me," I said, suddenly calmer. "Last night, when I got here, Skye and I went for drinks at the hotel bar. We talked for a while, and then she got up and she . . . she just disappeared. She never came back. And she meant to come back. She left her purse at the table, with her wallet and credit cards and passport and medication and . . . look, she left everything behind. No one has seen her since. I don't know what's happened to her, but I'm scared for her. The hotel won't do anything and the police here are . . ." My voice trailed off.

"Don't worry, sweetheart. I'll make sure my people take care of everything." It was the verbal equivalent of a pat on the head and it made me want to lash out at him.

"What people do you have taking care of *anything*? Gavin Stroud? Apolinar Muñoz? You may as well throw dimes down a wishing well. When are you going to get the police involved?"

"If there's one thing I've learned about doing business, it's that you don't want any contact with the police. That's certainly been my experience in Mexico."

"Your experience? Based on what?" Irritation crackled in my voice. "Gavin told me you were too much of a coward to set foot in Mexico."

"Did he really?" Martin's voice was still quiet, but there was something slyly dancing at the edge of it.

"He didn't call you a coward. *I'm* calling you a coward," I clarified, guilty at the thought of getting Gavin in trouble with his boss. "Gavin told me about the kidnapping threat, and that you wouldn't come to Mexico."

"I see."

I tried to keep my voice steady, even though my blood pressure was surging. "Martin, there's something seriously wrong here. Gavin wants to think Skye went to another hotel, but she didn't just run off. I think she might have been targeted for kidnapping because of her relationship with you."

"Her what?" He sounded genuinely perplexed, but I knew what a good actor he could be.

"Don't start, Martin. I don't care."

"But I—"

"I don't want to hear it. I just want you to lean on Gavin and Apolinar."

"All right, but I want something in exchange," Martin said.

"Do you really? What might that be?"

"I want you to be ready to leave Mexico at a moment's notice."

That stopped me short. "What? Why?"

"I can't explain right now, except to say you're in a very dangerous spot. Whatever you do, don't get into a taxi or a car with anyone you don't know. I'm going to get you out, but the devil's still got the details knotted up."

"Do you think someone wants to kidnap me?"

There was a long pause. "Yes, Lily. In fact, I know someone does. But don't breathe a word to anyone, especially not Gavin. Try to act as carefree as you can."

"You want me to act carefree?" Incredulity curdled my voice. *Carefree* brought to mind the Fred Astaire movie, which had Ginger Rogers sailing through much of it in a hypnotist-induced carefree trance. "Skye has been kidnapped, and I should be . . . carefree?"

"For now, yes. Don't let your guard down with anyone. And stay away, as far as you can, from Gavin."

I was speechless. Martin was acting as if he were in the same Cold War spy movie that Skye had seemed to think she was in on Friday night.

"Martin, I don't know what the hell is going on, but all I want is for you to make sure your people look for Skye."

"I will. But, sweetheart, please don't be difficult—"

"Martin, don't ever call me sweetheart again," I said, and hung up.

# 25

The restaurant was a mirror image of the nightclub, with identical wrought-iron grilles, but the walls were painted bright turquoise. It gave the effect of standing inside a fishbowl, one with bars over its glass. Denny was waiting for me just inside the door.

"Lily, can I talk to you for a second?" she said, touching my elbow. I followed behind a privacy screen of carved dark wood. Through small openings in the floral design, I could see that Ruby and Roberta were already seated at a table on the far side of the room, well out of earshot. "Let me preface this by saying that I know this is total crap, but there was a complaint made about you."

"What complaint? Are you kidding?"

"Pete Dukermann is claiming you came to his room and trashed it."

I almost laughed. "That's insane. I went to his room, but he'd already demolished it. It looked like a hurricane had hit. There's broken glass everywhere. He punched a hole in the wall." I lowered my voice. "He's got cocaine in there. He's out of his head."

"I know he is," Denny said. "I swear, no one is taking him seriously. I'm trying to get him out of the hotel, actually, because he's a creep and a slimeball and he's only going to cause problems. The only thing is . . . you went to Pete's room?" Her expression was incredulous. "Why on earth would you do that?"

I dropped my head, embarrassed to my core. There was no shame in the travel-writing world greater than a visit to a hotel guestroom inhabited by Pete Dukermann. "I wanted to see if he'd gotten any emails from Skye. He hadn't, but he showed me pictures he'd taken of her yesterday. Then I saw a necklace exactly like the one Skye was wearing last night, and Pete claimed she'd given it to him."

"Excuse me? Skye gave *Pete* a necklace?"

"Pete said it was because his wife dumped him, and Skye didn't want the necklace because she was mad at her boyfriend . . . it was a ridiculous explanation. I thought he might have done something to Skye, so I went storming through his suite. I know it was stupid. You don't have to tell me that."

"Don't worry about it. You didn't do anything wrong." A waiter walked over and Denny looked up at him. "Oh, hi."

"I wanted to let you know that everything is ready." He glanced at me, looking me over, before turning back to Denny. "Do you want us to start serving lunch?"

"Give it a couple more minutes, Guillermo. Thanks."

He turned and walked back to the kitchen.

"There's one other thing," I said. "Have you seen Pete? He has scratches on his arms and hand. I can't help but wonder if it might have something to do with Skye."

Denny's face was pale. "Do you think he hurt her?"

"I don't know. In a way, I can't imagine it, but then again . . . I just don't know." The truth was, everything was happening so fast and everyone was acting so suspiciously that I couldn't tell which way was up anymore.

"Don't even think about Pete. By the time you get back from the tour this afternoon, I'll have you, Ruby, and Roberta in another hotel. Things are moving slowly, but that's going to happen." She looked at her watch. "I've got another call to make on that front. Let the maitre d' take you to the table. I'll be right back."

Before I could protest that I could find my own way to the table—the restaurant was virtually empty, after all—Denny patted my arm and went through the door. The maitre d' gave me a gracious bow. As he led me to the table, I noticed that the sky had darkened again and rain was starting to tap lightly on the big umbrellas over the tables outside. As I got closer to the table, I realized Gavin was sitting there, across from Ruby. He stood and held out a chair for me. I would be seated next to him, and across from Roberta. *Don't let your guard down with anyone. And stay away, as far as you can, from Gavin.* That was what Martin had advised me. *So much for listening to Martin,* I thought, taking the seat next to Gavin and trying to smile.

Ruby didn't smile back. "Well, look who's here. Maybe now we can order something. I'm starving!"

"Sorry, I didn't mean to keep you waiting," I murmured.

"It's fine. You didn't keep anyone waiting, Lily," Gavin said.

"It's not fine!" Ruby said. "Young people don't know how to tell time today. Plus, they got no manners. You'd think they were raised in barns."

Everyone, even Roberta—who'd been staring at her water glass sadly, as if waiting for the miraculous appearance of wine—looked at Ruby.

"I can tell you what happened," Ruby added. "It's all on account of TV. People watch actors being all stupid on there, and it's monkey see, monkey do." She shook her head. "It's like bringing Satan into your living room."

Gavin signaled the waiter, clearly avoiding eye contact with Ruby.

"Satan?" I asked.

"Lucifer. The devil." Ruby eyed me, as if unsure whether I was disagreeing with her or simply slow.

"I know who Satan is, though I don't think we've been introduced," I said. "I meant that I didn't understand how he lives inside a television. I think he can do better."

She rolled her eyes. "Well, you're the funny one, aren't you?"

"Not really. It's just that whenever anyone starts talking about Satan, I think of Vincent Price playing Mr. Scratch," I explained.

"*The Story of Mankind*!" Ruby's voice rose, and she let out a wheezy, cackling sound. It took me a second to realize she was laughing. "That was a fine movie."

Why was I surprised that she knew the film? She'd probably seen it when it was first released in 1957. To Gavin, I said, "Any word about Skye?"

His mouth twitched. "No. I told you, I don't really expect anything."

Ruby's ears perked up. "Skye McDermott? She's here?"

"No," Gavin said, and the same moment I said, "Yes."

Ruby looked back and forth between us. "Well, which is it?"

Gavin's words tumbled out, clipped and rushed. "Skye had to bow out of the press trip because of a personal issue."

He shot me a warning look, as if challenging me to contradict his official version of the story.

"Skye was here, in the hotel, last night," I said. "We were sitting out on the balcony around ten. Then she went inside and she didn't come back. She just vanished."

Ruby frowned, but before she said anything, Gavin filled the empty air. "Lily's getting spooked by our resident ghost."

"The hotel has a ghost?" Ruby said. "I don't truck with places that have ghosts."

"It's part of a local legend."

"Whatever has happened to Skye isn't a local legend," I snapped. "It's not part of a ghost story. And it hasn't been properly explained."

"Legend has it that the man who built the hotel was in love with a woman who was married to another man," Gavin said, as if I hadn't spoken. "He built this estate to be their castle, where they could meet. Then, one night, she came here to meet him, and discovered he'd been murdered. She ran away, into the night, and was never seen again. Some people say they've seen her walking on the cliffs, or they hear the scream she made when she discovered her lover's body."

Before I could say a word, Ruby spoke up. "That's a stupid story. The man was probably a gangster. The same people who killed him probably killed her, too."

"People have different theories about what really happened, of course," Gavin allowed.

"I say it's *stupid*." Ruby raised her voice for emphasis. I couldn't help but smile at her.

Whatever argument might have erupted was halted by Denny's arrival. "Oh, I'm glad everyone's here!" she said, looking far happier than she had reason to with the group gathered at the table. "And I'm so pleased to see that Gavin

Stroud, managing director of Pantheon Worldwide's operations in Mexico, has joined us."

"Managing director of Pantheon Worldwide's operations in Latin America, Denny," Gavin corrected her.

"I'm sorry," Denny said, giving Gavin a searching look. "I didn't realize that news was official yet."

"It's official if I say it's official, isn't it? You're going to have to keep up if you're going to work for me, Denny." Gavin looked around the table, taking in everyone's startled expressions. "I've been managing director of Pantheon's Mexican division since its inception. More recently, I've taken on the role of managing director for all of Latin America. I'm glad to have all of you here." Gavin smiled at me. "To celebrate your arrival at the Hotel Cerón, we're going to have a champagne toast, followed by lunch."

On cue, two waiters came out, one carrying a silver tray with crystal flutes. I noticed the glasses were already filled, which suggested that this was more of a cheap-sparkling-wine toast than a champagne one. As if reading my mind, Denny said, "We were going to do a rosé champagne, but the crate is stuck in customs at the moment, so this is Taittinger's Blanc de Blancs."

My eyebrows went up. That was an expensive wine to pour for us, especially at lunch. "Oh, delicious," Roberta said as a waiter set a flute down in front of me.

Ruby glanced at Roberta, then at me. She tilted her head in Denny's direction, and I noticed that Denny was still standing, and her eyes were on Gavin. Denny's hands gripped the chair in front of her, as if she needed to hold on to something solid. Her face was blank, but her mouth was open slightly, as if she wanted to answer Gavin's curt words but didn't know where to begin. Gavin, while being courtly with me, seemed to enjoy being abrasive with her. It made me wonder if Gavin, after years of being the underling, was showing his teeth now that he was top dog.

The maitre d' intervened, pulling the chair out for Denny with an exaggerated flourish. "Thank you," Denny said, taking her seat, but not looking at all sure about being at the table.

"It's a pleasure to meet all of you." Gavin lifted his glass of champagne. "Here's to your stay in the historic resort city of Acapulco. It's famous for having been a playground for movie stars and important people in the past. However, I hope that you will find much to interest you in the present day."

I took a small sip of champagne. It was delicious, but I set the glass down quickly. The last thing I needed was something to dull the edges of the fear that had grown inside me; I regretted letting my guard down the night before, and I wasn't going to repeat that. As if I needed another cautionary tale, the sight of Roberta gulping down her champagne in one frantic swoop reminded me of my mother. Not that my mother ever bothered with champagne; her poison of choice was gin, though she also gravitated to cheap red wines. There was a fine edge between savoring a drink and needing a drink, and I was determined to stay on the side that let me remain in control.

While the first course—a gazpacho with chunky mounds of tomato and cucumber rising artistically in the center of the bowl—was served, Denny chatted about the clean-up of Acapulco Bay and how clean the water was today. Gavin leaned over and whispered, "Is there something wrong with the champagne?"

I shook my head.

"I only asked for it to be served because I know you like it. At least, I thought you did."

"That was kind of you, Gavin." I took a miniscule sip. I'd

noticed Roberta, across from me, eyeing my almost-full glass intently, and as I set it down, I leaned forward to obscure Gavin's view. "What's the next resort over called?" I asked him, staring out the window. His gaze mirrored mine, and as he answered, I slid my glass toward Roberta. The next time I looked at it, the glass was empty and returned to its original position.

The odd thing was, I'd started feeling strangely lightheaded for someone who'd only had two tiny sips of champagne. Gavin pressing me to drink only made me suspicious. Maybe he didn't want good champagne to go to waste; fair enough. But perhaps there was more to it than that. Martin's words played in a loop in my head. *Don't let your guard down with anyone. And stay away, as far as you can, from Gavin.* He was paranoid about security, I knew that, and I understood that he was afraid the kidnapping threat directed against him could boomerang in my direction. But warning me away from Gavin wasn't part of that. Between Gavin's angry words about Martin and Martin's not-at-all subtle warnings about his onetime protégé, I was beginning to suspect that the two of them were at war.

"When did you become head of Pantheon's Latin American division?" I asked.

"A month ago. I should say I'm the de facto head of Pantheon's Latin American division. The board of directors hasn't made that official yet." He lowered his voice. "I'm doing the work, I just don't have the title yet. The truth is, it's a belated recognition of my work in Mexico. No new Pantheon venture has ever performed like this one."

"But the hotel's so empty," I pointed out. As I said the words, Denny's head whipped around, but she didn't say anything.

"Oh, that's only because of the renovation and restoration work," Gavin said.

"Are elves doing the work?" I asked. "Because I don't see any sign of it."

Gavin's eyes held mine, and that tight little smile reappeared. "Then we're doing our job, keeping everything quiet and under wraps. Of course, the more obvious work won't start until next week, after you've left. In November, we'll be relaunching under the Pantheon banner. The hotel is already booked solid for the winter months." The pride in his voice was unmistakable.

I started to ask another question, but the room seemed to spin and my head started to pound. "Excuse me," I said, standing.

"Is there something wrong, Lily?" Gavin asked. "Are you feeling quite well?"

"Fine. I'll be right back."

It was horrible, trying to stroll along as if everything were normal, when I felt suddenly sick. I had a quick vision of Ava Gardner at the end of *The Killers*, when she was meeting with the insurance investigator and trying to pretend everything was fine; she was nervous, though, and even before she got up to go to the bathroom, the investigator knew something was wrong, so he was ready when the hit men showed up. Only I didn't feel like Ava's predatory character in that movie; I was pretty sure I was the chump. When I looked back, everyone at the table was staring after me.

In the bathroom, I rested my head against the cool aquamarine tile of the wall. My insides were quivering. Skye was missing. Martin was telling me I was in danger. My body was telling me something was wrong. Two sips of champagne. Really? I didn't know enough about knock-out drugs, but it was hard to believe that was enough to do it. On the other hand, I felt as if someone were beating my head in with a hammer. Could I have picked up a flu bug? I'd felt a bit off on Friday night, but I'd assumed that was because I was worried about Skye. Now I was cold and shaky and, when I looked in the mirror, my skin was covered with a sheen of sweat. My stomach knotted so tightly it made me gasp and double over. I rushed into a stall and threw up. Afterward, I rinsed out my mouth and applied fresh lipstick. *A fresh coat of paint isn't going to cover up what's wrong with you,* chided Claudia's voice.

*Maybe Martin was right after all,* I thought.

*If you're starting to trust Martin, there's something wrong with your head again,* said the voice. *You're the only person who cares about finding Skye. If you leave, Gavin and Apolinar will drop it. No one else cares what happened to her.*

*But I don't want to be responsible for her,* I argued back.

*You didn't want to be responsible for me, either.*

That was true, but it didn't feel like a fair accusation. No one had ever asked me if I wanted to take care of my sister, but I'd done it. Reluctantly, resentfully, reproachfully, and I hadn't done a very good job of it. When I looked back, I wondered what I could've done differently, and if there were a way things could have worked out differently. The thought that crushed my heart as if it were in a vise was a sneaking suspicion that if I'd given up what I wanted in order to take care of Claudia, she would probably still be around. If I'd devoted myself to being her caretaker, that situation might have gone on indefinitely, or at least until I killed myself to get away from it. I was that selfish, I realized; I wouldn't have been able to spend a lifetime taking care of her.

The face that stared back at me from the mirror was a lot

like my sister's; with the clammy pallor, it wasn't unlike Claudia's when she was sick with longing for a fix of heroin. *Are you giving up already?* a voice in my head demanded. Only it wasn't a slithery, guilt-inducing whisper. It was my own conscience. *You're on your own here. Jesse isn't coming to your rescue. Neither is Bruxton, nor Martin. You're it.*

I crept back into the dining room, my eyes on the only occupied table. Denny was chatting away again, but Gavin was staring intently at his Blackberry. Ruby was chewing on a piece of fish. Roberta was looking from one end of the table to the other, as if watching a tennis ball in play, and before I got to the table, a waiter brought over a fresh glass of wine for her.

"This is just a spritzer." Roberta sounded disappointed. I noted that drinking my glass of champagne hadn't knocked her out, and I started to feel foolish. She was drunk, yes, a little wobbly—her natural state—but perfectly fine otherwise. My stomach twisted and I realized it was possible that I'd eaten something earlier that wasn't agreeing with me. It wasn't easy to avoid Montezuma's revenge in Mexico, and I'd been traveling so much lately that I could've picked up a bug anywhere.

I was just about to excuse myself when Gavin said, "Lily, what's wrong? You don't look well at all." He glanced at Denny. "That's not a problem with this afternoon's trip, is it?"

"No," Denny answered. "Lily, do you want me to call a doctor?"

"My, Denny, you are quite the hypochondriac, aren't you?" Gavin said.

"I'd rather be safe than sorry, Gavin."

Gavin looked at me. "You need some rest, Lily. We have dinner here at eight tonight. If you're feeling up to it. Let me take you up to your room."

With every bit of determination I could muster, I planted a smile on my face. It was irrational and borderline insane, but I was afraid to be alone just then, and I'd be damned if I was going anywhere with Gavin. There was something frightening about having hours stretching out ahead of me with no one expecting me anywhere. I could disappear, just as Skye had. If I did, no one would even know.

"And miss the zocalo?" I said, fighting to stay upright. "Not a chance."

# 26

While everyone else had dessert, I went to the lobby to wait for the minibus. Sitting on a sofa, I let my head drop in to my hands and took deep breaths. What was wrong with me? Skye had been so nauseated that she'd been on medication for it; no wonder she couldn't keep food down. I felt cold and clammy and was haunted by a suspicion that someone could have poisoned Skye and was now trying to poison me.

That was ridiculous, I knew. It was on a par with some of the crazy things that used to fall out of my mother's mouth, about how people would take Claudia and me away from her. Sometimes she would get into such a panic about it that she would lock us in a closet or cellar, telling us it was for our own good. Claudia and I would whisper to each other, her voice in the darkness not unlike the one that lived in my head. That was how I became so good at reciting lines, I realized. We both loved Poe. *The angels, whispering to one another, can find, among their burning terms of love, none so devotional as* . . .

I pulled my mind back from that pit. For a moment, I was certain I was going to throw up again, and I put my hand over my mouth. It took some time for the queasiness to subside. Someone put a hand on my back and rubbed gentle circles.

"Are you sure you're well enough to do this, Lily?" Denny asked.

"Yes," I croaked. But I wasn't. My head swam when I looked up, and my eyes couldn't meet Denny's apprehensive gaze for more than a second. "I just need a minute," I whispered.

"I'm worried about you. I really think we should call a doctor."

"I'm fine. Or I will be in a few minutes. Can we talk about something else?"

"Sure. Um, any requests?"

"Talk about something that won't make me dizzy."

"I can tell you what we're going to see this afternoon. You'll love Acapulco's Cathedral. It was originally a movie set from the 1930s."

"Really? What movie?"

"No idea. I think it was Mexican, so maybe it's one you haven't seen." She was quiet for a moment. "It's funny, how Acapulco came up. The city only grew when people started building hotels. There was a businessman from Texas, Albert B. Pullen, who built up much of what is now Old Acapulco."

"Like Bugsy Siegel in Las Vegas?"

"I don't know if he was a gangster," Denny said.

"Sometimes, there's little difference between businessman and gangster."

Denny was quiet, and I thought of Martin. How little difference there was between entrepreneur and criminal, in that case. His face blurred into the image of another man's. That was Leonard Wolven, whom I'd encountered in Peru. Even now, the memory of him sent a shiver up my spine. There was a strain of ruthlessness that was required to succeed on a grand scale, the way they'd both done. I didn't know enough tycoons to generalize about the species, but the ones I'd come across were sociopaths. They both had a soft spot in their hearts for their own offspring, but that seemed to be where their human qualities ended.

"When did you start to feel sick?" Denny asked.

I'd felt unwell since I'd arrived at the hotel, I realized. Pretty as the place was, there was something unhealthy about it. Early on, I thought it was nerves. Now, I knew something more tangible was at work. The nausea and headaches had come in little waves before, but they'd gotten stronger.

"Last night," I said. Lifting my head took a lot of effort, but it helped me tamp the crazy notions down. Getting sick while traveling was an occupational hazard. Why was I stuck on the idea that someone was trying to make me sick? I blamed Martin for planting paranoid ideas, and—to a lesser extent—Skye, for disappearing in the first place.

"Did you eat or drink anything before it started?" Denny asked.

"I had a drink at the bar, then dinner in my room." When I thought about it, it was after dinner that the first uncomfortable sensations had crept into my head. That memory was interrupted by Gavin.

"How is my guest of honor?" he asked.

"She needs a doctor, Gavin," Denny answered for me.

"Nonsense. It's unfortunate, but many travelers get sick in Mexico. It's often from ice in drinks, you know. That's rarely made from bottled water. Antibiotics won't help. All you can do is stay hydrated." He cleared his throat. "I'm sure a lie-down would be helpful. Let me take you to your room, Lily."

"Good idea, Gavin. You take Lily up while I call a doctor," Denny said.

"You will do no such thing," he barked at her. I caught the fury in his eyes, but his face quickly rearranged itself into serene blandness. "Why are you harping on about this, Denny? People who work for me need to learn when to hold their tongue when I've made up my mind."

I waited for Denny to snap back and remind him that she didn't work for him, but all she said was, "I'm just worried about Lily."

"I'm sure she'll be fine when she gets some rest," he answered. "Let me take you upstairs, Lily."

"No," I answered.

There was a stunned silence. Guests could disappear from the Hotel Cerón, but rudeness wasn't allowed. "You're welcome to sit here as long as you like, of course." Gavin sounded hurt.

"Denny, will you take me up to my room?" I asked.

Gavin's eyes shifted from me to Denny and back again. "I'm happy to—"

"Thanks anyway, Gavin." I willed myself to stand. The effort drained me. I was not so much dizzy now as weary. Just breathing was an effort.

I could feel Gavin's eyes on us as we slowly made our way out of the lobby and to the elevator. As I stepped inside, I started to lose my balance and grabbed her arm, making her shriek.

"I'm sorry." I steadied myself against the wall. "I didn't mean to hurt you."

"You didn't," Denny said. "I was just terrified you were going to fall."

The elevator started moving upward. "Why does Gavin think you work for him, Denny?"

She looked away, as if suddenly embarrassed. "He offered me a job."

"Working for him in Mexico?"

"Not exactly." She gave me a sheepish look. "He said I'd be perfect for vice president of marketing and publicity at Pantheon."

"Is that his come-on line?" As soon as I said the words, I felt awful, because Denny appeared stricken. "Of course you could do the job," I corrected, "but someone is already in that job, and that's not going to change without Martin's approval."

"I know. Maybe . . ."

The elevator doors opened on the fifth floor. "Maybe what?" I asked.

"Gavin's got a lot of pull. Maybe he thinks he can influence Martin." Denny looked up from the floor and changed the subject. "Are you okay walking?"

"Yes." I wasn't ready to drop the Pantheon conversation. "I thought you loved running your own business. Didn't you tell me you'd rather have your freedom than a job at a big company?"

"I go back and forth about it," Denny admitted.

"Why?"

"Things haven't been going well lately."

"What happened?" This conversation was like pulling teeth. Clearly she didn't want to talk about her business troubles with me.

"It's no one thing. There are just a lot of things that have piled up. People think PR is one of those easy, fun jobs where you get to travel and write press releases. They don't think about screaming clients refusing to pay you because you didn't get them featured on a TV show." Her face was tense. I didn't think she was speaking hypothetically.

When we got to my door, Denny asked if I wanted her to come in and get me settled. I said no, and watched as she retreated down the hallway. With her head bowed, shoulders stooped, and arms crossed, she looked as if she were shrinking into herself. The toxic gloom of the Hotel Cerón had worked its way into her veins, too.

# 27

Alone inside my room, I kicked off my shoes at the door and staggered along the hall, touching the wall for support. I made it to the bed, where I curled up in a fetal position. I didn't feel sleepy, just headachy and frail. Thinking about Skye made it worse, but I couldn't help it. *The thing is, I know how to get even with him. I'm going to destroy him professionally, and he'll never even see it coming. This isn't about revenge. This is about righting wrongs. Illegal wrongs, Lily. I can deal with my hurt feelings, but he can't be allowed to keep on doing the things he does.*

I couldn't see how Martin taking Skye out to dinner a couple of times would give her such an appetite for revenge. Even if he'd slept with her and never called again, would she really devote herself to destroying him? I didn't believe that. Yet Skye's craving to get even had consumed her.

My cell phone rang. I rolled over and pulled it out of my bag. "Bad news," said a rough-edged voice.

"Brux?"

"Yeah, it's me. I'm calling to tell you I suck."

"What's wrong?" I asked.

"Remember how I had you forward me those emails this morning? Tech guy laughed his ass off when I showed him."

"I don't understand. Can't he do it?"

There was a pause, and I knew he was dragging furiously

on a cigarette. That would normally have set off my own cravings, but the swirling sickness had knocked those out.

"Stupid, lousy computers," Bruxton said. "So, it turns out, if you want to find all the info I thought you could get, you actually have to do it from the computer receiving the email."

"You mean, I'd need to send my laptop to New York for the tech to look at?"

"You got it a lot faster than I did."

"There's nothing they can do?" Every time I turned around, there was another problem, another puzzle, another wall. I couldn't get anywhere.

"The tech had a couple ideas. One was that you can remotely turn over control of your computer to him."

"What?" The note of alarm in my voice was so obvious that Brux let out a low growl that was his attempt at a chuckle.

"Yeah, see, I knew you'd say that. Miss Lily Moore doesn't like anyone poking around her business. Especially me. She's got secrets." The way he said *see-krits* with his upstate New York accent sounded like a schoolyard taunt.

"Be quiet. You said he had a couple of ideas."

"Next one's even better. You could do the search yourself."

"How would I do that?"

"He emailed you instructions. I told him there's no way you're that big a nerd."

"I love a challenge," I said. "I can't believe you think I'm as dumb as you are."

"I'd love it if you proved me wrong." There was a pause. "I think we should make a bet about it."

"What kind of bet?"

"You're coming back to New York after this, right? So, if

you manage to do it, I'll take you out to dinner wherever you like."

"What if I fail?"

Even though I couldn't see him, I could picture him, in the silence that followed, blushing to the roots of his close-clipped blond hair. "I'll think of something," he muttered.

"I know you will," I teased. Bruxton, for all of his macho posturing, was prone to getting flustered whenever we segued from caustic banter to flirting. I still felt a little off-balance when I was around him, but mostly because I'd finally let myself enjoy his company. I hadn't let down my guard, not completely, but I allowed myself to enjoy him. We hadn't slept together, and he'd barely even kissed me—unless you counted a quick clinch two days ago that Jesse had accidentally interrupted. But it felt, more and more, as if it were just a matter of time.

He changed the subject abruptly "So, what's Acapulco like?"

"I have absolutely no idea. I've barely left the hotel. It feels like a big, exotic prison." I didn't want to talk about the Hotel Céron itself; Bruxton wouldn't react well when Martin's name came up. I had a fleeting image of Brux storming over to Martin's apartment in the Dakota; he would shake the truth about my ex's relationship with Skye out of him, but then Brux would be suspended and sued, if not jailed. Part of me wanted to confide in him about how fearful I felt, but another side of me worried that he'd want to run from me if he discovered how crazy and paranoid I really was. "Could you check something else for me?" I asked instead.

"What now?"

"Has Skye McDermott ever been arrested?"

"Sorry, you have to fill out a form and cut a check to the Criminal Records Section."

"What if I buy you coffee instead?"

"That's bribery. But it'll work," Bruxton said. "Also, I'm way ahead of you. I already checked her out. She was arrested in April for driving under the influence. No jail time, just rehab and community service. She was lucky."

For a moment, I couldn't catch my breath. Part of me had wanted to believe that Pete was right and Denny was wrong about Skye. But Denny had been telling the truth about Skye's DUI.

"Lily? You still there?"

"Yes. Just in shock, though. Could you look up one more thing for me? Please?"

"You like pushing your luck?"

"There's a photographer named Pete Dukermann on this trip. I know him going back years, and he's a creep."

"Violent creep?"

"More like an octopus. He's always coming onto women on press trips. He likes to brag about his open marriage. He and Skye spent yesterday together. Today, I discovered he's trashed his hotel room, and he has Skye's necklace and a pile of cocaine."

"What the fuck?"

"I know. It's crazy. And then he told Denny—"

"No, Lily. What were you doing in his room?"

"I wanted to know if he had an email from Skye. Then he showed me photos he'd taken of her yesterday."

The silence on the other end stretched out. "Let me get this straight. You want me to check into Pete Dukermann to see if he's got a rap sheet, find out if he's dangerous. Meanwhile, you're hanging out in this guy's room."

*Inhale, count to three, exhale.* "I know you're saying that because you're concerned about me, Brux. I know you're not trying to suggest something repulsive."

Now the silence stretched out on the other side. Bruxton's ex-wife had cheated on him with his best friend, and I knew he had his own issues as a result. He was also a hothead who was prone to flying off the handle. Those facts had given me pause about him, but his brilliant NYPD partner, Norah Renfrew, had taken me aside one day. *He's one of the best men I've ever met, but his heart has been stomped to pieces,* she'd said to me. *You're not going to add your footprints are you, Lily?*

Bruxton exhaled loudly. "That didn't come out the way I meant it at all."

"I know."

"I act like such an asshole sometimes. Why do you even talk to me?"

"So you can look things up for me, of course."

He laughed, but the sound came out with a rough-edged rasp. "I deserved that. Okay, spell out the name for me."

I did. "Thanks, Brux. You know I appreciate it."

"Just be careful. And promise me you won't go into any other strange rooms. Especially ones with men in them."

# 28

As cheerful as I'd tried to sound on the phone with Bruxton, it took all of my energy to get my laptop out of the safe and onto the bed. At least I wasn't dizzy anymore. The pounding in my head was probably from my paranoid delusions. Had I really thought someone was poisoning me? That was pure paranoia, and if there was one thing that terrified me above all else, it was the idea that I might end up like my mother. She was a drunk, but that wasn't the worst of it. My mother had paranoid delusions that sometimes made her abusive, though she wasn't completely crazy. She was also incredibly manipulative, and she had a talent for getting under my skin, and Claudia's, wounding us with barbed words that went in like arrows and couldn't ever be cleanly extracted. The last thing my mother ever said to me was, *You only care about yourself, you selfish little bitch.* I used to spend a lot of time wondering if she'd really meant that, or if she'd simply relished wielding words like weapons. Then I'd made the decision to put her out of my mind, and I did my best to stick to that.

Resting against pillows and the headboard, I balanced the laptop on my legs and opened it. Brux was good to his word, and there was a detailed list of instructions from the tech guy, Santos, and a note at the end, telling me he would be at a family wedding for most of the day, but I could call someone named Christy Hintz if I needed help. I read the instructions over, and they seemed pretty clear: first get the email's "full headers" displayed, find a string of numbers in the "originating IP," and then plug them into a site called Network Tools. That sounded easy enough. For all my adoration of retro things, I loved modern gadgetry, too.

*Try it on your own email first,* Santos had also written. *That way you'll know you're doing it right.* So I did, and I instantly hit a speed bump, because it took me a while to figure out how to see the full headers. Once I got it, my screen was filled with long strings of letters and numbers, broken down into groups with odds names. *X-Apparently-To. Return Path. Received-SPF. Authentication Results. X-Cloudmark Score. Content-Transfer-Encoding.* What the hell was all of this? But I spotted *X-Originating-IP* as well, highlighted the string of numbers that followed it, and copied it into the search box on Network Tools. A split second later, the site told me *The IP address is from Mexico(MX) in region North America,* and poured out what looked like an endless string of numbers that took over my screen again. What was I supposed to do with any of that? But I scrolled down, and kept scrolling as I discovered text that started to make sense. *Cablemas Telecomunicaciones (Acapulco),* it finally revealed, identifying both the Internet Service Provider and the location. Success! I felt like I'd figured out a big puzzle, even though all I'd done was plug some numbers into a search box.

My prideful feelings didn't last long. I repeated the process with Skye's email and got exactly the same result I had with my own. *Stupid computer,* I thought, silently cursing it out. *You are useless.* I noticed that the Network Tools site had a caveat near the top: *Network Lookups may be blocked by the various registries. The direct links for IP address network lookups are: Americas (ARIN) | Europe (RIPE) | Asia-Pacific (APNIC) | Africa (AfriNIC) | Latin American and Caribbean (LACNIC).*

So much for my computer skills. I called Christy Hintz and left a message for her. Afterward, I stared at my screen. What if the computer was actually right? Gavin Stroud believed that Skye had decamped to another hotel in Acapulco. I hadn't taken him seriously, but he might have been right about that after all.

Pushing the laptop aside with reluctance, I pushed myself off the bed and made my way into the living room. Skye's two Frakker's guidebooks were still on the table. I'd planned to give them to Gavin with the rest of Skye's things, but when I'd discovered she'd marked all the Pantheon properties, it had made me so curious about what she was up to that I held them back. Part of me felt guilty; after all, the books could have held her travel plans. But I didn't think she'd circled the Pantheon properties for that reason. Whatever the story she was working on happened to be, I suspected it involved those hotels in some way.

I dragged the books back to the bedroom and the relative oasis of the bed. Then I gave myself a minute with my eyes closed—all the while hoping whatever gorilla was sitting on my chest would go away and leave me in peace. Not likely, I realized, finally opening my eyes. When I started leafing through the Mexico guidebook, I looked for the hotels she'd circled. None of the others was in Acapulco, but there was one in Mazatlán, which wasn't far from Acapulco. I dialed the number on my cell phone.

"Hola, estoy llamando a uno de los invitados a su hotel," I said when a clerk answered. *I'm calling for one of your guests.* "Skye McDermott."

"Se equivocó de número," he said immediately. *Wrong number.*

I sat up straighter; he hadn't even bothered to check the guest registry. "Me gustaría hacer una reserva en el hotel." *I would like to make a reservation at your hotel.*

He hung up without another word.

I stared at the phone in my hand, and at Skye's note in the margin of the book. She'd scrawled *PW*—for Pantheon Worldwide—and a skeptical *FULL???*

My disbelief grew as I called each Mexican hotel Skye had circled. Some didn't answer at all. A couple of them told me they were full and would be for the foreseeable future.

With a gnawing sense of trepidation, I leafed through the Eastern Europe guidebook. In addition to marking the Pantheon properties, Skye had made a funny mark I didn't recognize next to some of them. Before I could find a pattern, my cell phone rang. "Hi, this is Christy. Santos told me you might be calling," said a woman with a warm voice and a cheerful Midwestern accent.

"Thanks for calling me back on a Saturday," I said. "He wrote out instructions for me, but I think I'm messing them up."

"Okay, let's go through this." Christy led me step by step through the process, and I got the same result with Skye's email.

"Maybe your friend really is in Acapulco," Christy said.

"Is that why the originating IP address has exactly the same numbers?"

"Exactly the same numbers as what?"

"Santos said to do a test first with my own email, to make sure I was doing it right," I explained. "I used an email I sent this morning. The IP address on Skye's is identical."

"Lily, every ISP customer has a different IP address. If the IP address is identical, your friend sent her email from the same place you did."

"That doesn't make sense. That would mean—"

Christy finished my sentence. "She's in the building with you."

# 29

I didn't know what else to do, so I called Gavin. This was his hotel, and he needed to know what was going on. He didn't answer, and I ended up leaving a message saying I urgently needed to speak with him.

When I hung up, my doorbell rang, and then I heard a whirring sound and a click. Too late, I realized I hadn't put the deadbolt on; someone had opened the door of my suite. I swung my legs over the side of the bed, even though I felt too weak to make it to the doorway of the bedroom. It was a relief when Denny poked her head inside.

"Sorry to bother you!" she said. "I wanted to check on you. I hope you don't mind, but I brought visitors."

Ruby and Roberta were right behind her. "Are you feeling better, Lily?" Roberta called.

"Yes, thank you."

"You look like something the cat dragged in," Ruby added.

"Thanks for nothing," I said. "I think it was something I ate at lunch."

"We all ate the same thing, and no one else barfed."

Denny came into the room and set several bottles of mineral water on my bedside table. "We thought we'd get you some food that definitely won't make you sick."

"You gotta take this, too." Ruby crab-walked in and handed me a bottle. "Activated charcoal. That's what they'd give you at the hospital if you went in sick like you are. I never travel without it."

Denny opened a bottle of water and I swallowed a few capsules. "You guys are the best."

"I've got some protein bars," Ruby said. "You want to see if you can keep one of those down?"

"I am kind of hungry," I admitted. She handed me a bar in a foil wrapper and I tore it open.

"I'm glad to see you eating," Roberta said. "I was a little bit worried about you, to tell you the truth. I thought you might be one of those anorexic-bulemic girls."

That was hilarious. Roberta the lush was worried about me? "I love food, but sometimes I forget to eat when I get stressed. On this trip, I seem to get sick *when* I eat."

"My daughter's nervous like that," Ruby said. "Only she crossed over into actually having a real disorder. There was nothing anyone could say to convince her. Even when she was a bag of bones in the hospital, she was saying she had tree-trunk thighs. Can you believe that?" Ruby shook her head.

"Did she . . ." *Did she die,* I wanted to ask, but Ruby misunderstood my question.

"She got better. I wouldn't say she's completely well, but she's on track and she sees a therapist to keep her that way. She got married last year, so now she's got someone else to watch over her." She sighed. "For a long time, I felt responsible. I was a dancer when I was younger, you know."

"We know," Denny and Roberta answered at the same time.

"Yeah, well, I was obsessive about what I ate. I guess I thought I transferred that into her head," Ruby said.

"That wasn't your fault," Denny argued. "There are a million different ways women get the message that they should be thinner."

"I used to watch over her like a hawk though. I'd say, 'Don't eat that, it'll make you fat.' You want your kid to turn out well, you know? But you never know how what you do will affect them. But I was a single mother long before it was fashionable, and I just bumbled along."

As Ruby was speaking, I thought of my own mother. Most of the time, I banished her from my mind. Even though I knew that my sister and my father had their flaws, I was able to accept them and love them anyway. Claudia had lied and stolen to support her addiction, and my father had been a womanizer. But my mother was another case entirely. When I remembered her, it was like thinking of a terrible injury, and all I could do was wonder how I got through it. My mother was either self-absorbed and feeling sorry for herself, or else obsessing about Claudia and me and doing lunatic things as a result. Either way, she was drinking. When I was growing up, all I could think about was getting away from her.

"I'm sure you tried your best," I said. "I bet your daughter is grateful for what you did for her."

"Maybe. Who knows?" Ruby said. "Sorry to be so depressing. It just preys on my mind, and I wonder if I could've done things differently. Done them better, I mean."

It was a funny thing, but moments like this were what I really loved about press trips. When you were on the road, far from home, it was possible to become very close very quickly to people who were strangers to you a day earlier. Travel stripped away routines and habits, making you more vulnerable and more aware of your surroundings, and more open than you would normally be. There was an intimacy created simply by being together in an unfamiliar place. Sitting in my bedroom, with Roberta perched near the foot of the bed and Ruby and Denny standing in the doorway, was the first time I felt relaxed since coming to Acapulco.

It didn't last long. There was a whirring sound and a click. We all heard it, and stopped speaking. "Was that the door?" whispered Roberta.

The door closed with a quiet click, and then there was the clack of the deadbolt. Ruby's eyebrows shot to the ceiling. It was perfectly normal for the hotel's staff to come in for a variety of reasons, but strange that no one knocked first. There were footsteps, then a pause, as if the intruder had paused to listen for any sound, and footsteps again. Then Gavin appeared in the doorway.

Gavin was at least as astonished to see Ruby, Roberta, and Denny as they were to see him. He dropped the large bouquet of flowers he'd carried in, scattering long-stemmed lilies all over the floor. "Damn it," he muttered, stooping to pick them up. "What are you doing here?"

"What about you, sneaking in here without ringing the bell!" Ruby yelled at him. "What were you, raised by wolves? Did nobody ever teach you manners?"

Gavin's face was bright red when he stood. He glared at Ruby but didn't answer.

"We all wanted to see how Lily's feeling," Denny said, breaking the tension.

"She needs rest, not a lot of chatter," Gavin said.

"What's in that box you're holding?" asked the eagle-eyed Roberta.

"Nothing," Gavin muttered.

"Did you bring Lily a present? That's so sweet!" Roberta, for all of her boozing, was quite possibly the sharpest tack in the drawer.

"A present! How romantic!" Ruby's beady eyes were bright, as if she were on the trail of some particularly juicy gossip.

The pair of them had successfully thrown Gavin off his game. Without a word, he handed me a shallow, wide box that was black and white, and tied with a red ribbon. The name *Elisabeta Joyería* was printed, in white script, on the ribbon. The name seemed familiar, but I couldn't place it.

Gavin had crept into my room, bearing flowers and gifts? I was thoroughly creeped out, and all I wanted to do was to change the topic of discussion. "Gavin, are you here because of my message?" I asked.

His blank expression made it clear that he had no idea what I was talking about, but he leapt at the opportunity to save face. "Yes, of course."

"What I wanted to tell you is that I was able to check the IP address of the email that came from Skye's account this morning. From that, I was able to tell that Skye's message was sent from inside this hotel."

"What?" The red drained from Gavin's face as if he were being bled. Denny's expression was aghast. Ruby and Roberta looked confused.

"There are two possibilities," I explained. "Either Skye is in the hotel, sending email, or someone else in the hotel has her computer and is sending email from it."

"Are you quite sure, Lily?" Gavin asked. "I don't mean this as a negative comment, but aren't you up on 1940s films rather than modern technology?"

I pretended to smile. "I can understand your doubting that. I had doubts myself, which is why I called a friend at the New York Police Department. She was able to confirm it."

"So Skye is still here. She never left." Gavin's voice was quiet, almost musing. "And she *couldn't* have left today. How completely in character for that stupid, selfish, narcissistic little—"

He caught himself before an epithet crossed his lips, but the damage was done. His cold contempt for Skye took my breath away and dropped the temperature of the room by several degrees. Everyone was speechless. Surprisingly, the person who found her voice first was Roberta.

"Skye is a very sweet girl. If she's having a personal problem, we should be kind." Roberta's voice was calm and dignified as ever, but there was a steeliness in her eyes as she addressed Gavin. "Cruelty is the worst vice of all."

Gavin didn't answer that. Instead, he cleared his throat and turned to the one person he was able to order around. "Denny, I need to speak with you," he said. "I strongly suggest that the rest of you leave Lily alone and allow her to rest."

"Oh, please don't leave," I said to Ruby and Roberta. "I like having you here." Especially since I was worried that Gavin would creep back into my room at his first opportunity.

"Very well," Gavin agreed, but his tone was grudging. "Come along, Denny."

She rolled her eyes at me but followed in his wake. The door of my suite opened and closed before anyone said anything. "Would you mind putting on the deadbolt?" I asked them.

"Sure thing," Ruby said.

Both she and Roberta left the room, and I heard them whispering and giggling. When they returned to the bedroom, Roberta nudged Ruby. "Told you so."

"Yeah, yeah, yeah. A greedy eye sees far." Ruby shrugged. "Magpie here thinks Gavin Stroud has the hots for you."

"It's just the way he talks about you," was Roberta's prim rejoinder.

"What did he say?"

"Well . . . at lunch, he was telling us about something you said at breakfast this morning."

"What?"

Roberta and Ruby exchanged a brief glance. "He went on and on and, well, I don't even know what the point of the story was, except to make it clear you two were on a date."

"An all-night date," Ruby added, wriggling her eyebrows for clarification.

"The worst part was when he said he loved having breakfast in bed. Remember?" Roberta looked at Ruby and shuddered.

"That's disgusting," I said.

"Yeah, but he oversold it when he said that," said Ruby. "I knew then and there he was full of crap. I told you he wasn't her type. He's one cold fish."

"Gavin's a strange man," Roberta said. "He's rigid, but he's not as controlled as he wants to be."

"He looks like he's itchy all the time, but he'll be damned if he'll scratch." Ruby cocked her head, making her appear like a bright-eyed bird. "Looks like he's really making a play for you, though. Flowers, presents. I wonder what's in the box?"

"Here, if you're so curious, you open it." I handed it to Ruby.

She pulled the bow loose and opened the box, lifting out a long strand of reddish orange stones. Fire opals. That was what Skye had called them. My jaw dropped when I realized that the necklace was exactly like the one I'd seen Skye wearing the night before.

# 31

"Holy moly. Would ya look at that?" Ruby said.

"I told you so," Roberta added. "His eyes light up when he talks about Lily. I think he's obsessed with her."

"Yeah, but it's not like he only says nice things about her."

"What does that mean?" I asked.

"Okay, at lunch, when you went off to toss your cookies, Denny said she hoped you'd be well enough to go to Taxco tomorrow, and Gavin said he doubted it. Then he said you've been so sick since your sister died."

"He said what?"

"Gavin made you sound like you were some sad shrinking violet boo-hooing in the corner," Ruby said.

"Oh, do you remember when Denny said Lily was perfectly fine, and any normal person would be sad about something like that?" Roberta asked. "Gavin said it wasn't normal to be hospitalized for depression."

"I was never hospitalized for depression!"

Ruby's expression suggested she was puzzling something out. "I thought it was weird of Gavin to say that. I mean, you almost married his boss, so if it gets back to Martin Sklar that he's badmouthing you, his ass is gonna be kicked to the curb." It was embarrassing to realize that my failed romantic life was common knowledge among travel writers, but before I could say anything, Ruby went on. "Roberta and I talked about it. She said, maybe your ex wants Gavin to badmouth you. But I pointed out to her, Gavin keeps going on and on about how he's running the most profitable division of the company, blah blah blah. He's trash-talking you *and* his boss."

That was the moment everything came together in my mind. I wasn't worried about being paranoid anymore, even if my thoughts seemed outlandish. For the first time, I realized that Gavin had deliberately lured me down to Acapulco. The press trip—if I could even call it that—was window dressing.

"I can't believe this," I said.

"I thought it was off when I got here and saw you in the lobby," Roberta mused. "I was thinking, why would Lily come to a Pantheon hotel?"

"You knew this was a Pantheon property?" I was almost shouting. "How?"

"I'm a member of their points program," Roberta said. "You get an email when a new hotel is added."

"But how did you know we were staying here? Wasn't this a last-minute change?"

"Well, everything was very last minute, but on Monday I asked Denny for some information for my magazine. Her assistant sent it over, and the name of the hotel was in there," Roberta said.

I couldn't believe it. "Denny's been trying for months to convince me to come to Mexico," I said. "First it was Cabo, then Cancún, then Monterrey. There were a few other places." It hit me, as I said the words, that they were all places where Pantheon had properties. The hotels I'd called that afternoon—the ones that had been brusque and told me that they were fully booked up—were all in places that Denny had tried to lure me to.

"I didn't get asked until a week ago," Ruby interrupted

my train of thought. "I don't get many invitations anymore, so I said yes. No wonder the arrangements have been so cheap."

"Cheap? Are you kidding?" I shook my head. "They flew me down in business class."

"What?" Ruby's face turned so red, I thought she might explode. "I was in a crappy middle seat in coach! It was the pits."

One cardinal rule of travel writing was never to let the other journalists know what the host did for you, because they gave certain perks to their favorites. But putting me in business class and Ruby in coach was too big a gap. I remembered that she and Roberta had come in together, which was standard for journalists arriving from the same city. I'd been flown in the night before. I was willing to believe Gavin had tricked me into coming to Acapulco, but it was painful to realize that Denny was involved in that deceit, too.

# 32

When Ruby and Roberta left my suite, I locked the deadbolt behind them. Then I threw my things into my rolling suitcase and zipped it up. The Elisabeta Joyería box mocked me from the bedside table. I was repulsed by the idea that Gavin had been able to fool me, but even angrier that I'd made it easy for him. After all, how hard had it been to trick me to come to Acapulco? All he'd had to do was throw an expensive airline ticket my way and promise me a luxurious stay at a resort. The only tough part was that he needed an assistant to bait the trap for him.

I had a sudden impulse to rip the necklace and let the beads scatter around the room. But when I picked the long strand up, all I thought about was Skye. Had Gavin bought her an identical necklace? Had she been involved in the trap, too? It hit me that her disappearance may have been by design; after all, I wasn't going to run out of a hotel—even a Pantheon hotel—if I thought a friend was in trouble. It struck me suddenly that her disappearance was the one thing that made me reluctant to leave. That had been a brilliant move on Gavin's part.

I dropped the necklace back into its box. The lid had the address of the shop printed on the inside, and I realized Elisabeta Joyería was inside the Hotel Cerón. That made it easy for Gavin, didn't it? He was far sleazier and shadier than I ever imagined.

Leaving the suite without a backward glance, I rolled my suitcase down the hallway. The elevator seemed to take forever. Downstairs, in the lobby, the clerk gawped at me. "Miss Moore, where are you going?" he called, but I ignored him. Outside, the bellman turned to stare at me.

"I'd like to get a taxi to the airport, please," I said.

They looked at each other. "Of course. Let me make a call," said one. He pulled out his cell phone and walked away. I couldn't hear a word he was saying.

"Why are you leaving, Miss Moore?" the other one asked. He had a soft voice and a slight lisp, like a Mexican Mike Tyson; he was about the same size as the boxer, too.

"Something has come up."

"That's too bad, Miss Moore."

It was a little creepy, the way he kept calling me by name. And even eerier to realize that everyone at the hotel seemed to know me by name.

"A taxi should be here in an hour, Miss Moore," the other bellman called, pocketing his phone.

"An hour?" I looked around. "What about the hotel car that picked me up?"

"It is not available right now."

The vehicle was parked down the driveway. "Isn't that it?" I asked, pointing.

He shrugged. "It is the driver who is not available."

I was determined to leave. "Fine." I started walking, but they blocked me.

"Where are you going?" one asked.

"I'll hail a taxi on the road."

"Oh, no, Miss Moore. You cannot do that. It is not safe."

Martin's warning echoed in my ears. *Whatever you do, don't get into a taxi or a car with anyone you don't know.* I didn't care. "Get out of my way."

"Sorry, Miss Moore."

"You don't seriously think you're going to block my way, do you?"

"Orders are orders," said one.

"It is not safe," said the other.

I tried to move around them but couldn't. The entire situation felt ridiculous, as if I were Alice in Wonderland encountering Tweedledee and Tweedledum as a pair of hulking hoodlums in hotel uniforms.

We faced off for a while, but I couldn't make them budge, and their combined bulk was like a brick wall in my path. "Why not wait inside for your taxi?" one finally suggested. I stormed back into the lobby, feeling trapped.

"Would you like something to drink, Miss Moore?" asked the clerk at reception.

"No, thanks." I didn't add that I wanted to avoid being poisoned. The combination of the charcoal, protein bar, and water had made me feel better. I'd rather go hungry—and thirsty—than sample anything that came from the Hotel Cerón's kitchen. If that was paranoid, so be it.

"What is wrong, Miss Moore?"

"Family problem," I lied.

"I am sorry to hear that. Perhaps you would like to read a newspaper?"

I abandoned the lobby just to get away from the cloying staff, leaving my suitcase near the exit. Retracing my steps to the spa, I found it locked up and its lights off. Next to it was a tiny shop. The gilt-edged sign in the window spelled out ELISABETA. The sign on the door said CERRADO. Closed. An elderly woman came out of a back room with a box and set it on a counter. She was petite, maybe all of five feet tall, and her shoulders had caved in, leaving her back rounded. Her lips were painted red, and her black-and-gray hair was pulled back into a bun with a pink flower. She could have been anywhere from sixty to eighty.

I tried the door, but it was locked. When I knocked on it, she turned, her face showing obvious surprise. Moving slowly, she crossed the door and pulled the door open. "Hola. Welcome."

"Hola," I said, stepping inside. "Esta es una tienda preciosa." *This is a lovely store.* The walls were painted a soft, buttery yellow and had delicate white molding looping around the top, grazing the ceiling. The floor was plain white tile, and the cases that stored the jewelry looked like antique dressing tables. The dark wood of the cases was pitted and gnarled and scratched if you looked closely, but it was well polished and had delicate silver flowers painted on it. Whoever had restored the pieces had done so with a reverence for their age and with a whimsical sense of beauty. The three-part silver looking-glass dominated one end of the room, and there were smaller mismatching mirrors dotting the other walls.

"Thank you," the woman answered, in English. "I apologize for this mess. We are being forced to close the store and I must pack everything up. But you are welcome to look and to shop."

"Why are you closing?"

"We have no choice. That horrible man forces us out."

"Which man?"

"Gavin Stroud." She pronounced his name the Spanish way, with the V sounding like a B. *Gabbin Estroud.* Her contempt for him was made clear in four syllables. "Since he took over, it is a disaster for everyone. The past year has been hard."

"But Pantheon only bought the hotel recently, didn't they?"

"Pantheon? Ha!" Her laughter was laced with chagrin. "Mr. Alvarez bought the hotel, many years ago," she explained. "Such a good man. But he died last year, and now his son ruins everything. Not son. *Hijastro.*"

"Stepson?"

"Yes. He is the devil. My daughter, Elisabeta, this is her shop. Now, she is sick with cancer and cannot work, so I watch her shop. But he—the devil—forces us out. He forces all the shops to close."

Gavin had mentioned that his mother had married a Mexican, but not that his father was in the hotel business. That intrigued me. Gavin had made such a big deal about the Mexican hotels he'd acquired doing so well; how many of those properties were really his stepfather's?

"You know him?" she asked.

"Yes."

"You do not like him," she observed.

"It's that obvious?"

"He does not have friends. Except for the girlfriend."

"The girlfriend? Gavin has a girlfriend?" I couldn't imagine anyone getting close to Gavin. It would be like cozying up to a statue.

The woman's smile broadened. "Would you like to try on a necklace?"

*So, that's how this is going to work,* I thought. She knew she had me hooked. "Yes, of course."

Looking down at the tray she'd placed in front of me, I examined the beads. They varied between orange and red, and some stones seemed to have an uneven hue, as if the color had been bled out of them. I picked up a necklace. "Are all of these fire opals, or are other stones mixed in?"

"Oh, no, that is pure fire opal. The stone gets its color from the iron in it, but it also has a high water content. It is a soft stone. The best ones come from dry places, like the desert. Those fire opals have better color. They can be cut to show off their inner fire." She picked up another necklace. "You see how these stones are cut? There is a limit to what you can do because of the softness of the stone. They are fire opals, but not so . . . hot." She smiled at her own joke. "I know you like jewelry. Your silver bracelet is beautiful."

"Thank you." I knew I wouldn't be able to leave the shop without buying something. If my friend Jesse were there, he'd tell me how weak-willed I was. My income had shrunk in recent months, but so had my expenses, since I no longer paid the rent on an apartment in New York. I still felt as if I had more money than before. "Did Gavin buy one like that?"

"More than one. I saw his little blond friend wear it."

"His . . . blond friend?" My brain struggled to process this information. I hadn't had trouble seeing Skye with Martin. Gavin was another question entirely. Had she dated Martin, then traded down for Gavin? I could hear her voice so clearly. *When the two of you started dating, you kept it quiet for a while, didn't you?* she had asked me about Martin at the bar. Then, *I'm in a situation like that right now, and I'm kind of sick of it, to tell you the truth. He's secretive about everything.*

It had never occurred to me that she was speaking about Gavin.

The woman pushed the tray forward slightly. "What do you think of the earrings? Beautiful, yes?" She brought a gilded hand mirror out from under the counter, as well as a bottle of rubbing alcohol and some cotton balls. She let me try on several pairs, cleaning each before and after I had them on.

It was difficult pretending to be fascinated by the jewelry when all I could think about was Skye. She'd dated Martin and Gavin? I wondered which one she wanted revenge on. Her life seemed more and more like a chaotic whirlwind, especially since Ryan was still in the picture, handing out credit cards to Skye. It made me think of Barbara Stanwyck's character in *Baby Face*, trading up from one man to the next. Not that Gavin was a trade-up, but he seemed to have delusions of grandeur.

*What do you care?* whispered that voice in my brain. *Let them tear each other up.*

The beauty of the fire opals started to grow on me, and my greedy, jewelry-loving magpie side surfaced. I really was as superficial as Claudia always said. Finally, I settled on a pair of earrings that had a faceted bright orange stone dangling from a silver thread. The woman wrapped them up for me, in a package that looked just like the one Gavin had given me, only smaller. I paid with a credit card.

"Can I ask you something else?" I said. "How did Gavin force the shops to close?"

"There are no guests."

"None?"

She shrugged and lowered her voice again. "I thought he might be working with the Zelas. Drugs, you know. Drugs are behind most of the crime in Acapulco now. Most of my family has left because of it. My cousin's grandchildren can't even go to school anymore, because there are kidnapping threats against the teachers. Many schools wouldn't open."

"You think Gavin is involved with a cartel?"

She shook her head. "It makes no sense. You can recognize the men in the cartels by how they walk, how they dress. They do not come here." She stared out the window of the shop, into the hallway. "I know something is wrong, I just do not know what."

# 33

I was embarrassed at not guessing sooner that Gavin and Skye were romantically involved. The clues were all there. When I thought back to my conversation with Skye on Friday night, I could see where I'd gone wrong. She'd talked about little else but Martin, and because she'd known the details of his schedule, I'd assumed she had a relationship of some sort with him. But Gavin would have an insider's knowledge of Martin's schedule, and he was Skye's conduit for information. I couldn't say that Skye had lied to me, exactly; I'd jumped to mistaken conclusions all on my own. That wasn't true of Gavin, though. He'd deliberately misled me. *I only know Skye through her relationship with Martin.* He'd been lying through his teeth. He had his own relationship with her, but he was keeping that under wraps.

The problem was, I couldn't imagine Gavin in a romantic relationship, period, and that was a blind spot I regretted. He was, as Roberta had said, a cold fish. But that was just the surface, and I'd never guessed at what was churning underneath.

That thought stopped me dead in my tracks. Skye had disappeared and Gavin had wanted to pretend that he barely knew her. That wasn't an accident. He'd lied to me, bold-faced. I was no expert, but even I knew that, when a woman disappeared, the first person the police looked at was her lover. The fact that Gavin was preemptively denying their relationship was inherently suspicious.

There was another possibility. Gavin had wanted to play-act at seducing me, and Skye didn't want to stick around to see that. Ironically, the only thing Gavin hadn't lied about was when he said he thought Skye was cooling her heels at another hotel in Acapulco. They'd fought, and he assumed Skye had run out instead of hiding somewhere in the hotel. Maybe her disappearance was meant to punish him. It didn't matter anymore. All that mattered was getting the hell away from the hotel.

I wondered what I owed Martin. As much as I'd come to despise my ex, Gavin's crafty lure of me to Acapulco made me detest him even more. Had he poisoned me somehow when I'd sat next to him at lunch? Not with anything deadly, of course, just enough of something to put me in bed so that he could come surprise me with flowers and jewelry. Oh, how I hated him.

In the lobby, I checked for my cab, but of course it hadn't arrived. When my cell phone rang, I almost ignored it. I wasn't in the mood to speak with anyone in the world. But when I saw the name on the display, I realized there was one exception.

"So, you havin' fun without me in Acapulco?" My friend Jesse's warm, deep voice made me smile, in spite of everything.

"I hate it. It's horrible. Everything about this place is a disaster." I was dimly aware that I sounded like a particularly petulant thirteen-year-old. "I'm just about to make a run for the airport to get the first flight home."

"Holy moly. I knew you'd be missin' me, but never reckoned it'd be that much." He dropped his exaggerated Oklahoma accent. "So, I've been readin' the latest news from

Acapulco, and it's got me more than a little unsettled. There's a lot of decapitation goin' around in those parts, Lil."

"I don't even know where to start. I should have run last night, when I discovered Pantheon had bought the hotel."

"What?" Jesse yelped. "Pantheon? Your ex owns the hotel? Get the hell outta there, Lil!"

"I'm going to, believe me. Only Martin's not even the problem right now."

There was a scream, and a woman ran into the lobby, sobbing. "Ella está muerta. Ella está muerta," she repeated, over and over. *She's dead.*

"Jesse, can I call you back?"

"Sure thing. Just get outta Dodge, okay?"

The woman's sobs were so loud they seemed to reverberate throughout the entire building. Was this some kind of trick? I'd come to the realization, much too late, that Gavin Stroud was capable of anything.

The clerk was trying to comfort the maid. Out of the corner of my eye, something slithered along the tile floor. When I turned my head, I didn't see anything. Either I'd missed it, or it had been a mirage. I had no way of knowing.

"What happened?" I asked the clerk. He stared at me blankly, until I repeated the question in Spanish.

"La mujer desaparecida . . ." *The woman who vanished.* He took a deep breath. "They found her."

When I got to the fourth floor, I found that
the lights were off, just as they had been the night before.
The maid had wailed that the dead woman was in 423, but
before I saw the number I saw the glow of artificial light
spilling into the hall from a lone doorway. That gave an illusion of warmth, but as I stepped inside, the room felt like a
refrigerator. Someone had turned the air-conditioning on
full blast, and for the first time since I'd arrived in Acapulco,
I was chilled by something other than dark thoughts.

The first person I saw was Apolinar. He was just past the
long entryway to the room, with his back to the door. His
right arm was extended, and as I got closer, I saw that his
hand was on Gavin's shoulder. "I'm so very sorry, my
friend," Apolinar was saying.

As if he had eyes in the back of his head, hidden under his
sleek, pomaded black hair, Apolinar dropped his arm and
turned around. "What are you doing here?" he whispered,
his expression genuinely stunned as he stepped toward me.
"You shouldn't be here."

"Is it really Skye? What happened?"

"Gavin instructed the maids to enter every guest room in
the hotel. He wanted to be certain no one was hiding out.
When a maid came in here, she found Skye McDermott dead."
Apolinar crossed himself. "That is all I can tell you. Not

because I don't want to tell you more, but I don't know anything else."

"I want to see her."

"Can't you leave anything alone?" he hissed, blocking my
entrance. "Go away."

I tried to brush by him but he grabbed me, holding me
back firmly, but not roughly. He leaned so close his lips
touched my ear. "Don't be stupid, Lily. Get out," he whispered. His voice was so soft I could barely hear him, but his
eyed flicked over to Gavin, who wasn't paying any attention
to us.

Before that moment, my desire to see Skye had been wa-
tered down by fear. Apolinar's refusal to let me inside the
room crystalized my determination. I was hopelessly con-
trary. "Take your hands off me or you'll be looking to get
your old cliff-diving job back."

I don't know who was more surprised by my threat, Apolinar or me. "You are making an enormous mistake," he
breathed, but he let me by.

The walls of the room were tangerine and the carpet
was scarlet; together, they gave the effect of standing inside a fire opal. A pair of cast-off black skyscraper heels
lay under the table; they were small enough—and high
enough—to be familiar. An open bottle of wine sat on the
coffee table, accompanied by a pair of wineglasses that had
rusty red stains in them. Near the door to the bedroom
was a leopard-print suitcase with clothes spilling out of it.
I recognized a pretty pink cardigan with bows at the neckline. It was vintage, and I remembered coveting it when I'd
seen Skye wear it on another trip. That seemed like a lifetime ago.

From the doorway, I looked into the bedroom. Gavin stood at the foot of the bed, hands clasped in front of him. Skye lay prone on the floor, frozen and beautiful; her head was turned to one side, and I could see her red lips, parted as if she were about to speak, and her wide eyes staring ahead. She looked like an angelic doll, her platinum hair fanning out like a halo.

From behind me, Apolinar said, "Please do not touch her, or anything else. The police will be examining the room."

"She's wearing the same dress I saw her in at the bar," I said. No one answered me. I swallowed hard. "Has she been dead since last night?"

"No one knows," Apolinar said.

It wasn't until I knelt beside her face that I noticed the blood. Because the carpet was red, it was hard to make out, but as I leaned closer, I saw that someone had bashed the left side of her head. I must have made a little sound, because Apolinar was suddenly beside me, pulling me back. "Don't look too closely," he said. "It is awful." I smelled his cologne again, that woodsy, musky scent, and I was oddly glad of it, because I thought I'd throw up otherwise.

I looked around the room, needing to focus on something—anything but Skye's body—until I caught my breath. "What is that?" I asked, pointing to the nightstand. There were a couple of glassine envelopes lying there, next to a razor blade. It brought to mind the drugs I'd seen in Pete's room.

"The police will investigate," Apolinar said. "Please, let me take you out of here now."

"How did she get in here?" I asked.

"Either she had a key or someone else—"

Gavin spoke softly, but his words silenced us. "I thought she ran away because we'd fought. She told me she hated me. I thought . . ." His voice trailed off.

"It's a tragic accident," Apolinar said. "She must have fallen down and hit her head."

His suggestion was so ridiculous, I couldn't even answer it. I leaned forward again, close enough to touch Skye but holding my hand back. I'd confronted a dead body before—more than once—but it hit me with a rush that I'd never been near Claudia's. There were good reasons for that, given what had happened to her, but, emotionally, it was painful. I didn't know what closure was supposed to be, but I hadn't had any. My sister was in the world, and then she wasn't, and even though I knew she was gone, all I had to hold on to were strangers' accounts of what had happened. Now Skye was gone, too. The woman I'd seen less than twenty-four hours before, whom I'd known for years and traveled with so many times, this woman who'd talked and smiled and been as full of life as a person could be, was gone. What was left was this broken shell, suddenly so disconnected from the soul that had inhabited it.

A familiar voice whispered, *Would things really be different if you'd seen my body, Honey Bear?*

*Probably not,* I admitted. But that impulse to touch her skin and her hair, and to kiss her cheek, was still in me. The sensory memories, good and bad, lingered as well, deceiving me into feeling, sometimes, that if I put my hand out I'd be rewarded with a familiar touch.

Now, I put my hand forward, toward Skye, and no one said anything. It was as if they were all holding their breath. My hand hovered in the air near her, and I blinked. Touching a finger to her arm, I shivered. Skye hadn't just died; she was practically frozen.

"Don't," Apolinar said.

But it was too late. I'd already seen that her painted red nails were broken, as if she'd tried to fight off her attacker. A fleeting image of Skye screaming and trying to save herself flitted through my head. It was so vivid it made my heart palpitate. The fourth floor had been dark when I'd accidentally stopped on it the night before; if I'd stepped off the elevator and started down the hall, would I have heard her screams? It was shattering to think of her fighting for her life and losing. Skye was so slender and tiny; the odds were stacked against her in any face-off.

Apolinar handed me a handkerchief. When I touched my face with it, I found it was wet. I hadn't realized I was crying; I was still too much in shock.

"Come on, Lily" he said. "Stand up."

As I did, I heard a ragged gasp escape from Gavin's throat. But when I looked at him, his face was a pitiless mask that was devoid of emotion. The only hint of a feeling was in the tightness around his eyes and mouth. Whatever feelings he had were shunted aside.

"I'm sorry, Gavin," I said.

When he turned his head, the darkness in his face frightened me. "Why are you apologizing to me, Lily?"

"You were involved with her, Gavin. Don't you feel anything?" The words were out of my mouth before I could stop and reconsider them.

"Tell me, Lily. What am I supposed to feel?" Gavin spoke coldly, but there was something crackling underneath. He made me think of a lake covered in ice that was on the verge of shattering. He turned on his heel and stormed out of the room, leaving Apolinar and me alone with Skye's body.

# 35

I watched and waited from the hallway for a long time, even though there was nothing I could do. The paramedics who finally arrived approached the suite slowly, wheeling a stretcher with somber determination. They already knew there wasn't anyone to be saved.

Skye was gone, and I found that impossible to accept. Less than an hour earlier, I'd been reeling, almost sick with a desire to punish her for what she'd put me through. Now that I knew she was dead, I was guilt-ridden. Why hadn't I gone through the hotel to look for her? Why didn't I insist on bringing the police to the hotel immediately? I'd thought I was helping her by prodding Gavin and Apolinar and Denny, by calling Martin, by calling the police in New York. Everything I'd done had been futile. Skye had been dead since the night before. For all I knew she'd died minutes after I saw her. Or was it an hour or two later? Was she meeting someone she knew, or was she surprised by a stranger?

"Perdón, Miss Moore." A man's voice interrupted my thoughts. "Mr. Stroud would like to speak with you downstairs, in the bar."

"All right," I answered, without thinking. Moving on autopilot, I got myself downstairs and through the lobby before I realized that the waiter was still beside me.

"It is a sad day for all of us," he said.

"It is." I didn't have anything to add. My mind was whirling in other directions. Why would Gavin want to talk to me at the bar? Had he discovered something about Skye's attacker? Part of me was already convinced that he was Skye's attacker. *Tell me, Lily. What am I supposed to feel?* He barely seemed human.

The waiter and I were both quiet as we walked along the final, curving passageway. He held the door open for me and I walked inside. The lights were on, and beyond the glass of the balcony doors, the sky was dark gray. The rain was coming down so hard that the balcony was a blur. I looked around, but I didn't see anyone sitting at a table. The only face I saw was the monstrous plaster one above the bar, the one Skye told me was copied from the ruins of Xochipala. Its fanged, screaming mouth was even more terrifying by day.

"Where is he?" I asked.

"Down one level, miss."

I walked to the railing, then turned back. An eerie sensation shivered through me, as if someone were about to push me over the wrought-iron railing. But the waiter was nowhere near me. He was fussing over a table with a half-empty water glass on it. I looked down again, but the place seemed empty. I brushed against the railing and jumped back. For the first time, I noticed that its ironwork was shaped into intertwining serpents with sharp forked tongues.

"I don't see him," I said.

The waiter came over and looked down. "This way," he said, heading toward the staircase. I followed him down, and we circled around to a table that had one chair pushed back. The napkin was on the seat, as if someone were coming right back, and two flutes of sparkling wine, untouched, sat on the table.

Surely Gavin wasn't drinking champagne just then.

"Perhaps he has been called away," the waiter said. "Let me check."

He moved off, and I turned, staring into the shadowy corners of the room. My skin had been crawling since I'd stepped into the bar. My mind was crowded with twisted thoughts, possibly influenced by the ghosts I didn't believe in. I didn't want to be there. It was all wrong. I rushed up the stairs and to the door. Just as I was about to touch it, an arm wrapped around my neck from behind. *The screen,* I thought. He was hiding behind the screen.

"Don't fight me," he said in Mexican-accented English. "Let's make this easy."

I screamed as loud as I could and he tightened his grip around my neck. His forearm was braced against my windpipe.

"Are you going to be good?" he asked.

The next sound that came out of my mouth was choked and weak.

"Is that a yes?" he whispered, loosening his grip slightly.

"Yes," I whispered back.

He moved one hand and I felt something sharp against the back of my neck. "Here's what we're going to do. I'll—"

"Why are you doing this?"

"I'm your best friend," he answered. "I'm giving you a muscle relax—"

Before he got all the words out, I screamed as loud as I could and clawed the side of his face. He gasped and stabbed my neck with a needle. A current of heat ran through me, searing pathways from the top of my spine to the tip of each finger, and deadening everything in between. My head was suddenly disconnected from the rest of me.

"We could have done this the easy way," he said. "You chose this."

Whatever poison he'd injected me with was slithering inch by inch through my body. His arm held my throat too tightly to breathe. At that moment, I wanted air more desperately than I'd ever wanted anything in my life. Air meant staying conscious. I thought of Skye lying dead on that floor upstairs. Air meant a chance to fight back.

"What do you want?" My voice had withered away. The sound I made was broken in unnatural ways.

He didn't answer. His silence haunted me. He felt no need to threaten me, and that was more terrifying than any words he could utter.

He was holding me just a little more roughly than a lover might, and waiting for me to fade to black. My thighs were growing numb, and it was getting harder to stand. I tried to turn my head, but he held me fast. I could turn my gaze up or down, but not to the side. Up, there was just the wash of color, which was fainter than I'd thought. Muted, almost pastel now, but with wavy lines drizzled across it, like the reception my old television set with the rabbit ears used to get. Down, and I could see my feet, toenails painted red, one foot twisting in my shoe sideways, as if it had already gotten bored and dozed off.

"Stop," I said, but no sound came out. His arm around my midsection suddenly looked like two, as if this attacker were an insect with multiple limbs. The only thing I was certain of was that my consciousness was going to cave in on itself, buried under the onslaught of a drug that was turning off my nervous system piece by piece. I couldn't run; I couldn't scream. He was lowering me to the ground and there was nothing I could do to stop him.

There were footsteps running in the hallway.

"Me lleva la chingada!" he cursed. He dropped me and ran. I heard him running but I couldn't turn to look. I closed my eyes for what I thought was a moment, but when I opened them, the man who'd attacked me was gone and Apolinar was kneeling in front of me.

# 36

"I don't understand how this happened," Gavin said.

He stood in his office, appraising me with the same robotic detachment he'd shown toward Skye's body. I tried to remember how I'd gotten there. Closing my eyes, I had a fleeting memory of Apolinar carrying me in and gently depositing me on a sofa, as if I were some Victorian maiden who'd just suffered a fainting spell. I must have been slipping in and out of consciousness; I'd heard Apolinar speaking, but couldn't remember what he said.

"Why would anyone attack you, Lily?" Gavin demanded.

"I don't know." My mind retreated from the memory of what had happened in the bar. I didn't want to think about it, or Skye, or the Hotel Cerón. Instead, I let my brain wander, trying to come up with an Ava Gardner film in which she played a sick person, laid out on a sofa like I was. My favorite actress was a vamp, a seductress, frequently a bad girl with a heart of gold, but I couldn't think of any roles where she was ill. Ava wasn't like Bette Davis, who played dames with ailments both mental and physical—think of *Now, Voyager*, or *Dark Victory*—or Olivia de Havilland, who played such otherworldly good girl roles that she was often viewed as too good for the one she was in. Ava was too worldly, and earthy, to be painted that way.

"Don't go swooning off again!" Gavin barked at me. His jagged voice jolted me back to the present. I remembered that I didn't want to be there.

"She may need more rest," Apolinar said.

Even in my zoned-out state, I caught the searing look that passed like a shadow over Gavin's face.

"Let me see if I understand what you and Apolinar have told me," Gavin said. What had I told him? My mind wanted to drift away, but his voice kept forcing me back into his airless office. "You were told that I wanted to meet you in the bar. Preposterous as that must have sounded, you went along. Then a man you didn't see grabbed you and injected you with what he said was a muscle relaxant, but he ran off when Apolinar came to your rescue. Did I miss anything?" He stared at me before turning to Apolinar. "For the first time, I understand why Goethe called earth the mental institution of the universe."

"You make it sound ridiculous," Apolinar argued. "It was a serious situation. That man could have killed her."

I yawned. "What time is it?"

"Seven-thirty," Gavin snapped.

My mental calculations were slow, but they creaked along. "I've been unconscious for an hour and a half?"

"You've been awake for the past half hour." Gavin's voice was cold. "Don't you remember?"

"Not really."

"You told us about the attack," Apolinar said. "But you weren't able to identify the man. You—"

"Thank you, Apolinar," Gavin cut him off. "You may go now."

"But sir—"

"I told you to get out."

Apolinar exited without another word, pulling the door closed behind him.

Gavin hovered over me. "Now it's just you and me, Lily." He spoke slowly, as if savoring every word. His stony expression unnerved me. It wasn't so much the flat hardness of his eyes that did it; it was his rapid breathing. He couldn't hide his excitement anymore.

I started to sit up, but Gavin put his hands on my shoulders and pushed me back. It wasn't painful, but there was enough force behind it to keep me from trying that again. The last thing I wanted was Gavin touching me, and that realization made me determined not to retreat into the deliciously drowsy ether. I had to force myself to stay awake.

He knelt next to the sofa, putting his face so close to mine that I could see the fine lines around his eyes, and the deeper, unforgiving ones around his mouth. "What I don't understand is how Martin got a man inside my organization," Gavin said. "I run a very, very tight ship. I keep a close watch on everyone. I learned that from Martin, you know. He's very jovial, when people meet him, but he's deeply suspicious."

"What does Martin have to do with any of this?" I understood every word Gavin said, but I couldn't make sense of them. Part of me wanted to blame the muscle relaxant, but enough of it had worn off that my brain could focus. Gavin's preoccupation with Martin, and his paranoia, made him seem mentally unbalanced.

Gavin's eyes traveled over my face, as if trying to determine the odds that I was as baffled as I seemed. "Martin has everything to do with it." He stared at me for a while, as if hoping for some telltale sign. I felt like a butterfly pinned under glass. Every instinct I had screamed at me to run away, but I didn't believe that the drug still ping-ponging through my system was going to let me make a speedy getaway.

Finally, Gavin got to his feet and shuffled to a console against one wall. He poured himself a glass of some colorless liqueur with bits of gold drifting in it, downed it, and poured another. "Would you like a drink, Lily?"

"No, thank you."

He held up his glass. "Goldwasser from Gdańsk. Not to your taste, is it? You're a champagne girl, through and through." He smiled. "I'd be happy to have someone bring a bottle up."

"No!" My reaction was as virulent as if he'd offered me cyanide. Belatedly, I added, "Thank you, Gavin."

"Such lovely manners. It was always clear why Martin loved to show you off."

"Why do you keep talking about Martin?"

"Do you have any idea what it's like to work for Martin?" Gavin asked, coming back to hover over me. "He thinks he owns people. There's no privacy, no respect or regard. You're nothing but a puppet who exists to do his bidding, and he'll mock you while you're doing it. He keeps chipping away at you until you're hollow inside." Gavin raised his glass at me. "Aha. I can see from your expression that you know precisely what I mean."

"I can imagine he wouldn't be easy to work for," I allowed. I didn't agree with Gavin's assessment, partly because I'd seen Martin's largesse toward his employees. It came out in the form of gifts and bonuses over Christmas and New Year's, but there was more to it. I remembered one Pantheon employee adopting a baby girl from China with his partner, and Martin giving the man a paid six-month paternity leave.

There was no doubt in my mind that Martin would be demanding and exacting, but he showed his appreciation for people, too.

"Robo-Rex." Gavin gave me a tense imitation of a smile. "I know that's his nickname for me. You know it, too, Lily. Anyone who has had any dealings with Pantheon knows exactly what kind of abuse Martin dishes out to those who work for him. He gets inside you like a cancer. Even when he's not in the room, I can hear him mocking me."

"You hate him, don't you?"

Gavin sat on the sofa, his hip touching my waist. He leaned forward so that we were almost nose to nose. "Don't you, Lily? You would if you ever opened your eyes. You know how much he loathed your sister, don't you?"

That rattled me. "Yes."

"He wanted to pay her off so she would get out of your life, but he also said she was a parasite who'd never leave you alone. He talked, many times, about making her go away." His eyes slid over my face, taking my reaction in. The friction between Martin and Claudia had been painful to navigate, partly because neither of them was ever completely honest with me. Each had plotted against the other, neither one ever thinking about the position that put me in. Did Martin's hatred of Claudia burn so hot that he'd confided in his lapdog? Or was Gavin just clever enough to realize it was a wound in my heart that was easy to open up? *Gavin's more clever than Martin*, whispered that voice in my head. *He's more subtle. He's used to working around Martin to get what he wants. Be careful.*

"Did Martin tell you that himself?"

"No," Gavin admitted. "I'm just a useful idiot to him, not a confidant. But what I'm saying is true. If you doubt it, look into a man named Gregory Robinson. Martin hired him to take care of the Claudia problem."

I didn't have to feign my horrified reaction; I knew who Robinson was. I'd encountered him while searching for my sister. "Martin's done some terrible things, hasn't he?" I whispered.

"Martin is an evil man. He's going to suffer for all that he's done."

"What do you mean?"

"Nothing at all." Gavin stared at me. "I am truly sorry about what happened to your sister, you know. *In pace requiescat.*"

I turned my head around to stare at the back of the sofa, so Gavin couldn't see my expression. All *in pace requiescat* meant was "rest in peace," but Gavin's phrasing jolted me and made a memory twitch deep in the back of my brain. What was it? I didn't want him to see that it bothered me, so I touched my face as if brushing tears away. "It's still so hard for me to talk about her," I whispered.

If I'd hoped an emotional reaction would put him off, I'd miscalculated. The next thing I knew, Gavin was stroking my hair.

"You can always talk to me, Lily. I think we could become very close, couldn't we?"

There was something especially chilling about Gavin when he was pretending to be romantic. He was like a creature who had seen human beings interact and wanted to copy the gestures, even though the sentiments eluded him. Gavin had lured me down to Acapulco not because of love or even lust; there was no raw desire emanating from him. He wanted to sleep with me because I had been Martin's. Gavin wanted everything Martin had ever had.

"Did you like the necklace, Lily? I thought it perfect for you, with your dark hair and fair skin. I know how you do love jewelry."

I wondered what he'd said to Skye when he'd given her the same necklace.

"I don't know what to say." My voice was slightly breathless—it still felt as if a gorilla were testing his strength on my ribcage—but that wasn't a negative in this case. If anything, it helped me sound as if I were overwhelmed with emotion, or at least, a sentiment that wasn't revulsion.

"You don't have to say anything, Lily." Gavin loomed over me and I knew he wanted to kiss me. I coughed and kept talking.

"Gavin, I'm so flattered. I never would have imagined—"

He lifted my hand and kissed it. The gesture was something Martin had done, many times, and I'd always loved it. But with Gavin, I wanted to rush to the nearest bathroom and scrub my hands. It was one thing to play along with his delusions with words, but my body had other ideas. I flinched.

"Poor Lily. You're not a very good actress, are you?" Gavin dropped my hand. For a moment, I thought he was going to hit me, but instead he stood and smoothed out the creases in his trousers. "Don't worry." His voice was alarmingly casual. "Everything will be resolved soon, I promise."

"What does that mean?"

"You want to leave the Hotel Cerón, don't you?" He gave me that awkward hint of a smile. "Then just do exactly what I tell you to do."

# 37

"Let me take you upstairs, Lily," Gavin said. "Do you think you can walk, or shall I carry you?"

"I'll walk." The muscle relaxant had mostly worn off, leaving me oddly refreshed. My body, from the neck down, felt like it had been on vacation, while my head was ready to explode from the tension.

In the lobby, I found myself staring through the glass doors to the outside world. I was desperate to get out of the Hotel Cerón's twisted orbit. I had to escape its sickly sweet smells and suspicious staff and ever-present atmosphere of doom.

"How lovely it would be to escape right now," Gavin said, as if he were reading my mind.

"What?"

"Isn't that what's going through your head at this moment, Lily?"

"I was thinking about Skye. I can't believe she's dead."

"Really? I certainly can. The wonder is that no one killed her before this. I thought about it on several occasions."

I stared at him in mute horror.

"Don't be a hypocrite, Lily," he chided. "Don't tell me you didn't want to kill her when you found out she and Martin had been an item."

He put his hand on my back, but I flinched again.

"You're determined to be difficult, aren't you?" Gavin looked me over while a muscle twitched at his jaw. "Very well. Shall I summon your friend Apolinar to take you up to your room?"

"All right." Anything was better than fending off Gavin's clumsy attempts at seduction.

Gavin spoke to the clerk, and Apolinar appeared in the lobby a minute later.

"Take her upstairs," Gavin instructed. "Make sure she's comfortable and has whatever she wants. But keep in mind, you're accountable for her. If she gets away, I'll know it was you who helped her."

Apolinar looked affronted. "I'd never—"

"Just do as you're told," Gavin said. He walked away.

Apolinar didn't speak to me in the elevator. "Do you know who attacked me?" I asked as we got off on the fifth floor.

"No. How would I?" His voice was steady but he kept his face forward, glancing at me only out of the corners of his eyes.

"Funny, how the man got into the hotel and then out again, isn't it?"

"We will find him. He can't get away."

"Not without help," I added.

Apolinar opened the door of my suite with his own key card, which didn't make me feel reassured about my safety. I followed him inside. "Why did you let him get away?"

Apolinar's face was serious. "He had the opportunity to run because I grabbed you to keep you from collapsing. I thought you were badly hurt. That's how he got away."

"Oh." I took a breath. "Didn't anyone try to stop him while he ran out? The bellman wouldn't let me get past the door."

"There are other ways out of the hotel."

"Such as?"

He shook his head. "Gavin isn't about to let you leave. He has moved heaven and earth to bring you here."

"What do you mean?"

"He is a very bitter man," Apolinar answered.

"Gavin's obsessed with Martin Sklar. I think he slept with Skye because Martin took her out. I know his only interest in me is because of the relationship I had with his boss."

"We have a saying in Mexico. *Árbol que crece torcido jamás su tronco endereza.* Do you understand?"

"A tree that grows bent never straightens out."

Apolinar nodded "That's right."

"Meaning?"

He looked around, as if someone might overhear. "Gavin's father, his birth father, I mean, used to beat him. He beat Gavin's mother, too, and that's why she fled from him, but she left Gavin behind. Then his father died, and Gavin came to live with his mother and her new husband in Mexico. Mr. Alvarez was a very caring man, you know. I worked for him for many years. Gavin thinks his stepfather was cold, but Mr. Alvarez did everything to educate him, and he spoiled Gavin in some ways. But Mr. Alvarez had his own young son, Tomás, and he doted on him."

"You're saying that Gavin is still fighting old battles with his father and stepfather through Martin?"

"Mr. Alvarez believed in Freud. He thought Gavin searched for a dominating father figure. It's a love-hate relationship, and it obsesses him. Mr. Alvarez used to say, 'Perhaps, when I am dead, Gavin will finally be free.' But he is not. If anything, he's worse."

"When did Mr. Alvarez die?"

"Last November. It was a long time coming. Mr. Alvarez had Parkinson's Disease. He allowed Gavin to take over the business before he passed away. He hoped Gavin would be his own man, but instead, Gavin sold the hotels to Pantheon at the first opportunity." Apolinar shook his head. "Mr. Alvarez wanted him to be able to stand on his own, but he came to see that Gavin can only survive in the shadow of a larger man."

"But you said Mr. Alvarez had another son. Why didn't he take over the business?"

"Tomás died in a swimming accident some years ago. Gavin was with him. I have never been told the details of what happened. Mr. Alvarez had his heart broken then. He was never the same. His wife—Tomás's mother, as well as Gavin's—died of an overdose not long after."

"Are you saying that Gavin killed his brother?"

"Those were not my words," Apolinar answered. "I worked for Mr. Alvarez, and now I work for Gavin. I do that because Mr. Alvarez asked me to. I could not say no to him. Mr. Alvarez took me out of the slums of Barra Vieja and educated me. He paid for me to go to school. He even sent me to America to learn English. My loyalty is to Mr. Alvarez and to his family. Gavin is all that is left of Mr. Alvarez's family. So, when Gavin gives me an order, I obey, even if I regret it." Apolinar took a deep breath. "I am telling you all of this so you will understand. You are a smart woman. Let what I have told you guide your actions. Do not make Gavin give me an order that I would regret."

**38** After Apolinar left, I reached for my cell phone and found it was gone. The last time I'd used it had been when Jesse called me, and I'd tossed it back into my bag. I still had the purse, but spilling its contents over the bed only confirmed that the phone wasn't there anymore. I collapsed on a chair and stared into space, noticing that my carry-on suitcase had been quietly returned to my room and was standing against the wall. That felt like a taunt, reminding me there was no way out. It was already eight o'clock. I'd been at the Hotel Cerón for twenty-four hours, and in that time, Skye had died and I'd discovered I was a prisoner.

As an afterthought, I picked up the room's phone, feeling briefly reassured by the dial tone. I wasn't cut off from the world.

*Sure, but you can be monitored,* Claudia's voice reminded me. *The room phone? They can listen in on that. They can keep you from calling outside the hotel. And they will know if you call anyone inside the hotel.*

I returned the receiver to its cradle. The obvious alternative was email, but when I tried it, it told me I needed a code to access the Internet. The system hadn't been password-protected before; the fact it was now wasn't a coincidence. I didn't have a way to contact the outside world. My claustrophobia usually came to the fore when I was confronted by dark, enclosed spaces. But I could feel my pulse quickening as the old, familiar fear started to fill me.

I pulled off my dress and slipped into my jeans, T-shirt, and ballerina flats, then added a cardigan for good measure. I examined my neck where my attacker had injected the muscle relaxant; there was no visible wound except some prickly red skin around the puncture. He'd known how to do his job. But what job was that? My paranoia was in full bloom. What had always inhibited its growth was the idea I'd replicate my mother's mistakes, seeing the darkest possibility inside every shadow and hiding from the world. But everything around me had turned to dust, and suspecting the worst was the only reasonable response I had left.

I pocketed my passport along with my driver's license, credit cards, and cash. My silver bracelet was on my arm, and I stroked it as if it were both armor and an amulet. Putting my key card into my back pocket—I didn't want to return to my room, but knew I might have to—I shut the door with the quietest of clicks, then crept past Denny's, bowing low enough that I wouldn't be visible through the peephole. *Now that's lunacy,* I thought, but Denny was working with Gavin, which meant I couldn't trust her. Would she help me out of the hotel? Maybe, but it was just as likely she'd turn me over to Gavin. I had no idea where her loyalties really lay, and I didn't want to put them to the test.

When I got to Ruby's room, I rang the bell.

When she opened the door, she did a double take. "Are you done packing already?"

"Packing for what?" I asked, stepping inside without being asked to.

"For moving hotels, of course. You're not on the sauce, are ya?"

"No. Did they tell you about Skye?"

"Yeah. It's just awful. They said it was an accident."

"An accident?"

"She fell and hit her head." She peered at me closely. "Why, what did you hear?"

I thought about telling her the truth and realized that would only cause her trouble. "I just heard that she was dead. I still can't believe it."

"It's unreal. Denny was crying but that creep Gavin was just like a stone statue, maybe some kind of gargoyle. I tell you, that character is a freakin' weirdo. I'll be damned glad to get out of here."

"Ruby, do you have a cell phone?"

"No way. Those things give you brain tumors. I told Roberta she was lucky she lost hers."

A chill ran through my spine. "When did she lose her phone?"

"She noticed it was gone after lunch. But who knows? Maybe she left it on the plane." Ruby shrugged.

A thousand awful ideas crowded in my head. Any notion I'd had about using Ruby's land line went out the window. Gavin was controlling enough to spy on everyone in the hotel. Maybe Roberta really had dropped her phone somewhere, but I was certain she'd had an assist from Gavin.

"I need you to do something for me." I wrote down three sets of names and telephone numbers on a pad on Ruby's desk. The irony of the customized stationery—HOTEL CERÓN was emblazoned in black at the top, along with an artist's pen-and-ink rendering of the main building—wasn't lost on me. "When you get to your new hotel, you have to call these people."

"But you're coming, too?"

"I'd love to be wrong, but I'm not sure if that's going to happen." I held out the paper and Ruby took it. "The first one is a New York police detective named Bruxton—"

"That his first or last name?"

That got a brief smile out of me. Bruxton hated his given name, but I thought it was romantic. He shared it with a handsome leading man of the 1930s who'd died during the Second World War when Nazis shot down his plane. "Last. He'll hang up on you if you call him by his first. Tell him what's happened here. Then there's my friend Jesse Robb—"

"That's a cute fella. Photographer, right? Looks like Gregory Peck. Not quite so fine as John Wayne, but close."

"Right. Just call him and tell him . . ." Guilt surged through me. I'd dragged Jesse into enough messes with me; if he got hurt again, as he had in Peru, I'd never forgive myself. "Tell him I'm sorry I didn't call him back, and that I love him. The last one on the list is Martin."

"Your ex?"

I nodded. "Tell him everything you tell Bruxton, but warn him that, whatever he does, he can't come to Mexico."

"Why not? He's exactly the guy who could fix Gavin's little red wagon."

That was exactly what I was afraid of. *Martin is an evil man. He's going to suffer for all that he's done.* Gavin's gray eyes were filled with fire when he'd said that.

"It's dangerous for him here. He'd get hurt."

"You sound like you're still involved with him," Ruby observed.

"I thought keeping him out of my life permanently was going to be easier than it's been, at least in the past couple of days."

"It's never easy," Ruby said. "I avoided my ex like the plague for twenty years after we divorced. Hated his guts. But the day he died, I broke down and cried like a baby."

That resonated with me. "Thanks for helping, Ruby."

"You bet." She walked me to the door. "Hey, what do you think they're doing with Pete?"

That stopped me suddenly. I'd forgotten all about Pete Dukermann. "I don't know. Nobody mentioned him."

"I hope they're not moving him with the rest of us," Ruby grumbled. "That guy has B.O."

*He also might have a cell phone*, I realized. Gavin had seen Ruby and Roberta in my room, and he knew I'd turn to them for help, but Pete was a wild card. "His room is at the end of the hallway," I said. "I'm going to stop by and see him."

"I'll come with you," Ruby volunteered.

"I'll be fine."

"You've been sick. Pete'll take advantage of that. You need a bodyguard."

I wasn't going to argue with her. Thanks to the way the building curved, it was impossible to see Pete's room until we were almost there. If we'd arrived a moment later, we would have missed Gavin Stroud stepping out of the suite directly across from Pete's, putting a key card into Pete's door and opening it. I realized Pete hadn't been lying when he said he'd seen Skye come out of a room near his. She'd been with Gavin, and since Pete was a surprise guest, booked into the hotel at the insistence of the New York office, he'd caught Skye off guard.

"Gavin," I called.

"Didn't I tell you to—" He caught sight of Ruby, and his perfectly chiseled features froze, except for his jaw, which had a muscle throbbing against it. He cleared his throat. "I believe you are supposed to be resting, Lily."

I was relieved that Gavin was still trying to keep his mask up in front of Ruby. He'd lost his inhibitions around Apolinar, Denny, and me.

"We're looking for Pete Dukermann," I said. "I guess you're visiting him."

"No, I . . ." Gavin's eyes drifted to Ruby and color crept back into his face. He shut Pete's door with a firm click and turned to face us directly. "I have no idea where he is, as a matter of fact. I was informed that he destroyed his room, and I came up to inspect the damage."

"What does he think he is, some kind of rock star?" Ruby interjected. "How bad is it?"

"Terrible, actually. Pantheon will certainly be taking legal action against him." Gavin ran a hand through his hair. "Why don't you both go back to your rooms? I believe everyone else is packing right now."

"Please open the door, Gavin." I spoke slowly, letting my words wash over him and watching the color trickle from his face. For once, my voice was calmer than his.

"What? Don't be silly. I can't just let you into a guest's room, Lily."

"That so?" Ruby said. "Are you running this place, or are you just someone's errand boy?"

If I'd stood there thinking all night, I couldn't have come up with something more provocative to say to Gavin. His mouth opened and shut without a word, like a ventriloquist's dummy.

"Gavin, I'm really worried about Pete," I said. "His marriage broke up and he's depressed and . . . I'd just like to see that he's all right."

"He isn't in his room, Lily."

"Would you open the door? Please, Gavin?"

"No."

I wondered what he'd do if Ruby weren't beside me, challenging him in her smart-mouthed way. Having her there was a mistake, I realized. Gavin was going to let Ruby and Roberta leave the hotel, but he could change his mind at any time.

"Okay, Gavin. Come on, Ruby. Let's walk back to your room."

"No way. I'm gonna—"

Pete's door opened. "I didn't find anything else," Apolinar said. "But I think that's Skye's laptop in here."

Apolinar belatedly caught sight of Ruby and me. "What are you doing here?" he demanded.

Gavin looked at Apolinar, then back at me and Ruby. He sighed. "It doesn't matter. Let's all step inside."

Pete's entryway was dark, but a light was on in the living room. It was a shameful mess; somehow Pete had found ways to make the room even worse than it had been that morning. The bedroom door was open and a light was on inside, but it was empty, too. The bed was unmade and there were pills on the nightstand, along with a mound of white powder that I took for cocaine. The closet doors yawned wide open, and the empty hangers looked forlorn. Pete's clothing lay on the floor, shed like snakeskin.

"Pete isn't here, Lily." Gavin's voice was behind me. I turned and saw him leaning in the doorway, arms crossed. He looked like his bland, unruffled self, almost languid now.

I stepped into the bathroom. It was empty, of course, though the signs of Pete's drug use were even more readily apparent. The counter was littered with hypodermic needles, small bags filled with some kind of white powder, and a couple of spoons. It looked like a heroin junkie's shooting den, except that the powder was white.

"It appears that he has been shooting cocaine into his veins," Gavin said. I could see him in the mirrored wall of the bathroom, standing just behind me. For once, his face wasn't just a bland mask; suddenly it was a kaleidoscope of emotions, shifting from revulsion to contempt to fascination. "Can you imagine? What kind of maniac does a thing like that? He's obviously out of his mind."

"There's no—" I thought twice and stopped speaking. *There's no cotton* was what I was about to say. The garbage bin was empty, as if Pete had consciously decided to deposit his trash everywhere except the proper receptacle. But there wasn't any cotton on the countertop either. It was one of those tiny details that was so easy to overlook; if you didn't know anyone who injected drugs, it would never cross your mind. But addicts didn't just need the cotton for preparing the fix, they hoarded used cotton, because it was saturated with the drug and could be used for an emergency high.

"There's no what, Lily?" Gavin's brow furrowed.

"There's no way one man could have all of these drugs for himself, is there? Do you think he's a dealer?"

"I don't care what he is," Gavin whispered. "When I'm through with him, it won't matter anymore."

"Would you look at this place?" Ruby called. "It's like that house on *Jersey Shore*."

Apolinar said something to her and they both laughed.

In the mirror, I watched Gavin's hungry, hollowed-out face, and I felt truly afraid of him for the first time. He was always Martin's obsequious, accommodating, self-effacing creature, one who never made any demands. But that had just been a spectacularly clever disguise. Martin's outsized ego needed to be stroked; pretending to be a lapdog was a very clever way of manipulating him. And the wolfish gleam in Gavin's eyes told me that was exactly what he had done.

Gavin stared back at me in the mirror. "You're shaking like a leaf, Lily," he murmured. He placed his hands lightly on my shoulders.

"I'm not feeling well. I don't know what that man injected me with, but it's made me feel so sick. I need to go to the hospital. Please, Gavin."

"I'll let you go tomorrow. After Martin gets here."

"Martin?" I turned to face Gavin.

"He's on his way to Acapulco as we speak. I'm sure everything will be perfectly fine after he arrives. But before that, you're not going anywhere." Gavin wrapped his hand around the back of my neck and pulled me forward. He wasn't pretending to be gentle anymore. "You have a choice, Lily." His breath was hot against my face. "You can tell those two foolish old biddies that something is wrong. But then I'll keep them locked in the hotel with you. Would you like that?"

He presented it as a choice, but I had no option at all. "Please let them go. I won't say anything."

"I'm glad to hear that. I don't want them around." He loosened his grip. "Do you know how I can tell that you didn't say something to them already? They're not intimidated by me at all. That old hellcat was willing to take me on in the hall."

"I don't think anyone would believe me even if I told them."

"You're probably right." He let go of my neck and played with my hair. "I didn't bring you down here to hurt you, you know. That was never my plan."

"What was your plan? Trick me to coming down here so I would be bait for Martin?"

Gavin smiled. "Something like that."

"Hey!" Ruby called. "Check this out." Both Gavin and I looked over at her. "There's a silver computer and a black one. Apolinar says the silver one is Skye's . . . *was* Skye's, I mean."

"Pete's computer is black. I saw it when I was in here this morning." I was grateful for any excuse to get away from Gavin. I brushed past him, moving through the bedroom and peering into the living room. Pete's laptop was still on the desk. I lifted the top and it hummed back to life. It was open to his email inbox. At the top was a message from . . . me. My heart missed a beat, but I caught my breath as I realized it was just my auto-reply, telling anyone who emailed me that I was on the road. Still, that meant that Pete had recently sent me a message. I clicked into the sent folder and found it. His latest sent message had a subject line of just one word: *Sorry.* I clicked on it:

> Lily I'm sorry for what I did. I just couldnt see any way out after what happened with Skye. I knew youd find out sooner or later. I promise you I will never hurt anyone again

My brain creaked along, processing the lack of proper punctuation and strange syntax. I remembered seeing missives from Pete in the past, and they looked vaguely like this. He wrote the way other people texted. But he'd never emailed me in his life, and the messages I'd seen from him had been on travel-writing boards online, and they ran along the lines of "cant wait to see everyone in aruba." This message made the hairs on the back of my neck stand up.

"I don't believe this," I said. Gavin, Apolinar, and Ruby were all staring at the screen of the other computer, completely mesmerized.

"I told you," Apolinar said. "It's Skye's laptop. What's it doing in his room?"

"I'm going to kill him," Gavin breathed. "I'm going to spike his heart with adrenaline so he remains awake and alert as I cut him apart from limb to limb."

"I can't believe he killed her. That rotten bastard," Ruby said, fury overtaking her shock.

"Why would he take her computer?" I asked.

"He wanted to send messages to pretend Skye was still alive," Apolinar said.

I stood beside Gavin, watching his hand tap lightly over the keyboard, revealing Skye's Facebook page and news stories she'd left open. He clicked on her email and her inbox immediately appeared. Like me, and everyone else I knew— except Martin—Skye left herself permanently logged in to her account.

What stunned me were the subject lines. *Fraud at Pantheon* appeared in the headers of several emails. I only saw the words for a split second before Gavin slammed the top closed and grabbed the laptop. "Ruby," he barked. "Go to your room and take everything you don't want burned to the ground out of there. Apolinar, go help her."

She was so surprised, she didn't even argue. "Okay." She gave me a long look with her penciled-in eyebrows lifted to the ceiling before exiting. "See you in the lobby, Lily."

Apolinar followed her out, a frown creasing his forehead. He kept his eyes down, not looking at Gavin or me.

Gavin's expression was as remote and detached as ever, but the laptop in his hands was almost vibrating. It was the only sign of emotion in him.

"You don't think Pete attacked Skye?" I asked.

"The clues all seem to point in that direction, Lily. What other explanation is there?"

There were a few I could scare up, starting with the real murderer wanting to cover up his tracks. I didn't believe Pete wrote me that bizarre note of apology, and I didn't think it would be hard to set him up. On the other hand, there were the marks on his arms that made it clear he'd been in some kind of battle.

Gavin's voice went on. "The drugs in the room where Skye was found. Her computer in his room. Pete's arrest."

"What do you mean?"

Gavin blinked. "Didn't your friends at the New York Police Department tell you Pete had just been arrested for beating his wife?"

"No!" I don't know why the news startled me, but it shook me to my core.

"I suppose that's why he came running down to Mexico," Gavin mused. He turned to me. "We're going to your room, and I'm taking your computer."

"Like you took my cell phone?"

That made him smile. He was enjoying this. "There will be a guard posted at your door. You will stay in your room, or I'll find somewhere to keep you. I promise you, you'll find that latter option far less pleasant."

The whitewashed facade had dropped, and now even Gavin was admitting the truth: The Hotel Cerón was a prison, he was my jailer, and I was completely trapped.

**40** Without any more words between us, Gavin marched me back to my suite at the opposite end of the hallway. He snatched up my laptop but froze when he saw the pair of Frakker's guides.

"Where the hell did you get that?" he demanded.

*That?* I thought. There were two books. Which one was he fixating on? "From Skye," I admitted.

He grabbed both and piled them onto the computer. Then he waited silently until another man showed up to stand guard duty. Even without words, I could read the ruthless determination in his face. Whatever course he'd charted, he was following it through.

After he left, I turned and slid my back against the door until I collapsed on the floor. All the time I'd been afraid for Skye, worrying that she'd been kidnapped by people who wanted to get to Martin, it had never occurred to me that I might be used as a pawn for the same reason. In my own mind, the end of my relationship with Martin was so final and irrevocable that the idea of using me as a bargaining chip was preposterous. *What was your plan? Trick me to coming down here so I would be bait for Martin?* I'd been incredulous as I'd said those words to Gavin, but he'd been smugly superior as he answered, *Something like that.*

He understood something about Martin that I'd willed myself to forget. For all of his countless faults, Martin had one impressive virtue, which was a dogged devotion to the people he loved. It didn't mean that his behavior was impeccable; Martin was entirely capable of lying to his loved ones, misleading them, even cheating on them. But he would never abandon them. I'd known that when I'd decamped to Spain. I'd left him in the lurch, planning our wedding and then never coming home. I'd known he would come after me, and he had. Even though I'd never acknowledged it, I'd wanted to test just how deep his devotion ran. Now I knew.

I stared up at the ridiculous floral display Gavin had ordered for me. It was oversized and showy and signified nothing but a desire to impress. Would he let me go when all of this was over? Maybe, if he decided no one would believe the story I had to tell. In the meantime, he seemed amenable to leaving me alone. Grateful as I was not to be in the same room with Gavin, I knew I couldn't bide my time inside a cage. I had to get out of the hotel and warn Martin he was walking into a trap. I owed him that much.

My laptop and phone were gone, I reminded myself as I got to my feet and made my way down the hall. The room phone was dead when I lifted the receiver. I shouldn't have been surprised Gavin had shut it off. What was the point of listening in on my conversations now? I stared out the window, wondering how hard it would be to make it down five stories, then gulping when I realized how bad my odds were. I did the only thing I could think of, opening the interconnecting door between my suite and Denny's. Hers was locked, but I knocked over and over, and finally Denny opened it. She was flushed and breathing hard, and tracks from fresh tears and mascara marked her face. Normally so unflappable and crisp, she looked rumpled in her black dress and cardigan. She had a red flower pinned to the neckline of her dress, but it was wilted and shriveled, as if the Hotel Cerón had gotten to it, too.

"I need to talk with you," I said.

She nodded, then turned and walked back along the corridor to the living room, leaving me to shut the door and trail after her. Heading into the living room, I almost tripped over her luggage, lying open like a pit.

"Denny, why did you want me on this press trip?"

She bent down to pick up an espadrille that was lying on the floor and hurled it into her suitcase. "You already know the truth, don't you? It was Gavin. He wanted you down here. Everything was his idea."

Her words hung in the air between us. "Everything?"

"This was his show. He suckered me into it." She wiped her face.

"You lured me down here! You lied to me, Denny."

"I'm so sorry, Lily." The look on her face was pure misery. "I swear to you, I had no idea what Gavin really wanted."

"This whole press trip is a sham, isn't it? Is Mexico Tourism even involved?"

"Gavin's underwriting the cost of everything. His only priority was getting you down here."

"So, each time you invited me to Mexico this summer, you were working for Gavin?"

"I thought he was in love with you!" Denny said. "He was totally obsessed. He wanted to know everything about you, he read every word you ever wrote, he would talk about you for hours. He was desperate to get you to Mexico. He made it sound like he wanted to show off for you, that he was going to impress you with the way he was running his own show here."

"Gavin isn't obsessed with me, he's obsessed with Martin. He thinks he should be running Pantheon."

"I know. That's all Gavin can talk about now, knocking Martin off his perch. It's scary. He knows how tightly Martin controls the company. Even if Martin is off his game, I still don't see how Gavin thinks he can do it."

That took a couple of seconds to sink in. "Martin's off his game? What do you mean?"

"Things have changed a lot at Pantheon in the past couple of years," Denny said. "You know I used to work there, and I still talk to some people. They say Martin got distracted by issues in his personal life. At first, it was all about his son. Then there was everything that happened with you. Now, things have gone off the rails."

"How?" My heart seemed to thud to the floor and the room was suddenly unbearably hot. "What the hell are you talking about?"

"I don't have details. But Martin has totally fallen off the radar. People can't believe it. This is a man who used to inspect every Pantheon hotel site before, during, and after construction. He hasn't done that in months."

"But he was just in Burma. Maybe he's just focusing on new destinations?" My words were hopeful, but hollow. Martin was always exploring new destinations, but that never kept him from micromanaging other aspects of his business.

"Sure, Burma. Just like his trip to Bhutan, and Nepal before that. Do you see a pattern, Lily? He claims he goes to these exotic, underdeveloped places, but no one ever sees him. No deals have come out of these trips." She paced in front of me, clearly preoccupied with the question. "It's like he's hiding out, and no one can figure out why. Some people joke that Martin's actually dead, and his son is pretending he's alive so the money keeps flowing."

I collapsed on Denny's sofa. Everything around me was moving in slow motion. Was something wrong with Martin? Had he had some kind of breakdown? *Fraud at Pantheon* flashed through my mind. Martin's company was in trouble. Skye had known it, she'd struggled to prove it, and she had died. That fact made me terribly sad, but as the picture became more complete, the truth about Skye made me resentful at the same time. *If anything, you're the person who could help me with the story,* she'd told me the night before. All those questions she had about Martin, and I'd stupidly assumed her interest was sexual. But Skye had been hunting for evidence, and testing me out to see if I'd be willing to help. *So you two really are through?* Skye was trying to gauge how much distance there was between Martin and me, and how much hatred. She'd been trying to figure out whether I'd betray him.

I couldn't tell Denny any of that. "Do you think there's something wrong with the company?" I asked her.

"There is some kind of fraud going on. Skye knew it, but she never told me what it was about. Maybe Martin's stolen money from the company, and because of the economic downturn in so many countries, he can't hide that anymore."

"So, Gavin wants to take over the company, and he thinks he can take advantage of the fact that Martin is distracted to become CEO?" *Clash of the titans,* I thought. I was sure that when Martin's father founded the company, he never would have imagined his son battling for his position. Or his life. "What I don't understand is what's in it for you, Denny? Were you really willing to go along with all of Gavin's craziness just to get a job at Pantheon?"

"You have no idea how cutthroat PR is, Lily. Even when there was plenty of money being tossed around, it was hard. But now, everyone has cut back so much . . . if someone flashes a dollar, it's like a feeding frenzy for sharks. The only places that pay big money for travel PR anymore are places with such bad reputations that no one wants to go there. I thought I was going to hit the big time with my own boutique publicity company. It hasn't worked out that way. Some hotels I worked with went belly-up and never paid me. One destination sued me because of a problem with their campaign, something that was out of my control. It's been hell." She looked teary again. "My mother keeps telling me what a failure I am. 'You forty-one, you have no husband, no job, no children. You boyfriend just using you till ex-girlfriend come back. You live in Brooklyn!' " Denny mimicked a pidgin English accent. "That's my Tiger Mother."

"I'm sorry." Sometimes I wasn't sure what was worse: having a mother dedicated to making you miserable, or not having one at all. Occasionally, when I was feeling really sorry for myself, I thought I'd been orphaned at thirteen. That was when my father had died and my mother had disappeared down a gin bottle. Having her around for the next five years had been harder than her death actually was. *Maybe for you,* called that voice from the back of my brain. Claudia was two years younger, already on drugs and in trouble. Maybe I *was* just as selfish as my mother claimed. Maybe what Claudia always said was true. *Deep down, you're pretty superficial.*

I took a deep breath. "According to Gavin, Martin is on his way down to Mexico now. Do you have any idea what Gavin has planned for him?"

"Gavin doesn't tell me much of anything. What little I know comes from his moments of grandiosity, when he wants to show off. He said he's going to force Martin to give him control of Pantheon."

"How? Do you think he's going to make Martin sign succession papers? You think that would stand up in court, anywhere in the world? One minute after Martin leaves Mexico, the paper wouldn't be worth anything, except as proof that Gavin was guilty of extortion."

"He . . . I don't know what he'll do."

"Denny, the only way Gavin's plan works is if Martin never leaves Mexico alive. You know that as well as I do."

She nodded. "I never believed he'd be capable of that, but after what happened with Skye—"

"What are you talking about?"

"Gavin murdered her," she whispered.

# 41

Every nerve end in my body fired up. "I suspected it, but . . . are you sure?"

"I'm not sure of anything," Denny said. "But Gavin's trying to get me to believe that Pete Dukermann killed Skye, and I don't believe it. It's almost like . . . like he thinks he found a perfect scapegoat."

"Did Skye tell you about her relationship with Gavin?"

Denny nodded. "She swore me to secrecy about it. She was always pissed off that he wouldn't be seen with her in public, that he kept so many secrets from her. She told me she wondered if the only reason Gavin was interested in her was because Martin had taken her out. She thought he was proving something in his own head."

"That's probably true."

"Skye got so bitter about it. She kept talking about how she was going to get revenge on him. She was going to destroy him."

As Denny said the words, Skye's voice in the bar came back to me. *The thing is, I know how to get even with him. I'm going to destroy him professionally, and he'll never even see it coming. This isn't about revenge. This is about righting wrongs. Illegal wrongs, Lily. I can deal with my hurt feelings, but he can't be allowed to keep on doing the things he does.* Afterward, I'd believed she was talking about Martin, but I was wrong. It was Gavin she'd wanted to get even with.

"How was she going to do that?"

Denny shook her head. "She kept saying all she needed was an inside source at Pantheon. Then she could nail it. But she was also half-hoping to get back together with Gavin. Last night, when I saw her, she was going to see Gavin. She stopped at my room to show me what she was wearing. She said they were going to get married, or else she'd see him in hell."

"What time was that?"

"Just before seven, I think."

That fit what I knew. I'd seen Skye in the lobby on Friday night around eight. She'd been red-faced from crying, which told me exactly how that ultimatum had turned out. "Has Gavin ever mentioned Skye to you?"

"When I asked about her on Friday night, he told me she'd left the hotel. He called her all kinds of awful names. At the time, I thought it was because of her ultimatum, but now . . ." She gulped. "When he told me tonight that Skye was dead, he was so . . . controlled. It was like he was talking about a pet he didn't really care for. All I could think was, he's truly a sociopath. He has no feelings at all, except for himself."

"That fuels his rage. Gavin feels very sorry for himself." I thought of how he'd wanted to enlist me as an ally against Martin, as if Martin had screwed us both over and Gavin was going to get even. But I'd only glimpsed the fury underneath Gavin's cool, polished surface. *Martin received a kidnapping threat last year, when we opened our first Mexican hotel, the one in Cabo. Of course, Martin was perfectly fine with sending me here in his stead.* I could picture Gavin's face as he said it, the way his eyes burned and his mouth twisted.

We were both silent for a moment, lost in the undertow of our dark thoughts.

"Where's your phone?" I asked.

"Gavin took away my cell when I got here. Lily, he's watching everything and everyone." The expression on her face was bleak. "Martin Sklar is a control freak, but Gavin is so much worse." She eyed me, as if unsure how much she could say to me. "Gavin's similar to Martin, but more tightly wound and extreme. They're like peas in a pod. Oh, on the surface, they couldn't be more different. Martin's all charm, and Gavin's all serious. But underneath, they're both . . . watchful. They don't trust other people."

"Denny, you have to get out of here and call the police."

"Gavin knows all the people who are important to know around here—the police and everyone else. He's got excellent connections in Mexico. No wonder he wanted to lure Martin here. For all intents and purposes, this is Gavin's home playing field."

"Then call Pantheon's board of directors. Someone has to be able to stop him."

The doorbell rang.

"I have to get that. Gavin will let himself in here if I don't answer quickly," Denny said. "Hide!"

"Where the hell can I hide?"

She looked frantic. "Anywhere! Look, there. Closet. Go!"

My body reacted before my mind did, racing into the bedroom and pulling the door shut. I hated tight spaces and it had been a long time since someone had gotten me to enter one willingly. For a moment, time froze around me and I was a child again, locked in a closet with my sister while my mother battled her own demons. Some of them were real— like the child services people, who knew something wasn't quite right at our house—and some of them were imaginary. The latter lived at the bottom of bottles of gin, and I never knew when they might come out. Sometimes, my mother drank and drank and drank and fell into a kind of forgetful stupor, in which she didn't seem to know that she was anyone's mother. Not mine, and not Claudia's. She thought we were strangers, or friends, or even incarnations of her own dead relatives. My whole body trembled.

*Get a grip, Honey Bear,* hissed a familiar voice. *Nothing has happened to you. At least, not yet.* I heard Denny opening the door of the suite. *Okay, now you can start panicking.*

*Thanks for the vote of confidence,* I thought.

"I was wondering if you were still here. You need to go, Denny. Before he kills you, too." It was Apolinar who was speaking. I thought about stepping forward, but I was curious about what he'd say if he thought I wasn't around.

"He's crazy," Denny answered. "But I don't think he would—"

"You didn't see Skye's body, did you? He smashed her head in, like she was an insect. This silly girl, who was in love with him and followed him around like a dog, no matter how badly he treated her. He did that to her. Gavin could do anything to anyone. He is a man without conscience."

"I've got stuff everywhere. I just have to pull it together."

"Leave it and get out while you can," Apolinar said.

"I have to get Ruby and Roberta."

"Already done. I had one of my men take them over."

"Gavin's left them alone at another hotel? No one's watching?"

"Are you joking?" Apolinar said. "They have a TV, but no phone, no Internet. That *pinche culero* Gavin is nothing if not thorough."

"You should be careful what you say. I wouldn't put it past him to bug my room."

"I'd know about it if he did. One of my men would have to do the work." Apolinar lowered his voice. "He's got one of my men working that pathetic slob Pete Dukermann over right now."

"Why?"

"Why do you think, Denny? Let me tell you what Gavin did. He says to me, come, let's look at Pete's room. So we go and look around, and what do I find there? Skye's computer. Just sitting there, all nice, like it's praying to be discovered. Then I show Gavin, and he starts talking about how he's going to cut Pete into pieces."

A sob burst out of Denny's chest, halfway between a wail and a scream.

"Shh. Calm down. Gavin has a man watching Lily's room. You want him to hear you?"

"I'm sorry. It's just . . . when I got involved, I never imagined things would end like this."

"Gavin is fucking crazy," Apolinar said. "What did you think would happen?"

"I thought he'd get Lily down here and he'd come onto her and she'd slap him. Then she'd leave and all of this crap would be over. Why did Pete even come to this hotel? He could've stayed anywhere! He should never have been here."

"None of us knew this would be the week Gavin would go back to his old habits," Apolinar said. "Gavin has what we call *cara de muerto*. Death face."

"Old habits?" Denny's voice was terrified. "You're saying Gavin's killed people before?"

I thought of what Apolinar had told me about Gavin and his half-brother, Tómas. Who else had Gavin murdered?

"Forget it. But Denny, you must get out while you can."

"What about Lily?" Denny asked.

"I've got an idea how to get her out of the hotel."

"And then?"

"Look, I can't stay. I wanted to make sure you leave now. Gavin is going to torture Pete. If Martin Sklar shows up here, he's a dead man. That's a lot of blood already on Gavin's hands. Do you think he'd hesitate to kill you to keep you quiet?" Apolinar's voice got softer. "I knew what Gavin was planning was awful. All along, he's plotted to kill Martin Sklar, but no one else was supposed to die. Everything is spiraling out of control and I don't know where it will end."

"How will you get out?"

"I can't," Apolinar said. "Gavin needs to keep me around to do his dirty work."

Their voices receded, and I opened the closet door. A moment later, the front door to Denny's suite opened and closed, and she came into the bedroom. "I don't know what that sounded like to you, Lily, but I promise—"

"What do you plan to do?" I asked.

"I'm getting out of here now, before Gavin decides to kill me because I know too much." She grabbed her purse and rifled through it, pulling out a black key card. "Take this. It's an all-access pass to every room with an electronic lock. You can find a place to hide. There's also a staircase for the staff. It's behind a regular door, one that doesn't have a number on it. It's on the far side of this floor."

"Thanks, Denny."

"Just don't let Gavin find you," she said. "And if he does, please don't tell him how you got that card."

"Do you think he wants to kill me, too?"

"I never imagined he'd kill Skye," Denny said. "I don't know what he's capable of anymore."

# 42

When I went back to my suite through the connecting door, I looked around, wondering if there was anything I should grab before making a run for it. I had to wait for a few minutes for Denny to get rid of the guard outside my door. He tried to argue with her when she told him to carry her suitcase downstairs, but he finally obeyed.

As I walked down the corridor, holding the key card, I noticed that the lights were turned very low, making the angles and corners suddenly spooky. This really was an old castle, even if it had been turned into a playground for tourists. There was blood in its history, if the sad story behind its ghost was to be believed. I thought of Skye's body, abandoned in a moldy, dusty room. There was blood in the Hotel Cerón's present, too.

Near the elevator, I felt like tiptoeing. The card burned hot in my hand. What if this was just another wild goose chase? I was Gavin's prisoner, and there I was, wandering around the floor like a child playing a game. Or worse, a madwoman who'd been locked away. I thought of Poe's Madeline Usher, buried alive in the mansion she shared with her brother. In the story, her brother claimed the house was sentient. The two of them were tied to it in life and death. Somehow the endless gloom of the Hotel Cerón had made itself at home inside of me.

As I rounded the curve on the opposite end of the hallway, in sight of Pete's room, I noticed a door without a number. I tried the key, saw the blink of the green light, and heard the whirring of a door unlocking. I slowly pushed it open. Inside was a yawning black pit that reeked of damp earth. A metal cord dangled against the inside wall, and I pulled it. Somewhere below me, a light went on, its yellow glow illuminating a wooden staircase. The rickety, splintery stairs were nothing like the opulence of the Hotel Cerón's public facade. It was as if a third-world village were hiding inside the splendid palace.

Letting the door close behind me, I tried to steady my breathing. The smell of the moldering wood and plaster didn't help. *Pretend you're a ghost; maybe if you move like one, you'll get out of here,* I told myself. Or maybe Claudia's voice said it; I wasn't sure anymore. The darkness in my mind was mirrored by the world around me, and my own ghosts had slipped from whatever tethered them to me. They were everywhere.

I walked down flights of stairs, but that seemed only to take me one story down, judging from the big, red "4" written on the wall. More flights down led to a "3." Progress, at least.

There were lights on the landings and a few bare bulbs hanging by wires along the walls, but much of the space was dark. It was hard to imagine the Hotel Cerón's staff trudging through here, day after day, while guests meandered through broad, gilded hallways. Would it really offend anyone's sensibilities to see a maid walking by with a stack of towels? Even in the low light, the steps felt as if they were turning to dust under my feet. There were cracks on the walls, splintering out like the branches of a tree. The grand edifice of the hotel no longer felt so stable.

*Keep going,* I told myself. There was nothing to do except move ahead.

I made my way farther down. The tightness of the space and the lack of light made it feel as if things were closing in on me, and that made it hard, in turn, for me to get enough air into my lungs. It was my old foe, claustrophobia, but there was more to it than that. There was a scent of decay that got stronger with each step down. It filled my nostrils and seeped into my bloodstream, making me feel dim and light-headed. Forcing myself to continue, I noticed a whirring sound. Was I imagining all of that? It was hard to tell fact from fiction. I was inside a castle, and I'd found my way into its dungeon; I wondered if I would be able to walk out of it again.

There was a chain attached to the wall, and the sight of it stopped me midstep. I couldn't see a purpose for it; maybe it didn't have one anymore. I viewed the Hotel Cerón as a modern-day House of Usher, but the chain pushed that out of my head. All I could think of was another story of Poe's, "The Cask of Amontillado." As much as I loved Poe, I'd never liked that tale, because I couldn't understand why the narrator wanted revenge on his friend. He started out saying there were a thousand injuries, but he couldn't take the insult; it was never clear what the friend had done. Still, those transgressions were the reason the narrator lured his friend into a catacomb, chained him to a wall, and buried him alive. Naturally, Claudia had loved the story. *You don't understand it,* she'd told me. *He didn't need a reason to kill his friend. He already had his justification.*

In some ways, she'd been a very wise child. I had a feeling that eleven-year-old Claudia would have seen the truth about Gavin long before I did. He didn't have a reason for what he was doing, but he had an arsenal of justification. He'd shown me that over breakfast. What had he said about Martin? *He'd love for everyone to think he does a great job running Pantheon, but the truth is he's just extraordinarily talented at claiming the credit for other people's work.* I'd realized then that he hated Martin, and I'd found it amusing when he called Martin "Pharaoh." I should have found it threatening. Taking on a pharaoh meant using whatever he loved against him. I knew Gavin was cozying up to me, but I'd been unwilling to see myself as a mere pawn.

*In pace requiescat*, I remembered suddenly. That was what Gavin had said in his office. Those were the final words of Poe's story, too.

When I finally reached the next landing, I found I had nowhere else to go except a tunnel in front of me. The whirring was louder, and the air smelled a little sweeter. Breathable, in any case. It wasn't until I got to the lighted doorway that I understood why. I was in the basement of the Hotel Cerón, and I'd discovered its laundry room; one big washing machine was working away. A maid sat dozing in a chair. I backed out, relieved she hadn't seen me, until I felt something scramble over my foot. It wasn't a snake this time, but a rat. I gasped and watched it twitch its tail dismissively at me before scurrying down the corridor and through a hole in the wall. There were other rats around that hole, I realized, coming and going as if Grand Central Terminal lay just behind it. I edged my way along the other wall, holding my breath for fear of plague or hantavirus or whatever the hell they carried, and I kept my eyes on them. The hole in the wall had a rock tucked into it, but that wasn't exactly barring rodent access. The rats looked at me, and it seemed as if their beady black eyes were weighing me, considering how good a meal I'd make, before they lost interest.

I kept my hand on the opposite wall, for fear of falling, and my fingers slid into a crevice. Jumping back, I pulled my hand away, afraid of being bitten or worse. The wall was a mass of giant fractures, like a piece of shattered glass that was still barely held together by inertia. Looking around, I realized that the other wall, with its rat hole, was at least as bad. It was impossible to reconcile the glamorous, gilded world above with this rancid pit below.

*No wonder the place doesn't have guests,* I thought. *It's rotting from the inside, and it's going to fall apart one day soon.* Pantheon never would have bought it if they'd inspected it. Even if Gavin were to succeed in getting rid of Martin, his Mexican empire was already crumbling.

When I got to the next staircase, I rushed up the fragile steps as quickly as I could. Part of my brain feared the rats giving chase; I also wondered if the foundation would crack apart and fall in before I got upstairs. Whatever areas of my brain that weren't consumed by those fears pondered whether I'd find a door to the outside world, or if I'd be trapped and have to run the gauntlet of rats and corroded concrete again. When I finally found the exit, I almost wept with relief. Shoving open the door, I gulped warm, humid air into my lungs before noticing two men who were waiting just beyond. They were holding guns.

One of the men smiled at me, revealing gold teeth under a caterpillar mustache. The other just stared. They pointed me up a short flight of whitewashed cement steps, opening a door inside and taking me down the long, winding corridor, past the jewelry shop and the spa and the other dark storefronts. There was nowhere to run. One man led; the other stayed behind me. There was nothing I could do but follow.

In the lobby were half a dozen men, all of whom had guns. I felt as if I were marching into the O.K. Corral; visions of John Wayne movies and a shimmering image of Gary Cooper in *High Noon* played in my head. It was High Midnight in Acapulco, apparently. Glancing at my watch, I saw it was only ten o'clock. Clearly my muscle-relaxant-induced nap had messed with my internal clock. I wasn't tired, but I was suddenly starving.

I recognized a couple of the men. One was the big-bellied loudmouth who'd accosted me with a gun on the hotel grounds, when I discovered the field of half-built bungalows. The other was the fiftyish waiter who'd served me in the bar when I was with Skye. I didn't see the clerk from reception who'd checked me in the night before.

"*Buen trabajo*," the waiter said, congratulating them on capturing me.

The waiter led the way behind the reception desk and knocked on Gavin's office door. When Gavin told him to come in, the waiter opened the door. "Hello, sir. Look at what the dog dragged in," he said.

"The *cat*, Eduardo. It's look at what the *cat* dragged in." Gavin took a last, long drag on a cigarette and dropped it into a glass. I'd never seen him smoke, and I wondered if this was a new habit for him, or something he'd hidden along with his true character.

Gavin stood, pulling at his clothing in a vain attempt to reverse the creases that were piling up. At ten o'clock at night, he was still wearing his suit jacket. It didn't look so formal now; there were deep creases and dark splotches on it. I didn't want to think about what the splotches were from.

"Come in," Gavin said. As we stepped forward, he put one hand up. "No, wait. Let's go to the Urdaneta Room." It reminded me of how he'd changed his mind that morning, when he was ordering breakfast. As organized and robotic as Gavin was, perhaps not every decision he made was scripted. "How does that sound, Lily?"

"Fine." If I was going to be in a prison, it might as well be a beautiful one.

Gavin picked up a laptop bag and walked beside me down the airless hall. Eduardo the waiter was a few steps ahead, while the two goons still shadowed us.

"Do you really need three men with guns to protect you from me?" I asked Gavin.

"You're more dangerous than you look."

"Then carry your own damn gun."

"That's not what a gentleman does," Gavin shot back.

He really was like Martin, I realized. His claim made me remember something Bruxton's NYPD partner, Norah Renfrew, said about Martin. *Mr. Sklar doesn't seem the type to do his own shooting, know what I mean?* Carrying a gun and doing the dirty work, those were jobs for underlings. The man at the top could order up whatever horrible thing came into his head, but as long as he kept his own hands clean and his suit pristine, he could go on thinking of himself as a gentleman.

At that moment, I was filled with hatred for Gavin, but also for Martin and for everyone who ran Pantheon. There they were, calling themselves gods—a pantheon was, literally, a collection of gods, after all—and they behaved as if they were unaccountable to mortals. *Fraud at Pantheon?* No, it was more like Pantheon was a fraud.

"Here we are," Gavin said as we got to the door. Eduardo held it open for us. "We'll be fine, I'm sure," Gavin added, not even bothering to look at the goons. "Wait in the hall."

"Yes, sir."

The Urdaneta Room was only dimly lit, and Gavin turned up the overhead lights. Even without natural light, it was a lovely space, but its charm was lost on me. The flowers were cloying and oversweet, and the iron trellises over the windows resembled elaborate prison bars. One time, when I'd visited Toronto, I'd toured the Old Don Jail, which had metalwork in the shape of stunning dragons and snakes; that didn't make it any less of a prison.

"Do you mind if I smoke?" Gavin asked.

"Go ahead. I didn't know you smoked."

"I like to be private. Cigarette?" he offered.

"No, thanks." I looked around the room. Was the only exit really that lone door to the hallway? I stared at the windows, wondering if the glass could be knocked out. The trellis was too tightly knit in most places to squeeze through, but if there weren't any glass—

"There's no way out of this room but the door," Gavin said, as if reading my mind. "The glass is so completely bulletproof you could fire a machine gun at it and there'd be no cracking. It's also got a special coating so that no one outside can peer into the room."

That made sense; when I'd walked around the hotel, I hadn't seen the Urdaneta Room from the outside. "I was wondering about ventilation. Cigarette smoke isn't good for that painting you're so proud of."

"Ah, Proserpine." Gavin set the laptop on the table and walked up to the painting, staring at it while smoke swirled around him. "Do you know what the strangest thing is, Lily?"

"I have a feeling I'm about to find out."

"Oh, you *are* charming. I used to think that luxury meant opulence, and having everything you want. But I've found that all of the pleasure is in the hunt. I don't really care to keep things. They become this awful responsibility, almost a millstone around one's neck." He moved closer to the painting. "Even the finest things are just things. You can destroy them if you wish, and no one else can ever have them again." He turned to look at me and gave me that grim smile. *Death face,* Apolinar had called him, and I understood exactly what he meant. There was an appetite for destruction inside Gavin, and it was insatiable.

"Is that why you killed Skye?" I asked.

"I didn't kill her."

"You expect me to believe someone else did?"

"I don't care what you believe. What I know is that the man who killed her was just the instrument. If I had to guess, I'd say the idea wasn't his."

"What does that mean?"

He dragged on his cigarette, staring out the window. "I had no idea how ridiculous and sentimental Skye was until recently. I suppose that happens when you only see each other for a week here, a weekend there. I thought I knew her. I believed we were on the same page, that we might actually want the same things."

"Imagine that."

"Do you know what she really wanted? Marriage and a family. Can you picture that? What would I want with a child? How stupid was Skye to think that?"

"Naive. Hopeful. Optimistic," I said. "Not stupid."

"She wouldn't have gotten pregnant if she'd had a working brain."

That floored me. "Skye was pregnant?"

"Yes. You didn't know? She blindsided me with the news last night. She knew what I was planning, and she knew how much it meant to me, but she decided to be a fool and confront me with her preposterous ultimatum."

"What did you say?"

"I told her to get rid of it, of course. I certainly didn't want it. She wailed like a madwoman, carrying on about how she would raise the child without me, and I'd be sorry."

"That was why you killed her?"

"Are you deaf? I told you, I didn't do it." He glared at me with bloodshot eyes. "I wanted to strangle her last night. But she went storming off and I was relieved. I thought she'd gone away. I had no idea she was still inside the hotel."

"If you didn't kill her, who did?"

"Martin."

His accusation didn't rattle me; it was utter nonsense. "Skye died in this hotel, Gavin. You're the one standing here, not Martin."

"I didn't say he magically appeared and did the job himself. Martin's always got someone working for him on the inside. That's another thing I learned from him." Gavin gave a joyless laugh. "You know, I actually thought it might be that lumbering fool Pete Dukermann. It seemed highly suspicious that he just happened to run in to Skye in the zocalo, and then, when Denny told him he couldn't stay here, he called someone at Pantheon's PR office who forced us to let him in." Gavin shook his head. "I'm almost disappointed to find that he isn't Martin's man, after all. That would have been impressively creative on Pharaoh's part."

"Where is Pete now?"

"In one of the bungalows. We gave him rather a working over, I'm afraid. Of course, he's another detail I'll have to deal with later."

"So you know he didn't kill Skye?" I pressed.

"There was a nanosecond when I thought it was possible that he'd killed her," Gavin said. "Until I realized poor, hapless Pete was the recipient of the world's laziest frame-up job."

"Who would frame him?"

That earned a smirk. "My dear Lily. Always the last to know." He dropped his cigarette on the floor and lit another. "You know what's disappointing to me, Lily? I know there's nothing, absolutely nothing in this world, that would devastate Martin as much as the thought of you in my bed. Yet here I am, and there you are, and the thought of sleeping with you doesn't appeal to me at all."

"I'm crushed."

"At first, I thought it was because I don't go in for brunettes. I always think the blonder, the better. And while I do very much approve of the way you dress, there's something very tough and low-class behind it all. I can see why Ava Gardner appeals to you. What was it she was called? Grabtown Girl. That's you to a T, Lily."

At one time, not that long ago, the idea that someone could see past the surface polish to the depths of my grubby roots would have been painful to me. Then, after Claudia's death, I'd given up my glamorous facade for a while, and I'd been surprised to find I missed it. Instinctively, I'd gravitated to it again, but my reasons had changed; I enjoyed glamour, simply because I loved beautiful things, especially when they had history. But I didn't need to hide behind them anymore.

"That's the biggest compliment you could pay me, Gavin."

"Don't make me start in on your personality." Gavin shrugged slightly. "I tried to get my mind around it. It would drive Martin mad to think of us together."

"Is your entire life about Martin?"

"Now you sound like Skye. I admit, I am preoccupied with him. But I've been waiting in the wings long enough. It's my time now. We just have to wait for Martin to get here. Ah, speaking of which . . ." Gavin went to the table and opened the laptop. "He should be arriving soon. Of course, he'll have his little army with him. He's just terrified to come to Mexico, you know. We can watch for him together."

Gavin turned the laptop slightly so I could see it. There was a black-and-white image of the front of the Hotel Cerón. I moved closer and saw it was a live feed.

"I just realized, I'm being a terrible host. I've decided I'm not drinking any alcohol tonight, but you can have whatever you like. Champagne, perhaps? I can have the chef whip up some dinner for you, too."

"How thoughtful, Gavin. Is this so you can poison me again?"

Gavin turned and stared at me. The smile that crept over his face was the first big, genuine expression I'd ever seen there, and it frightened me. "Clever, clever girl. I'm rather surprised you figured that out."

"How did you do it?"

"There are so many poisons to choose from, you know. All you need is a little something to mask the taste or color. The poison was in your soup at lunch, by the way, not the champagne. I don't think it's appropriate to adulterate champagne."

"What did you use?"

"Don't look so worried. It wasn't plutonium. You'll be fine."

I remembered reading about a Russian spy who'd been poisoned with plutonium, and his agonizing death in London. Gavin looked pleased with himself, having thoroughly unnerved me.

"Why?" I demanded. "You already had me here. Why poison me?"

"I didn't want to be obvious about keeping you a hostage," Gavin explained. "My hope was that you would be too sick to get out of bed, and hence you'd be less of a security concern. Also, your illness would be perfect cover for making you disappear suddenly, if I needed that to happen."

"But the police would know—"

"They would do damn all."

"But they know about Skye...." The words died as I caught Gavin's expression. "Wait, the police don't know about Skye? What about the paramedics who took her body?"

"Lily, don't you understand anything about the hotel business?" Gavin ground out one cigarette and lit another. "Do you think I want the police poking around here under any circumstances? I'm already up to my eyeballs in bribes I have to pay. I really don't need more complications."

"What did you do with Skye's body?"

"My people will make it look like another cartel killing. There are so many of those around here, no one will notice. Or care."

"She was your lover," I said. "She cared about you."

"I know. I can't let myself think about her just now. It's too hard. I suppose I revealed as much of myself to her as I ever have to anyone." He said this quietly, as if it were a guilty admission. "But it was also exhausting. Keeping up pretenses, I mean. Pretending I cared about the meaningless things she cared about. She was a child in so many ways. All of the idiotic, romantic ideas she carried around ..." His breathing was ragged. He wasn't as self-controlled as he believed. "Mind you, she lied to me, too. All these months, I believed she was only seeing me. She had some other man lined up to raise the child with her if I wouldn't." He stared at the painting of Proserpine. "I suppose we've both been spinning our webs around each other all this time."

It sounded awful, but it also felt familiar. How many couples had lies piled up between them, so large that they overshadowed the relationship itself? What could you do but pretend you didn't see them, unless you wanted that relationship to crack apart?

"I don't understand why you think Martin killed her," I said. "What could he possibly gain?"

"Skye thought she was so clever. She was going to write this big tell-all about Pantheon if I didn't marry her. She'd dug up quite a lot of dirt, actually. It would've destroyed my career and landed me in jail. Of course, it would've done the same thing to Martin. He might have killed her for that reason alone. But, knowing him, I believe it was more personal. He was furious that I'd gotten you down here, and that was his way of showing me he was still in control."

"I don't believe that for a second."

"How sweet, Lily. You still defend him."

"It's a crazy theory."

"Be that as it may, I will avenge her death," Gavin said. "I promise you that."

"You were already going to kill Martin," I pointed out.

"That's true." Gavin looked thoughtful. "But he won't be the only one to die."

I didn't ask if he was going to kill me. That was something I took for granted.

It was one in the morning when three SUVs pulled up in front of the Hotel Cerón. "Here we are. The grand duel is about to begin," Gavin said. We watched on the computer screen, and it felt like an old movie. A bald, black man in a dark suit got out of the middle SUV, walked to the other side, and opened the door. The man who got out was dressed as Martin dressed, but a brimmed hat shielded his face from view. As he moved away from the vehicle, it was obvious that he wasn't Martin. He moved hesitantly, without Martin's bravado and confidence. And even though he was roughly the same height and build, he was much too thin.

"Son of a bitch!" Gavin yelled. "It's a trick!" He grabbed my arm. "Did you know Martin was sending someone in his stead?"

"No. I haven't spoken with him since this afternoon. You're the one who told me he was coming here. I never heard that from him."

"I can't believe it. That lying bastard!" Gavin was on the verge of tears. He picked up the computer and smashed it on the tile floor. While he was stomping it and cursing, there was a knock on the door.

"Mr. Sklar is here, sir." That sounded like Eduardo.

Gavin let out a string of curses before he opened the door. He froze, as if turned to stone.

"Hello, Gavin," Martin said. "Long time, no see." He peered into the room. "Lily, sweetheart. You have no idea how happy I am to see you."

If he hadn't spoken, I wouldn't have recognized him. My former fiancé had always reminded me of Tyrone Power, the matinee idol who'd starred opposite Ava Gardner in *The Sun Also Rises*. But Martin had become a gaunt shadow of his former self. He was still impeccably dressed, as he always was, wearing a trench coat thrown over his shoulders, a well-cut black suit and white shirt, a pale blue scarf tied at his throat, and a matching pocket square. It was if he were planning to attend a yacht party after he took care of this bit of business. He smiled at me, but his face looked sunken and lined. I felt an unfamiliar sensation of pity for him wash over me. I'd wished terrible things on him after Claudia's funeral, and I'd hoped his empire would crumble to dust, but I'd never wished for this.

"Martin." My voice was breathy, like a starlet over-reading her lines. I couldn't help it. "I can't believe you're here."

"Well, I had no choice but to come to Mexico. Not with everything that's been going on at the Hotel Cerón." He shot a look at Gavin, who was standing near him, looking as tense and taut as a hawk watching its prey.

"You're not pronouncing the name correctly," Gavin said. "The emphasis is on the second syllable in Spanish. I can't imagine you haven't learned that by now."

"You're the expert on Mexico, Gavin." Martin's tone was mild.

"I'm rather an expert on many things." The self-satisfaction in Gavin's voice was impossible to miss. His self-possession was returning, after that terrible outburst before he'd opened the door.

"Yes, we'll be speaking about that," Martin said. "But there's no reason to bore Lily. Sweetheart, I have a car waiting outside. Would you go, now, please?"

"No, Martin, that won't do. Lily is going to stay put." Gavin was slyly confident. "What I can't believe is that you brought three carloads of bodyguards with you. You are getting more paranoid every day." From the motion of his head, I could see he was trying to look down the hallway and count how many there were.

"You've got plenty of armed guards right here, Gavin. Or is that a new development, since people started dying at this hotel?"

"You don't like having your own methods used against you, do you, Martin?"

"No, I suppose I don't. Look, let's work this out like reasonable people. Lily will go outside and get in the car. My bodyguards will stay outside with yours and they'll wait while the two of us talk privately in this room." His eyes swept over the interior again, and I knew he was trying to check if any guards were inside with me.

"All right, we'll have your bodyguards and the hotel's guards stay outside," Gavin said. "However, Lily stays in the room. Apolinar, come here."

"That's one of *your* guards," Martin said, his expression grim.

"He's a business associate. The fact that he handles security for the hotel is a plus."

"Fine. Mr. Muñoz can stay. But Lily goes outside."

Gavin shook his head. "I'm afraid that's out of the question." He turned to his own guards. "You can go outside with Mr. Sklar's men."

"That okay with you, Mr. Sklar?" asked a man with a deep baritone.

"It's fine, Nevins. Thank you," Martin answered. He turned to look at me. It was hard to return his gaze. I hadn't ever planned to see him again, for so many reasons. Now that we were in the same room, my heart ached because he looked as if he were dying. It wasn't just the muscle and tissue that had wasted away; Martin was normally so animated. Now his hands hung at his sides, as if it would be too much trouble to lift them. His eyes were still startling, green the shade of natural absinthe, and they were steady and serious. I was more afraid for him than I was for myself.

# 45

After Martin and Apolinar stepped into the Urdaneta Room, I heard footsteps marching out of the hallway, presumably moving toward the lobby. Gavin looked around the room. "Well, now. How cozy that it's just us." His voice was cool and smooth. He was so pleased with himself that he was almost purring.

"Knock it off, Gavin," Martin said.

"I don't think so. I know how tiresome you find it when anyone else talks for more than a minute in a meeting, Martin. You're the only one who gets to drone on and on endlessly. But think of this as my meeting. I'm the one running it."

"You've done a hell of a job running the show down here, haven't you?"

"I've been taking care of matters at Pantheon for some time now, while you lope from crisis to crisis in your personal life. I admit, it's a shock to see you looking so ghastly. I was already going to suggest that you make a plan of succession, but it's obvious that one is absolutely necessary."

"I see," Martin said. "Undoubtedly, you've got papers ready for me to sign."

"As a matter of fact, I do."

"Then what?"

"If everything is in order after that, and you don't try anything clever, I'll let Lily go," Gavin said. He didn't say a

word about what he had in mind for Martin; he didn't have
to. The air was heavy with it.

"I'll leave the cleverness to you, Gavin. Here's the problem. I can't put you in charge of the company. I don't get to
appoint the next CEO. The board will have to vote."

"You can suggest it in the strongest possible terms, and
the board with go along with it," Gavin said. "I have strong
support on the board already. This will just make the transi-
tion a certainty."

Martin laughed a little, but the sound he made was dry
and crackly and not at all convincing. "Gavin, you made a
good lieutenant for years. I acknowledge that. But you in
charge of the operation in Mexico has been a disaster."

"Really? Why do you say that?" Gavin's jaw was so tight
the last word was almost hissed out. "I've made money here
hand over fist."

"I'm not going into the whys and wherefores—"

"Because they bloody well don't exist!"

"No, Gavin. I won't because Lily's here. If I start explain-
ing where you've gone wrong, you'll become increasingly
reluctant to let her leave." Martin's voice was surprisingly
understated. He had to be furious, being held hostage, for all
intents and purposes, by his employee inside his own hotel.
But he didn't show it.

"You're just an empty suit and an empty brain," Gavin
sniped. "The only reason you're running the company is because your father founded it. You have no talent or expertise
at all."

"I built it up. I made Pantheon into a global empire."

"I did that for you. I've worked like a dog for years, and
you get all the glory. You need people around you, all the

time, to keep you amused and to keep all of your anxieties and insecurities at bay."

"Gavin, you can keep insulting me all day if you like. But Lily should leave."

"Absolutely not. You know, Lily and I had the nicest chat this morning. It was all about what a coward you are. Isn't that right, Lily?" He didn't wait for an answer. "It would be a surprise to her to learn you're completely gormless. But perhaps she'll find this amusing. That kidnapping threat that's kept you out of Mexico? I was the one behind it."

The silence in the room was deafening, until Martin said, "I know."

"The hell you did!" Gavin yelled. "You knew damn all."

"I didn't realize it at the time. It took me a while to piece it together. In fact, it was only recently that I did. It hit me one day, how funny it was I could never go down to Mexico. I had to trust you to run the show for me here. Gallant Gavin, such a stand-up guy, willing to brave great danger for the company. And those profits! You just kept them climbing. What a great show."

This enraged Gavin more than anything had. "You knew nothing."

"I didn't keep tabs on you the way I should have. But when I started looking . . . let's just say you weren't good at covering your tracks. You were sloppy, Gavin."

Gavin stepped forward, punching Martin in the chest. Martin reeled and went down.

"You think you're good at figuring things out, Martin? Let me give you a little lesson. I'll show you who's sloppy." Gavin put his hand out. "Apolinar, your gun please."

"What?" Apolinar looked anxious.

"Gun." Gavin put out his hand.

Apolinar took the gun out of the holster at his waist and handed it over. Gavin tested the weight in his hand. "Is the safety on?"

"No."

"Good." Gavin pointed the gun at Martin, then swiveled around. He shot Apolinar in the stomach and the man fell back and hit the ground. Apolinar lifted his head, touching his hands to the hole in his gut. They came away red. His mouth was open, but no sound came out.

"That's what you get for being Martin's spy," Gavin raged.

Apolinar was trying to say something, but blood bubbled to his lips. He looked at me and mouthed something, then closed his eyes. He was clearly in agonizing pain. I went to Apolinar, kneeling on the ground beside him. I didn't know much about him except that he'd done some vile things in his time; he'd known Gavin planned to murder Martin, and he was prepared to help. But he'd also cared about getting Denny and me out of the hotel, and he was loyal to the memory of the man who'd lifted him out of the slums. That was enough to make my heart ache. I touched his forehead and he opened his eyes.

"What did he promise you, you greedy fool?" Gavin shouted. "More than I was paying? I hope you enjoy it in hell."

Gavin turned back to Martin, who was still on the ground. Only now, Martin was holding a gun in his hand.

"Isn't this an interesting turn of events?" Martin asked.

"That looks like a stage prop in your hand," Gavin taunted. "I know how to shoot. My father taught me long ago. You don't."

"Ank," Apolinar whispered, blood dribbling from the corner of his mouth.

"What?" I whispered.

Gavin kept up his taunting. "Look at your hand, Martin. How it quivers. My, but you're frail. How I wish the entire Pantheon board were here to watch this. They would be lining up to put a bullet into you."

Apolinar moved one leg, and I realized what he meant. He had an ankle holster. I grabbed the gun purely on instinct and raised it. Gavin's head turned in my direction. Martin fired, and Gavin went down.

# 46

Time slowed to a standstill. Martin was on the floor, breathing hard. Gavin was sprawled out, staring at the ceiling. Apolinar's eyes were open wide and fixed on the ceiling. I touched his eyelids to close them, then went to Martin's side.

"Can you get up?" I asked, still in shock.

"You're still holding that gun," he pointed out.

"Oh!" I bent down, setting it on the floor. Martin grabbed it, making it disappear into a coat pocket.

"Just give me a moment, sweetheart."

"What did I tell you about calling me sweetheart?" I knelt beside him and resisted a sudden urge to touch his face. His skin was so dry it looked as if he were at risk of flaking apart.

"Do you hear any shooting out there?"

I strained my ears. "Nothing."

"Good. Hopefully my man out there is earning his keep."

"You *do* have someone working for you."

Martin nodded. His breathing was short.

"But I thought that Apolinar—"

"Apolinar turned down my offers. I made quite a few, but he was firm."

"A man lured me into the bar late this afternoon," I said. "I think he was planning to—"

"Help you escape? Exactly." Martin put one hand on his chest, pressing on it. His breathing eased a little. "If you hadn't resisted, you'd be in New York now and we'd be toasting Gavin's gullibility." He shook his head. "Or maybe we'd still be here. Gavin had guards all over the grounds, so smuggling you out was going to be damn near impossible. Maybe this is where we'd have ended up, no matter what. You're not hurt, are you, sweetheart?"

"No." Dazed and confused, but not hurt. I was trembling. "Don't think I won't kick you when you're down. Just keep calling me that."

Martin moved into a crouch and I helped him up.

"Can you stand on your own?" I asked.

"Yes. No. Give me a moment." His hat was on the ground and his face was resting on my shoulder. At that moment, we were holding each other up. My eyes were fixed on Gavin, lying on the ground in a pool of blood. He looked so pathetic and forlorn, his face still registering disbelief.

The door opened. "Mr. Sklar! Are you hit, sir?"

"No." Martin lifted his head and looked at me. "We need to get out of here, Lily."

"We can't leave!"

"You're shell-shocked. Take a deep breath." He draped his trench coat over my shoulders.

"Martin, we can't just leave. We've got to tell the police what happened."

"Lily, if we stay now, we could end up staying forever."

"You're being melodramatic. The Mexican police are not going to detain us forever."

"No, but it could be months. If my doctors are to be believed, I don't have many of those left."

That hit me like a slap, and I turned my head away so that Martin wouldn't see my expression.

"Pete Dukermann is in one of the bungalows," I said. My heart thudded in my chest, and my voice came out dry and dull. The reality of what had just happened in the room was finally sinking in. "Ruby and Roberta . . . I don't know where they are. Gavin had them moved somewhere."

"We'll find them."

I looked around the room, feeling helpless. I didn't want to stay, but I was afraid to go, too. Someone had to stay to piece this together.

"There's a plane waiting. We need to go, Lily." Martin took my hand, and we walked out together. I couldn't look back.

Martin's driver took the roads to the airport at breakneck speed. The sky was black and it was raining again. I stared out the window, more panicked than I'd been at the Hotel Cerón. I could see Martin's reflection in the glass. He was slumped against the seat, with his head back and his eyes closed. His breathing was labored. Part of me had hoped that he wasn't sick, that it was all a ruse for sympathy and reconciliation. But he couldn't fake that he was wasting away and there was no point in pretending otherwise.

When we arrived at the airport, one of his guards opened my door and immediately led me to the plane. "What about Martin?" I asked, not understanding what was happening.

"Don't worry," the guard said, before lowering his voice. "He's been up way too long. He's gonna need some help getting on the plane. Don't look. He'll be embarrassed."

'd like you to tell me when you first noticed the symptoms of the poisoning." Dr. Revery was a tall, broad-shouldered man with copper skin and a slight Southern accent. His words crept out of his mouth at a leisurely pace, which was oddly calming in spite of everything that had happened. We were in the air, probably still over Mexico. I hadn't seen Martin since I'd been on the plane; all I'd been told was that he was resting. I didn't have to ask why Martin had a doctor there; that was painfully obvious.

"I thought I was imagining things," I admitted. "I started feeling nauseous after Skye vanished on Friday night, but I figured that was because I was worried about her. I thought my heart was going to pound out of my chest, but it calmed out eventually. When I went to bed, I felt as if I were freezing. But it wasn't until this morning—I mean, Saturday morning—that I realized something was wrong. During lunch, I threw up. My vision seemed blurry. I had an awful headache and chills. I had trouble moving. It was like having the worst case of the flu ever."

"Was there some specific pain you felt, anywhere at all?"

"No, it was a sense of total exhaustion. It was hard to breathe."

"There are so many possibilities, and this is not my area of expertise," Dr. Revery said.

"What is your specialty?" I asked.

"Oncology."

That went into my heart with the speed and force of a bullet. Oncology meant cancer. Just looking at Martin, that was what I'd feared.

Dr. Revery's voice broke through my thoughts. "When I say poison, I'm not talking about arsenic or belladonna or any of those Agatha Christie methods. I can't perform all the tests I need to on the plane, but your blood pressure is unusually low, which is another symptom of many types of poisoning. I'm going to start treating you here, but you're going to have to promise me you'll cooperate when I check you into a hospital in New York. Someone will need to perform gastric lavage."

"What's that?"

"My fancy-pants way of saying someone will pump your stomach." I must have made a face, because he smiled. "Yeah, that's the look people get when you mention stomach-pumping."

"But I'm still up and walking around," I pointed out. "Doesn't that mean I'll be all right?"

"It means you're tough as old leather, but it's no guarantee. You were poisoned more than once. You probably had just a drop the first night. I'd say you were hit with at least two doses the next day. There may have been more than one poison involved. It's possible that they tried one poison, which only hit you slightly, then got you with something stronger."

"I thought I was being completely paranoid. It seemed crazy." I closed my eyes. The conversation I'd had with Gavin in the Urdaneta Room played through my mind again.

*How thoughtful, Gavin,* I'd said. *Is this so you can poison me again?*

*Clever, clever girl. I'm rather surprised you figured that out.*

"Is there any way of proving I've been poisoned?" I asked Dr. Revery.

He shook his head. "It's tough to prove with a live patient. Your body is moving the poison out of your system right now. The evidence is disappearing, and that's a good thing. Now we need to focus on keeping you alive."

# 47

After Dr. Revery gave me a handful of pills—expensive versions of the charcoal pills Ruby had given me, I was sure—I sat staring out the window. He'd asked if I wanted to lie down, and I'd told him I was too keyed up to rest, but that wasn't true. I was so bone-weary and emptied out that I could have fallen asleep on a bed of nails at that point. But in the back of my mind was a worry that, if I drifted off, I wouldn't wake up again. Part of me knew that, when I dreamed, at some point I would see Skye and Apolinar and Gavin again, and I didn't want to chance that. I was busy wrestling my own fears and demons.

"I don't want to bother you, but I needed to see how you are." Martin's voice caught me by surprise. He'd slipped into the seat across from me, without my noticing. Even in my hazy state, it was impossible to miss how frail and haggard he looked.

"I'm fine. Did your doctor give you a report?"

Martin hesitated. "I hope you don't mind."

"It's fine. I'm just not looking forward to having my stomach pumped." It wasn't the physical discomfort that unnerved me. My mother had had her stomach pumped on several occasions because of her suicide attempts. I'd spent most of my life avoiding the long, ominous shadow she cast. However inadvertently, I seemed to be following in her footsteps.

"I owe you an apology, Lily. I know, I owe you much more than that, too, but I—"

"An apology for what, Martin?"

"For your being dragged into this mess. For putting your life in danger. Gavin knew that if he lured you to Mexico, he could lure me, too. I'd told him so much about you, and about us. I made it easy for him."

"That's funny. I thought you might want to apologize for wanting to kill my sister."

The look on his face was both painful and priceless. Back in January, when I'd confronted him, he'd never actually admitted what he'd done. He'd danced around it. He'd equivocated. He'd flat-out lied. I'd been able to force certain admissions from him, but never that he'd planned to kill Claudia.

Martin stared at me. I watched him without saying a word. We stayed locked in battle for some time, until Martin said, "If I could go back in time and change one thing I've done, that would be it."

"You don't get to go back and fix it, Martin. No one does."

"I know that. But it doesn't stop me from wishing I could."

I nodded. "I wish you could, too."

We sat quietly; I was staring into space, trying to keep my composure. For some reason, seeing Martin turned my internal clock back by months, to when I was still raw with loss and guilt.

"Do you know what the worst part is?" Martin asked. "I'd gotten used to the idea that your sister was always going to be in the picture. I knew she'd keep on making you miserable, and I was going to live with that because there was no other way to have you in my life. I'd made peace with it, as much as I could. It was only because I thought she was threatening Ridley—"

"I know, Martin. I understand that part."

"You do?"

For a moment, I didn't see how thin and aged Martin had become. I only noticed his eyes, which were as vividly green as ever. They didn't make my heart do its shivery little rhumba anymore, but the light behind them made it warm up in my chest.

"Thank you, Lily. You have no idea what that means to me."

"How are you feeling?"

He shrugged. "Given that I could just as easily be a corpse right now, I'm feeling pretty damn good." He gave me a shy wraith of a smile. "You have no idea how sorry I am about all of this."

"I don't blame you for what Gavin did, Martin."

"I didn't have a clue what he was doing until you were already in Acapulco." His mouth puckered slightly, as if he'd tasted something sour. "I gave Gavin too much freedom. It was only when the board made him head of the Latin American division that I started looking at his operation. You know that saying about not looking a gift horse in the mouth? I almost wished I hadn't."

"What did you find?"

"A giant mess that could potentially destroy the company. I had trouble believing it, and I was still working out what to do about it. Once I realized you were in Acapulco, I knew what Gavin was up to. I have to admit, it was an inspired move on his part. He knew there was nothing I could do to get you out of there safely, and I would have to come to him eventually."

"You tried to get me out. I didn't cooperate."

"It was a stupid idea. I should have flown down immediately." Martin stared into the distance again, his expression disbelieving. "I'm to blame in all of this. I just don't understand how everything went so bad so fast. I'm an idiot for having faith in Gavin."

"I was surprised just how much you trusted him. Gavin tried to turn me against you by telling me about Gregory Robinson."

Martin's face contorted; for a second, I thought he was having a heart attack. "He *what*? I never told him—" His voice cracked and whatever else he'd been about to say was buried under silence. I didn't say anything. On some level, I didn't think Martin understood how much Gavin truly hated him, or how far he would have gone to destroy him.

He touched the back of my hand with his dry, dusty fingertips. "If you'd died, it would have been my fault." Martin's voice was a dry croak. He stared at me, and there were tears in his green eyes.

I didn't want to talk about how close we'd both just come to dying. "What will you do about the Mexican police?" I asked.

"What do you mean?"

"When they find Gavin's body, and Apolinar's."

"They're not going to find their bodies."

It took a moment for that to sink in. "You really think you can bury this?"

"I do."

I stared at him. It was impossible not to think of what Gavin had said. *Martin's always got someone working for him on the inside.* He hadn't been wrong about that. In fact, Gavin was more right than he knew.

"Do you think you can bury the fraud at Pantheon, too?" I asked him.

He gave me a long, dark look. "Yes." A moment later, he got to his feet and shuffled away without another word. I didn't see him again for the rest of the flight.

# 48

In typical dramatic style, Martin had an ambulance waiting for me at New York's John F. Kennedy International Airport. That might have seemed like a luxury, but after a doctor administered a numbing gel to suppress my gag reflex and made me swallow a plastic tube, I was desperately wishing I were back at the airport, waiting in the customs and immigration line.

"It's been more than twenty-four hours since your last dose of poison, if Dr. Revery's estimates are correct," the gastroenterologist told me. "My guess is you'll be okay, but I'd like you to keep checking in over the next three days."

"Does that mean I have to come back to the hospital and have my stomach pumped again?" I asked. "Because my answer to that is no."

"Just call in every four hours. This is my direct line." She handed me an embossed card with a number scrawled in ink. Doctors had such lousy handwriting that I wondered if it was a med school requirement. "If you have any recurrence of symptoms—nausea, chills, headaches, vomiting—or anything at all feels off, call me immediately."

"Sure."

"In case you don't, I've instructed your brother in what to watch out for. I've also told him what you can and can't eat. Be sure to drink plenty of water, and stick with yogurt and plain crackers today. A light broth is fine, but nothing heavy or greasy or spicy."

"My brother?"

"He's waiting for you in the lobby. You can go home with him now. Get plenty of rest."

When I finally emerged from the hospital, I was cranky, sore, and in need of a serious toothbrushing. The only thing that lightened my spirits was the sight of my best friend waiting for me on a vinyl couch in the visitors' lounge.

"Well, dear sister, it's good to see you again," Jesse said, without a hint of his Oklahoma accent. He sounded like an actor on Masterpiece Theater.

"Jesse! How did you get in here?"

"I got a call from someone I ain't too fond of, but who was tryin' to do the right thing," he drawled, sounding like himself again and pulling me into a giant hug. Jesse detested Martin, so that was as far as he'd go in giving him credit.

"I've missed you so much," I said.

"You only left on Friday morning."

He was right. It was Sunday afternoon, but it felt as if a lifetime had elapsed since I'd last set eyes on him.

"I know, but it's good to be home."

"You hear that?" Jesse called over his shoulder. "I told you New York is always home to her."

Pulling back a little, I turned to see who he was talking to. Bruxton was standing there, wearing jeans and a black T-shirt that showed off both his muscles and his tattoos, which started at his wrists and crept up from there. If you looked closely, there was a bulldog and an eagle—both beautiful, intricate designs—but the cumulative effect of all that ink was thug-like. His blond hair was cut to a length that would've been approved by the military. His face was arranged in its usual fierce expression, as if the snarl he'd perfected on perps had seeped into his everyday life until it was normal for him. A muscle in his jaw tensed and I realized he was biting down on nicotine gum.

"Hi." To my own ears, I sounded like a shy, and probably slow, child. I wanted to exude glamour and mystery, but proximity to Bruxton short-circuited that. Suddenly embarrassed, I realized what a mess I looked like.

"Hey." Bruxton's expression seemed to soften a bit, and he took a step forward, but then he stopped.

There was an awkward pause before Jesse said, "What's wrong with you two crazy kids? Y'all know it's legal to hug each other, right?"

He gave me a little shove and nudged me into Bruxton, who put his arms around me. My face rested against his neck, and the scent of him—a mix of soap and shaving gel tinged with tobacco—was intoxicating. I would've stayed there awhile if Jesse's heckling hadn't continued.

"Don't you two look cute. Guess I'm your fairy godmother."

"Thanks for meeting me," I said, pulling away with reluctance.

"Oklahoma Boy told me you'd be here. I was getting worried about you." There was something wary in his voice. I felt like a jerk. Whatever madness had happened at the Hotel Cerón, I'd sought out Bruxton's help and then dropped him. It was true that Gavin had cut me off from the rest of the world, but I hadn't been completely honest with Bruxton before that happened.

"I'm glad to see you. Both of you," I said.

Jesse arched an eyebrow at me. "You better be happy to see me. You had me worried there for a while."

"It was insane at the hotel. You can't even imagine. . . ."

"I got a pretty big imagination. Try me."

"I don't even know where to start," I said. "It's a long, complicated, sad story."

"Well, you gotta cough up the details sometime, Tiger Lily."

I knew Jesse was right, but I really didn't know how to start. Instead, I let Jesse fill in the spaces with his usual cheery chatter. Bruxton was silent as he took us down the FDR Drive. It was a sunny day with a bright blue sky, and I felt as if Acapulco were on another planet. I stared toward the East River, taking in Roosevelt Island and bits of Queens. Even the Pepsi-Cola sign over the now-defunct bottling plant was a welcome, familiar sight. I was home, and I could forget about what had happened. I was in sunlight again, and I never wanted to leave.

By the time Bruxton took the exit at Fifteenth Street, even Jesse was subdued. The tiny stretch of road before you got to Avenue C was a wasteland of empty lots and wire fences.

"That SUV's comin' up behind us real fast," Jesse said.

Bruxton pumped the gas pedal, but even as we shot forward, the black SUV that had followed us off the highway caught up to the car and slammed into the back. We weren't hit hard but the jolt still came as a shock.

"What the fuck is he doing?" Bruxton said.

We looked back. The SUV was revving toward us.

"Both of you duck," Bruxton ordered.

I didn't see what happened next, but I heard gunshots. Then the car ground to a halt while squealing tires took off.

When I looked up, the SUV was half on the sidewalk and half on the road, disappearing onto Avenue C.

"Is everybody okay?" Bruxton asked. We were shaken but unharmed. "Lily Moore, that was one hell of a welcome home."

Officers in patrol cars turned up almost immediately and took our reports. Emergency medics checked us out. When they finally let us go, I was shaking badly. Jesse hugged me, but that didn't calm me down.

"Tiger Lily, you have any idea what that was all about?" Jesse asked.

"No."

"That's what I was afraid of."

A tow truck wheeled Bruxton's car away. The windows were broken in bits over the seats. It was a miracle that the flying glass hadn't cut any of us. A cop drove us over to Jesse's apartment building at Broadway and Eighth.

"You going to be okay?" she asked me as I got out.

"I wish I knew," I said.

Upstairs, Jesse vanished into the kitchen, saying he was going to call a deli to deliver some food. As soon as he disappeared, Bruxton turned to me and put his hands on my shoulders.

"You have any idea who that was? Because I don't believe in coincidences," he whispered.

"No. I can't even imagine. Everything happened so quickly."

"I understand that. But the cop part of my brain—which is most of my brain—can't help but think about the fact that you get off a plane from Mexico with your shady ex-boyfriend, and on your way home somebody ambushes you."

"There was a man named Gavin Stroud who wanted Martin dead. But he's dead now, so—"

"How'd he die?"

"I . . . um . . . I'm not sure how much I can tell you."

Bruxton's expression was as skeptical as if I'd been a crook he'd caught red-handed. It made me feel ashamed, because it synced with the part of my brain that told me I should come clean. "Did your shady ex have him killed?"

"No! He wanted to shoot Martin but Martin shot him first."

"When did Sklar become Quick-Draw McGraw?" Jesse asked, stepping out of the kitchen.

"I know you two both hate Martin, but this wasn't his fault," I said.

"You gotta lot of 'splainin' to do," Jesse said.

It was only after the food arrived, and we sat down in the living room to eat, that I started to tell them what had happened in Acapulco. They were both quiet. Jesse gave me encouraging glances, but Bruxton's hard eyes never veered from my face, which unnerved me.

I told them the story in all of its confusion and madness. There were things I couldn't explain, and I didn't even try. When I got to the part about Gavin shooting Apolinar, and Martin shooting Gavin, Bruxton got riled up.

"I can't believe what I'm hearing. You know there's never going to be justice for any of these people. Martin Sklar is going to walk away unscathed, yet again."

"He shot Gavin in self-defense. He had no choice. Gavin had already killed Apolinar. He was going to kill Martin and then me."

"You're actually defending your ex," Bruxton said. "He killed a guy, and you're okay with that?"

"A guy who killed Skye, tortured Pete, killed Apolinar?" I demanded. "I was there. Gavin Stroud poisoned me."

"It's a good thing Sklar shot that lowlife Stroud, 'cause it saves me from havin' to go after him." Jesse touched my shoulder. " 'Cause you know I would."

"I know." I hugged him, grateful to always have him in my corner. "There was nothing else anyone could do. Gavin lured me down there because he wanted to kill Martin. He was going to kill me, too."

Bruxton looked away. He'd reminded me of a pit bull the first time we'd met, and he did so again; even though his eyes were on me, he wasn't making eye contact. "I'm going to make sure there's a cop detail watching this place for the next few days. I don't think you should go out, Lily."

"I was a prisoner in Acapulco. I'm not going to be a captive here, too. Look, Gavin Stroud is dead and so is the man he relied on to do his dirty work."

"What, you think he only had one?" Bruxton asked.

"There's no way he gave an order to have someone follow me from the airport. He was planning to kill me in Mexico."

"What about Skye's killer?" Jesse asked. Both Bruxton and I turned to stare at him. "Don't y'all give me the hairy eyeball. Lily, you said you didn't reckon Gavin killed her. Who do you think did?"

"I have no idea," I admitted. "Gavin had a lot of people working for him in the hotel. Any one of them could have been the killer."

"Yeah, but not many of them could get someone to attack you in New York. That's got to narrow it down," Bruxton pointed out.

I ran through the list in my head. "I honestly can't think of anyone."

"Keep thinking," Bruxton said, getting up. "I need to get going."

"I'll walk you out," I offered. I shadowed him through the living room into the alcove of the foyer.

"So, I guess I'll be seeing you around," he said. For some reason I couldn't explain, that caught me in the chest like a punch. *See you around* sounded like a brush-off.

"You'd better. When?"

He looked at me. "That's up to you, Lily."

"You're always asking me when I'm coming to New York. Now that I'm here, you don't know?" I tried to keep my voice cool, but I was hurt. My nerves were still jangled and I couldn't hide it.

"Tell me something. Why didn't you leave Sklar's hotel when you found out he owned it?"

"I wanted to, but it was late, and Skye had vanished, and I needed to make sure she was all right."

"You sure that's the real reason?"

"Is that what you're upset about? The fact that I didn't run screaming out of the hotel?"

He flushed, and I braced for a biting comeback. "I never thought you'd make up with that bastard. I don't care how nice he dresses or how swell he talks, he's a scumball."

I started to argue but Bruxton put up one hand, palm forward.

"I know he didn't kill your sister. But he's a bad guy. And now you're talking about him like he saved your life. Like"— Bruxton stared into my eyes—"like you still love him."

His honesty caught me by surprise. "Seeing him was hard," I admitted. "He's sick, and he looks like he's got one foot in the grave. I can't pretend that didn't affect me. It made me sadder than I ever imagined I could be for him."

"He went running down to Mexico to get you out of there. I know I should give him props for that. But it just makes me hate his guts."

"Why?"

"Because I wish I'd been the one who went down there to save you."

I was touched and flattered and annoyed all at the same time. I hadn't realized it at first, but Bruxton was seething; everything I said about Martin was making it worse. Ingrid Bergman had once been quoted as saying, *A kiss is a lovely trick designed by nature to stop speech when words become superfluous.* There were no words I knew that could help me, so I leaned forward and kissed him. He pulled me against him and kissed me so hard that I moaned.

"Well, you two don't waste time gettin' reacquainted, do you?" Jesse said. Bruxton and I moved apart, as if jolted by electricity. Jesse laughed and disappeared back into the living room.

"I'll call you," Bruxton said, opening the door. "Make yourself comfortable with New York's finest watching you twenty-four-seven."

"Brux."

He turned to look at me.

"Just for the record, Martin didn't save me."

We stared at each other.

"I almost forgot," he said, breaking the spell. "You wanted to know who Skye called on Friday night, before she disappeared." He reached into his pocket and pulled out a folded slip of white paper. *Ellis Burke,* he'd written in blue ink, with a phone number after it.

*I'll be back in a couple of minutes,* Skye had said. *I just need to call m— um, someone.* I'd wondered if "m—" meant Martin. Had I misheard her? It didn't matter anymore. Skye was dead and there was nothing I could do to help her now.

"Who's that?" I asked.

"You tell me." He reached for the back of my neck and kissed my forehead. "Be careful." A muscle in his jaw twitched just before he turned and walked out, closing the door behind him without another word.

**50** "Lily and Bruxton sittin' in a tree. K-I-S-S-I-N-G," Jesse taunted me, putting his long legs up on the coffee table.

"How come you spell out the G but you never say it?"

"That's culturally and linguistically racist, y'know."

His breezy tone didn't make the heavy weight in the middle of my chest any lighter. "Do you think there's anyone running around New York who wants you dead?" I asked.

"Nope. I'm as lovable as it gets."

"What about Bruxton?"

"I don't reckon there are many folks who'd take him on in broad daylight."

"So that leaves me as the target."

"Which is not to say you're not lovable, 'cause you are. But you got a knack for gettin' into trouble."

"All I did was go on a press trip!" I protested.

"Yeah, this one ain't your fault. It's your ex's. You know what freaks me out most in all this? I'm feelin' sorry for Sklar and that monster kid of his." Jesse's mother had had cancer, and her death, when he was eighteen, was still a subject that could bring him to tears.

"I know. Ridley is only sixteen. He's not a monster. He's sweet but a mess." As I said the words, I wondered if that was why Martin didn't want to talk about the company. *Do you think you can bury the fraud at Pantheon, too?* I'd asked, and Martin had simply said *Yes*. Was Martin trying to do something with the company so that Ridley would be taken care of after Martin was gone?

"Okay, Ridley's a sweet monster," Jesse allowed. "What are you gonna do now?"

"Run back to Barcelona. Think about getting another job. I love to travel, but I'm sick of travel writing. There's got to be something else I can do."

"Like what?"

"I have no idea. Writing is the only skill I have."

"We could start a magazine," Jesse said. "I'd call it *Truth in Travel*, 'cause we all know there's not much truth to be had out there, 'specially in travel. All this glossin' over the problems in a place. 'Hey, don't mind them guards with machine guns, they're just protectin' this beach from poor folks.' "

"That is the truth." I yawned, and tried to remember when I'd last slept. No wonder I was about to drop. "One of Martin's people said I'd get my computer back. Gavin confiscated it. I think he stole my cell phone, too."

"Well, if you ever wanted to be incommunicado, here's your chance. But you're welcome to use my computer, Lil, and you can call in for your messages from my phone."

"What would I do without you?" I asked him, not for the first time. He passed me a cordless receiver, and I dialed my number and got into voice mail. There were several messages waiting for me: a brief one from Martin, saying he was on his way to Acapulco and to hold tight; an equally brief one from Bruxton, wanting to know if I was okay; and one from Ruby, who'd called that morning, wanting to know where the hell I was. Then there was a message from a voice I didn't recognize at first. "Hello, Lily, this is Ryan Brooks. You telephoned me yesterday. I've been trying to reach Skye but I'm only getting her voice mail. Can you call me, please?"

I listened to his message over and over, with my heart feeling heavier each time. I'd forgotten that I'd called Skye's former fiancé, and the realization that he—and Skye's friends and family—didn't know she was dead made me want to run away. Gavin had told me he'd disposed of Skye's body, but I had no idea what he'd actually done. The people who loved her wouldn't know the truth. Would they take my word that she was dead? Would I have taken someone's word that Claudia was dead, if I hadn't learned the truth? Part of me would have wanted to continue on in hope and desperation, walking that fine line between heaven and hell, unable to let go.

Jesse listened to the message. "You want me to call him?" he offered.

"No, I have to do it. I was there. I need to tell him how it all happened." The prospect only made me feel empty. Maybe calling Skye's former fiancé wouldn't be so bad. Maybe he had a new girlfriend and the call wouldn't leave a gaping hole in his life. But I found that hard to believe. Knowing that Martin was sick had affected me more than I could put into words. It didn't matter that I wasn't in love with him anymore. I had loved him, and that feeling had mutated and transformed, but it hadn't died.

Dialing Ryan's number, I held my breath. When he answered on the first ring, I tried to keep my voice steady. "This is Lily Moore. I just got your message."

"Have you heard from Skye yet? Is she all right?" His voice was frantic; I could picture him waiting by the phone for news about her.

"I am so sorry to have to tell you this, but Skye is dead," I said. "They found her body in a room at the Hotel Cerón yesterday afternoon."

Ryan's ragged breathing made him sound almost like an obscene phone caller. It was a full minute before he said anything. "The Hotel Cerón. That's a Pantheon hotel, isn't it?"

"Yes."

Ryan let out a cry of pure anguish. "She was murdered," he gasped. "I told her if she kept digging, she could die. That bastard Martin Sklar killed her."

# 51

Jesse wouldn't let me go out to Brooklyn alone. "You got rocks in your head again?" he mocked when I told him I had to see Ryan Brooks. Instead, he got the apple of his eye—his baby blue 1968 Camaro, Ginger—out of the garage down the street and steered us over the Manhattan Bridge. A police car followed us at a not-so-discreet distance.

Even though the Brooklyn Bridge was considered the iconic one, the Manhattan was the one I loved best. It marked the point where my old neighborhood, the Lower East Side, bumped into Chinatown. Driving east on Canal Street, we could see the gleaming white arch and colonnade, the Beaux Arts style so distant from the neon-lit buildings standing near it.

"I love this," I said. "I miss seeing it every day."

"Well, there's only one remedy for that. You think when you move back to New York you'll want to be on the Lower East Side again?"

"Who said anything about moving back?"

"You said you missed it."

"If I were to move back, there are things about Barcelona I'd miss, too."

"Uh-huh. Remember back in Peru, when you told me that Elinor Bargeman lady compared you to a mule with a nail in its head? You got all huffy about it, but she ain't wrong."

He teased me all the way across the bridge, but got quiet as we turned onto Tillary Street in Brooklyn. It was a short drive from there to Ryan Brooks's building. Seventy-five Livingston was part of downtown Brooklyn's Skyscraper Row, and its Art Deco facade matched the grandeur of any downtown Manhattan tower. It reminded me of the Woolworth Building, with its bands of neo-Gothic detailing. But whatever charm it had held for me in the past had evaporated by the time we parked the car, waved to our new cop friends, and walked along Court Street. I was afraid to go upstairs and hear what Skye's ex had to say.

"You look real nice," Jesse said in the elevator. "Did I mention that already?"

"Do I look that nervous?"

"Yep." He shrugged. "But purdy anyway."

The doorman had called upstairs, and Ryan Brooks was waiting with his apartment door open. He was on the short side and heavyset, with wire-rimmed glasses and curly black hair. His eyes were half-swollen, no doubt from crying. We introduced ourselves and shook hands; he looked so forlorn I wanted to hug him.

"I can't believe she's gone," Ryan said, after we got inside. The apartment was a riot of Elsie de Wolfe–inspired design: heavy drapes swagged over tall windows, pale green walls holding molded white rectangular panels, antique wood furniture and leopard-print accents. There was a portrait of Skye hanging over the mantelpiece; in it, her hair was still golden blond, and she was wearing a strapless lavender ball gown. She was unbelievably gorgeous, but the picture didn't hint at her personality; it was like one of those old MGM studio shots. There were gold-framed photographs of her dotting every table in the room. Ryan, in his well-worn jeans and black T-shirt with ARCADE FIRE embossed on it, stood out against his surroundings as the one thing that didn't belong. The apartment felt less like the place where he lived and more like a shrine to Skye.

"This must be such a terrible shock," I said.

"You may not know this, but Skye was pregnant."

I nodded. "I did know that."

"We were talking about baby names just before she left for Mexico," Ryan said.

"You were?" My voice was more than a little incredulous, and I flushed with embarrassment. "I'm sorry, I just thought, um . . ."

"You're aware the baby wasn't technically mine," Ryan filled in. "I understand. Some people might find this surprising, but I didn't care. I've always wanted children."

I was speechless. It wasn't hard to understand how you could meet someone and love their kids as your own, but I couldn't grasp how Ryan was able to accept what Skye had done. It made me sad to think of her demanding that Gavin marry her, while knowing she had Ryan in her back pocket in case that didn't work out. She really was manipulative with the men in her life.

"I wanted to ask you about the story Skye was working on," I said. "All I know is that it was about Pantheon's being involved in some kind of fraud."

"I'm surprised she revealed that much," Ryan said. "Skye only told me because she needed help. It was a sign of how desperate she was. She'd broken up with me for an Englishman named Stroud who worked for Pantheon, and there she was, coming back to get me to piece together a financial puzzle for her."

"Can you explain it to me?" I asked.

"I'm not real good with numbers, so talk slow," Jesse added.

Ryan turned to me, studying my face. "How much do you know about money laundering?"

Jesse and I looked at each other. "Go on," Jesse said.

"The basic principle is simple." Now that Ryan was in technical mode, his voice was stronger. "Criminals have cash, but they need to hide how they got their money, so they run it through legitimate businesses."

Jesse shook his head. "How would you do that through a hotel? Anyone who sees it is gonna know there's something fishy with guys cartin' around bundles of cash."

"You're not comprehending the scope of the operation," Ryan said. "After Skye fell for this Stroud character, she began to travel just to see him. That was when she noticed something fishy about certain Pantheon hotels. She said you'd be blind not to see they didn't have guests. So, she did a little digging. She'd be the first person to admit that she didn't have a financial background and she could barely do long division, but she saw the books that were full of ghost guests who'd supposedly stayed at the hotels. That meant gobs of money were being laundered through the hotels day after day."

"So that's why the hotels all claimed they were full," I said. "They didn't want anyone staying there to see that they weren't."

"If you think about it, an expensive hotel can rake in money," Ryan said. "Imagine every room is full each night, and those rooms have a rack rate of, say, a thousand a pop. Then let's say the restaurant is full, the bar is full, the spa is full, maybe there's a per-guest daily resort fee. Everyone's getting a room-service breakfast each morning. Add it up."

"But the hotel would be paying tax on all of that revenue," I pointed out.

Ryan's cell phone rang. He picked it up and glanced at the screen. "I should grab this. Hold on. Hello, Denny? It's good to hear your voice. I was worried about you." There was a long pause. "Lily told me what happened. I can't believe it. Yes, Lily Moore. She's here right now. You're welcome to come over." Another pause. "Okay. I'm going to need your help with the memorial service. I just want it to be perfect for her. Okay. Take care. Get some rest. Goodnight."

"That was Denny Chiu?" I asked.

"She's a good friend. I was trying to call her when I couldn't reach Skye. She just got back to New York. She's really shaken up." He rubbed his forehead. "Okay, where were we? This is where creative accounting comes in. The hotel has to pay its employees. Imagine there's a whole army of phantom employees. They need to buy food for all those meals. They need to do maintenance on the building and make repairs. Maybe they say there's a problem with the elevator, the water system, whatever. It doesn't really matter what. The point it, those expenses add up and most of the profit disappears. They'll pay something in taxes, but nothing substantial."

Something Pete had said about Skye came back to me. *She asked what I thought the flowers cost. You know, the flowers in the lobby. She asked if they were worth ten thousand a month. I'm, like, this is Mexico. Are you crazy?*

"Another thing to consider is that the hotel can increase its revenue stream in fraudulent ways."

"Like what?" Jesse asked.

"Well, Skye told me about a bunch of shacks the company put up in Monterrey. They were of poor quality, and she couldn't believe anyone would stay in them. When she asked Stroud about it, he said they were presold and that many of Pantheon's guests liked a rustic setting." Ryan shook his head. "That English guy fed her a line of garbage and she ate it up. I told her that it sounded like he was the one running the scam, and she got angry at me. She said no, that she'd seen other Pantheon hotels outside of Mexico and they were run the same way. She said Martin Sklar was a mean bastard who would do anything to keep his hotel business afloat."

"So the Hotel Cerón had ghosts, after all," I said. "But they were phantom guests rather than a resident spirit." Martin was so proud of his company, but in a teetering global economy, with travel revenues down, the business undoubtedly needed a boost. Pantheon Worldwide was a high-profile operation. It wouldn't look good to have the luxury brand squeezed by hard times. Had Martin hit on the idea of turning his properties into money-laundering pits?

"Skye snuck around, getting scraps of information," Ryan went on, "A couple of weeks ago, she found a source connected to Pantheon. She was expecting to get some solid information that way." Ryan's face got tight. "The last time I talked with her, she told me that if anything happened to her, it would be because Martin Sklar was determined to protect his interests."

# 52

We made the drive back to Manhattan without a word between us. The car wasn't silent, though. Jesse put on a Sarah Vaughan album and turned the volume up. The first song that came up was "Fool's Paradise," and I wondered if that's what I'd been living in. Skye had been blind to Gavin's faults. In the back of her mind, she must have known he was guilty of a great many things, and the mental contortions she went through to hide that from herself would have been extensive. But was I any different? Was I any less of a fool for Martin than Skye had been for Gavin?

When we got back to the Village, Jesse gave me some juice and crackers and dialed the deli around the corner for himself.

"I know you just went through a nightmare, but you have to cheer up a little," he said. "You look like somebody just shot your dog. Or your best friend. And since I'm your best friend, I'm hopin' to high heaven not to get shot again."

"You're never going to let me live that down, will you?" I asked.

"Prob'ly not."

"For the record, I yelled at you not to come into the room that time. You wouldn't have been shot if you'd listened to me."

Jesse patted my head. "You keep tellin' yourself that."

After the food was delivered, he dragged me to the table, but I didn't want to eat. As Jesse set a bowl of soup in front of me, I thought of the soup that had been served at lunch on Saturday. Skye was already dead by then. Gavin was a corpse less than twenty-four hours later.

When Jesse asked what I was thinking, I told him. "Boy, I'm sorry I asked." He went back to eating his soup. "Okay, if we can't have a civilized conversation, let's have an uncivilized one."

"What does that mean?"

"You don't think Gavin killed Skye. Want to explain?"

"Gavin is cold . . . was cold, I mean. But I think he cared about Skye, in his own strange way. He was embarrassed to admit he felt anything for her. I think she might have actually loved him. What I find hard to accept is that Skye knew he was going to do something to me, but she stayed with him anyway."

"Maybe she thought he wouldn't do anything bad if she were around," Jesse offered.

"She knew. And she didn't leave." I took a sip of broth. "If Gavin was going to get rid of her, he wouldn't have waited until I arrived. There was too much risk she'd say something to me."

"That's a fair point." Jesse chewed slowly, a sure sign he was deep in thought; normally he was a speedy eater. "So, Skye was hangin' in with Gavin, even though she didn't like what he was up to."

"Skye was working on a story about how Pantheon is using its hotels to launder money. That would destroy Gavin—and Martin. Not only would he have to step down, but he'd end up in jail."

Jesse started to cough, and took a long swallow of water. "You're sayin' Sklar had all the reason in the world to shut her down, Lil. He had a motive for murder."

"But I don't believe he'd do it for the company," I said. "The only time I know for sure that Martin wanted someone dead was because she was a threat to someone he loved."

"Then you're saying Sklar wouldn't murder Skye, because he wouldn't kill for the company," Jesse pointed out. "I can believe that. He's not some marauding maniac. So why do you look so worried?"

"Because Martin is someone who'd kill to protect a person he loves. And I know he loves me. If there was ever a way of showing that, coming down to Mexico and putting his life in danger was it."

"I see your point. But if you ever go back to him, I'll put a nail in your mule head myself."

I shook my head. "You don't quite get it. Martin killed Gavin. That was self-defense. But, even if Gavin hadn't had a gun in his hand, I think Martin would have killed him, because Gavin had tried to hurt me. From Martin's point of view, if Skye were involved with Gavin's plan, then she would deserve to die as well."

"Okay, but that doesn't explain why an SUV tried to crush us like a tin can today," Jesse said. "I'd love to say Sklar put somebody up to that, but he didn't, not any more than I did. So what does that leave?"

"Somebody who wants to hurt Martin," I said.

"And who's that?"

I racked my brain. "I don't have a name, but I have an idea. Gavin was sure that he had the support of key members of Pantheon's board. He never named anyone in particular, but what if one of them was backing his power play?"

"Silently backing it," Jesse pointed out. "Someone who'd let Gavin do the dirty work, and pull strings from the background."

"There was one thing that was completely out of place in Skye's bag. She had a guidebook about Eastern Europe, and she'd marked the Pantheon hotels in it."

"You find out who's runnin' that part of the show, you got the silent partner."

I picked up the phone and dialed Martin's number. "Lily. How are you sweetheart?"

"You never stop," I said. "I have a strange question for you. Who runs Pantheon's Eastern European division?"

"That's an interesting question. The territory is divided between a Russian woman named Svetlana Khorkov and good old Josef Dietrich."

"Josef Dietrich," I repeated, remembering the times I had met him. He was a decade older than Martin and heavyset, with a hearty manner and a ready smile. I remembered Gavin mentioning a Josef—that was the friend who'd sent him china from Prague.

"You know him," Martin added. "He's the only true friend I have on the Pantheon board."

Apolinar had said something about Gavin always looking for father figures. *Mr. Alvarez wanted him to be able to stand on his own, but he came to see that Gavin can only survive in the shadow of a larger man.* "Is there a chance he could have been helping Gavin set up his hostile takeover of the board?"

There was dead silence on the other end for a full ten seconds. "No. Of course not." Martin was almost spluttering.

"What about Svetlana Khorkov?"

"She's no friend of Gavin's. She voted against him heading up the Mexican division. She's prone to temper tantrums, so I'm not sure if she dislikes him for a reason or because she can make him cower. You have to take a hard line with her."

"Does Svetlana or Josef know how sick you are?" I asked.

"I tell Svetlana nothing. She'd use it against me. Josef knows about the cancer, not the rest. He's the only one on the board who does."

"I think, if you look into it, you'll find he was close to Gavin."

"No, that's impossible. I made a mistake in trusting Gavin, but Josef—"

"Martin, someone tried to kill me and two of my friends just off the FDR Drive today," I said.

"What?" Martin sounded like an electrical current had been shot through him. "Lily, are you all right?"

I told him I was and explained, as best I could, what had happened. The news shook him and his breathing became harsh and irregular. I was torn between worry for him and for myself. "That wasn't Gavin or any of his henchmen," I told Martin. "Gavin had to be working with someone else."

"I'll find out who it is, but I can tell you it isn't Josef."

"How can you be so sure?"

"When my father died, Josef was the one who guided me through the business. I couldn't have done it without him."

*He was like a father figure to Gavin, too,* I thought. But what I said was, "Whoever it is, just find out soon. If Bruxton hadn't been there this afternoon, I think I'd be dead right now."

# 53

Ellis Burke's office was on Union Square West, which made me think it would be some sort of grand edifice. But when I walked into the building on Monday morning, the sleepy attendant barely nodded at me, but he took notice of the cop I was with. The elevator jolted and buzzed on its way up to the thirteenth floor. Its lights blinked a couple of times, but the car finally creaked into place and the door opened. The corridor was grim and gray, and it smelled like old onions. When I got to Ellis's door, I tried the handle, but it was locked. I knocked and waited, then knocked again.

Finally, I heard footsteps, and then a froggy voice. "Who is it?"

"Lily Moore. I called this morning."

"Are you alone?"

I gave Bruxton's friend a pleading look and he rolled his eyes but took a few steps away from the door. "Yes," I said. There was a long pause, and what sounded like whispering. Then a couple of locks turned and the door opened a crack. A man's face peered out, his eye just above the brass chain.

"Yeah, that's Lily Moore all right," he said.

I couldn't see who, if anyone, he was talking to. "Are you Ellis Burke? I'm here to talk about Skye McDermott."

"Oh, I bet you are." His voice was ominous. "I bet you are." He looked me over. "Huh." He shut the door, took the chain off, and opened it again. "You can come in, I guess. But don't touch anything."

He stepped back and I moved inside. I saw something move out of the corner of my eye and noticed a pretty blonde in jeans and a black T-shirt with a giant silver skull emblazoned in sequins on it. She was clutching a cell phone. "It's okay," Ellis said. "She's alone. And she probably won't shoot us."

"Okay," she said, pressing a button on the phone, making the screen go dark. She smiled at me and came forward, holding out her hand. "Hi, I'm Manda."

We shook hands, and I noticed she was wearing a silver goth ring with spikes coming out of it. "My sister would've loved that," I said, forgetting myself for a moment.

"Thank you. I was just admiring your dress." She smiled, which made her look about a decade younger. She was probably a college student.

"Manda's one of my interns," Ellis said, bringing me back into the present.

The little I had been able to find out about Ellis online told me he was a veteran of print magazines including *Fortune, Forbes,* and *Smart Money,* and that he'd left the business to create an online magazine that was such a top-secret project it didn't even have a name.

"I want to talk to you about the piece Skye was writing for your magazine."

"I bet you do. I bet you do." He glanced at Manda. "How about you get us some coffee? From Starbucks, I mean."

"You can just tell me to go outside," she said, turning on her high heels rapidly and heading out the door.

"But I really did want coffee," Ellis whined. He sighed. "Okay, let's sit down." He led me over to a metal table that sat in front of a high window. It had matching metal chairs.

Everything smelled new and looked as if it had come from Ikea. Ellis sat on one chair, then put his legs up on the one next to it. "So, what brings you here?"

"I want to talk to you about Skye's story on Pantheon."

Ellis laughed. "That's rich. Also lame. Why would I tell you anything?"

I leaned forward. "Because Skye's dead and she won't be writing the story."

"Skye's dead?" That got his attention. "Since when? Who told you that?"

"I saw her. We were both at the Hotel Cerón in Acapulco. She disappeared on Friday night, and her body was found the next day."

"She was murdered," Ellis whispered. "Do they know who did it?"

"No."

"Making Martin Sklar the next logical suspect."

"How's that logical? Skye was working on a story about Pantheon, but all of the dirt she'd dug up was about Gavin Stroud."

"The money laundering? Yeah. But there's a lot on Sklar himself. Like the laws he broke, building a hotel on an archaeological site in Thailand, burying a report about a hotel he built in China being on a toxic dump, the bribes he's made to officials around the world."

"It sounds like you've got a dossier on him."

"It's all up here." Ellis tapped his temple with a forefinger. "That way, no one can break in and shut down my operation."

"And what an operation it is."

Ellis gave me a sour look. "I've heard all about your smart mouth. I also heard you pistol-whipped Martin Sklar when you broke up with him."

I tried to look bemused. "Now, where would I get a pistol from?"

"If you were a corporation, I'd move heaven and earth to find out. But since you're just a travel writer, I'll keep on being curious."

"Just a travel writer? Wow. You must've been a real peach for Skye to work with," I said.

"What is it you want, anyway?"

"I'm interested in Skye's story, because someone needs to write it."

Ellis let out a low whistle. "I didn't know you hated your ex so much."

"I don't mean a piece about Martin. I mean an article about the money laundering and whatever Pantheon has been up to."

"What do you need?"

"Skye knew something was wrong with a few of the properties in Eastern Europe. Did she tell you what?"

"Yeah. They don't exist."

"What does that mean?"

"Do I need to draw you a picture?" Ellis asked. "They're money-laundering pits, just like Mexico, but the guy running them is cunning enough to skim so much of the profits that it isn't obvious. Dig?"

"Got it. Why did Skye call you on Friday night?"

"She told me she was with you in Acapulco. She said she thought you might have some information about when Sklar started laundering money, and which properties were involved, and she wanted my okay to bring you in. I told her I thought that was a crap idea, because you'd probably go running to Sklar about the story, but she said you wouldn't."

"She was right," I said. "What else did she say?"

"She found another source," Ellis said. "But she mentioned that the source's info might be a little out of date."

"So, maybe someone who used to work for Pantheon?" *Like Denny,* I thought.

"Could be."

"Was there anything else? Anything at all?"

"Just that she was going to stick close to you all weekend because she knew you were in danger," Ellis said.

That made my heart ache. I hoped Ellis couldn't see how those words affected me. If I cried in his office, that would be filed away for reference, no doubt.

# 54

It took more nerve than I thought I had to step inside Martin's apartment building again. The last time I'd visited was just after I'd found out my sister was dead, and I pieced together the lies Martin had told me about her. He wasn't responsible for what happened to Claudia, but he'd made my search for her more difficult and, if anything, more painful. But the memory that haunted me was how Martin had made me lose control. I'd struck him across the face several times, knocking out teeth. At the time, I felt justified in my rage, but time had only made me see myself as a fool.

Whatever I'd done, Martin's standing instructions to let me come upstairs were still in effect. The doorman greeted me and sent me upstairs, though he rushed for the phone before my back was turned. I could only imagine what he was saying.

Ridley, Martin's son, had the apartment door open and was waiting for me. He was even taller and broader than when I'd last seen him, and he still had trouble making eye contact. But he gave me a big hug. "Hi, Lily. You smell nice."

"Thanks, Ridley. Have any football teams tried to recruit you yet?"

He made an odd sound, as if he were clearing his throat, but I knew him well enough to know that was how he laughed.

"How's your dad?"

"He's resting right now. It might be a while before he's up. There's a nurse here, too."

A solidly built woman with her hair in dreadlocks came into the room. "That's my cue," she said. "I'm Anne. I already know you're Lily. Martin talks about you all the time. Anyhow, I would've recognized you from the photos he's got."

"He still has those up?"

"See for yourself," she said.

As I walked in, I saw that she was right. There were pictures of me, and of Martin and me together, and of us with Ridley, looking like a family. If anything, Martin had more pictures up than when we were actually a couple. Looking at one of them, I realized that it wasn't my imagination that Martin's appearance had changed so dramatically. In a few months, he'd aged rapidly and dropped a shocking amount of weight. The gaunt man I'd seen in Mexico was a shadow of the Martin I'd known.

"How bad is it?" I asked.

"It's bad," Ridley said. "He should never have had—"

"Hush, your papa's a private man."

"He's secretive about everything."

"I'm not supposed to talk about it," Anne said. "I had to sign so many confidentiality agreements when I started working here, I think he could put my ass in jail for telling you."

"I probably could," Martin said, standing in a doorway and leaning on the frame. He was wearing a pair of monogrammed pajamas he might have swiped from Cary Grant in *Indiscreet*. "Hello, sweetheart."

"I guess I can't threaten you for calling me that while I'm standing in your home, can I?"

"It would be a little bit rude."

I moved closer to him, but stopped short of actually touching him. This was a stage of our relationship I'd never envisioned. Should I kiss his cheek or hug him? A handshake would only be sad. I looked at him, knowing he was thinking the same thing.

"Ridley, would you mind going for a walk with Anne?"

"Okay, Dad. You want me to pick anything up for you?"

"Thanks, son, but no."

"You probably need a new book to read," Ridley said. "I'm going to get you one."

"That sounds good."

Ridley hugged his father, which was something I'd never seen before. Over the years I'd known them, Martin tried to hug his son but Ridley usually pulled away. I knew he had a lot of issues with his father, but there was something incredibly sweet seeing them together now.

After Ridley and Anne went out, Martin and I stared at each other silently. There was so much between us, some of it good and some horrible. "How sick are you?" I asked finally.

"Sick enough that it's incredibly boring to talk about." He made his way to the sofa and sat down. He sighed. "I'm a bad host. I should've asked if you wanted something to drink before they went out."

"I'm fine. It's you I'm worried about."

"Is that what you came here to talk about, Lily, or is there something else on your mind?"

"There's a lot that's on my mind." I sat in a chair across from him. "Starting with why you would want to kill Skye."

# 55

Martin didn't answer that. Instead, he leaned back so that his head rested against the top of the sofa.

"Martin, I know about the fraud. The money laundering."

"You think I had Skye killed because of that?" Martin looked at me again. "That's insulting, Lily. I didn't kill her."

"You could have had someone do it."

He sighed. "If you believe that about me, I may as well end it all right now." He lifted his head. "Do you?"

"No," I admitted.

"Well, that's something." He settled back against the sofa and sighed. Then he closed his eyes and pinched the skin over the bridge of his nose. "Ask me anything."

"You knew about the money laundering?"

"Not until recently. But I knew Gavin was making the company a fortune, and I didn't bother to stop and think about how. If I'd looked, I would have seen that the Mexican division made boatloads of cash because it wasn't in the hotel business. It was in the money-laundering business. It was inspired of Gavin, in a way. Think of it. No cash spent on wooing visitors, or catering to guests. No people to worry about at all. Just a skeleton staff to maintain the property, and a big pile of money into the coffers on a regular basis."

"You're saying the money-laundering business was Gavin's? Was no other Pantheon hotel involved?"

"No."

"What about the hotels in Eastern Europe. Are all of those aboveboard?"

"Yes." His voice quavered, just a little. "I think."

"You don't know."

"I don't keep moles at Josef's properties."

"You have *spies* at your hotels?"

"Of course. How do you think I'm able to run things with such a tight rein?" He gave me a full-wattage smile that, in healthier days, would have made him look like Tyrone Power; now, it only highlighted how weak he'd become.

"That's horrible. Also, brilliant," I admitted. "Except that you need more Eastern European spies."

"I'm not in the running for any Person of the Year awards," Martin answered. "I just know how to run great hotels. Or I did."

"Before you got sick." My voice was quiet. "I know you have cancer. Will you talk about it, please?"

He smiled again, more gently. "I always wondered if I might drop dead suddenly of a heart attack, like my father did when he was fifty-three. But cancer found me first. Only, it's not the real problem anymore."

I closed my eyes, but I couldn't keep my composure so I jumped up and walked quickly to the window. Staring down at Central Park, I struggled to keep my breathing steady.

"What does that mean?" I asked him, wiping my eyes.

"It started out as lung cancer."

I turned to face him. "But you don't smoke. You never did."

"Sweetheart, I hate to break it to you, but any doctor will tell you, there are a lot of people who never smoked with lung cancer these days. It's not just me."

"Is it because of secondhand smoke?" I stared at Martin, languid on the couch. I'd walked in, intent on making him confess that he'd committed murder; instead, I was thinking about how I was going to be responsible for his death.

"Lily, please come here."

I was rooted to the spot, and when I opened my mouth to answer, nothing came out.

"I would come over there, but I can't." His voice broke as he said that last word. "Please."

My feet moved me toward him, and I sat on the sofa beside him, moving gingerly in case I made things worse.

"Lily, you know that saying, 'It is what it is'?"

"That's a stupid saying."

"But kind of true. This isn't about secondhand smoke, or about all the time I've spent checking out construction sites, or the time I've spent in polluted cities. It just is."

We sat for a long time like that, gazing at each other. It was hard to reconcile the life I'd once imagined having with him with where we'd landed instead.

"When you said that wasn't the problem anymore . . . the cancer spread?"

"I kicked cancer's ass," Martin said, sounding almost smug. "What happened was my doctors didn't realize I never should have had chemotherapy. Have you ever heard of a disorder called Charcot-Marie-Tooth?"

I shook my head.

"It's a hereditary disorder, but a lot of people who have it don't know it. It affects the nerves, especially in the feet and legs, hands and arms. It's kind of a bastard, because it erodes muscle tissue and kills touch sensation, while leaving you with all of your pain receptors intact."

"That's horrifying."

"People who have it aren't able to have chemo, but no one knew I had it. It's almost impossible for me to walk a block now without falling down, unless I'm wearing metal braces on my legs. I still have most of the function in my hands, but the doctors say I'll lose that soon."

It was too awful to take in. Waves of emotion beat against my chest, and my eyes were watery. Martin stroked my hand.

"How can you run the company anymore?" I asked. "Why don't you quit and focus on your health? Just keeping up the pretense that you're working on hotel business must be exhausting."

"I'm down, but I'm not out. I'm tougher than you think."

"The story about the money laundering is going to come out, you know."

"I know. Sooner or later."

"Sooner, because I'm going to write it."

He swallowed hard. "Is this your way of getting even with me?"

"No. I'm well past that point." I curled my fingers around his. "It's my way of giving some kind of meaning to Skye's death. She's the one who uncovered it."

"I suppose you'd like some hard evidence to do with that theory. Would you mind getting my laptop for me?"

I went into his bedroom to retrieve it; I stared at the large photograph he had of me on the wall, and the smaller ones on the night table and dresser. It made me think of Ryan's shrine to Skye, and that made me sad. It was as if both he and Martin were frozen in time, refusing to move ahead, denying a new course needed to be charted.

When I came back, Martin told me what files to delve into, then said, "You do the scrolling. I need a nap."

"You can go to sleep, if you like."

"Did Ridley mention I now sleep sixteen hours a day? That makes me a sloth. But I'd rather stay awake and watch you. Unless you want to nap with me."

"Is that your best offer?"

"A few of my nerve endings are still in working order, sweetheart."

I did my best to look affronted, then turned my attention to the files.

"Martin, why did Denny leave Pantheon?"

"She was passed over for a promotion. She ended up trying to sneakily undermine her boss. She would be very sweet to this woman she hated, then tell everyone else terrible things about her. She loved to talk about the woman as a manipulator, but it was really Denny who was masterful at playing all sides."

A wide swath of goose bumps, running from my tailbone to the nape of my neck, lit up. "Denny kept telling me how manipulative Skye was."

"Really? What would she gain by doing that?"

"It was in the context of Skye's relationships with men, and how she mistreated them."

"Why would Denny care?"

"I don't know. It was mostly about Ryan, Skye's ex-boyfriend." What had Denny told me? *Sorry, just thinking about their psychotic relationship ties my muscles up in knots. I'm supposed to be her friend, but I feel terrible for Ryan. He's a really good guy. He deserves better.* "Denny kept talking about how Skye used him and abused him."

I tried to remember the first time his name had come up with Denny. *I think the person who gets it worst is Ryan. He's such a sucker for her. She breaks up with him, sleeps with strings of guys, tells him all about it, then asks him for money. And he gives it to her.*

"Denny wasn't lying, though. Skye was giving Gavin a marriage ultimatum while talking baby names with Ryan." I stopped and thought about it. Ryan. Denny was always talking about Ryan.

"Could Denny have been jealous of Skye in some way?"

"Skye was stuck on Gavin. What would there be to get jealous about? Anyway, Denny and Skye were close friends."

"How do you know that?"

"Well, Denny mentioned it. A few times."

"Do you have anyone's word for that but Denny's?" Martin asked.

"Skye's ex, Ryan. He mentioned that they were friends." I remembered him saying Denny was a good friend. That made it sound as if she were his friend, rather than Skye's.

"When did he say that?"

"Jesse and I were over at his apartment on Sunday night when Denny called him."

"She called him? To tell him about Skye?"

"I think she wanted to come over to his apartment."

Martin laughed. "Oh, Lily, this is ironic. I can't accept the truth about Josef, and you can't about Denny."

"Hold on. It sounds like your opinion of Josef has altered a bit. What changed your mind?"

"I keep thinking about Gregory Robinson. I never told Gavin what I did. I never told anyone. You know, and Ridley does. Neither of you would tell Gavin a thing. So, I started to think about who it was who first put me onto Gregory." Martin sighed. "That was Josef."

"Was that part of his fatherly advice?"

"I'm ashamed to say it was. My father never did business like that. He was a very tough man, but honorable." Martin closed his eyes, as if he were about to drift off, but he kept talking. "We were never close. I don't know why. He was a hard person to get close to."

"Like father, like son."

"Maybe." He was silent for a moment. "Josef was the opposite. So warm. So easy to talk to. He knew how the world really worked. He wanted to help me."

When I'd been trapped at the Hotel Cerón, I'd believed Denny wanted to help me. She'd argued with Gavin about having me see a doctor; she'd been worried about what Gavin would do to me, and she tried to protect me. I'd known her for a long time, and I knew her to be thoughtful and generous. That made me so reluctant to be objective about her now. "The worst part is that they seem so kind," I said.

"We're both willfully blind, Lily. We want to believe we know them. We think we know the truth about them, but we don't. We're just comfortable with our illusions."

He was right, but when I opened my mouth to say so, it was hard to breathe. *Ryan keeps bailing her out of things. She knows he'll always catch her, no matter how far she falls.* Means, motive, opportunity. Denny had them all.

**56** Denny wouldn't meet with me; I couldn't even get her to answer my calls. *There could be a good reason for it,* I told myself. Maybe Josef Dietrich's henchmen were after her, too. It didn't take me long to be disabused of that idea. Martin's people found Gavin's correspondence with Josef; Gavin had been the one to sound the alarm about me, but he didn't mention Denny. What shocked me was the timing: Gavin sent the message on Saturday evening, just after he'd taken away my laptop and Skye's guidebooks; *Frakker's Eastern Europe* had been a solid clue after all. Gavin didn't say what to do with me; he only provided my address in Barcelona and Jesse's in New York, as well as a list of known associates and haunts.

I finally got Denny to meet with me by employing a subterfuge not unlike what Gavin had done to me. I got Ryan to call her and ask her to come over to his apartment. When she arrived, I was waiting in the living room for her. Jesse was in the next room, pretending to be my bodyguard but mostly just indulging his love of eavesdropping. The police were downstairs, shadowing me as they had since the incident with the SUV. I didn't expect her to confess and go running into the arms of the NYPD. But I couldn't let what I knew crush my conscience without saying something.

I got to Ryan's very early, which was lucky, since the pouring rain that day only got harder after I arrived. By the time Denny walked in, soaking wet in a black trench coat, pulling a black head scarf off, I was seated on the sofa, sipping a glass of champagne.

"You have your own key?" I asked. "That's very trusting of Ryan."

"What are you doing here, Lily?" She dropped her umbrella and tossed her coat over a chair next to mine. She was wearing a black pencil skirt and printed blouse that I was pretty sure I'd seen in a Prada display. She was as chic as ever, but there were dark pouches under her eyes, and her skin had broken out so badly that cover cream couldn't fully hide it.

"Here's to being alive," I said, lifting my glass. "I appreciate that more and more these days. Don't you?"

She pushed her glasses up to the bridge of her nose, trying to hide her discomfiture. "I'm still pretty shaken up about everything."

"Are you really? I guess murder could affect you like that." I took a sip of champagne while she stared at me. "Skye's murder," I clarified. "It must weigh on your conscience."

"Lily, you're sounding more than a little deranged. I know you've been under plenty of stress. But you can't—"

"Are you afraid I'm wearing a wire, or carrying a tape recorder?" I shook my head. "I wish. From what I've been told by my friends in the NYPD, even if I get you to confess, no one will prosecute you for a murder in Mexico when the victim's body hasn't even been found."

"Where's Ryan? Does he know how crazy you are?" Her voice was acid.

"Ryan went out. He's a gentleman. I don't expect you to admit you murdered Skye. It's enough for me to know you did. How are those scratches you were hiding in Acapulco healing up? I'm glad you don't have to wear that same ratty bandage all the time."

"I don't know what you're talking about, Lily." Her voice was cautious. "Are you sure you're feeling all right?"

"Well, I'm much better now that Gavin isn't poisoning me anymore. That made me feel pretty awful in Acapulco."

"Did Gavin do that?" There was some genuine surprise in her voice. "I wondered when you got sick at lunch. The way he was talking about you . . . .I had a feeling he was up to something."

"Yes, Gavin had all kinds of wrong ideas. Which is, I suppose, why you two got along."

She stared at me, her face a mixture of sullenness and fury. "I don't need to listen to this," she announced, grabbing her coat.

"Oh, yes, you do. You want to hear how I figured out that you killed Skye. It's got to be weighing on your mind. What if the police find her body at some point? It would be best to know the case against you."

"You have no proof of anything," Denny said, but she set her coat down again and planted herself in a chair. She wanted to know what I knew.

"Here's what I've got. On Friday night, you were already at the Hotel Cerón when I got there. You were planning on getting rid of Skye before the press trip even started. You knew Gavin wouldn't miss her. The timing was great."

She didn't say anything, but her eyes stayed on mine, and she didn't blink.

"You told Skye that you had information for her about Pantheon. That's how you got her to go upstairs with you, to the fourth floor. You knew that whole floor was empty. And you had an all-access key card, so you had your choice of rooms. All you had to do was lead her to one of them, then surprise her by smashing her in the head. By the way, what did you use? I was thinking a candlestick, but I suppose there were all kinds of possibilities."

"Do you think you're being funny?" Denny asked.

"So, you hit Skye, and she fought back, but all she can do is scratch you before you take her out. What I wonder is, do you think that hitting her killed her? Or was she in shock and did she lie that way until she bled out?"

"That's a horrible thing to say. Skye was my friend."

"Kind of, sort of her friend. I knew you two were close, but I had no idea you were dating the same man."

"If you think I was involved with Gavin, you are out of your mind, Lily."

"I mean Ryan."

Her eyes turned anxious and she clasped her hands together on her lap, but she didn't speak.

"I thought about what your mother said to you," I explained. " 'You forty-one, you have no husband, no job, no children. You boyfriend just using you till ex-girlfriend come back. You live in Brooklyn!' Did I miss anything?"

"No." Her voice was so soft I barely caught the word.

"I guess that big portrait Ryan has of Skye on the wall right behind you is a hint that he's still in love with her, isn't it?"

Denny swallowed hard.

"Ryan was surprised when I asked if you two were dating. He said you're friends who see each other from time to time. It didn't sound like he thinks of you as his girlfriend."

A plump tear slid out of her right eye and snuck under her designer frames. "You don't know what it's like," she whispered. "He lives and dies on a word from her. Every time she had a problem, she went running to him. If she needed money, he was her bank. She treated him like trash, and all he would say was that her parents' marriage broke up when she was in college, and that messed up her view of the world. That was the great tragedy of her life, and it was supposed to explain every mean, rotten thing she did." She wiped the tear away. "She cheated on him when they were together. She was evil, and he couldn't get her out of his life. I couldn't even talk to him about it. He would say someone had to be there for her."

She made a choking sound and touched her chest, hand over heart. "It was never going to end. She got herself knocked up by Gavin on purpose, because she thought that might make him marry her, the stupid bitch. Gavin wanted her to have an abortion. But Ryan . . . he was waiting in the wings, ready to swoop in and take care of her and her bastard. No matter what awful, manipulative, evil thing she did, she was going to hang around Ryan's neck like a millstone for the rest of his life."

It wasn't an admission of guilt that would stand up in court, but it was a confession. Her hands shook and she took off her glasses and rubbed her eyes.

"Here's the funny part," she added. "One time, I told Ryan how to keep her. I said if he acted superior, and cheated on her, and occasionally slapped her around, she'd be hooked on him. As long as he still had his money, of course."

"Why didn't you leave, Denny?"

"I love him. It's as simple as that. He's such a good man." She took a deep breath. "What are you going to do?"

"There's not a lot I can do. Except tell Ryan what I know."

"Why would you do that?"

"He deserves to hear the truth." I picked up the glass and

put it down again, without drinking. "Here's what I wonder, Denny: is it all worth it? Now that Skye is gone, are your problems fixed?"

She held my eyes for a moment, but her face crumpled and her shoulders sagged. "Ryan is devastated by her death. He told me he'll never be able to love anyone else." Her words were punctuated with little gasps. "Why would you tell Ryan anything? I helped you in Acapulco, Lily. You know that. I wanted to get you away from Gavin, when I found out what he was really doing. I was worried when you got sick, because I knew he was behind it. I tried to help you!"

"I know you did, Denny."

"Do you know what Skye did? On Friday night, when she came upstairs with me, she was telling me how awful she felt because Gavin was going to hurt you. She wouldn't tell me what he was planning, only that you were going to suffer. I told her we had to get you out of the hotel, and do you know what she said? It was too late, and Gavin would kill her if she said anything."

My mouth went dry. I didn't answer.

"She knew Gavin was going to hurt you, but she didn't care. You know what else Skye said? She was sure she could get you to help with her story before Gavin got rid of you."

It took me a moment to find my voice. "You're not trying to convince me that you killed Skye for me, Denny, are you?"

"What does it matter why she died? You can't bring Skye back."

"The truth matters."

Denny laughed. "The truth is that Skye got what she deserved. What does it matter to you? Why can't you leave this alone?"

I set my glass down and got to my feet. "There's a man

named Josef Dietrich who wants me dead because I stumbled on part of Pantheon's money-laundering operation. He tried to have me killed when I got back to New York. The police have been watching my back and I have to be chauffeured everywhere I go. The police are keeping an eye on Jesse's building, because Dietrich's people know I'm staying there and strange men from Little Odessa are constantly checking it out. I can't walk down a street because Josef Dietrich wants me dead. Do you know when I'll feel safe again? When I publish the story about what he's done. Once the truth is out there, he can't touch me."

"So, tell your story about him. Leave Ryan and me out of this."

"What do you think will happen if I do that? Will you and Ryan live happily ever after?" I waved my arm around the room. "How would you feel about being the caretaker of Skye McDermott's shrine for the rest of your life?"

"Without her around, everything will be different. He just needs time."

"Your entire life would be based on a lie," I said. "You talked about Skye lying to him. You said Ryan deserved better. Is what you're doing better?"

"Why do you even care?" she yelled, launching herself toward me. I was sure she would hit me, but she stopped short, looking me over. We were the same height, both slender, both relatively fit. She'd killed someone, but I was willing to bet I'd been in more fights than she ever had. Skye had been tiny and delicate, and she'd been sick when Denny killed her. The medications Skye had been taking were for an extreme form of morning sickness that had left her emaciated and weak.

"You didn't just kill Skye," I said. "You also framed Pete. You wrote emails on Skye's laptop, and then you planted her computer in his room. That was a clever touch, since you'd already put some of Pete's drugs in the room where Skye died. Pete was tortured because of you."

"You can't blame me for what Gavin did!"

I remembered when Apolinar had come into Denny's room, telling her she needed to leave. *Let me tell you what Gavin did,* Apolinar had said. *He says to me, come, let's look at Pete's room. So we go and look around, and what do I find there? Skye's computer. Just sitting there, all nice, like it's praying to be discovered. Then I show Gavin, and he starts talking about how he's going to cut Pete into pieces.* I could still hear Denny's agonized wail. She knew what she'd done to Pete. She was cold enough to frame him, but not cruel enough to avoid feelings of guilt afterward.

"You pointed Gavin in Pete's direction. You knew Gavin was crazy enough to hurt him."

"Why can't you leave everything alone?" she screamed.

"That was what I used to do." My voice was quiet. "I left things alone, because I didn't want them to be my responsibility. Looking back, I wish I'd done things differently. I can't go back, so all I can do is change what I'm doing now."

"I never meant to hurt Pete. I was terrified of Gavin."

"Pete's in a coma. The doctors don't know if he's going to come out of it."

"Don't you understand? I had no choice. If Gavin had suspected me, he would have—" Her voice broke and she started to sob. "I can't sleep," she said. "I think about Pete . . . and Skye. Even though she deserved it, I can't . . ."

I didn't say anything. I couldn't comfort her, and I couldn't think of any other words.

It took her a while to regain her composure. "So that's it," she said, wiping her face. "You're going to ruin my life?"

"Like you said, Denny, I have no proof. Maybe Ryan won't even believe me."

"Don't do it before Skye's memorial," she said. "Please."

"Why should I wait?"

"Don't interrupt Ryan's mourning with this. He's already suffering so much. Please don't do that to him. Hearing this would kill him."

"For all I know, Josef Dietrich's people will kill me before Skye's memorial," I said. "I can't promise you anything."

We faced off silently. She surprised me by picking up the champagne flute I'd left for her and downing it in one long swallow. I heard a sound and suddenly Jesse was in the doorway.

"Sorry, but I got kinda worried. It was too quiet," he said.

Denny stormed out of the apartment, slamming the door behind her.

"I guess that went about as well as anyone could hope for, huh?" Jesse asked.

"I don't know what I expected," I admitted. "I half-expect her to come back and shoot me."

"Does it make you feel all important, havin' all these people want to kill you?" He grinned at me. "I gotta hang out with you to get excitement in my life, y'know."

"All I want is peace and quiet."

"Ha. You know who you remind me of? Al Capone. He once said, 'I want peace and I will live and let live!' Somethin' like that, anyways. You couldn't do it any more than he could. You'll be stirrin' up hornets' nests wherever you go."

"Do you want some champagne?" I asked him.

"Nah. Too fancy. Do we have to wait for Ryan to come home or can we go?"

"He gave me a key. I just have to leave it with the door-man. Give me a minute, okay?" I went down the hall, turning into a bathroom that was painted the dusky pink of a Carib-bean sunset. I closed the door and braced myself at the sink.

*She was sure she could get you to help with her story before Gavin got rid of you.*

I didn't want to believe that. There was a good chance Denny was lying, or at least exaggerating. Why that one line rang through my head, I couldn't explain. It wasn't that it was true, it was just that I feared it was, and that made my eyes hot and watery.

There was another version of the story. What had Ellis Burke said? *She was going to stick close to you all weekend because she knew you were in danger.* For all I knew, Skye had said both things, and meant them. It didn't matter; I knew which one I'd keep.

I heard a phone ring; Jesse answered it and laughed, mak-ing me smile.

*Just breathe, Honey Bear.* Sometimes I had to be reminded of that. I splashed some cold water on my face. There wasn't anything more I could do for Skye.

When I came out of the bathroom, Jesse said, "You wanna hear somthin' funny? The cops called up to check if you were still here. They wanted to know if you snuck out."

"Why would they think that?" I was baffled.

"I guess girls in leopard-print trench coats all look alike to them, at least on a dark and stormy night. Ready to go?"

"Sure."

"Woohoo. Hey, where's your coat?"

"Right there." I stared at the chair where my raincoat had been. It was a bright leopard print; in this room, given Skye's own love of the pattern, it didn't stand out in this room as much as it would have on the street. But it was gone, and I only saw Denny's black trench coat, still sopping wet.

"How could she grab the wrong coat?" Jesse asked.

I stared at it. Denny and I were wearing black boots and black skirts; she'd had a black scarf over her hair, as I had over mine, and a black umbrella. It took a moment for what she'd done to sink in.

"She didn't take the wrong one," I said. "I think Denny knew exactly what she was doing."

# EPILOGUE

On the day that my piece about the money-laundering operation at Pantheon was published, Martin stepped down as CEO of the company. He made a terse statement about how Pantheon needed a thorough housecleaning, and how he welcomed a government investigation and would do anything necessary to cooperate. He would be bringing in a CEO from outside the company, since the current board had resigned under duress and was under investigation. Josef Dietrich had made front-page news on two continents by dying in a swan dive from the balcony of a Pantheon tower in Budapest; he'd been drinking heavily that night, so there was much speculation over whether it was an accident or a suicide.

Martin didn't make any comment about his illness, but his public appearance set tongues wagging. He was as stylish as usual, and as irreverent. He added, as a parting shot, that he was staying on as chairman of the board. I took that as a nod to Frank Sinatra—whose nickname was, in fact, Chairman of the Board—and it made me smile. Afterward, he and Ridley had lunch with Jesse and me at One If By Land, Two If By Sea. It was a savvy move on Martin's part. It showed that he approved of the story I'd written, and it made him look stronger than he felt. I couldn't help but watch his hands while we ate. His left had developed a twitch, and I knew enough about the disorder to realize that the nerve endings were being stripped away. He didn't talk about it, but I couldn't help wonder what his life would be like when the only sensation he was left with was pain.

"Poor fella," Jesse kept saying afterward. "I'm prayin' for him."

Jesse and Martin were two of the only people who realized the significance of another story that had appeared in New York papers a couple of days earlier. BEAUTIFUL PR EXEC DIES IN HIT-AND-RUN, it screeched, above a particularly gorgeous photograph of Denny Chiu. I couldn't bring myself to read it, so Jesse supplied the details. She'd been hit outside of Washington Square Park, just a couple of blocks away from Jesse's apartment building. She'd died immediately at the scene.

"She took my coat and went to your building," I said. "What was she thinking? I told her Josef Dietrich's men were watching it."

"She was havin' trouble with the guilt. You know that. She couldn't live with it. She knew her life was over when you spilled everything to Ryan, anyway." He looked at me seriously. "You tell Ryan who really killed Skye?"

"No."

"You still plannin' to?"

I studied Denny's picture and put the paper down. "I don't think there's any reason to tell him anymore."

"Then I reckon Denny got what she wanted."

The day of Skye's memorial was also the day Pete Dukermann finally came out of the coma he'd been in since he'd been evacuated from Mexico. When I went to see him in the hospital the next day, he was surprisingly upbeat. "I thought I was a goner," he admitted. "But it all worked out in the end. And you know what? Donna and I are back together." He beamed from ear to ear. "Isn't that awesome? Who knew being in a coma would fix all my problems? Plus, she's going to get counseling."

I imagined the poor woman needed a lot of help, being married to Pete. "Maybe you could go together?"

"Yeah, we'll do that. But she's going to get anger-management counseling for herself. She's promised."

My mind went back to the scratches and marks I'd seen on Pete in Acapulco. "Wait a minute! You mean—"

"Don't say anything. It's kinda embarrassing," Pete said. "But we're gonna get things set right. It was like a vicious circle. I'd get high, or I'd travel, and Donna would get mad. Sometimes she'd lose control. Then, with that last fight, I hit her back and got arrested. It was the lowest point of my life. I never hit a woman before."

I hoped, for both their sakes, they were ready to get help. "Maybe Donna could start coming with you when you travel."

"You know, I think I'm done traveling. At least for a while," he admitted. "Don't you feel sick of it?"

"No. I don't know if I'll ever want to go back to Acapulco, but I'd still go to hell in a handbasket, if I got the chance."

"That's wanderlust. Exactly how I used to feel. Only I don't anymore."

"Maybe I'll wake up one day and decide that I don't, either," I said, but somehow, I doubted it.

I was going back to Barcelona, I told myself, even as I changed my return date not once, but twice. Bruxton and I spent some time together, but he was so emotionally aloof I was never sure where I stood with him. Finally, on the night before I was supposed to fly back to Barcelona—third time's the charm—I decided to take the direct approach. We were supposed to have dinner together; instead, I discovered that was just a ruse. Jesse had planned a surprise going-away party for me, and when I walked out of his guest room, wearing my vampiest black cocktail dress and open-toed slingbacks, there were thirty people jumping out at me in the living room, shouting, "Surprise!"

"Gotcha!" Jesse said. "Bet you never saw that comin'!"

"No, I did not."

Bruxton, standing against one wall, shrugged at me. It was a what-can-you-do gesture. I didn't like it one bit.

By nine-thirty, I'd had enough. "Let's go for a walk," I told Bruxton.

"You sure you want to leave? You're the guest of honor."

"They'll have plenty of fun without me."

Outside, it was a cool night. Without discussing it, we headed toward Washington Square Park. I'd walked by it several times since Denny had died, thinking about her. Bruxton offered me a cigarette, then lit one for himself. He put his arm around me and rubbed my bare shoulder. Maybe I wasn't the only one who'd waited for this. "You cold?"

"No, I'm fine." Except that I wasn't. "Brux, do you remember when I came back from Acapulco, and I kissed you?"

"Hell, yeah."

"Why haven't you tried to kiss me?"

He looked away. "You've been spending a lot of time with your ex, Lily. I don't feel right, getting in the way of that."

"Getting in the way?"

"He's sick. He's probably dying. He needs you more than I do."

"He asked me to marry him again. Do you know what his argument was? That I'd be a very rich widow soon. I passed."

"But still you spend time with him."

"Brux, you have a son, so I didn't think I'd have to explain this to you, but apparently I do." We stopped in the middle of the sidewalk, facing each other near the park's gleaming white, triumphal arch. "If anything happens to Martin, I'll be Ridley's guardian."

"Doesn't the kid have a mother?"

"Yes, but she's been in and out of rehab. Right now, she's in again. Not exactly the influence Ridley needs."

"You'd, what, act like Ridley's mom?" Bruxton was taken aback by the idea. He was a perennial cynic, but this was clearly a scenario he hadn't envisioned.

"I don't feel ready to be anyone's mom. But I'd take care of him." I took a breath. "If things had worked out differently, I'd be his stepmother. Claudia was close to him, too. She thought of him as a kid brother. One way or another, he's always going to be part of my life. He's family to me."

"Does that make Martin family?"

"In a way." I tried not to smile at his sour expression. "He's my ex. I'm not in love with him anymore, but I'm not ashamed to admit I still feel a kind of love for him."

"What would Claudia think of that?" His voice was harsh, even raspier than usual.

"I think she'd understand. She'd know how hard it is to lose someone you love, under any circumstances." I tossed our cigarettes in the gutter and put my hands on his chest. He was almost ridiculously overmuscled and inked. I'd caught sight of his tattooed torso once and I wanted a better view. "Claudia would be thrilled that the romance is gone.

She'd definitely understand that I feel a duty to Ridley. She would have, too."

"Yeah. I can picture that." His hands gripped my waist, and he pulled me close. "I still hate the idea of you flying off tomorrow."

"What reason have you given me to stay?" I teased, putting my arms around his neck.

"You sound like you want to be convinced." His hands were moving along my body, as if trying to memorize every inch of me, every curve. He leaned forward and kissed me hard, clutching me against him. My body was so hot it seemed as if I were melting into him.

"Get a room!" called a man walking past.

"Get a life, asshole," Brux called after him. The man turned, took a good look at Brux, and hurried off.

I couldn't help but laugh. "I love your chivalrous side."

"Yeah, it comes out a little too often." He leaned forward and kissed me again. "So, what do you want to do?"

"You, obviously."

"You serious, Lily?" He put his forehead against mine. "You want to come back to my place tonight?"

"More than anything."

"I'm not going to want you to leave," he whispered.

"I bet I won't want to." I pulled back a little. "But I will."

"Can't I convince you to stay?"

I shook my head. "But you can convince me to come back."

He put his hand on the back of my neck, his mouth working mine over intently. He tasted like coffee and cigarettes, and that went well with the musky aroma of his skin. "I'm gonna make the best damn argument I ever made."

"Good. I hope you can drive fast."

"Damn straight." He started to pull me down the street, but he stopped and picked me up, spinning me around and making me laugh. "You're crazy, you know that?"

"I do." I leaned forward to kiss him again. "Deep down, I'm pretty superficial."